I HOPE YOU GET THIS MESSAGE

FARAH NAZ RISHI

HARPER TEEN

An Imprint of HarperCollins Publishers

Library of Congress Control Number: 2019941390
ISBN 978-0-06-274145-5 (trade bdg.)
ISBN 978-0-06-298183-7 (special edition)

Typography by Catherine San Juan
19 20 21 22 23   PC/LSCH   10 9 8 7 6 5 4 3 2 1
❖
First Edition

For Shaz—
I hope you found your light,
but I hope you know
you were mine.

The stars will be watching us,
and we will show them
what it is to be a thin crescent moon.
You and I unselfed, will be together,
indifferent to idle speculation, you and I.
(Kulliyat-e Shams, 2114, by Rumi)

THE OFFICIAL RECORDS OF
THE INTERPLANETARY AFFAIRS COMMITTEE

TRIAL: TERMINATION OF PROJECT EPOCH
DURATION: EIGHT DAYS

ANNUNCIATION AND ROLL CALL: The Interplanetary Affairs Committee (IAC) designated this unit, Unit 212-G, to take these minutes as official record.

Thirteen (13) Scions—randomly selected citizens of Alma—compose the grand jury. The trial will be overseen by an Arbiter chosen by the IAC. Their task is to determine the fate of Project Epoch, a long-standing experiment to test the sustainability of life on another planet, which according to the results of Public Referendum 5571a is now up for review and potential termination. For the purposes of anonymity, the names of the 13 Scions will be omitted from these records.

TRANSCRIPT
EXCERPT FROM TRIAL

ARBITER: Our objective here is simple: to decide the fate of the experiment known as Project Epoch. There has been much discussion in the public sphere regarding the role of this grand jury in a philosophical sense. Should we consider ethical factors in our decision? Morality? Politics? Or are these simply distractions? Let me be clear. Our laws state that the primary role of this grand jury is a pragmatic one. Our task, therefore, is to reconsider the continuation of Project Epoch in terms of what is best for the practical situation of our sovereign planet, Alma, and the future of all its citizens.

SCION II: But doesn't our conclusion depend on the viability of other alternatives? If we can remotely sabotage the Anathogen diffuser before it activates, do we propose new reinitialization sites?

SCION 2: Are there even new reinitialization sites to propose?

SCION I2: We have deployed probes to alternative reinitialization sites, but none has proven as viable a habitat as Project Epoch, or as time efficient.

And given our own planet's precarious status, time is no longer on our side. Terraforming, reinitializing, even colonizing—those are no longer realistic options. Epoch remains the most feasible choice for a new home unless we allow the specimens of our experiment to destroy its delicate equilibrium.

SCION 6: That is precisely why our scientists implanted the Anathogen virus. They foresaw the local population's failure to ensure the Project's long-term sustainability. It is tempting to give the local population the benefit of the doubt, but their enduring inability to cultivate the planet is the most damning argument against its continuation.

SCION 10: We are in agreement on one thing: it is time to step in. We can no longer afford to be naïve in this matter—or allow our investment in the Project to be so drastically compromised.

SCION 4: The population of Epoch may have already received communications confirming our planet's existence. Everything has been compromised.

[The jury bursts into inaudible murmurs.]
ARBITER: Order, please. Order, or I will shut the feeds. [More muttering, gradually subdued.] I

will remind the tribunal and those witnessing our deliberations that whether Project Epoch is aware of the trial is irrelevant. The deliberations will go on, and our decision will be made. That is our task. The question remains: Should we continue to monitor Project Epoch and sustain the only other intelligent life that remains in the galaxy? Or do we allow the implanted Anathogen virus to disperse in eight days, as scheduled, and terminate the Project for good?

I open the floor to testimony and opinion.

Dear Joanna,
You're right. I did take those aquamarine earrings back in college. I just wanted to be a little more like you.
I'm sorry.

Dear Taylor,
I hope you get this message. Mom and I forgive you.
We love you. We want you to come home.

Dear Lucy,
No, you know what? YOU'RE the bitch.
Love, your sister

Mama,
It's Lynn. I'm sorry I've been a shitty daughter.
If I don't get a chance to talk to you before,
then know that I missed you every day.
Goodbye.

Emmy,
I was too much of a coward to send you that song
I promised. I'll always wonder if we could have
been something more.

G—
I don't know where you are or if you'll even care
to hear from me, but meeting you was the best
thing that ever happened to me. Thank you.

To the girl with the yellow backpack
on the weekday morning Q train,
You calmed me down when we got stuck underground, and I've
been crushing on you so hard ever since.
If I get a chance to see you one more time,
I'll tell you in person.

Dear Flynn,
You were right—it was yours. I'm so sorry.

Mom, Dad, Sammy, Shan:
I don't know if any of this is real,
but just in case: I love you. So much.
I'm praying for your safety.

Jeb,
I told you this would happen. I TOLD YOU.

Dearest Devi,
I screwed up real bad when we said goodbye.
No matter what Ajay's told you,
know that I loved you more than anyone.

Khalil,
I faked it the whole time. Peace out, asshole.
I hope the aliens probe you first.

1

JESSE

"Don't you dare," Jesse muttered. But the closeness of Ian's mouth on his neck killed his willpower, making his threat weak, and his knees weaker. Ian was teasing him, definitely teasing. And although it felt kinda good—okay, really freaking good—he didn't exactly like being at someone else's mercy.

Especially Ian's.

Teeth grazing. Mouth tightening. Jesse could practically hear his skin pop as he watched his own breath come out in clouds against the cold September night air. But as Ian's hand explored down his arm, as his fingers brushed against the leather cuff Jesse wore around his wrist and reached for the hem of his T-shirt, pleasure slipped into annoyance.

Jesse threaded his own fingers between Ian's, keeping them in place.

Jesse had two rules: his clothes stayed on—well, except for his pants, currently unzipped, if that even counted—and no touching the cuff.

And then it was over. Ian pulled away, smiling. The lime-green *Close Encounters* sign gave Ian's cheekbones a neon cast as it flickered and buzzed. Jesse was surprised the sign stayed lit at all; the place, like many others in Roswell, had closed down months ago.

Jesse's skin burned where Ian's mouth had been. He released Ian's hand and pressed his cool palm against the sear.

"Jesus. Really? A hickey?" He zipped his pants.

"Didn't hear you complain." Ian's smile faded. "Plus"—he looked away—"I wanted to leave you somethin' to remember me by."

For the last few months, Jesse and Ian had been meeting in the back of Close Encounters to have close encounters—of the casual kind. Before Ian, it was Joey behind the Arby's—his choice, not Jesse's. Before Joey, it was Ryan in the UFO Museum parking lot. Etcetera. Jesse was good at picking out the tourists who seemed a little more interested in *him* than the souvenirs he used to sell at the Roswell Plaza Hotel gift shop. Usually, it didn't last. The tourists left. That was the great thing about tourists: built-in security.

But Ian wasn't one of the usual picks, in part because Jesse had lost the gift shop gig. Ian went to the same school as Jesse, and thanks to Jesse's poor attendance—and his "behavior challenges," as his principal called it, Jesse was held back the year before, which made them both juniors now. He had seen Ian around; he just didn't realize Ian was interested in him until recently. Turns out Ian was just as good at keeping a low profile as Jesse was.

Jesse had wanted to—meant to—end it a while ago, but he hadn't gotten around to it yet. Besides, with the extreme lack of tourism these days, Ian grew more and more . . . convenient.

That's all, Jesse told himself. *Convenient.*

So here they were again, in the most run-down part of Roswell, in the middle of the night, flat desert spread around them both like a musty hotel blanket. A seemingly normal night, even if the wood fence behind them was covered in graffiti depicting green aliens in sombreros.

Except that it wasn't like Ian to leave a trace on him, and he knew damn well how Jesse felt about anyone staking a claim on him. Claims meant emotional investments. And investments meant living up to someone's expectations.

And expectations would only disappoint.

Jesse knew. He'd disappointed enough already.

"I have to tell you somethin'." Ian spoke gently. His accent was more intense tonight, which meant one of two things: (1) Ian was angry, or (2) Ian was nervous. Either way, it wasn't a good sign, and it put Jesse on edge. "There's—there's been a change of plans."

Jesse knew that tone of voice. He knew *plans*, and how they *changed*. His throat tightened. "Spit it out."

"We're leavin'." Ian sighed. "Tomorrow. I'm leavin' tomorrow."

A flare of pain shot through Jesse's chest, but he immediately flashed his trademark cover-up smile. "Oh. Good for you, man."

"We're headin' to my grandpop's place in Nashville. I mean, I can't blame them. Roswell's a hellhole, and it's only getting worse. My dad's shop hasn't had a car come in for weeks." He brushed a clump of sweaty bronze strands off his forehead. "Blame NASA, I guess."

It had been three months since NASA and some other science-y, alien-seeking organizations had supposedly discovered a nearby planet they called Kepler that could sustain life—that *did* sustain life. Two weeks since scientists supposedly intercepted an encoded radio message from the planet itself. The bunch of static they picked up was apparently more than just, well, static. What it meant was anyone's guess.

But it didn't matter if NASA hadn't yet figured out how to decode the message, if it even was that. It didn't matter that the whole story was probably cooked up bullshit, more government distraction tactics. All anyone ever wanted to talk about now was *real* aliens. Not the big-headed stuffed ones you could win at Close Encounters if you had enough tickets, back in its heyday, or the cardboard cutout you could take a picture with inside Pluto's Diner, where Jesse's mom worked.

Fake aliens weren't all that exciting anymore, hadn't been for decades, and it wasn't long before tourists, as few as there were, stopped showing up. Even Roswell's small local population had begun to dwindle to near-ghost-town numbers. Jesse's mom had called it the end of Roswell as they knew it—a total exaggeration, Jesse had thought at the time.

Now he was changing his mind.

Jesse shrugged. "No need to explain yourself to me. Your life is none of my business." The words fell from his mouth faster than he could stuff them back in. His counselor would shake her head if she could hear him. He'd just seen her yesterday for their weekly at La Familia Crisis Center, and the sound of her featherlight voice was still fresh in his mind. *Only five seconds of thought stand between you and a crap-ton of regret*, she'd say. Too late, though.

"None of your—?" Ian's fists curled. For a moment, Ian stared at Jesse, as though searching for something. Then he shook his head. "Ya know, I really liked you."

Jesse's skin prickled. He'd heard the same words come from Joey, from Ryan, from all the others who tried to stop him from pulling away from their lives. But the worst part about all this was that this time, it was *Ian* who was leaving.

Jesse should have broken things off weeks ago, when he'd first had the thought that maybe he *would* meet Ian's folks and stay for dinner, maybe he *would* hang around Mr. Keller's auto shop.

He'd been letting himself get too close.

"Yeah, sure. What we had was fun, and now what we had is *over*," Jesse said. And why had Ian thought it was a good idea to hook up one last time before dropping this news? Now Jesse just felt stupid. He pulled his leather motorcycle jacket—the one with the ugly crow patch on the front—closer around him. It was too big for him, but the extra leather felt good—protective, somehow. It's why he always kept his clothes on during every hookup. Most of them, anyway. "It's better this way," he said, forcing a laugh. "Trust me."

Ian was quiet for a while. He looked down and licked his dry lips. "It's funny," he finally said, in a way that wasn't funny at all. "I knew what people said about you, but I didn't care. I didn't believe 'em."

Jesse didn't need to ask what he meant. People were always running their mouths about him at school—whispering that he was white trash, that he was a thief, that he was a piece of shit. It wasn't even being gay that was the problem. Jesse's sexuality was like his tattered leather jacket: a part of him, nothing more. Just one of the many reasons people chose to keep their distance from Jesse, and Jesse chose to keep his distance from everybody else.

He rubbed at his wrist, at the raised scar tissue beneath his leather cuff. "Maybe you should have," Jesse said.

"Yeah." Ian's voice cracked. "Yeah, maybe."

Jesse almost said *I'm sorry*. And he was. The truth was that every fiber in his body screamed, *Please don't leave me behind.*

But what was the point? In the end, all he could muster was

an icy "See you around."

Ian managed a laugh that sounded like he was choking. "I doubt it."

There was nothing more to say. Jesse could feel the weight of Ian's gaze on his back, the heaviness of Ian's anger and pity. He took a deep breath, ignoring the twisting in his stomach. He would not turn around.

Ian would go to Nashville and forget all about Roswell and Close Encounters and the nights they'd spent touching each other under its fluorescent radiance. He'd forget all about Jesse.

And Jesse would stay here. Jesse would always stay here.

Above him, the stars were winking. Gloating, maybe.

Or maybe they felt sorry for him, too.

CATE

CATE'S BUCKET LIST FOR THE END OF THE WORLD
(IN PROGRESS!)

1. Actually go to a party
2. Sneak out (sorry, Mom!)
3. KISS JAKE OWENS!!!

One minute, Cate was straining over the pounding music to explain the difference between "literally" and "metaphorically," and the next, Jake Owens was holding her face between his sticky hands, pressing his beer-soaked lips to hers.

She stiffened in surprise. She was kissing Jake Owens. *She was kissing Jake Freaking Owens.* She'd had a crush on Jake forever. The guy had bright green eyes speckled with gold, played ice hockey (and had the body to prove it), and had those low eyebrows that gave him an expression remarkably like an adorable, sad puppy in an SPCA commercial. But all she could think was that his mouth tasted sour. Before she knew what she was doing, she put her hands on his chest and pushed.

"Wait." She resisted the urge to wipe her lips when he pulled away.

He frowned. "I thought you wanted . . . ?"

The rest of his words were lost beneath a surge of music. Around them, bodies undulated to the beat of some annoyingly repetitive dance song, and the bass thumped in uncomfortable syncopation with Cate's heartbeat. The floor, tables, and every available surface sprouted empty red SOLO cups. Someone—Ivy, probably—had set up a fog machine, cloaking the inside of Krysten Meyer's basement with a thick layer of white that swirled and shifted against the dancers, ghostlike.

A couple of days ago—a few *seconds* ago, even—Cate might have drunk it all in—literally *and* metaphorically—reveling in the freedom of just being here. But now it looked gross. Tacky. Like everyone was trying way too hard to look like they were having fun.

"Sorry," she said. "I—I'm not feeling great." Which was at least partially true. She hadn't thought kissing would taste so much like Bud Light.

"What?"

"I'm not feeling great," she shouted.

"Talk louder."

"I'm not feeling great!" This time, at maximum decibel levels.

The hunger in Jake's eyes vanished. "If you're going to puke, go outside," he shouted back at her matter-of-factly. "The upstairs toilet's clogged."

She stared at him in amazement. This was the guy she'd even told Mom about, who'd listened eagerly, *excitedly*. And she'd stared at him so many times—fleeting glances in the halls, in third-period Honors English and seventh-period World History—that she was startled to realize she had never *truly* seen what he looked like before. Maybe sad-puppy Jake from class had only existed inside her head. Now, up close, she noticed not one, but two thick hairs protruding from his nostrils like spider legs, and the noxious beer-and-cheap-cologne fumes wafting from his neck.

What would he say, she wondered, if he knew about Mom's condition? She didn't want to think about it.

"Thanks for the tip," Cate said. When she pushed past Jake, he didn't try to stop her.

She needed air. The music was giving her a headache, and she was dizzy—she'd only choked down a few crackers for dinner before the party. Her mom had thrown out the Chinese food she'd been planning to eat for dinner because she swore she "saw a camera hidden inside the lo mein."

She felt a bead of sweat roll down her back. It was too hot, too damn hot. She should never have snuck out in the first place. She should never have let Ivy convince her. Usually, she knew better.

Listen, Babe, Ivy had said, wrapping her arm around her. *The world is probably ending. Aliens on the march and all that. So why are you holding yourself back?*

It was typical Ivy exaggeration—the bunch of radio static or signal or whatever it was from the newly discovered alien planet Kepler-88a hadn't even been decoded yet, and for all they knew it was nothing more than an alien butt-dial, or maybe a simple *Hello, little Earthlings! Mind if we borrow some sugar?* Nothing to panic about.

Cate couldn't help but feel that this time, though, her best friend was right. Why else would aliens ever bother to contact Earth? And if it really was harmless, why bother encoding it? At this rate, the world probably *would* end before Cate's life had even begun.

And if that meant tonight would be one of her last memories, she *really* had to rethink her life decisions.

As Cate pushed her way toward the stairs, Ivy's voice reached her from across the room. "Cate! Get over here!"

Ivy glowed against the fog, and the way her smile crinkled the corners of her eyes made her almost painfully gorgeous. A girl in her element. A girl with no regrets.

And why would she have any? The girl knew how to live, how to grab everything she wanted; despite dealing with parents who argued more than they breathed, she was named captain of the debate team, snagged an early acceptance to Stanford, and had 100 percent certainty in her future career as an attorney just like her mom. She made it all look effortless, too. Soon, Ivy would be *free*. She'd deserved it.

When had their paths diverged so much? Cate was happy for Ivy, and proud as hell. But she couldn't help but feel left behind. Then again, it wasn't like Cate had much of a choice. She had to be there for Mom. Mom, whose tired eyes always held a glint of guilt whenever she looked at her, who always insisted that Cate stop holding herself back because of her.

But she had to. It was stupid to imagine, if only for one night, she could have anything resembling a normal life. How could she, knowing Mom would be home alone, fighting demons in her own head?

What happened? Ivy mouthed, flashing an all-knowing grin from across the room.

Cate smiled weakly. *Bathroom*, she mouthed back.

Ivy fake-pouted. "Fine, but hurry!" she shouted, cupping her hands to her mouth so Cate could hear her above the music.

Cate took the stairs two at a time, grabbed her jacket from the couch, and flung it over her shoulder. She dove through the crowd of classmates clustered in the front hall—some she didn't know; some she didn't care to know—reached for the doorknob, and plunged outside.

She wasn't going to the bathroom. She was going *home*.

The September chill made Cate grateful for the jacket

she'd brought. Light gray vegan leather, on sale. A certified Ivy Huang pick, like most of her best clothes, like her newest haircut, a cute bob. But she still couldn't shake off the cold that had crept on her skin when Jake touched her. She'd imagined her first kiss would give her a rush of butterflies, that it would feel sweet, like liquid gold.

Stupid.

She shot a text to Ivy to let her know she'd left the party, and took a deep inhale. An afternoon rain had brought out the scents of metal and oil and earth from the veins of the city. The night was unexpectedly clear, and the fog had rolled off the bay, leaving the stars intact, glimmering against the dark.

She used to like looking up at stars. She'd even talk to them, too; on nights Mom couldn't listen, Cate knew that at least *they* would. But ever since her Environmental Science teacher told her that by the time their light had reached Earth, the stars had already died, the night sky creeped her out. The stars she saw were shining corpses, echoes in a hollow sky. She might as well have been venting to dead people.

She wondered if the aliens on Kepler-88a had seen the same stars, before they had died. Were they even prettier back then, up close and brimming with life?

Immediately, she tried to quash the idea of alien planets and their stars. She had enough to think about, and until the little green guys showed up with neutron guns, she still had to go to school every day and grab groceries for her mom on the way home, still study like hell just to catch up, make sure Mom took her pills, make sure that she ate, make sure that she slept, make sure Mom held on to her receptionist job at Health First Medical, which she'd managed to keep for an entire nineteen months (and four days). As long as Cate helped her mom stick to their routine, things could be normal, *stable*. Otherwise, her mom would stay glued to the TV, absorbing every bit of information about the weird signal from the new planet, melding news with the false thoughts and memories that seemed to grow in her mind like fungus. Ever since talk of aliens had become the topic on everyone's lips, Mom's condition threatened to spiral out of control. While the rest of the world buzzed with excitement, Cate had fished softened peach-colored pills out of a toilet bowl with a pasta spoon strainer and begged her mom to take one, just one pill.

She turned the corner of Folsom, and the Citizens for a Safer World office came into view. Tonight, the lights in the windows were off, but the sidewalk was still littered with anti-alien protest signs from an earlier demonstration.

Earth First, most of the signs screamed.

Love Is Not an Alien Concept, a lone counterprotest sign retorted.

She'd been so caught up preparing for the party that she hadn't even registered the sounds of the demonstration, hadn't even known it happened. She'd been so stupidly filled with hope for tonight. For her first—

She stopped walking. She'd had her first kiss. She touched

her fingers to her lips. Did she feel different?

A little bit.

Maybe. But she was probably imagining it. Just like she'd imagined sad-puppy Jake.

Her house emerged over the lip of a steep hill, a tiny slice of building smashed between other narrow homes. Cate and her mom rented the bottom floor of a traditional single-family home, remarkable only for its lurid flamingo-pink paint, which always flaunted itself from a distance. Tonight, however, as Cate approached the house, number fourteen lit up different shades of red and blue, red and blue, flashing staccato in the rotating sweep of police lights.

Police.

Guilt squeezed at her lungs with an icy grip, leaving her breathless.

She should never have left her mom alone. *Stupid, stupid, stupid!*

She ran.

The slamming of car doors resounded in the quiet night air; two police officers in dark uniforms emerged from the police cars. Her mom, still in her pastel blue pajamas, was hailing the cops from the front porch as if they were arrivals on some cross-oceanic ship.

"Mom!" Cate gasped, finally reaching the front yard. She was always struck by how effortlessly gorgeous her mom was: sand-and-sunbeam-flecked hair, glimmering green eyes—neither of which Cate had inherited—and laugh lines like memories of happier times etched in her skin. But now Mom looked sickly pale, like she was straining beneath some invisible weight. She tilted her head, squinting, as though she didn't recognize her daughter.

And maybe she didn't. More and more often, Cate's strong and beautiful mom felt tucked away somewhere. More and more often, Cate came home to Molly.

No. That wasn't right. Dr. Michel had told Cate that different sides didn't split her mom into different people, that *everyone* had different sides to them, and that didn't make them any less whole. But Cate, she hated to admit, still caught herself calling this stranger by Mom's given name whenever she appeared: Molly, a stranger she found unpredictable, even frightening at times, someone who didn't respond when spoken to, or spoke in rhyming phrases and nonsense words. Someone who dumped pills in the toilet because the voices told her to. Someone who saw cameras hidden in the lo mein.

But no, Mom was Mom, full stop. She would always and only ever be Mom.

Even if, in the dark corners of Cate's mind, it sometimes didn't feel like it.

The two police officers turned at the same time. "This your mother?"

"What does it look like?" Cate snapped. She had to stay calm, she knew that—but sweat trickled down her back. She dodged the cops and leaped the porch steps, grabbing her mom by the elbow.

"Are you okay?" Cate asked in a low voice. "Are you hurt?"

Her mom shook her head, even as she began to sway. "Not yet. Not yet. But soon," she said dreamily. "The police *know*."

"*You* called the police?" She could only imagine what Mom had said to them on the phone.

"Your mother called to report some kind of home invasion," one of the police officers said. "Dispatch had trouble getting the story."

Cate pushed down another surge of nausea. Her mom had been worried for weeks about an invasion—but not the kind they meant.

"It's okay, we'll put your alarm on, all right, Mom?" she replied, keeping her voice as steady as possible. They had no alarm system, but whenever her mom was upset, the idea of an alarm had seemed to pull her back. "It's my fault. I didn't set the alarm. No one's going to get in." Cate clenched her mom's hand, pulsing it steadily one, two, three times. Again, one, two, three, just like Dr. Michel had told her. Thankfully, her mom started to squeeze back. That was a good sign. Cate turned back to the cops, flashing them a big smile. "We moved from a bad area. Lots of home invasions. My mom gets nervous."

The police officers exchanged a look. One of them cleared his throat. "So there was no burglary?"

Invasions and burglaries: Mom thought Kepler-88a had infiltrated Earth long ago. Sometimes she thought the aliens were snatching babies, stealing secrets, lifting thoughts, even from inside people's heads.

"I—I'm so sorry," Cate said quickly, pivoting toward a new

lie, a new explanation. "There's been a misunderstanding. See, what she told dispatch was probably that we moved from our *last* home because of a burglary. But she was calling this time because I snuck out without telling her and she was worried." She spoke in a fluid rush, hoping the police officers would miss the gaps in her story. "But I'm here! I'm fine. Everything's fine, see?" It was only a matter of time before one of the neighbors noticed the commotion. Cate had lost count of all the times she'd had to explain why Mom was wandering outside at odd hours: she was just forgetful, she'd had one too many mimosas, she'd chased off a raccoon. Her mom's behavior had made Cate a deft liar; she'd had more than enough practice for the inevitable day that cops would show up.

Finally, the second officer, a kind-faced woman whose badge read *Rodriguez*, sighed. "Just do me a favor and don't give your mom a heart attack, all right? That's what cell phones are for. You gonna be out late, you call her."

"I will," Cate said. "I promise."

She stayed there, holding her breath, until the cops had returned to their car. Only after their taillights had disappeared over the hill did she realize how badly she was shaking.

She let go of her mom, wiping her wet palms on her jeans, sick with relief and with terror at how close they had come.

"Come inside, Mom," she said.

"Why did you let the officers go?" Her mom's voice was sharp, escalating. Across the way, Cate thought she saw the neighbor's curtains twitch.

"They'll come back later. They're going to patrol for . . ." She couldn't bring herself to say "aliens." "They're doing a neighborhood patrol. They said to get inside. Let's stay inside and turn on the alarm, okay?"

She whipped her keys out of her jacket pocket with trembling, still sweaty hands and approached the front door. The tiny blackbird key chain her mom had given her, before the schizophrenia took an aggressive hold five years ago, thwacked against the door as she turned the handle. She had once truly liked her blackbird. Her dad had carved it by hand and given it to Mom when they'd first met. It reminded her of Mom's first story about Dad: that he was a shape-shifter who transformed into a bird and flew somewhere far away. But one day, he'd fly back home, she had promised. Now the key chain was a reminder. A reminder that her dad, whoever he was, would not come back. A reminder that the stories she'd loved as a kid were just signs of Mom's early delusions.

A reminder never to rely on anyone but herself.

She sat her mom on her reading chair in the family room before racing into the kitchen to find the pills she'd been drying out on a paper towel. After checking her phone again—Ivy still hadn't texted her back—she made the mistake of glancing up and catching her reflection in the mirror above the sink, bleary-eyed, her concealer faded to reveal the stress zits she'd painstakingly hidden. But at least she was home, and that meant Mom was safe now. That meant Cate could breathe. She could deal with smudged eyeliner later.

When she came back into the living room, Mom was pacing in front of the TV, gripping a folded piece of paper. Cate recognized the paper right away: a ripped sheet from one of the many marble composition notebooks Mom kept tucked in the back of the broom closet, filled with strange drawings and coordinates that made no sense to Cate. Cate had discovered them years ago, but when she'd asked her mom what they meant, her mom had only smiled and said, "It's a secret." Cate never looked at them again. Looking inside them felt too much like a window into Mom's mind.

The news was on now, but muted. The screen revealed a panel of experts in suits with furrowed brows and pursed lips. Below them, a ticker at the bottom of the screen displayed the headline: KEPLER-88A: ALLY OR ENEMY?

The screen cut to the president of the United States at a podium, and the ticker changed: POTUS AND HIS JOINT SECURITY COUNCIL BOAST PROGRESS MADE ON DECODING MISSIVE FROM OUTER SPACE. . . .

Before she could read any more, her mom stepped in front of the television, blocking it. Cate swallowed her irritation. Selfishly, she just wanted a second to wipe off the rest of her makeup, to get out of this stupid dress, to pretend that tonight never happened.

"I've got your medicine," Cate said. "You can take it and go to bed."

"I'm not tired," her mom replied flatly. She took a step forward and seized Cate's wrist, knocking the pills from her hand. Fingernails dug into Cate's skin. "Listen, Cate. I want you to promise me that if anything happens to me, you'll get this letter to your dad." She pressed the folded square of paper into Cate's hand. "He's one of them, you know."

Cate didn't have to look at it to know that what was written there would be more nonsense. She didn't have to ask what Mom meant, either. First it had been the guy behind the register at the grocery store. Then the little girl selling Girl Scout cookies to fund a trip to the space station museum in Novato. Then a random old woman feeding birds in the park. "Aliens," her mom had said. "All aliens." The invasion wasn't coming. It was already here.

"Dad was an alien, too, huh?" Cate bent to retrieve the pills. She hated having to talk to her mom like she was a child, hated having to pretend to take her seriously in moments like these, hated all of it—this disease that had invaded their lives, more terrifying and insidious than any aliens could be.

Worst of all, she hated that, despite everything, Mom still clung to her memories of Dad like a comforting blanket, still clung to her desperate hope that he would come back after all these years. Mom and Molly seemed to be in agreement about one thing: Cate wasn't enough to protect them. Maybe they were right.

No. Stop that.

But her mom didn't seem to notice her discomfort. "Tall, with thick brown hair and dark eyes," she went on. "He looked like us. Blended in. But I could tell he seemed different.

Special. Always had his eyes on the sky. I had no idea, of course, where he was from. Everyone in Reno is from out of town, you know. I was."

"Why don't you take your medicine," Cate said, handing her a single pill.

Her mom inspected the pill between her two fingers, gripping it like a diamond. Cate tried not to cry with relief when her mom brought it to her lips and swallowed, leaving the water untouched.

"My feet are cold," her mom added. "What time is it?"

"Almost midnight, Mom." Cate's voice cracked. "It's time for bed."

"You shouldn't be up this late," her mom said, as if suddenly realizing it.

"It's okay." Cate drew her mom into a hug. *This is my mom*, Cate repeated inside her head. *No matter what, this is still my mom.* "I will never let anything happen to us, okay? I promise. Nothing's going to happen."

Over her mother's shoulder, the news was showing another press conference, another parade of military higher-ups, another cycle in the endless rotation of frowning experts. She read the ticker: DEMONSTRATIONS ROCK THE COUNTRY, DEMANDING THE GOVERNMENT RELEASE ITS TRANSLATION OF THE KEPLER-88A SIGNAL . . . NORTH KOREA THREATENS BALLISTIC MISSILES IN RESPONSE TO "WORLDWIDE HOAX" . . . CHRISTIAN EVANGELISTS TAKE TO THE PULPITS TO DECLARE END OF TIMES . . .

Cate's mom pulled away. She was sweating, despite the coolness of the air. But her eyes, at last, found focus. "Nothing's going to happen to us, Cate," she said, her head tilted like a bird's. "Why on earth would you say such a thing?"

TRANSCRIPT
EXCERPT FROM TRIAL

SCION 3: I apologize for the interruption, but I fear we're talking in circles. I believe it would be far more fruitful to further discuss the concerns about the impact of the leak. The communication itself compromises not only the integrity of our deliberations but potentially our planetary security.

SCION 6: We've already established there is nothing to discuss. Your sentiments are nothing more than paranoia. The specimens of Epoch have repeatedly denied the possibility of civilizations that predate theirs, despite comprehensive evidence to the contrary. Even if they have the capacity to translate the leak, they can pose no risk to our people.

SCION II: Every moment wasted on conjecture brings us closer to the Anathogen virus, rendering this entire discussion meaningless.

SCION I3: [abruptly stands] I would like to propose

---

that a representative of Project Epoch—a human—
be present to speak on their behalf. Can it be a just
trial if the accused cannot bear witness?

[Let the record show the feeds crashed momentarily
due to an upsurge in traffic.]

ARBITER: Order, please, or we will cut the feeds.

SCION 13: Scions, we are deciding the fate of a species. The humans of Planet Epoch share 98 percent
of our DNA, yet we are discussing their potential
eradication as if they are no more than bacteria.
Do they not deserve a say in their own fate?

SCION 7: It would take more than eight days to
bring them here.

SCION 13: Then perhaps we should not be deciding
the fate of an entire species in a matter of eight
days.

ARBITER: Sit down, 13. [Scion 13 sits.] Unfortunately, the countdown for the Anathogen dispersal
demands a swift decision, and Alma grows ever
weaker with each passing moment. Let us continue.

3

ADEEM

"Earth to Adeem," Miss Takemoto's voice rang out from the front of the computer science lab, shocking Adeem into awareness like an electric jolt to his skull.

Adeem looked up, confused. At the front of the room, Miss Takemoto's hand was still gripping the Expo marker to the whiteboard where she'd begun writing a string of code. From the looks of it, they were reviewing arrays. Kindergarten stuff. He knew he'd zoned out for a reason.

"Glad you could join us again," she said as the class erupted in snickers. "Now if you could refrain from huffing on that applesauce pouch like a baby elephant, we can all get back to class."

Adeem shoved his red-rimmed glasses back into place and blinked in slow, clumsy realization. He pulled the applesauce pouch from his lips. He'd been sucking, not blowing—not that he was about to correct her, of course—on an empty pouch of Very Berry Applesauce for God knows how long. When had applesauce turned to air, anyway? Was that why he was so airheaded? The lack of sleep was affecting him more than he thought.

He'd been up all night listening in on ham radio nets— basically discord channels for radio junkies—on his shortwave radio. Ever since he'd overheard a former NASA engineer explain what he knew about the alien message on one of the nets, information not available to the general public, he'd been hooked. He'd even discovered the radio could allow him, if the timing was right, to communicate with astronauts on the International Space Station, people who'd reached the scientific equivalent of enlightenment. And they'd talk back, their voices carried by nothing but photons, almost three hundred miles from Earth. Who knew what else he'd find?

An embarrassed smile crept across his face. "My bad, Miss T."

She waved her hand impatiently. "Just toss it, please. How many times do I have to remind you there's no food allowed during class?"

As he stood and dropped the empty pouch with a *thunk* into the nearby trash bin, he could feel his classmates' eyes on him, wondering if Miss Takemoto would finally snap and write him up. It wasn't the first time Adeem had caused an interruption, after all. Once, he'd made a program on C++ to control her mouse cursor from his phone, forcing her to click on all the wrong programs; it'd taken her ten minutes to realize it was him. Then the other week, he'd made her computer meow whenever she pressed the space bar. But his grades had cushioned him from any kind of penalty, and he was pretty sure Miss Takemoto had been impressed he could pull those pranks in the first place. It's why she'd been hounding him since freshman year for his college plans, trying to get him to meet with an MIT rep, and throwing sign-up forms for code jams and national robotics competitions in his face—sometimes literally.

Even the applesauce pouches were her idea. Easy to eat when coding, healthy sugars and all that. "I'm not having you become one of those Mountain Dew–chugging zombies, not under my watch," she'd said before tossing him a pouch after school at Coding Club. Back when he actually showed up.

He took his seat in the back of the classroom. Beside him, Derek Robinson, his best friend since fifth grade, shook his head. *Idiot*, he mouthed. Adeem flashed him a grin.

Adeem normally spent his weekends at Derek's house, where they made their own video games. They'd work side by side late into the night before Adeem would call it quits and crawl to the kitchen to eat all of Derek's Corn Pops in the glow of the refrigerator, while Derek sat cross-legged on the countertop, adding final touches to some artwork on his tablet. Their latest project was a cat simulator game. Before that, it was a dating sim for AIs. A platformer. They'd done it all.

But the games never went anywhere, and Adeem's parents—and Miss Takemoto—were hounding him now with words like "wasted potential" and "future plans." They might have had a point. Making games took time, time that probably could have been spent doing homework or fluffing up his résumé or studying for the SATs. Things he never did. In the end, though, Adeem put their game-making on hold, if only to stop dragging Derek down with him, give him his weekends back. Even if *his* future was a black hole, Derek's didn't have to be.

Not that he'd told Derek the real reason, of course. As far as Derek knew, Adeem simply didn't have time to make games anymore now that his weekends were taken over by his newest weird hobby: amateur radio. Which was partially true.

It's not Thursday if you don't get dragged by Miss T at least once, Derek typed on a blank Notepad file on his computer—their way of passing notes, though they sat next to each other—once their teacher began lecturing again.

Adeem opened Notepad on his own computer. *She's just mad because I already finished her joke of a midterm.* He'd created a binary translation program using JavaScript. It had taken him two hours, a couple applesauce packets, and one tumbler of black coffee. He'd turned it in last night, and Miss Takemoto had replied with a single thumbs-up emoji; they both knew the midterm project was nothing more than a formality for him.

Derek's eyes widened. *Why do you even bother taking any*

comp sci classes when you're just gonna dominate them?

Adeem shrugged and typed: *And miss baby's first steps into programming? No way.*

404 Humor Not Found, Derek replied with a scowl. JavaScript Fundamentals was Derek's first coding class, and he wasn't shy about expressing his hatred of it to Adeem, much to Adeem's amusement. But for someone who only cared to do artwork for their games, Derek was actually pretty good at coding. It'd be fun having Derek in on his pranks, not that he'd risk getting Derek into trouble, too.

Miss Takemoto finished writing the array object and was now highlighting the various elements and variables in different-colored markers. But Adeem caught her glancing back at them, as if she knew he wasn't really paying attention. He batted away at the guilt buzzing in his head like a fruit fly that wouldn't die.

The thing was, Miss Takemoto had high hopes for Adeem, and he knew it. Adeem wasn't exactly a genius—and according to his mom, he was an idiot for not taking school seriously—but he'd always been pretty good at fixing things. It had started with him tearing apart his sister's old toys and putting them back together: a plastic "robot" dog, a canary-yellow drone, a remote-controlled R2D2. Then his dad's antique Philco radio, chipped at the left-hand corner from when his sister, Leyla, had once dropped it. He'd nearly taken apart the family computer until Leyla introduced him to programming, and he soaked up code like a sponge. He loved everything about it:

the fractals of scattered text across his white screen, the delicate architectural coherence of it all, and the looming threat it could all fall apart with a single misplaced symbol. Coding was like a game of chess, but he could make the rules. With his own imagination being the only constraint, coding was the closest he'd ever felt to having some semblance of control over something.

The skill had other benefits, too. Being the only two brown kids in school, Adeem and Derek were practically walking targets for people like Chris Wakely, the kind of kid who proudly hung a certain red baseball cap in his locker and grumbled, loudly, about the growing population of "Mexicans" during every school assembly. When Chris Wakely called him a terrorist in the hallway last year, Adeem hacked into Chris's email and created a macro that made every one of Chris's emails autosign as Shit Wakely. Coach Grier wasn't too thrilled; apparently, it had made Chris's college football scholarship prospects a little . . . strained.

But that was the extent Adeem had ever used his talents: making silly little games, pulling stupid pranks. As for anything else—anything *more*—some invisible weight was holding Adeem back.

How was he supposed to explain to Miss Takemoto and his parents that taking his coding talent seriously would mean that his future would forever be tied down to memories of his sister? Memories that still stung every time he saw the chipped Philco radio or wrote new code he was proud of.

Code that she would have been proud of, too.

If she'd cared enough to stick around.

The eighth-period bell chimed.

He turned off the computer and stood, racing to pack his notebook, when Miss Takemoto called his name, her voice only just bobbing above the cacophony of rustling backpacks and chairs scraping across the linoleum floor.

She was waving him over. Dread coiled down from his stomach to his feet, fastening him to the floor.

Derek looked at him sympathetically and shook his head but said nothing. Adeem breathed in, letting the oxygen settle before walking through the crowd of glazed-eyed students making their way out of the classroom.

"You staying after school for Coding Club?" Miss Takemoto asked as he approached, hastily erasing the whiteboard, leaving behind trace marks of code. It smelled sharply of alcohol solvent and ink, and made him dizzy.

Miss Takemoto was also the supervisor for Coding Club, and there was no way Adeem could deal with her any longer than he already had. He scrambled for an excuse. "Not today. I've got a . . . dentist appointment."

But Miss Takemoto suddenly spun to face him, her eyebrow raised. "*Another* one?"

Shit. Note to self: think of other kinds of appointments. "Yeah," he said with a laugh. "All that applesauce, I guess. Eroding my enamel."

She wasn't convinced. Her eyes bored through him, and

her face contorted as though it was straining to hold back her accusations. If he was lucky, the smell of alcohol solvent would hide the smell of his bullshit. Behind her, the flyer for the National Robotics Challenge still hung on the corner of the whiteboard. She'd probably put it there on purpose.

It was times like this he wished he could ask Leyla for advice. Leyla, the one person responsible for his love of computers and old tech. Leyla, the one person who could always make sense of him when he could not.

Leyla, the one person who he'd been sure would always be there. Until she'd ninja'd her way out of his life.

Adeem flexed his stiff fingers and smiled through gritted teeth. "I'll start showing up again soon. Just been busy with other stuff." *Like avoiding you.*

Miss Takemoto's expression was unreadable. "I'll hold you to it," she said. And Adeem knew she would.

Maybe Derek was right. He was starting to regret signing up for her class. He needed to avoid her altogether.

Derek was still standing by the doorway, waiting. He always waited. And it surprised Adeem every time. He was starting to get convinced Derek would always stick around, a feeling so uncomfortably unfamiliar to Adeem.

Because when Leyla left, Adeem was sure everyone else would, too.

Adeem grabbed his backpack off his chair and followed Derek into the hallway. They walked side by side, making their way toward study hall.

"Everything okay?" Derek asked casually, but his eyes spelled out worry.

"Oh, that. I'm grounded from applesauce, apparently. Guess I'll have to start bringing corn chips and Pop Rocks to class instead."

Derek snorted. "I honestly don't know why Miss T puts up with your ass."

"Honestly? Me neither." Adeem pulled his hood back down, letting cool air hit his neck. "Me neither."

ADEEM: CQ, CQ, calling CQ. This is Alpha Eight-Romeo-Delta-Sierra. Hello, world. This is Alpha-Romeo—

RESPONDER: A8RD . . . S? Is that correct?

ADEEM: Yeah. I mean, affirmative. Over.

RESPONDER: This is November-Seven-Foxtrot-Victor-India, coming in from El Paso, Texas.

ADEEM: N7FVI . . . got it. Okay. Uh, I'm Adeem, from Carson City, Nevada. I just got licensed. As an operator. So I'm just testing out CQ for the first time. Kind of amazed it actually worked. I mean, I've fixed radios. But never actually transmitted anything.

RESPONDER: Well! Nice to meetcha, Adeem. I'm Jim. Let me be the first to welcome you to the world of amateur radio. It's a fun little hobby we have here, but you never know when it might come in handy, and you never know who you'll meet. Go ahead.

ADEEM: Sounds like it. I heard you can talk to astronauts if you're lucky.

RESPONDER: That's radio for ya. It'll connect you to just about anyone. Got anything to report?

ADEEM: No. I mean, nothing yet. Was just testing it out, in case, you know? And I just . . . wanted to see if anyone could hear me.

RESPONDER: Ha. I know the feeling. Well, rest assured, you've been heard loud and clear.

ADEEM: That must be a first.

RESPONDER: Come again?

ADEEM: Nothing. Thanks, sir.

JESSE

The glass door chimed behind Jesse as he entered the Quik-Trip and narrowly missed slipping on a giant puddle—of water, he hoped—that someone had forgotten to finish mopping. A yellow *CAUTION: WET FLOOR* sign lurked stealthily to one side.

Great. Thanks.

He pulled his baseball cap farther over his face, his dark curls stubbornly peeking through, and peered at the counter. Monday meant Marco's shift.

Usually, when Marco wasn't out smoking, he was bent over his phone, or cabled to his earphones, listening to music on blast. But today he had his back turned to the door, and his eyes glued to the small TV wedged between stacks of shitty one-ply toilet paper in the corner. The usual crowd of reporters were working themselves into a lather over the same alien planet bullshit as always. Dimly, Jesse remembered hearing the president was meant to deliver some urgent message to the nation.

More scare tactics, he'd bet.

Marco was so engrossed, he didn't even glance over his shoulder when Jesse entered.

But just in case: "Hey, my man. Workin' hard or hardly workin'?" Jesse asked cheerfully.

Marco only grunted in response.

Jesse smiled. Ah, Marco. Always dependable. The manager, Randal, was onto Jesse, and if *he* was manning the storefront, Jesse'd have to scrounge for loose change to buy a pack of gum just to snuff any suspicion. A waste.

Long ago, Jesse had learned that swallowing his guilt, stuffing it deep down inside him, made for pretty good sustenance. And though his mom never knew why the bread and peanut butter kept popping up on the shelves even when she had no money to buy them, she never questioned him, and neither did Jesse's stomach.

After Dad died, Jesse's mom used to recite fortune cookie proverbs like, "You always have a choice in anything you do." Her way of doling out motherly advice, or comforting herself. But if they had a choice, it wasn't much of one. Money was tight, had always been tight. When the hotel closed down, one of Roswell's last, Jesse's part-time job prospects looked dim; almost no businesses in town were hiring, except for a new Citizens for a Safer World branch—and his mom called them a hate group, so Jesse steered clear. Even if it did make him feel helpless. Useless.

But his mom was already taking about a million shifts a week waiting tables at Pluto's, and there was a limit to how much he would watch her work herself to the bone for him. Even if his mom kept insisting she had everything under control, Jesse wasn't stupid. He'd seen the piles of used tissues in her trash can, heard the arguments she had with Mr. Donovan, the landlord, on the phone. Jesse *had* to pull his weight, somehow. Unlike Ian, Jesse and his mom couldn't up and leave when things got rough. They didn't have a grandpa in Nashville they could run to. They only had each other.

Now safely out of sight, tucked between the aisles packed with pork rinds and potato chips, Jesse surveyed the meager food options. His mom had never been a fan of white bread, but the QuikTrip carried nothing else. Maybe he'd get her a loaf of real bread from some bakery for her birthday. The fancy kind with poppy seeds on the crust, the kind that Dad used to get early in the morning every Sunday, when it was still oven-warm. When he wasn't on one of his "business trips" to California. Or when he wasn't obsessed with building his weird machines out of scrap metal in the work shed behind the house.

Poppy seeds always made him think of Dad. Poppy seeds,

lottery tickets, lug nuts, and Bud Light: dear ol' dad in a nut-shell.

Jesse shoved a loaf in one inside jacket pocket, a jar of Jif into the other. If there was one good thing his old man ever did, it was leaving behind his giant-pocketed, oversized motorcycle jacket with the ugly crow patch. That and his old shed full of failed contraptions and dented metal parts—a freaking temple of fool-headedness and rust.

If only the guy hadn't left behind a pile of debt, too.

Pockets full, all Jesse had to do now was casually exit without making Marco suspect a thing. It was all about attitude. He eyed the security cameras—no red light blinking; they probably couldn't afford to keep them wired anymore—and pulled his hat down even farther, just in case, as he slid once again into view of the counter.

Still, Marco didn't even glance away from the TV. Jesus. Jesse wondered how long it had been since he'd even blinked.

A gaudy wall of color behind the counter gave him pause. Rows of scratch-off lottery tickets, screaming promises of instant cash, including Lucky Star Lotto, the kind of tickets Dad used to buy compulsively and squirrel away in an old utility cabinet in his work shed, where he'd spent most of his time with those goddamned, good-for-nothing machines.

Once, when Jesse asked why, his dad grinned, revealing white teeth against his thick black beard. *Times can get tough, kid*, he'd explained, locking the drawer. *Luck is valuable. We gotta keep luck for a rainy day.* For all Jesse knew, his old man had never scratched a single one. It pissed Jesse off to think about it now. All that money his dad had thrown away, money that could have been used for bills, for family movie nights, for keeping his promise to take Mom to Cali with him one day. So much *waste*.

The door chimed. A guy in a navy-blue track jacket entered the store. Black hair, a sharp nose, a clean face—he didn't look much older than Jesse. Though the QuikTrip was thick with the smell of burned coffee, when the boy edged over to the coffee station, Jesse got a whiff of his shampoo: woodsy, like freshly cut cedar, mixed with something like vanilla.

He had never believed in things like "aura"—though his counselor had told him if he had one, it'd be the color of the night sky, dark blue and hazy purple. He wasn't even sure, sometimes, that he believed in souls. But if she was right—that some people did give off auras and presences and energies— then this guy's could only be described as a fiery-white, unrelenting orbit, a gravitational pull. And Jesse was caught in its path.

The boy filled his cup to the brim, and it took his long legs only two easy strides to bring him to the register. Marco tore himself from the TV and recoiled in surprise, as though he hadn't even noticed the guy come in, much less appear in front of him.

Marco scratched his chin, his expression returning to its usual state of vacancy. "You need a lid for that?"

"Nah, gonna chug it," the boy said. His voice was a smoky

vibration of bass, and something shivered down Jesse's spine. Did he go to a different school? Was he a tourist? Just driving through? He wanted to see his face, a want like a rush of blood to the head.

He tugged at the leather cuff around his wrist. *Impulsive.* The word rang in his brain. His counselor had called him that. *You lack impulse control. Like a dog chasing a car. Think about that the next time you're itching for a chase.* His fingers slid beneath the smooth leather, and he squeezed his wrist, hard.

The register dinged; Marco slapped the drawer to close it. Change exchanged hands.

"I've always wondered—does anyone actually buy those?" the boy asked suddenly. Jesse couldn't see what he was referring to, but Marco spun to see what the boy was looking at: the lottery tickets, glittering like jewels.

"Oh yeah. You'd be surprised."

"Yeesh." The boy ran his hand through his thick mop of hair. "Can't put a price on hope, I guess." His laugh was rich, buttery smooth. Like he put his whole soul into it.

He left as quickly as he'd come, leaving only the subtle smell of cedarwood. Jesse slipped his hands into his pockets, feeling the peanut butter jar and bread still snug in their place: weights that tethered him to his purpose. He started for the door.

Suddenly, the store phone started ringing at the same time that Marco's cell began blowing up with text message pings, the simultaneous sounds breaking through Jesse's mind-numbing daze and snapping him to attention.

"Oh, *shit*," Marco was saying to himself, not answering his texts at all, just staring at a news reporter on the TV screen. The show he was watching had been interrupted by a breaking news announcement. Marco turned up the volume.

It was live footage of the president himself, pink-faced and shaken as he read out an official statement. "... was decoded at fifteen hundred by US intelligence. Officials have confirmed that the alien planet calls itself Alma, and that the signal we received is indeed a message, a warning of an impending judgment ..."

The words seemed to blur in Jesse's head. Something about seven days.

A colony. Earth *was* the colony.

Termination, an experiment, an alien threat against humanity. The static was actually a *message*, the worst possible kind. He could barely keep up.

Then there was a rapid slew of information on new travel restrictions and security measures ... but it was like Jesse's brain had imploded.

Security measures? Was this a joke? What kind of security measures were you supposed to take when it came to freaking mass genocide by an alien planet? He felt dizzy. His thoughts were spiraling too fast to understand. The convenience store faded to white, falling away. Only the sound of his own breathing echoed in his head, drowning out the president's televised voice.

Seven days. Seven days. Earth might end in seven days. For practically as long as he could remember, Jesse had wanted a way out. But this was ridiculous. A conspiracy theory. It had to be.

Could it be real? He was a Roswell kid, for Christ's sake. Half the tourists that came through believed in little green men. He knew better than to fall for this shit.

And yet . . . this was different. This was the president. Would the president lie?

Okay, yes, maybe. But was *everyone* lying?

He wondered, fleetingly, whether his counselor had heard the news. He wondered how she would try and spin this one for the positive. How she would try and "turn loss into opportunity." How much loss would she face, would they all face, before she would admit it was nothing but bad luck?

His eyes trailed from the TV, and suddenly, the little gold stars on the lotto tickets were all he could see—glistening, blinding.

Times can get tough, kid. We gotta keep luck for a rainy day.

He ducked under the counter, as though he could feel the stars pulling him in like magnets. He peeked over at Marco, still glued to his screen. The cell phone in his grip lit up with more text messages.

Can't put a price on hope, I guess.

Jesse's fingers hovered over the scratch-offs, itching for the feel of their perforated edges. Itching to feel his fingertips skirt the surface of stars. He pulled at a corner ticket and tore.

"Hey!"

He swiveled around. Marco had turned and caught sight of him. For a second they were frozen there, staring at each other, while above Marco the corner TV still babbled the news of the maybe-end-of-the-world.

It was exactly like a dream.

Except that it wasn't.

Before Marco could say anything else, Jesse vaulted over the counter and bolted for the door.

Marco was right behind him. Jesse reached out and knocked over a magazine rack. Marco tripped over it but managed to grab the back of Jesse's jacket as he went down, pulling at it, almost taking Jesse down with him. But Jesse caught himself and jerked away. Marco was back on his feet, nimble for his size, just as Jesse regained his balance. In this small space, there was no way Jesse could outrun him; he'd have Jesse pinned to the ground a few feet out the door.

He was facing Marco now, who was breathing heavily. Jesse hadn't given him enough credit.

"Hand it over," Marco said.

When Jesse tried to pivot, Marco rushed forward and threw a punch. Jesse dodged it easily. His countless suspensions and occasional expulsions for fighting came in handy.

But all that was over now. Everything was over. The future looked like one split second of mushroom cloud. What the hell did Marco think he was fighting for? Why did he care?

Jesse was distracted, giving Marco a window to land a punch clean to the face. A hot explosion screamed through

Jesse's body, his jaw throbbing. He doubled over. Cradling his face, he almost smiled, relishing the pain that knocked Ian right out of his head.

That's when Jesse saw the bread and peanut butter; they'd been thrown from his pockets and landed a couple feet away. He dove toward them, but Marco seized him again, this time by the collar, and dragged him farther away from the food.

No. This was the one right thing he could do for his mom. He wouldn't let Marco take that away.

Instinct took over, and Jesse threw a punch as hard as he could. Marco recoiled and quickly let go. Jesse's mind was numb, scorched by an inner white blaze that had no beginning or end, leaving room only for the fire and fear and frustration he'd been suppressing for so long. Jesse advanced, punching him again. Marco staggered back, trying to raise a hand, trying to get Jesse to stop. But then Jesse kicked him in the stomach. Marco gagged and bent over.

"Stop–!"

Jesse couldn't hear. He swung his leg at the backs of Marco's knees and watched him slam to the ground.

"Please! Stop!"

This time, Marco's voice reached him, tunneled deep into Jesse's chest, made him freeze where he stood. He suddenly felt so cold. His mouth tasted like blood.

Marco was curled up in a fetal position, a huge crimson welt on his cheek, blood dripping from his split lip. His left eye had disappeared beneath a mound of deep purple skin.

With every gasp of air, his chest shuddered.

Jesse took a step back. What the hell had he done?

"I'm just trying to keep my job, man," Marco wheezed out. He had his hands in the air, like he was still worried that Jesse would attack him. "We're all just trying to survive."

"There's no fucking *point*," Jesse choked out. Tears burned at the back of his eyes. He almost said he was sorry. Like there would be a point to that, either. Like it would change what he'd done.

He picked up the fallen bread and peanut butter. In the distance, he heard the wail of a police siren—no telling where it was headed, but he didn't want to take any chances. He tore out of the store and through the streets until all he could hear was the slap of his shoes against pavement and the thud of blood in his ears. Every time his feet hit the ground, his jaw bloomed red pain behind his eyelids.

It was the least he deserved.

Finally, he slowed down to a walk and listened. No sirens. He'd half expected to find the world transformed, unrecognizable. But it was worse than that. The world hadn't changed at all.

Jesse looked up. The sky was clear and stars were bright. Maybe in another life, he'd find them beautiful.

The last time—well, second-to-last time—he and Ian had hooked up was in Ian's car. They had driven out into the desert until the city lights faded into the horizon, a blurred spot of hot light. They'd lain on the hood of the car after they fooled around and Ian had showed him where the planet was.

"You can't see it," he said, circling a wide area of the sky with his finger. "But it's somewhere in that general direction."

"I don't get why everyone's freaking out about it. It's just gonna be a glorified Earth."

"Maybe," Ian said, laughing, and squeezed his hand. Jesse liked the way Ian laughed. It was full and warm. "Maybe *we're* the glorified Earth. Ever think of that?"

Now Jesse took a slow sip of crisp night air. He shoved his hand in his pocket; the lotto ticket was still nestled inside. Gritting his teeth, he closed his eyes.

If there were aliens up there, he wondered if they were looking down at him right now. Maybe they'd be shaking their heads at him for stealing, for the depravity of humans like him. Then he'd forever be that guy: the reason humankind was destroyed. Of course, he knew he wasn't important enough to cause the apocalypse.

He wasn't even important enough to Ian.

"Nothing glorious about it," he said out loud. His breath seized on the cold desert air and then vanished.

BY THE POWER VESTED IN THE INTERPLANETARY AFFAIRS COMMITTEE OF THE SOVEREIGN PLANET OF ALMA:

HUMANS OF EARTH: You are hereby notified that final judgment will be issued in seven solar days under authority of Chapter 12, Article 8 of the United Galactic Assembly Agreement.

Offenses committed have been purported as follows:

1. Destruction of intergalactic environmental resources;
2. Unconscionable systematic abuses of its own people;
3. Gross disregard for the preservation and sustainability of future generations;
4. Incessant armed attack and devastation without provocation;
5. Subjugation and slavery of free-thinking organisms;
6. Elimination of a people's right to self-determination;
7. Disruption of the peace.

. . .

There is no need to attend the committee hearing to contest your liability. Sanctions are in effect until further notice.

SEVEN DAYS

UNTIL THE END

OF DELIBERATIONS

LYNNE, are you seeing what I'm seeing??

The news? Mark's flipping his shit. Do you think it's real?

I don't want to believe it, either. How is this happening?

I don't know. I can't think right now.

THIS ISN'T FUNNY, JEREMY. I'M LEGIT FREAKING OUT.

Yeah, but what else are we supposed to do
 lol

You need to take a flight home right now.

Don't worry about money, I'll cover it.

I've got midterms in like three days.

Your mom is worried.

Come home now.

Please.

If Alma's going to exterminate all of humanity . . .

That means animals will inherit the earth.

And for some reason, that makes me feel better.

Margot, are you high??

5

CATE

When Cate was nine, her mom had sent her to a summer camp called Camp Escondido, about an hour's drive south from where they lived at the time in Daly City. Cate had spent that summer learning how to ride horses, nursing her shredded knees from hours of rollerblading, and clumsily weaving friendship bracelets with all the other girls.

It was the best summer of her life.

When it was time to go home, she had cried—and didn't stop for a week. Not just because the camp was over and she missed her friends, but because *summer itself* was ending soon. It felt like she had glanced away for a second and the whole summer had slipped by her, like her mom had somehow tricked her, cheated her of something excruciatingly important.

It felt like that now. The world itself was ending. Summer was going away for everyone.

One week. They had one week to live . . . *probably*. How should she even begin to process that? It was as if the whole world had been walking on its merry way only to find it had stepped in something sticky. Now they'd reached that moment of hesitation—was it dog shit or simply a piece of gum?

Seven billion lives were at the mercy of some distant planet, a speck they could hardly see with even the best telescopes. What did they want, really? They said Earth was going up for judgment: But what kind of judgment? What more could they want? The whole thing felt unfair. And why even *send* a message of warning if humans could do nothing to change the outcome? She almost wished they'd just torch Earth while everyone was sleeping. Get it over with.

Schools across the state had been suspended in light of the news, and since Ivy had yet to respond to any of her texts, Cate couldn't even ask her what she thought about it all, though, knowing Ivy, even aliens wouldn't scare her. Some people on TV were suggesting the whole thing was one big scam, or a ploy by the government to distract from rampant unemployment and a massively unpopular new Supreme Court justice. But Cate wasn't optimistic or dumb enough to believe that.

It seemed to Cate no one in San Francisco had slept last night: everyone walked around like dull-eyed zombies. Maybe it was that no one could stand to be in darkness, or bear the inevitable *The Day After Tomorrow*–style nightmares. Apartment lights burned all night long, and as a result, the state was experiencing rolling blackouts. But some people were already accusing Kepler-88a—no, *Alma*—of interfering with the grid to cause chaos. It didn't help that the local government was silent about whether this particular blackout was a scheduled one. The government was silent, period. And that's what scared her most of all.

She was actually relieved when she got a request from Bethany, her boss at Lickity Split Creamery, for help: the freezers were dark and the ice cream would soon become worthless, watery milkshakes—if rioters didn't loot the place first. So Bethany had decided to pass out the inventory for free.

"Even the end of the world can't kill people's taste for good ice cream," she had said with a wink, and it was true. All day, there was a line around the block. Bethany turned up the radio extra loud, and the Creamery was filled by old Motown classics, the music pulling more customers inside. Some of the littler kids in line giggled watching Bethany overenthusiastically bob her head to the beat, and their parents smiled tiredly, perhaps grateful for the momentary respite.

Cate even recognized a couple of classmates who shuffled in joking about being called sinners by four different Jesus impersonators, though their faces were waxen with exhaustion. She didn't know their names, and they probably didn't know hers, but they nodded at her in acknowledgment, as if seeing Cate work a shift at an ice cream shop when all of humanity would be eradicated in a few days were the most ordinary thing in the world.

Working in the heat, talking to people, scooping until her bicep ached—Cate was just happy for the excuse to *do* something, to shut down her mind, to keep it from cycling around the same news like a fly headed for a bug zapper.

Was it possible—even remotely possible—that all human existence could end, just like that? The grocery store lines and the math tests, the basement parties and the beach concerts, summers at Fort Funston and the early morning rush—all of it just gone, evaporated, *extinct*? What would come next, if anything?

What could Cate say she had done in her life?

It was after six p.m. when Bethany told Cate to go home: they'd reached the end of the supply, and still people were coiled around the block. Cate knew they weren't there for the ice cream. They were there for a slice of summer, a slice of happiness, packed into a cone. A scoop of forgetting.

Ivy still wasn't answering any of her texts or calls. Cate's worry was slowly devolving to panic. Ivy's parents were always prone to fighting, and the news about Alma was bringing out the worst in everyone. With school canceled, Ivy couldn't exactly bury herself in schoolwork, or go to a house party veiled as a study session to avoid the fighting. And the last time she'd tried—and failed—to break up an argument between her parents, she'd gotten so frustrated, she stormed out and blasted through her allowance on a giant plum blossom tattoo at some seedy parlor in the Tenderloin. It would have covered her entire back if Cate hadn't made her reconsider.

But she told herself that Ivy could take care of herself. She always had.

Public transportation was down, and a logjam of traffic fleeing the city—as if there was anywhere to go—meant taking a cab would be pointless. She passed a prayer circle right in the middle of the street, cars honking and people shouting as their leader chanted. It all gave her the chills—she didn't know what to make of it and felt dazed as she floated through the city where she'd lived nearly her whole life, all of it transformed. At least it wasn't as bad as New York or Chicago, where they'd had to dispatch the National Guard to keep order.

Cate's legs ached. All day she'd been fending off the exhaustion of a sleepless night, and she'd been walking and weaving through the thin spaces between car bumpers for miles. She had to fight her way through some sort of spontaneous dance party in the middle of the street—hands trying to pull her into the throng of bodies. Her weariness was enough to make her forget for a second *why* it was all happening—why people were partying like it was the end of the world. Not metaphorically, either.

Literally.

When she got to her own street and saw more flashing

lights, she paused for a second, confused, thinking she was back at another party. And then suddenly her mind went clear and panic wormed into her gut. *Shit.*

Not again.

She broke into a sprint. It was uphill, and she was panting by the time she got to her address, where, sure enough, a police car and a white van were parked at the curb. She counted two police officers and another two people in dark green uniforms. One of them was escorting her mother into the back of the white van. She recognized the logo on the van now: Saint Francis Memorial Hospital.

"No!" Cate cried out. This couldn't be happening. Not again. Not so soon. She could barely bring herself to think about what this meant—two episodes back to back. Were the meds no longer working? "Please! You can't take her."

One of the officers got in her way before she could barrel past him to the door. His name tag said *Davis*, and she recognized him from the last time.

"It's Cate, isn't it?" He gently put his hand on her arm. She shoved his hand away. "Listen to me, Cate. We're going to help her, okay?"

Lies. "Let her go. You have no right."

"You've got to be strong now," he said. "Your mom needs help. She's a danger to herself. She's a danger to *you*."

"You're wrong. She wouldn't hurt me." *She wouldn't, would she?* They might only have seven days left together: it was impossible and true. There was no way her mom would spend it in the hospital. "She's already seen a doctor. She's on medication. She's just confused. It's all this planetary stuff. Please. You can't take her."

"It's for her own good. Believe me. And we'll be sure to notify . . . Dr. Michel, is it?" He briefly consulted his notepad. Cate wondered where he'd gotten the name.

"She's just going through a rough patch. It's nothing we haven't dealt with before." Her mind was spinning uselessly, but finally it landed on something Dr. Michel told her during one of their sessions. "B-besides, you can't hospitalize someone against their will. It's—it's the law." She knew it was probably silly to be lecturing the cops about the law, but still—desperation had forced her hand.

"She's agreed to go, sweetheart," the officer said gently. "She asked us to come here. *She* called *us*."

Cate froze. "What?" All at once, she understood how the cops had known about Dr. Michel.

Her mom was smiling weakly. Cate could see her softened eyes, the tears welling in them. She could see clarity returning to her. Mom was fighting back. She brought her hand up to the window. Her breath fogged the glass. Cate placed a hand on the window, too, as if she could press her way inside.

"It's okay, Catey. I—I'm sorry. I'm slipping . . ."

Cate felt tears spring to her eyes. She wrenched open the car door; Officer Davis made a move to stop her, and Cate expected he would yank her back, but he didn't.

She wrapped her mom in a hug. "Mom, please . . ."

"I'll be okay," she said, squeezing back. "Dr. Michel will be good to me. We don't have much time left. I can't have you holding on to regrets like I do."

"Regrets? What are you *talking* about?"

Her mom squeezed harder. "Listen to me, Catey. You've taken such good care of me, you know that? It's my fault you've had to grow up so fast. I was stupid and young and getting sicker, and when I left your dad, I didn't realize you'd end up shouldering everything. If I'd known . . ."

Cate stilled. "You . . . left Dad?" Her forehead began to throb, as though something in her skull was clawing to break free. "What do you mean? What—you told me he left *us*."

"Everything will be clear soon, I promise." Her mom pulled away. As the flashing red and blue police car lights played across her face, Cate saw her mom and Molly, Molly and her mom, chasing each other like shadows. She clenched her fist, trying to will the thought away. There was Mom, only Mom.

"Come on now," said Officer Davis, a hint of soft pity in his voice. He closed the door and Cate stepped back to stand beside him.

Officer Davis's team started the van and pulled away from the curb. Just before she was out of sight, her mom mouthed the words: *the letter.*

The van turned and vanished from view.

And then she was gone.

Cate stood there, empty, shocked, staring down the street. She was suddenly aware of all the lights that had come on at once—the electricity on the block had returned. She imagined the windows like eyes peering down at her.

"Is there an adult you can call? Someone you can wait with?" Officer Davis glanced uneasily past Cate into the lifeless, empty house. "Your mother mentioned you have grandparents in Connecticut . . ."

Cate gritted her teeth. "They won't help me." She and her grandparents barely spoke except on major holidays: deeply religious, they had cut off Cate's mother after she got pregnant out of wedlock.

"All right, then, why don't you come down to the station with me," Davis said, "and we can make some phone calls together?" It seemed more like an order than a question. Cate had no idea what to say. She was still a minor—could she argue to stay alone in their apartment? Then again, the world might be ending in a week. Did protocol really matter?

Did anything matter?

She wanted to sit down, take a moment to just breathe and think. But she was afraid that if she sat, she might somehow come apart—her body breaking up into a crumpled pile of limbs. She hadn't realized she was shaking.

"Okay," she said. Her mind was whirling, like a greased-up wheel skidding off its tracks. Time. She needed time. "Can I pack a few things first?"

Davis nodded. "Sure thing."

She had her first lucky break: Officer Davis followed her up the stairs but waited on the stoop when she fumbled open the door and slipped inside. She called Ivy as soon as she was in her bedroom and was hopeful when it didn't go to voice mail this time. But still, no answer.

Dammit, Ivy. Where the hell was she? If she were here . . .

Panic crawled its way from her stomach up into her chest, choking her, making it difficult to breathe. The world was ending. Now, here, this second.

What was she going to do?

Think. Think.

She stuffed a bar of deodorant into her bag. A wad of clean underwear. Some T-shirts. A toothbrush. Her unfinished bucket list, scrawled on some Ghibli-themed notebook paper Ivy had gotten her. She kept her eyes off the books on her shelf, the musical jewelry box her mom had given her when she turned fifteen. The things she'd have to leave behind.

"Cate? You okay in there?" Office Davis called in through the open front door.

"Coming!" she called out shakily. She was starting to cry. She was starting to come undone. This was the beginning of the end. She grabbed her keys from the top of her drawer and caught the blackbird key chain staring back at her with mocking eyes. Maybe the stress was making her see things, too. Maybe she'd end up in a ward right alongside her mom, and that's how they'd spend their last hours on this earth.

At least they'd be together.

Why was she bothering to even pack? Fury and exhaustion fought within her, and she swayed, just wanting to lie down on her bed and close her eyes and make it all go away. She nearly tossed her entire backpack into the trash can in her room when she saw the envelope her mom had labeled and handed to her yesterday. The letter to her dad.

The letter.

She grabbed the letter out of the trash. Her hands shook as her finger slid under the envelope fold and began to tear. She was almost afraid to read it. Afraid it wouldn't mean anything.

Afraid it would.

She unfolded the letter with trembling hands. She read it over and over, her mind struggling to catch up to her eyes, to process the meaning of the words. But they *had* meaning; it wasn't the nonsense she'd expected, not even close. Every part of her body throbbed with painful awareness; she could hardly breathe.

"Cate? I'm coming back there, okay?" Officer Davis's footsteps began moving away from the front door.

Cate shoved the letter, quickly, into her backpack. It was addressed to an apartment in Reno, Nevada. Wasn't that where her parents had met?

Just then, her phone buzzed. Cate's heart flipped when she saw that Ivy had finally written her back. It felt like a sign.

It felt like an opportunity.

"Cate?"

Cate made the decision in an instant. There was no way she could go to the station. Not now. Not with her dad out there. Not now that she finally had a chance—maybe her last chance—to find him.

Without a second thought, she grabbed her bag and crept out of her room and down the hall—toward the back of the house, where there was a separate entrance into the small yard.

And then she ran.

Garrett—

God, I hope you get this letter. There are so many things
I've wanted to say to you. But now that I'm writing this,
the thoughts aren't coming to me. So I'll keep it simple.
I'm so sorry. I'm so sorry I pushed you away with no explanation.
Maybe one day, I can give you the explanation I owe you.
But for now, I need to tell you that I was pregnant.
She was yours. But when I tried to find you again,
you already had someone else.

I want you to know I cherish our memories.

And I'll cherish our little girl.

Forever sorry,
Molly

P.S. Her name is Catherine. But she'd tell you she prefers
Cate.

6

ADEEM

When the doorbell rang, Adeem's heart leaped into his throat. He wasn't expecting anyone. Unless some soldiers in green uniforms were at his door for an evacuation order, leaflets falling from the sky like snow behind them. Or men with swastikas tattooed on their shaved heads, gripping AK-47s.

Adeem shuddered. He wouldn't even be surprised. Based on what he'd heard on the radio, the world was going *nuts*: almost a hundred people had gathered in front of the Vatican and threatened a mass suicide, to coincide with the day the decision was to be rendered on Alma. NATO had called an emergency meeting in Brussels. Roads across the country completely backed up by evacuations to rural areas. Several billionaires from Saudi Arabia were preparing to launch their personal spacecraft to Mars—their way of trying to escape judgment day, he guessed.

At least school was canceled until further notice—a small silver lining in the storm cloud of imminent, planet-wide extermination. Adeem's father, exhausted after a record forty hours at the hospital, had slept almost until noon, when Adeem's mom finally got back from an extra-long board meeting at the mosque. Later, with reports of grocery shortages and continued riots, and rumors of blackouts to come, Adeem's parents had hurriedly left for a grocery store on the other side of Carson City that was supposedly protecting its stock with armed guards.

While they were gone, Adeem had locked himself in the upstairs library, where Dad had let him set up his radio transceiver station. He'd last been listening to a report of the sudden increase in violence—specifically, violence targeting Muslim communities. Three prominent West Coast mosques had burned down, the target of fanatical arsonists who believed that the end of days was here—and that Muslims had brought it.

He braced himself.

"The end is nigh!" a breathless and sweaty Derek blurted when he opened the door. At least, Adeem was 98 percent sure it was him; he was gripping a baseball bat, even though he definitely did not play baseball, and his face was hidden underneath the dark motorcycle helmet Derek had spray-painted gold for their Daft Punk Halloween costume last year. Behind him, his bike lay forgotten on the front yard, as though he had thrown himself off the moment he saw Adeem's house. His brothers must have taken his car again. "Nigh as *hell*! And I haven't even told Mia Jimenez I like her yet!"

Derek had been crushing on Mia Jimenez—a junior and the current president of the Video Game Club—since day one of their freshman year. She was also why Derek had agreed to help Adeem made the art for their video games in the first place. *Babes love video games*, he'd reasoned.

Adeem pinched the bridge of his nose beneath his glasses and let out a long sigh of relief. "Why can't you text me before you show up, like a normal person?"

Derek peeled off his Daft Punk helmet. "And the worst part is," he continued, pushing past Adeem into the house, "she's already on the road to Houston with the rest of her family, and I don't even have her number." He set his baseball bat down and collapsed onto the couch. "What if she gets hurt? I mean, even my dad's freaking out. He got punched out at Walmart trying to buy one of the last spare tires. Then he tried to make me wear my brother's Dragon Age warrior cosplay in case someone wanted to mug me for my bike. He almost didn't let me come at all. It's *bad* out there."

A sudden chill bit at Adeem's arms. He was starting to think now was the time to get better about praying. "Wait, *what*? Is your dad okay?"

"He's fine now, but I am worried about Mia. Do you think I should call the fire department in Houston, maybe ask them to find her?"

"Riiight, because I'm sure the fire department has time for that now."

"I could tell them it's an emergency," Derek whined. "Tell them my heart's on fire."

"Gross."

Derek flung his helmet at him, and Adeem barely dodged in time. It landed with a loud clack on the rug.

"*Not* helpful. Can't you and your fancy-ass radios project a message of love to every town until she hears me?"

Adeem folded his arms across his chest. "It doesn't work like that. Besides, even if it *did*, your message would only get lost in the chatter."

Derek suddenly stood. "What do you mean?"

Adeem led Derek through the upstairs hall, past Leyla's closed-off room. The library seemed to hum with life, as if with the buzz of electricity. The walls were lined by bookshelves filled with Quranic translations and Urdu poetry—minus Leyla's favorite book of poetry, which she'd taken with her. His school backpack, covered in anime and NASA-themed pins, was shoved in a corner, forgotten; he'd never been good about doing homework, but he figured he wouldn't need to worry about that anymore. On the leather-topped office desk that sat at the back of the library, Adeem had left his equipment: a portable Tecsun shortwave radio, one of three he bought over the years on his allowance, still on. A notebook filled with frequencies and locations written in his tiny scrawl. A pair of tangerine-orange headphones—Derek picked these up, admiring them. Adeem's laptop, covered in game decals. Neatly folded strands of coax cables. And the chipped Philco radio, a sight that always caused a dull ache in Adeem's chest, but he couldn't bear to put it away.

Derek plopped into a chair. "She wouldn't listen to the radio, anyway. She's probably listening to the Legend of Zelda soundtrack on repeat. God, I love her."

"So you've said," said Adeem, pulling his laptop toward him.

He'd created an algorithm that cycled through various frequencies and recorded them 24/7 to his laptop. Usually, the recordings were just robotic-voiced numbers and static, sometimes old, tinny music from the '40s. But in the past few days, dead radio channels were suddenly crackling to life. Since NASA had translated the message from Alma, people were using the dead channels to broadcast prerecorded messages and local news reports to each other. A scattering of stars flickering back to life.

All day, he'd gotten lost in the sound. Listening to the messages was cathartic, captivating, even, a front-row seat to the world's slow unraveling. Strings of code, waves of voice: they were one and the same. Full of hidden meaning, if you cared to look deep enough. After tearing out the USB connecting the radio to his laptop, Adeem shifted the screen toward

Derek. With a double click, the audio file he'd downloaded earlier opened, and he fast-forwarded the cursor to the spots where the audio spiked.

10:33 a.m. at 1610 kHz: "Code 10-33. I've arrived at the scene and we've got armed suspects, mass attempted suicides. I'm trying to get in, but—"

Derek's breath stilled. Adeem shifted frequencies with a click.

11:42 p.m. at 6125 kHz: *"Algunos han dicho que el Papa planea declarar un estado de emergencia para toda la humanidad . . ."*

1:04 p.m. at 6950 kHz: "Alma: Friends or foe? And does it matter? We're lucky to have Keith Maloney, formerly an astrophysicist at SETI, here to give insight into the seemingly impossible technology necessary for Alma to have sent their message . . ."

4:17 p.m. at 9478 kHz: "In these approaching dark times, we invite you to shine the mighty light of the Gospel on your heart and keep America in your prayers . . ."

6:21 p.m. at 9565 kHz: "Officials from China, France, India, Israel, North Korea, Pakistan, Russia, the United Kingdom, and the United States will be meeting tomorrow to strategize ballistic missile defense systems in place in preparation for invasion . . ."

"What *is* this?" asked Derek.

Adeem paused the file. "Radio broadcasts—stuff you won't hear on the news. Not yet, at least." He stretched his arms over his head, and his shoulders popped gratefully. "This is just what I've picked up in the past couple hours. Haven't even cycled through it all yet."

Derek let out a long exhale.

"Sooo yeah, as you can see, we're all going to die, probably." Adeem kept his voice light, but all day, his stomach had hurt like he was stuck in free fall. In a way, he was.

Derek swallowed. "What else are people saying?"

Adeem moved the cursor farther across the lines of sound recording.

His speakers let out another crackle of static, and then, at 2438 kHz: "Think about it, how are we supposed to fight these things when we have no way of knowing how they'll get here? What if they don't need to get here? With the technology required to send a message that fast in the first place, they could use lasers—"

Click.

4082 kHz: "This is the BBC World Service, and as promised, we'll be counting down the next seven days with the seminal classic Danse Macabre by Camille Saint-Saëns . . ."

Click.

1020 kHz: "When whatever you want to do cannot be done," a woman's voice began, "When nothing is of any use; —At this hour when night comes down, When night comes, dragging its long face, dressed in mourning, Be with me, My tormenter, my love, be near me."

Her voice faded to static. Adeem was supposed to shift the

cursor again to the next spike in the waveform, but instead, he yanked his hand away from his keyboard as if it'd bitten him.

That voice. That poem.

It'd been one of her favorites, an Urdu poem—Dad had introduced her to it. They would recite it to each other, back when they were still learning Urdu, and she'd teased Adeem for his clumsy pronunciation. "How can you be so good at computer languages but suck so bad at your mother tongue?" she'd said, throwing her head back and laughing.

"Adeem?" Derek asked.

Adeem couldn't stop shaking. He was so cold, his blood making a hasty retreat from his head. His ears throbbed with his frantic heartbeat. Derek's voice sounded so far away.

Where? Where was it coming from?

Be near me.

He grabbed the notebook he'd filled with frequencies. No shortwave radio frequency operated twenty-four hours, so more often than not, Adeem wouldn't hear anything—at least, not until the revival of all the dead channels. So he'd filled the notebook with stations he'd pinpointed locations for, or ones that had identified themselves with call signs; it made it easier to track time zones, so he'd known exactly when to tune in to hear something.

His glasses drooped as he flipped a couple pages in his notebook. *1020, 1020 . . .*

Seconds dragged on and his heart wouldn't calm down,

bursting at the seams with a delicate hope, a longing that made it hard to breathe.

His fingers ran down the column of numbers before finally landing on a location.

Roswell.

"You okay?" Derek was squinting at him.

"Yeah," Adeem managed to say. "Yeah. Fine."

Of all the places in the world she could be, why would she chose *Roswell*, the weird little town filled with aliens and superstitions? Roswell had always been a joke.

But it wasn't so funny now.

He was sure of it, though. He knew that voice. It was deeper than he remembered, breathier even, a voice drifting like cirrus between his ears. With every day that had passed these two long years since she'd left, he'd been so afraid he'd forget. But no, he would always know that voice, more familiar to him than his own—how could he forget?

How could he ever forget his sister's voice?

The sun was lingering just behind the top of the giant oak trees that bordered the backyard by the time the garage rumbled open. The twilight gloom made everything blurry, dreamlike. Lately, even during those rare evenings when he and his parents were home together, a bleak and hollow silence remained, as though when Leyla had left, she had taken the sound with her.

Now, though, the quiet especially stung. After Derek left,

he'd sent countless ham radio transmissions back to the Roswell channel, only to get no response. Which meant the message was just a prerecording, a mirage of his sister he couldn't quite reach.

His dad finally walked into the kitchen, limping, clutching a single grocery bag. He looked exhausted.

"What happened?" asked Adeem. He was surprised by the force of his own relief. He was used to being alone, but it was good to see his parents back in one piece. He needed to research nearby fallout shelters to make sure his mom and dad stayed that way. Though, knowing them, they'd spend the next six or so days at the mosque. Praying.

His mom trailed in now, throwing her purse angrily onto the countertop. "Hell is other people—that's what happened."

His dad chuckled weakly. "People were acting like animals at Costco, fighting over every little thing." So much for armed guards. "I sprained my ankle trying to grab some bottles of water from some guy in a foil hat. Your mom had to beat some guy off me with her purse." His dad fell into a chair at the dining table. "There wasn't much left."

It was an understatement. His parents had only managed to get a few cans of nonperishables, a few rolls of toilet paper. Powdered milk packets, which Adeem made a face at. The water bottles, apparently, hadn't made it home.

"Will that be enough?" Adeem asked. Enough for *what*, exactly, he wasn't even sure.

"We'll be okay," his dad said.

We'll be okay. Adeem felt a vein throb beneath his brow. Did "we" include his sister?

Adeem took a deep breath. "What about Leyla?"

His question brought an instant chill. The awkward tension in the air was so palpable, Adeem could have plucked a blob of it and thrown it at his parents' blank faces. Start an awkward tension food fight. A mood fight, if you will. After all, there were many unspoken rules in this house, and he'd just broken unspoken rule number one: don't bring up Leyla.

"Adeem—" his mom began.

"Don't." He hated it when his parents started a sentence with his name. He almost never liked what followed.

"Of *course* we've reached out to her," said his dad, grasping for a newspaper that wasn't on its usual spot on the table; the paper had stopped being delivered. He pulled his hand back. "You know we have. We've *tried*. But she changed her number. She wants nothing to do with us anymore."

"So that's it? A couple texts and you give up? You don't think the end of the world constitutes, I don't know, more of a freaking effort?" He hated how his voice was dripping with sarcasm. He was taking out his anger on the wrong people; his parents were just as much in the dark as he was. But still.

The worst part? His parents hadn't even said the wrong things. It wasn't as though when Leyla had admitted in shaky whispers that her best friend, Priti, was way more than just a friend, they'd told her to leave and never come back. They weren't like Qasim Uncle, who'd cast out his own son a few years ago, openly called him horrible things in front of the whole mosque. Instead, his parents stared, mouths agape, as though she'd grown another head, all while Leyla stood in the kitchen, still in the crisp button-down and black slacks she'd wear for her part-time job at the Sunday school, and clutched her necklace—a silver chain with a crescent moon Priti had gotten her. He'd wanted to say something, anything, but even Adeem's brain malfunctioned, overheating from sheer panic over how his parents would react. They hadn't agreed with Qasim Uncle's actions, but they hadn't exactly publicly denounced them, either. He didn't even have time to process it himself, the thought bouncing too fast in his head for him to pin down and explain, but there it was just the same: Leyla is gay, Leyla is gay, *Leyla is gay*. And with *Priti*.

Before words could come to any of them, Leyla left.

She had just turned twenty-one then. Even if they'd known she wouldn't come back that night, his parents would have been powerless to stop her.

"*Effort?*" his dad parroted. "You're almost seventeen now. You could have been out there finding her yourself, but I've never once seen you make an effort—in anything. So don't tell us we haven't done enough."

Without a newspaper to hide behind, Adeem could see his dad's chest rising and falling quickly, in sync with his own. The words stung, both for Adeem to hear and his dad to tell.

Adeem said, "I heard her."

His mom nearly dropped the cans she was putting in the pantry. "What?"

"On my radio," Adeem continued. "I've been listening in on frequencies across the country, and I think I heard her. She was reciting a Faiz poem." *Be with me.*

He swallowed, his voice becoming smaller.

"I think she's in Roswell."

His dad looked at Mom. "Roswell?" His eyebrows crinkled in confusion. "Why *Roswell*? The last we heard, she was in Reno."

Adeem's breath hitched like a stone in his throat. Reno was only a forty-minute drive from their place in Carson City. She'd been so close all this time? "But if you knew she was in Reno, then why didn't you guys say anything?" Adeem squeezed his fist, stiff from hours of scouring the internet and radio for her. "Why didn't you tell me?"

His mom shook her head. "There was nothing to tell. Reza told us he'd seen her there, but then she was gone before he could do anything. That's when she changed her phone number. Apparently, she was trying to find a job, but . . ."

Reza. Adeem hadn't heard that name in forever. Reza and his sister, childhood friends, had once been thick as thieves—had been much more. That was before Priti came into their lives, before Leyla and Priti disappeared without a trace.

After she left, Adeem was convinced Reza would have been the *last* person she'd ever want to see again. And yet.

He ignored the pang of jealousy in his chest, and the fury

that his parents hadn't told him anything sooner. "Was she alone?" he asked.

His parents knew what he was really asking: *Was Priti with her?*

"Yes," his dad replied solemnly. "She was alone, as far as Reza could tell. Something must have happened."

The thought of Priti now made Adeem squeeze his fingers into a fist so tightly they went numb. He knew what happened wasn't her fault—it's not like she *made* Leyla gay, as if Priti were some kind of magical proselytizing queer unicorn. That wasn't the issue at all. The issue was that they'd *left*, and part of him couldn't bear the idea that it'd been *Leyla's* idea to run away without a word and break her family's—and Reza's—heart. It couldn't have been.

And yet it'd been two years, and neither of them had called. But if something happened between them, if Leyla was alone now, then why hadn't she reached out yet? And where was Priti, anyway?

He had to find the truth.

"Maybe Reza has an idea of where Leyla went," said Adeem. At least Reza might actually have some semblance of a trail he could follow.

His dad shook his head. "Reno, Roswell—if your sister wants to be left alone, that's her choice." But Adeem could hear the grief behind his words. Leyla's departure had aged his parents overnight. "Besides, you can't go hunt her down now. It's chaos out there already, and it's only going to get worse. We need you to be safe. You need to be with us right now."

"But you just said I haven't been making an effort. So this is me making an effort. I can find—"

"It's. Not. Safe," his dad snapped, punctuating every word. "For now, we wait it out. We just have to have faith everything will turn out for the best."

Hypocrite, Adeem almost said; it was his dad who always repeated the hadith "Trust in God, but tie your camel." Trust, faith—Adeem didn't have time to waste on things that wouldn't give him answers. He needed to know for sure what had happened. He needed to see her one last time.

The sun had disappeared now, and the kitchen was shrouded in darkness, casting them in their own family vortex of shadow and silence. But none of them moved to flick on the lights.

It reminded Adeem of one of the poems his sister had shared with him once, one by Rumi. In the poem, Rumi banters with God over life's usual philosophical questions: what to do with that pesky thing called a heart, where to focus one's eyes, etcetera, etcetera. But when Rumi asks God what to do with his pain and sorrow, God tells him, "Stay with it. The wound is the place where the Light enters you."

"Weirdly comforting, isn't it?" his sister had asked him dreamily. That dingus tended to swoon over poetry like she was a Sufi romantic herself.

Adeem had thought it was stupid, and when he'd said as much, she'd flicked his forehead. But the problem with visible light, he'd argued, is that as far as electromagnetic waves went, it never got very far. It was weak; it couldn't cross through walls, easily bounced off surfaces to oblivion. If God wanted to reach you, He or She or They wouldn't use light.

Radio waves, though. Radio waves had more energy, were more resilient, and in the right circumstances, could travel across the planet.

Well, if light couldn't reach her, then maybe Adeem would.

7

JESSE

The bright orange eviction notice was taped to the front door when Jesse returned home from his group session. Jesse saw it from half a block away. Subtle, it was not: the envelope screamed up at him in red letters. They had one week to pay up or be homeless.

Of everything that had happened in the past few days, *this*—the fact that they might soon be homeless—was the most unbelievable.

Also: the scariest.

Because now it was clear as day to Jesse that the whole Alma thing was a prank. A joke. A distraction from cruel reality. Maybe when Jesse was a little kid, he might have believed in something like alien planets. He'd have *wanted* to believe: because if aliens existed, hell, *anything* could happen. Of course, he'd grown up since then. Aliens were up there with Santa Claus and the Easter Bunny, as faraway and imaginary and impossible as he and Mom finally being free of Dad's debts.

If he'd gotten worked up over Alma at the QuikTrip, it was only because of his nerves, not because he actually believed in this bullshit.

But these days, people would buy anything they saw on TV. A bunch of especially inspired kids had managed to break into the International UFO Museum and move—or *fly*, one of them drunkenly claimed—the giant flying saucer replica through one of the windows, leaving behind mounds of broken glass and shattered beer bottles. Despite the destruction, tourists clad in starchy *GREETINGS, EARTHLINGS* T-shirts still trickled back in to the museum, convinced that the debris from the '47 UFO crash hoax had actually been a sign from Alma all along. They'd even made the Vulcan salute at Jesse as he'd made his usual Wednesday trek to La Familia Crisis Center.

It had taken every fiber of his being not to flip the bird back at them.

He should have been happy to see them: more tourists meant more jobs, more life. But he preferred the tourists *before* Alma, the ones who'd take a couple photos with rubber martians with painted mustaches in the Alien Zone and would buy commemorative key chains at the Roswell Plaza Hotel gift shop and leave decent tips, more out of pity than anything else. The tourists now didn't even seem like tourists so much as religious pilgrims.

Alma fever had even seeped into his group counseling session at La Familia Crisis Center. Normally, their counselor, Ms. K, started with affirmations or positive poems by Maya Angelou or Rumi, citing some "healing power of poetry" bullshit. But Tom Ralford was even more eager to talk than usual. Tom used to run the local UFOs & U program on the radio, which actually had a decently big cult following until he'd had a nervous breakdown on air. He didn't go out much after that.

"I just wanna say, I'm real worried about Alma, y'all," he'd said. His eyes glinted as he tilted his embroidered safari hat with the UFOs & U logo down his forehead, something he did, Jesse had noticed, whenever a bad idea was brewing. "With the kind of comms tech they got, they could invade us in hours. Zap us into dust in an instant. So, as many of you know, I've been working on a radio program of my own built with the best kind of comms tech there is: Love."

Jesse barely suppressed a groan.

"Now I've still got more than enough slots for any broadcasts or transmissions you need to send to your family, your friends. The sooner we swarm the ionosphere with our love"—Tom thudded his chest for emphasis—"I guarantee the sooner Alma will back off."

The sound of someone clearing their throat interrupted

him. Ms. K pulled her fingers away from her silver moon necklace she'd been gripping and rested her hands on her thighs. "Thank you so much for that offer, Tom." If the woman suffered from one thing, it was too much patience.

And Tom knew it. He continued. "I'm tellin' you, in the coming days, people will spend an arm and a leg just to get out their feelings. Just to be heard."

No one's desperate enough to send a message through your dumb radio channel, Jesse wanted to say, but the last time he ran his mouth during a session, Ms. K smiled at him so menacingly, Jesse thought her eyes might actually irradiate him.

Ms. K nodded. "Why don't you pass out your information to those who haven't taken you up on your offer yet, and then we can get this show on the road?"

But when Tom had passed out cards with his "business" contact information—embossed with silver UFOs—Jesse and Ms. K were the only ones who didn't take them.

Mom didn't believe the hype, either. "You wait and see, J-Bird," she had said late last night, wrapping her Pluto's Diner apron around her waist. "It's five to one the president's got some new tax up his sleeve, and all this nonsense is just meant to keep us sniffing around elsewhere. Street magicians, that's all these politicians are. Wave a hand here and slip off your watch while you ain't looking."

The truth was, Jesse and his mom were too broke to worry about aliens. Even conspiracy theory was a pay-to-play luxury these days.

In the silence of the morning, the blood rush to Jesse's ears was deafening. It made no sense. Why hadn't his mom said anything about the eviction notice? Sure, he and Mom had an unspoken rule about minding each other's business—it was why she didn't even ask about the bruise on his jaw, or the fading hickey on his neck, and why Jesse didn't say anything about how it killed him to see her throw her entire body at the grindstone; she wouldn't hear any of it. And after the incident that had landed Jesse in counseling, Mom had been especially careful to give Jesse the space he said he needed.

But this was different. They'd been a few weeks behind on rent sometimes, but never *that* late.

Maybe they could get away with ignoring the notice. If half the world believed Alma was going to obliterate them, then enforcing eviction notices would be the last of anyone's worries.

But then what about the inevitable *after*? What would they do when everyone crawled out from their fallout shelters and realized the world still spun on its axis, like it always did?

Life never gave out free passes. Their landlord, Mr. Donovan, wouldn't, either.

Where the hell would they get that kind of money in a week?

Despite the cool, early morning weather, he was sweating. Anger left a tight ball of heat in his chest. It was all Dad's fault—for leaving them nothing but ratty clothes, a stack of debts, and empty promises.

Jesse sighed and wandered around the side of the house to

find the decaying work shed in the backyard, filled with useless machines built from scrap metal and other crap pilfered from the nearby junkyard—towering sculptures of trash.

If they really *were* forced out of this place, would he have to clean out that dump, too?

As he stared at the crooked shed, slumped like a wooden giant that had fallen asleep, a weird thought tickled at the back of Jesse's head. He swiveled and grabbed a hammer from the toolbox rusting underneath the front porch. A dirt path lined in runty cacti led him through the dusty backyard and straight to the shed's entrance. The dark green paint on its planks of cracked wood had long begun to curl and peel. Even nature seemed to reject it; thistle and cheatgrass waged war at the shed's edges, reclaiming the wood for its own. The shed was a small gust of wind away from falling apart.

When he was a kid, Jesse was convinced that his dad was a wizard, not only because his dad had a habit of pulling disappearing acts to California, but also because his dad had magic hands: hands that could make ordinary playing cards come to life, hands that could make a piano sing, hands that could tinker with metal and make it bend. Half of his childhood, it seemed, Jesse had spent peeking through the cracks in the plywood, wishing so hard to be allowed inside, to be trusted with his dad's secrets. One night, when Jesse was maybe six years old, his dad caught him. Jesse stood frozen as the sound of his dad's boots came closer and closer, banging against the floor like a war drum.

His dad had only grinned.

"Well, well, well. What's this? A little bird seems to have lost his way." Dad bent down and ruffled Jesse's already floppy hair. Jesse had tried not to flinch; only a few days prior, he'd made the mistake of showing his dad a baby grackle he'd found on the road, fluttering warmly, like a small flame in his palms. But Dad made him throw it back in the cold, said it was the only way it'd ever learn to survive. Since then, his dad had begun calling him J-Bird. Like a cruel joke.

"I've been thinking. You should come see this. It'll be good for you."

His dad set Jesse down right in the middle of the surrounding chaos: tools—hammers and saws and other thingamajigs Jesse didn't know the names of—were strewn about, and nearly every square inch of space had been overtaken by strange tubes and wires. His dad opened his arms wide, dramatically, like a circus ringmaster. "Well? What do you think of my palace?" He chucked Jesse on the chin. "Soon everyone will know the name Hewitt, J-Bird. We dream big here. What do you think of that? Are you ready to be famous?"

Jesse could feel all his nerves catching fire. He was ready, for sure.

But over time, the machines grew bigger, and his dad grew more and more obsessed. Increasingly, Jesse found the shed locked. Jesse's father stopped showing up for work. He stopped sleeping. He even stopped eating, no matter how much Mom knocked on the shed door and begged him to come out.

And then he died—drunk off his face in the middle of the night, going 100 mph on I-285 on his way to God knows where. *Maybe*, Jesse thought, *he was trying to die.*

Maybe those memories were better off dead, too.

The sun was beginning to rise. He gripped the hammer in his hand, anger distilling to heat and sweat at his fingertips.

He lifted the hammer and took the first swing at the padlock.

Ten years had really done their damage. Cobwebs had claimed the corners of the shed, their white gossamers glowing like filaments under the beams of early morning light that now punctured the shed's suffocating darkness. Rusted gears and pipes, and lines of colored wires intertwined and wove between them all like Christmas garlands hung on the rotting wall. The tiny, lone window had been left shuttered; corpses of dead flies littered the sill.

Dusty tarps concealed his dad's machines. He lifted one, using a hand to cover his mouth from the cloud of dust. A rusty metal box with an old green computer monitor for a face stared back at him. Worthless.

He straightened up. As he pivoted, he bumped into something hard and angular—the old worktable.

Stuffed in the drawers were stacks and stacks of blueprints: ideas that had come to his dad as easily as breathing. Well, no wonder they had—they were all useless. They weren't inventions. They were delusions.

His hand grazed the surface of the worktable, leaving

fingerprints in the dust. He remembered the drawer that had once contained all of his dad's old lottery tickets, all that unused luck. But the drawer was unlocked. Jesse's hands trembled. Relief and hope swept through him. This is what his dad meant by a rainy day. There must have been thousands, roped together with elastic—at least one of them had to be a winner.

He seized the pile and his heart sank. Of course. All of them had been scratched.

Not one of them a winner.

Mom. It had to be her. Recently, maybe. She must have been desperate to save what was left of their home, crouching in the shadows of Dad's memories, frantically scratching every single ticket. Still hoping, despite everything, Dad had left them a chance.

He could hardly breathe. The atmosphere was suffocating him. With a few hard tugs—maybe harder than necessary—he pried open the shutters. As harsh light flooded the shed, he noticed something enormous—far bigger than all the other machines—lumped in one corner beneath a black tarp. Beside it lay a metal toolbox; his dad hadn't even put the wrench back inside.

Jesse peeled back the tarp. The giant machine rested on its side, parts exposed, unfinished. Its rusted, rounded frame was massive—maybe six feet tall if it were standing upright. Maybe it once had a crisp white body, shiny from some acrylic paint, but it had long been chipped away at by time, coated with unsightly cracks like the shell of an egg. Embedded in its face were several damaged LED displays, surrounded by thick square buttons. Red, blue, and yellow wires, some of them ripped, had been woven between the screens, and they disappeared into various ports to create little ringlets. Other wires simply flowed down the machine and pooled next to it on the floor.

Jesse's heart began to beat faster. He was still gripping that hammer.

His father had believed that his machines would transform Roswell, turn it once again into a hub for extraterrestrial intelligence.

A crazy thought came to him: What if *he* could convince everyone to believe the same thing?

The idea spread through him like a glorious flame. He, the one and only Jesse Hewitt, could offer them a kind of salvation that no one else could offer. He'd give the people what they wanted. Yeah, that's what he could offer: a chance for people to send out a message in a bottle. Into the ionosphere, into space. To beg for forgiveness, pardon, whatever.

Tom had said it himself. *I'm tellin' you, in the coming days, people will spend an arm and a leg just to get out their feelings.*

Jesse slowly let the hammer drop to the floor by his side. He'd come in here . . . who knew why. To gawk, maybe. To satisfy some sick curiosity. To say goodbye.

Maybe to bash all of it to pieces, one last "eff-off" to his dad.

But now, he saw, he'd come in here for a reason. A calling.

He stared at the massive machine, his mind spinning faster than electricity.

All he had to do was clean it up a little, right?

Maybe repurpose some of the junk in Dad's shed to make it look legit. He knew how to sound convincing. He could build it up a little taller. Jesse had spent enough time in here growing up that he thought he could do it. He had everything he needed right here.

He knew people would fall for it. People always looked for something to do, something that made them feel like they were in control somehow. It's why locals hunkered down in homemade fallout shelters made with stolen mattresses and metal siding panels, and wore tin hats. Roswell was once holy ground for people like that, before the real aliens showed up and the exodus of tourists began. Maybe he and Mom only had a week to pay off their landlord, but what better week than *this*, when the whole world would be desperate to throw their money away for a chance to be saved?

If he could get the word out, if he could lure enough people here for twenty bucks a pop, they'd be rich. The world was supposedly going to end in a little less than a week. He'd have less than a week to get more tourists, bring a little life into this godforsaken town. But that was enough. If he played his cards right, he'd not only have enough money to save the house but maybe take Mom somewhere warm, like a California beach. Give her the vacation Dad never could.

Mom would finally feel taken care of. Lucky, even.

Impulsive, he heard Ms. K say in his mind. But what was that saying about desperate times?

Already, the plan was forming. First, he'd take the machine out of this wooden prison and let it breathe. Let the neighbors see it; let them do the marketing for him. He'd turn the whole Alma thing on its head.

It was like he'd heard that kid say back at the convenience store: *Can't put a price on hope.*

But Jesse sure as hell could try.

SIX DAYS

UNTIL THE END

OF DELIBERATIONS

TRANSCRIPT
EXCERPT FROM TRIAL

ARBITER: Silence. The local population is aware of our existence, yes, but this should not distract us. Their knowledge of us is irrelevant to our decision.

SCION 2: Apologies, Arbiter, but I must disagree. The reports show that the message was sent just before this trial began, which means that whoever sent it was trying to influence our decision, make it harder for us to choose. It's a mockery of this entire process. For all we know, one of the members of this jury is a biased Epoch sympathizer, which means we simply cannot move forward until they are rooted out.

SCION 4: Our sensors have determined the leak has caused a planetwide frenzied search for a potential weapon from an exo-civilization. The Anathogen diffuser could now be at risk.

SCION 7: No one here will admit to being the traitor. Perhaps the trial itself will force them to reveal themselves.

ARBITER: It must. We have no time to perform a full-scale investigation.

SCION II: My intent is not to condone the traitor's actions, but this gives us a clean slate. Epoch now knows it is being watched and judged. Maybe it will change for the better.

SCION 9: Morality should exist whether or not you are being watched. The population of Project Epoch has no excuse for its actions of the past.

SCION 13: You speak of morality, and yet, is it moral to exterminate an entire species from afar?

SCION 9: Humans are responsible for the extermination of 150 species on their own planet every day. Our scientists designed the Anathogen to render human termination painless and nearly instant, which is far more than they deserve.

ARBITER: May I remind you that our primary function is not moral or ideological? We must solely focus on whether the humans of Planet Epoch have exhausted their purpose. Can they teach us anything new? Or have we simply seen everything of them, every dimension and facet of human life that there is to see? I ask that you now turn your attention to our focus group, a random selection of humans whose behaviors may further elucidate these discussions.

8

CATE

"Are you sure this is it?" Ivy squinted through the windshield at the chipped gold *4C* lettering nailed on the apartment door.

Despite the warm weather, Cate's skin prickled. The doors leading to other apartments were all in various states of decay: peeling blood-orange paint, streaked and uneven, and mismatching doorknobs and knockers. A man in stained shorts, leaning against his balcony railing, scratched his swollen belly as he leered at the girls in their car.

Was this really where her dad lived? Suddenly, she wished she hadn't come.

The one other time Cate had tried to find her dad had been when she was twelve. She had tracked down her aunt

Lily—Mom's younger sister—despite the fact that she'd seen Lily only once or twice before in her life. Cate wasn't sure what had happened between her aunt and her mom, but Lily had just made a face and packed Cate back onto the bus that would take her home. *Your mother made her bed*, Lily said, *and she sure as shit got to lie in it.* Lily didn't seem to realize that she'd forced Cate to lie in it, too.

The blaring honk of an eighteen-wheeler made Cate jump in her car seat.

Ivy gently elbowed her. "Why do you look so nervous? He's not going to eat you." Then, "I didn't crawl through apocalyptic traffic for you to punk out now, girl."

This morning, they'd told Ivy's parents that they were going to the hospital so that Cate could visit her mom—which in all fairness *had* been the plan, at least until Cate called the inpatient psychiatric unit at the hospital, and a nurse abruptly explained her mom was in no condition to take visitors yet. Mrs. Huang, distracted by her phone, didn't question their lie. They had their own problems to deal with. Ever since the news of Alma broke, the Huangs stopped fighting long enough to agree to hide out in a safe house in Arizona owned by Mrs. Huang's law firm partner. But then the safe house had gotten overrun with seven other families looking for shelter, leaving the Huangs scrambling to find potential alternatives nearby. Cate tried to ignore the pang of guilt in her chest as she'd watched Ivy sneak her little brother, Ethan, a quick hug before leading Cate to the garage. She hated having to rely on

Ivy like this, but Ivy was the only one she knew with a license and a car, and the only friend she'd ever trust with bucket list goals. Plus, the drive to the address in Reno she'd found on Mom's letter was only four hours from San Fran. She told herself they'd be back before nightfall.

At least, it *should* have only been a four-hour drive, but even Google Maps couldn't predict just how bad traffic on the interstate would be—they'd been bumper-to-bumper for most of it. Every time Cate thanked her—almost every thirty minutes—Ivy assured her it was fine, that "this is just what best friends do."

Cate knew, however, that this wasn't a best friend thing to do. This was an *Ivy* thing to do.

Now, as they hopped out of Ivy's bright blue Miata—Mrs. Huang's gift to her daughter when she'd gotten her Stanford acceptance letter—Cate almost wished that Ivy had refused, that she had tried to talk Cate out of this idiotic idea, that they had gotten stuck in traffic and been forced to turn around. Then Cate wouldn't feel so guilty.

"Want me to come to the door with you?" Ivy asked, and Cate shook her head.

"Definitely not." What if her dad wanted nothing to do with her? She knew she wouldn't be able to stand it if Ivy was next to her to see the whole thing. She forced a smile. "I'll be fine." An army-green helicopter flew just above them, almost too close; the wind whipped Cate's hair as she got out of the car. The smell of fire burned her nose. Apparently, Reno wasn't safe from the riots and looting, either. They'd heard about it on the radio, until Ivy had insisted on plugging in their phones to play music instead.

If the world's ending, she'd said, *it will* not *end before I've listened to Beyoncé's new album another seventy-two times.*

Cate slammed the car door, but the window rolled down.

"Wait," said Ivy as she dug through her purse. "Just in case." She pulled out a small yellow tube and presented it to Cate.

"Is that *pepper spray*?" Cate was horrified.

"Just take it, okay?" Ivy shoved it in Cate's hand. "Listen to your auntie."

Cate rolled her eyes. But she pocketed the pepper spray anyway, tucking it beside her mom's letter. She'd learned long ago that sometimes it was better not to argue with Ivy.

Cate counted each step to the apartment—calming counts, Dr. Michel had called the technique—and knocked on her dad's apartment door. No response. Cate bit her lip and knocked again. Still nothing. Ivy gave a tap on her car horn. Cate turned around and shrugged.

"Not home," she called out. She felt a tremendous wave of air leave her lungs, like she'd just dropped from a height: she didn't know whether to be relieved or disappointed. Another green, unmarked helicopter flew overheard. The other day, Cate saw a squadron of military planes fly across the sky from her window, and even on the drive here, Cate counted twelve Humvees driving along the highway. It made her stomach churn. She guessed she'd better start getting used to them.

She gave the door one last pounding for good measure, to prove to Ivy—and to herself—that she had really tried. But before she could turn around, a raspy voice resounded from behind the door, and the urge to flee jolted her legs like an electric shock. "I'm comin', hold your horses."

A woman slowly pried open the door a couple inches, a grimace plastered on her face. Upon first glance, she looked fairly young—late twenties, maybe, but weariness had cut premature crevices around her mouth and eyes. She'd propped a dazed baby on her hip, the child's still cheek stained with old tears. The smell of stale cigarette smoke stung Cate's nose. "Can I help you?" asked the woman, in a voice that sounded as though she really hoped she couldn't.

Cate's heart leaped into her throat, choking her. "I–I–" She glanced back at Ivy, who was leaning against her car, for help. Ivy waved a hand encouragingly. "I'm sorry to bother you—"

"If you're here about that break-in down the street, I didn't see nothing."

"No, no," Cate said quickly, before the woman could shut the door. "I'm looking for, um, Garrett?" She wished she had a last name, but the letter hadn't told her. "Does he live here?"

The woman looked faraway for a moment, deep in thought. "Garrett, Garrett . . ." She swept Cate again with her eyes. "The only Garrett I can remember was the landlord, years ago. Bearded guy, right? Kinda looks like a bear?"

Cate's mind blanked. She hadn't the faintest idea what he looked like. All she had was the letter in her pocket. The only things Mom had ever told Cate about her father was that he was a possible animal shape-shifter or a magician-pirate hybrid whom Mom didn't trust with the news of her pregnancy. That and, lately, an "Almaen," otherwise known as an alien.

So she only nodded.

"Shit. Haven't thought about him in forever. Garrett . . . Holloway? Harrison? Can't remember the full name. I was a just a kid when he was around—maybe twenty years ago." The young woman rubbed her sleepy baby's back. "Fixed one of my toys for me, back in the day. He was . . ." The woman hesitated, but whatever she thought of saying, she swallowed. "Sorry, but he doesn't live here anymore."

Numbness extinguished Cate's disappointment before it could even take root. It had been, what, sixteen years since Mom had last seen her dad? Of course he had moved. Of *course.*

She'd made Ivy drive all this way, too, and for nothing. Cate clutched her stomach, feeling queasy, dizzy. True, she hadn't asked Ivy to do any of this, but still. She felt even more guilty than before.

"I see," Cate murmured. "Would you happen to know where he went?"

The woman's eyes narrowed. From afar, Cate could hear the echo of police sirens, a sound that made her tense all over again.

"No. I was only a kid when he was here," the woman repeated, straining her voice over the sirens. "But . . . you know what? I think he may've sent my mom a postcard once. I wanna say it was from Roswell." She brightened a bit. "Weird thing covered in green aliens, looked like he drew it himself. My mom kept it on her fridge for years—that's how I remember. Of course, I guess it could've been from someone else. But pretty sure it was him." The baby on her hip cooed, and she rubbed its back. "It's not much, but that's all I know. Sorry."

"Do you still have it? The postcard?"

"Sorry," the woman repeated, shaking her head. "I'm sure it's been gone a long time."

"That's okay. You've already been really helpful," Cate said, as gratefully as she could, even though she knew the chances of getting to her dad were next to nothing now.

The woman began closing the door but stopped halfway. "Hey, do me a favor, will ya?"

"Yeah?"

"Be safe out there."

Cate looked at the woman now—really looked at her: the crust that lingered at the bottom of her swollen eyelids, the gauntness of her cheeks. The signs of someone who hadn't slept in days. Someone who'd be up watching the news, maybe until the very end.

"You, too," Cate replied, finally, before the woman closed the door.

When Cate returned to the car, Ivy had one of her bright blue debate notebooks in her hands. "All right," she said. "So maybe we reorder a few things . . ."

"What are you talking about?" Cate asked tiredly.

Ivy folded the notebook to show off her handiwork. In her messy scrawl, the page read:

CATE'S BUCKET LIST FOR THE END OF THE WORLD, REDUX

1. FIND DAD
2. ~~Actually go to a party~~
3. ~~Sneak out (sorry, Mom!)~~
4. ~~KISS JAKE OWENS!!!~~
5. Kiss someone for real!!!
6. Pet more puppies
7. Steal something!!
8. See the world

"Honestly? Three out of eight ain't bad. Though it's a little too short for my liking."

"You can't make my bucket list for me," Cate said. She couldn't help but laugh. "Besides, I'm still working on number one."

She slid her phone out of her pocket and opened Google Maps, impatiently zooming into Roswell even if she knew she wouldn't see him, like on a Harry Potter–style Marauder's Map. If she could, she'd reach her hand inside the map to yank him out, look him in the eyes, and demand to know why he'd ever let Mom fall apart on her own. Why he'd let his family fall apart.

Ivy leaned over her shoulder to peer at the screen. "Roswell? As in, *New Mexico*?"

"It's twelve hundred miles away. I can be there and back in a day." Cate took a deep breath. "I know it sounds ridiculous. But it's now or never, right? And Mom really wanted me to find him."

"Cate, your mom isn't exactly . . ." Ivy broke off just in time. Cate felt cold. "What? My mom isn't what?"

Ivy only gave her a pitying look that was worse than anything she could possibly say. "You said so yourself. Your mom has been slipping recently. You can't even reach her right now to get answers."

Cate turned to the window, blinking back the urge to cry. "She wasn't slipping when she wrote this letter," she said, trying to control her voice. "She wasn't slipping when she told me it was important."

"Cate." Ivy gently took Cate's hand. "Roswell's a big place, and we don't even know if . . ."

"I know, I know. But I can find him. I know it. Mom's never asked for much, but she asked me for this." Cate realized, in an instant, that that was it: the heart and root of the whole thing. Her mom had asked her for one thing. Maybe the last thing. Cate hadn't been able to save her from getting sick. But what kind of daughter would she be if she couldn't even deliver a letter? If this is what she had to do, she'd do it alone. "You don't have to drive me. I'll take a bus."

"You think buses are still running?"

"I'll find a way," Cate insisted.

For a long time, Ivy was silent. Cate looked down at her lap. She felt herself deflating beneath Ivy's stare. She knew Ivy was right. What she wanted to do was irrational, too big of a risk. But if there was ever the time for taking a risk, it was now.

And what did she have to stay for?

"Look, if this is what *you* want to do—and I mean you, *Cate Collins*, not your mom or anybody else—then I'm not going to stop you. Just . . . please think about it, okay?" Ivy reached over to squeeze her hand. "I'll follow you to the ends of the earth, literally, but I don't want you making rash decisions just because E.T. and all his friends are probably going to invade the planet."

This, at last, made Cate smile. "Are you, Ivy Huang, really telling me not to make rash decisions?"

"Yes. And that's why you need to listen to me. Rash decisions are kind of my wheelhouse."

The sun lingered just beneath a billboard—Ataputs Apartments—staining the cloudless sky in soft pink and violet and orange brushstrokes. But thin white streaks, left by another squadron of army planes, split through the sky like scars.

"Speaking of," Ivy said, with a trademark smirk, "*since* we drove all this way . . . I think we owe it to ourselves to have a little fun."

Mom, Dad—

Before you freak out and call the police/FBI/CIA/all our family in Pakistan, please know I am safe. I have my phone, but who knows if the aliens will blow up all the cell towers (just kidding, I think?).

Anyway, please don't freak out. I promise I'll be fine.

I'll come back soon, a day, tops.

And I'm bringing Leyla with me. You'll thank me later.

Duas much appreciated.

Love,
Your favorite son

9

ADEEM

From the ten-foot printed sign outside the Methodist church, Reza Sultana's filtered, clean-shaven face grinned at Adeem.

Adeem hadn't seen Reza in years.

Reza was the closest thing Leyla had once had to a boyfriend. They'd met in Sunday school, and, halal questionability aside, all the aunties in the southwest Nevada Muslim community had decided those two had a definite *shaadi* on the horizon. And Reza was one of those rare, genuinely good guys—volunteered at homeless shelters, actually kept up with his prayers, looked you in the eyes when you talked. He would always pull these lame card tricks that failed half the time just to get a laugh out of people. It was no surprise to

Adeem that Reza had now become something of a Muslim youth organizer. The guy was practically a saint.

And stupidly, even though one had nothing to do with the other, this made Leyla's coming out all the more of a shock.

Seeing Reza now, on poster board so big Adeem could see it from across the church's enormous parking lot, made Adeem nervous for reasons he couldn't totally name. It was like returning to your childhood home only to find a real estate agent in the middle of an open house. It didn't matter if everything looked the same. The *central* thing was different: suddenly, "home" was something in the past.

Reza was hosting a youth retreat here, at a church, as a show of "interfaith solidarity in a time of no faith"—not that the terrorists who kept burning down mosques seemed to have much interest in mending fences. Other religious leaders, like a local pastor and a rabbi, were due to arrive later with their people, if the traffic didn't stop them. But the location of the retreat wasn't exactly ideal; the church was tucked beside a casino with only sparse pine trees and a couple hundred feet of land to divide them. Consequently, the back of the church parking lot was already occupied by the cars of tourists too cheap to pay for the fancy casino parking garage. Adeem knew this because he saw a half-drunk couple stumble out of their car, the straps of the woman's dress hanging off her shoulders, and wobble toward the row of pine trees not yet tall enough to obscure the towering Atlantis Casino on its hill.

Adeem glanced at his phone. Five o'clock, still light outside. Churches and casinos. Two kinds of people.

And the ones in between.

Adeem parked his dad's Acura TSX, leaving the baseball bat Derek had insisted Adeem bring with him for safety, and followed a flock of retreat attendees to the nearby church entrance. There must have been hundreds of them.

Now that Adeem knew his parents were still in touch with Reza—that he'd actually seen Leyla—he was starting to regret not sending him a text before he'd just shown up like this. But every message he'd drafted sounded idiotic. *Hey, Rez, I know we haven't talked in, like, two years since my sister dumped you and ran away with Priti, and I was too chicken to reach out because I'm a guilty, awkward mess, but now the world is ending and all, so can you help me find her now, maybe?*

Yeah, he was better off just ambushing Reza in person. It's not like he had much of a choice; Adeem had already tried contacting the radio channel in Roswell where he'd heard his sister but had still gotten no response. Reza was his only lead.

Adeem signed in at the front desk, ignoring the cheerful volunteers who offered to take any luggage, who asked how he was, if he was excited, though Adeem wasn't sure if anyone could be excited with Alma breathing down everyone's necks. He reached the crowded main hall. Wood beams lined the arched ceiling, amplifying sound and rattling his head, and the stained-glass window behind the pulpit appeared dull and dusty without sunlight to set it aglow.

Adeem lingered behind the last row and took a place behind a pillar, choosing to stand. So many kids. Most of them seemed to have brought their friends, laughing and chatting away—and most of them were his age. He spotted a skinny brown kid who reminded him of himself, staring anxiously at his lap until a cute ponytailed girl with a gold hoop nose ring playfully slapped his back. A volunteer, as indicated by her jungle-green shirt. She offered the kid a Jolly Rancher, and he broke into a smile. None of these kids were nervous at all, like it was just another day at Sunday school.

It didn't matter if the world was ending outside these walls. The thing about Reza is that he made you feel safe, regardless.

"Welcome, welcome!" a voice boomed from the left wing of the stage, and the prattling from the pews ceased. Reza crossed the stage and raised his arms dramatically. He leaned casually against the pulpit, taking in the applause, and adjusted the tiny microphone that hung off his collar. A line of smiling volunteers in their green shirts, including the cute girl with the nose ring, gathered behind him like an entourage. He was as popular as ever.

Adeem's stomach clenched. Seeing Reza affected him more than he'd expected. Because when he thought of Reza, he thought of Leyla, the two of them once a package deal in his mind. Reza had already been becoming something of a big brother to him. Had Leyla known? Had Adeem been pressuring her without realizing it? He'd never even bothered to ask her what she *wanted*. He'd just assumed. Hoped. Not

Instantly, Reza's face changed. "Get everyone to the basement. We're on lockdown, too. Go."

Now a flood of volunteers appeared suddenly, corralling the tense-faced audience members out of the main hall toward the stairwells leading to the basement, waving their hands like air traffic controllers.

Reza seized Adeem's shoulders. "*Inshallah*, I hope you find her soon." He stepped out of the darkened hallway toward the flood of people and stood directly underneath a series of stained-glass windows, his chin lifted toward a sky clouded with incoming rain. For a brief moment, his face was illuminated in the palest ray of green light. "We might not have much time left, after all."

Reza beckoned him to follow, but Adeem couldn't move. Couldn't think. What about Leyla? Roswell? Everything was happening too fast. He begged his rooted legs to move, his knees to bend, but they refused. There was a deafening silence in his head, a sudden emptiness that left him dizzy.

Reza disappeared, swallowed by the crowd, and Adeem ripped his feet from the floor—and forced himself through the doors, into the fading sunlight.

10

CATE

"I don't remember this being on my bucket list," said Cate, narrowly missing a pile of what she hoped was spilled food and not vomit on the ornate red-and-gold-carpeted floor.

"Nope," replied Ivy with a smirk. "That's because it's on *my* bucket list."

If there was a fire code for maximum occupancy in Atlantis Casino, Cate imagined they had long surpassed it. Despite the colossal, carpeted expanse of the casino floor, bodies crammed every available inch, making the air hot and viscous. With six days left on Alma's doomsday clock, everyone who'd clutched their money tightly to their chests and kept their pockets full of unused luck probably no longer saw the need. And Atlantis—named after a city that survived its own little apocalypse—was the perfect place to spend it.

The muted ceiling lights brought out the neon glow of hundreds of machines, surrounding her; a fast-paced, atonal scale played from a nearby slot machine before bursting into an excited ringing. It was a miracle this place hadn't been touched by the power outages.

Around her, she caught snippets of conversation—hints of other lives. A man in a feathered fedora and pin-striped suit grunted a low "Gimme another" to a blank-faced dealer whose concealer did little to cover his black eye. A woman with a still-raw tattoo of a cobra peeking from the front of her glittering red dress squealed drunkenly as she yanked the lever on a machine, while a small man ogled her nearby, the front of his pants stained with what Cate hoped was booze. She cringed as a shirtless boy, probably Cate's age or even younger, took a swig from a purple drink half-filled with colorful gambling chips; the liquid dribbled down his chin. To avoid the pile of wet chips at his feet, Cate walked into a cloud of cigar smoke, making her head cloudy with its rancid, peppery scent.

A smell of desperation. Of emptiness.

She could barely believe these kinds of people actually existed. Where had they been hiding all this time—had Alma brought them all out?

Or had she been so sheltered, so focused on her mom, she just hadn't seen them?

After four rounds of blackjack, Ivy lugged her casino chip pail away from the green-felted table, satisfied. It wasn't exactly full—in fact, far from it—but they'd still made a handful, and that was more than either of them had expected. Now Ivy took in the sights around them, hungrily searching.

"There! Dance floor, starboard!" Ivy exclaimed and grabbed Cate's arm. "This place is so damn big, I thought we'd never find it."

"For the love of God, please, no dancing," said Cate, groaning. They'd been at the casino for only a few hours, but it felt more like days. And she didn't like the way Ivy kept glancing at her phone only to silence all the incoming calls from her mom. Mrs. Huang must be worried sick. Maybe she'd finally secured a spot in a safe house somewhere, was desperate to have her daughter home so their family could find shelter together. The thought made Cate feel worse.

She yanked her arm from Ivy's grip and parked herself on an empty stool at the nearby bar. "We shouldn't even be here."

Ivy dropped her pail by Cate's feet and perched on the bar table beside her, ignoring the bartender's protests. "Aw, come on. You can count this as part of the mission. I mean, this is where your parents met, right? The place where it all began. Think of it as getting to know them better. And who knows?" she said, grinning as she locked eyes with Cate. "You might even have been conceived here. *Right*. Here."

Cate gave Ivy a shove. "I should never have told you that." This was exactly why Cate hated discussing her parents with Ivy. It was bad enough that her parents had met at a *casino*. Part of Cate had always hoped that their story was more romantic. More fairy-tale-like.

But Ivy only laughed. She beckoned the bartender with her finger. "Gimme a tequila and a club soda, will ya?" She caught Cate's glare and quickly added, "And some pretzels. Or any other snacks ya got. We're starving."

The bartender rolled his eyes, but almost immediately set two glasses on the bar and sloshed some tequila into one of them, bubbly soda in the other. He didn't ask for her ID. The people at the casino entrance hadn't even bothered to properly check Cate's and Ivy's fake IDs, either, and Cate knew damn well she didn't pass as twenty-nine-year-old Ethel Wellington. Getting into Atlantis, ordering drinks—it all felt too easy.

Cate hadn't even seen a single police officer or guard patrolling the casino, though after watching officers take Mom, she wasn't exactly upset about it. Guess they had bigger things to take care of.

Still, Cate felt a stir of unease. No cops. No rules.

No help if something went wrong.

The bartender slid them their drinks, one a sun-yellow liquid, rimmed with salt. Ivy swallowed her club soda in one go.

"Being the designated driver *sucks*." She slid the other glass into Cate's hand, a conspiratorial flicker in her eyes. "I'm living vicariously through you, girl."

The glass was cold against her fingers. Cate met Ivy's gaze and felt another stir of unease. "Can I eat first? All I've had today was half a granola bar."

She was well aware Ivy was no stranger to partying hard

and getting others to party with her. She had always been that way. If other people worked hard and played hard, Ivy worked her *ass* off—and played her ass off, too. It was, after all, her tried-and-true method of forgetting about her parents' issues. But *this* Ivy was . . . different. It wasn't like Ivy to push this hard, to constantly egg Cate on, to constantly push her to dance, to drink, to let loose—

It felt *off,* somehow.

And it wasn't just that, Cate realized. Ivy had said her dad took her phone after the alien message was translated, but what about before that? She hadn't checked in with Cate after the party, which wasn't like her at all. Ivy's silence in the car as they drove to the casino, and now her determination to do anything but talk—it all pointed to one thing.

Ivy was hiding something.

"No time!" She hopped off the bar abruptly and stretched her arms above her head. "Now, while you're here contemplating whether or not you're actually going to live for once, I'm gonna dance." She grinned wildly. "Start a tab!"

Ivy bounced into the crowd, her hips already swaying in perfect tandem to the beginning of a Drake song.

Cate took a handful of the pretzels the bartender set down. What was it that Ivy had said before? *I'll follow you to the ends of the earth, literally.*

She had sounded so sincere, so determined, then. But who was following who now?

The more Cate thought about it, the more she felt the

familiar angry buzz in her blood. She should have noticed it sooner. That faraway look in Ivy's eyes, ever since they'd left the apartment complex. It was almost as if Ivy was desperate for something, too, just like the other casino-goers—but for what? Even if she asked, she was sure Ivy wouldn't answer.

Cate eyed the drink in her hand once more, threw her head back, and downed the shot. The drink burned her throat as it slid down, like a rug burn on her insides. She slapped the empty glass on the bar and ran her tingling fingertips through her hair—half-surprised when her hair suddenly ended. She still hadn't gotten used to it; the haircut had been another one of Ivy's brilliant ideas.

They were all Ivy's ideas. Every single one.

Cate was struck by a sudden memory: Mom sitting on the bed next to Cate, braiding her hair, making Cate's scalp tingle beneath her gentle movements. She'd tell stories about Dad and his adventures, and Cate would listen. She always heard the longing in her voice, magnetic and warm, and it made Cate miss a man she'd never even met. Cling to memories she'd never had.

But in the end, they were all just silly imaginings and half-baked delusions. Her real dad wasn't a shape-shifting sky pirate who rescued decrepit towns from disaster. Cate sometimes wondered if her real dad even existed, if maybe he had been just a figment of Mom's imagination after all. But he had to be *someone*, didn't he? Unless Cate herself was imaginary, too, just a quiet figure living in the recesses of Mom's mind all along. Maybe Cate would wake up one day, look in the bathroom mirror, and find it empty.

She swallowed her thoughts. All that mattered was that her dad had a name now, and that made him real enough for her.

Garrett.

The base of her neck was slick with sweat. From the stress? Or the alcohol? She couldn't tell anymore.

Ivy reemerged from the crowd wearing sweat like a glistening second skin, the colorful disco lights refracting off the droplets on her body. Even her plum blossom tattoo, peeking from the back of her shirt, seemed alive. "I warmed up the floor for you," she said, breathless. "Now come."

The tequila was kicking in, lighting a warm, steady fire inside her. "Ivy. Why are we here?"

"What do you mean, why?" Ivy leaned her head, letting her long hair dangle to the side. "I told you. To have fun, for once. Carpe diem and all that. We didn't come out all this way for nothing."

"Exactly," Cate huffed. She could practically feel the letter throbbing in her purse. "We came to find my dad."

Ivy wrapped her arms around Cate, half falling on her. She was sticky. "I know, I know. We'll get down to business soon, my beautiful eager beaver, I promise, but look around! We're in motherfucking *Reno* with no supervision. It's time to cross some things off our bucket lists, babe. I need you to *live*."

Cate pulled away. She saw it written all over Ivy's face again. That look.

And suddenly, she understood. "You're hoping I'll just give up, aren't you?" she said. The words tasted bitter in her mouth. "You were hoping you could just make me forget."

"Finding your dad in Roswell is going to be like finding a needle in a shitstack—*if* he's even still there," Ivy continued, her shoulders slumped and her words coming as fast and unrelenting as punches. "It's not *worth* it. Remember when you finally found your aunt Lily and she said all that shit about your mom? You didn't want to go out again for weeks. You *cried* to me, Cate, and you *hate* crying in front of people." She took a deep breath. "I want to make sure you never get crushed like that again. Your mom wants you to deliver the letter. But the most important question is, what do *you* want?"

"It doesn't matter what I want," Cate said. Her pulse pounded in her ears over the drumming of the music. "I promised her."

"And that's exactly the problem! You don't care! You don't care about yourself *ever.* You only care about your mom. Even when it hurts. I mean, you have no time to study for the SATs because of her, don't have a social life because of her. You can afford to be a little selfish every once in a while, you know. Do you even know how to live for yourself? Because that's a thing, Cate. That's a thing people do. And now is kind of a great time to start."

"I *do* live for myself. I went to that party with you, didn't I?" Cate snapped.

"I practically had to force you to! You talked about your mom all night then, too, and then you ran off after an hour.

It's so hard to get you *out*, Cate." Ivy's voice rose higher and higher. "If you could get away with skipping school, you'd probably never leave your house."

Cate's jaw tensed. "I never asked for a last-minute life makeover."

"That doesn't mean you don't need it. As your best friend, I'm telling you this whole plan to find your dad is *ridiculous*. You need to learn to let go."

"Let go?" Cate's eyes burned. She blinked rapidly, trying to bring Ivy and everything around her back into focus. But her eyes kept blurring over, and now her throat felt tight, squeezed by an invisible force that made her want to cry even more. "That's easy for you to say. All you do is let go. But I'm not like you. I don't have the freedom to live for myself when my mom, in case you've forgotten, is *sick*. I don't have the luxury of a normal life like you—"

"Right, because my life is *so* luxurious." Ivy cut her off. "All I'm saying is, you've picked the literal worst possible time to make an impulsive decision. Even *I* can see that, Cate. But if you don't, fine. *Fine.* Go on your wild-goose chase. You're always running from something, anyway."

"What?" Cate could barely choke out the word.

Ivy picked up the pail and shoved it toward Cate. "Keep the chips. You're gonna need them more than I do." She spun on her heel and shoved her way into the crowd.

"Ivy!" Cate shouted, but Ivy either didn't hear or pretended not to. And Cate didn't have the heart to go after her.

Ivy didn't understand. Ivy had never understood.

Besides, Cate was used to doing things alone.

The pail was a heavy anchor in her hand. Ivy had covered the chips with a folded piece of notebook paper. Cate lifted the paper, unfolded it.

Her bucket list, the one Ivy had made for her. It was strangely short—Cate was surprised Ivy hadn't added an entire *tome* of all the things she wanted her to do before the end. This was the same Ivy who still made weekly, color-coded to-do lists for fun, the same Ivy who kept a shared Notes list on her phone of all the recipes she wanted to make with Cate.

So maybe Ivy had made the bucket list short on purpose. Maybe she'd wanted to leave room for Cate to add goals of her own.

Her heart jostled behind her ribs, rattled by the swirl of conflicting emotions: the cold grip of guilt, the lingering flare of anger, the black void of confusion. The paper suddenly felt heavier than the pail full of chips. But Cate had to focus. There was no time to let anything—or anyone—distract her.

Roswell was an eighteen-hour drive from Reno; she knew that much. With Ivy's chips, she'd have plenty of money for a bus. With any luck, she could do the trip straight and have three days with her mom.

Mom. She wanted to hear her voice so badly.

Cate still had the number for the inpatient psychiatric unit. Maybe she could call again, talk to Dr. Michel directly to get a better idea of when her mom would be well enough to take visitors. Cate was already pulling up the number when the music cut off with a screech. The lights came up abruptly, leaving everyone on the dance floor awkwardly blinking and embarrassed. The crowd on the dance floor suddenly looked like a crowd of pasty, confused grocery shoppers caught trying to steal something embarrassing. Even the bartender had stopped midpour, and now that the lights were up, Cate could see his yellowed, sleepless eyes and the angry rash crawling all over one side of his face.

And then everyone could hear it: the insistent, piercing wail of a fire alarm.

"It's Alma!" someone cried. "They're here!"

Just like that, all hell broke loose. People snapped out of their stupor, their screams and stomps all blending into a cacophonous flurry of sound. A rush of people thronged past the bar, one of them catching Cate in the face with an elbow. She stumbled off her stool and was immediately swept up into the flow of people. There was something else, too, another sound rising above it all, something that sounded terrifyingly like gunshots. The crowd swallowed Cate whole. Her limbs were pinned to her sides. She could hardly breathe.

"Don't you fucking touch me!" a man to her left snarled, crimson-faced. He flailed out with his fist and struck the nose of another man, releasing a tide of blood. Then Cate heard the gunshots clearer now. Debris fell from the ceiling like snowflakes. She thought she smelled smoke too. Screams crescendoed once again, the shoving growing more desperate.

Just how many shooters were there?

Cate's mind clouded with white panic. *It's okay*, she told herself. *It's okay, it's okay, it's going to be okay.*

But there was no room to turn around—no room to turn at *all*. *I can't go back*, she realized suddenly, remembering a snippet of knowledge she'd once heard during a fire drill. *I have to follow the crowd like it's a wave. So I don't fall. If I fall, I'll get trampled to death.*

Don't fall. Don't fall. Don't fall.

The crowd swept her along, unrelenting. All the way to the front of the casino, screams and shouts echoing in her ears the whole time. Until she and the crowd reached a bottleneck just inside the main exit. Her cheek was pressed into someone's shoulder blade, and by now Cate had been squished and pushed so many times she could hardly breathe. But she could see it: people were beginning to break from the crowd. Getting outside. The crowd here was so tight that it was almost motionless, and for a moment Cate felt almost surreally calm, as if she were just standing in the middle of a group of people, on a subway train, or something.

And then Cate saw it—an opening. She shoved forward with all her might, squeezed through a tiny gap between two large, sweaty men, and ran through the doors and out into the rain.

When Cate found a pocket of space between a row of pine trees that dotted the outskirts of the building, she stopped and took gigantic breaths, in and out, tears streaming from her eyes. Her lungs prickled beneath her chest, and her shoes were digging into the backs of her heels, but she barely felt the pain. She'd only run a couple hundred feet from the casino, half stumbling down the wet hillside until she reached the trees, until she reached the cover of their shadowy branches.

From a distance, Cate could still see the police and SWAT team members evacuating people, ushering them away from the casino entrance and toward the pine trees where she was hidden. She could smell smoke, too, and hear the wail of approaching fire trucks.

On the other side of the trees was the parking lot. She stumbled but somehow managed to stay on her feet as she willed herself forward, toward the first line of cars in the lot. She scanned them, unable to find that familiar shade of blue, and bolted deeper into the maze of cars. The lot seemed so much bigger than before, and she couldn't remember where they'd parked.

The crowd from the casino was close behind. Soon this parking lot would be utter chaos. There were too many rows and too many cars, many of them parked in weird, crooked angles in an attempt to make their own spots where there were none left. She doubted those cars belonged to people heading to the church.

But Ivy's blue Mazda was gone.

"Come on, come on . . ." She grabbed the door handle of another sedan and pulled. Locked. Of course. A fresh crowd of people thronged past her. One girl's face was streaked with soot and rust, or maybe blood. In the distance, smoke was unwinding from the casino roof.

She coughed. She was still having trouble breathing. Her head was full of thick clouds of smoke, with the clamor of the alarms, with the shrill, piercing wail of the approaching emergency vehicles. She just wanted to sit down somewhere. Somewhere dry and safe and enclosed—somewhere *quiet.*

Automatically, almost without thinking, Cate tried the hatchback on her right. Also locked. Cate went around to the next car, tried the door. Nope. She tried another, and then a pickup truck, and then another car, moving closer and closer toward the church until . . .

Click.

Thank God. Someone had forgotten to lock their Acura.

She scrambled inside, scattering a pile of papers and a portable radio across the back seat. She quietly closed the door behind her and locked it.

Cate flattened herself against the back seat of the car as frantic footsteps thundered past her. She felt light-headed and closed her eyes. She could feel the pinch of her blackbird key chain in her pocket pressing into her stomach, but her body trembled uncontrollably and she didn't dare move it. She felt a sob well up in her throat. The world was ending, and she was miles away from her mom, crying in a strange car that smelled faintly of mangos and hoping her best friend didn't hate her. And for what? To find a dad who'd never even bothered to fight to get Mom back?

Stupid. So stupid. But the stupidest thing of all was how

sure she was, even now, that she would have regretted not trying.

Footsteps. She heard more footsteps, a lone pair, slapping the pavement, getting closer. Was it more people from the casino, people like her, who were just trying to find someplace to hide? Or was it the shooter?

Please let me be safe.

She closed her eyes and prayed.

ADEEM

Smoke.

Adeem saw it the second he was outside; the back of the lot, where the cars were more packed together, was also full of people, many of them breathless and red-faced, as though they'd been running. And more were coming, bursting through the row of pine trees that divided the church grounds from the casino. Some were screaming, others crying. Dread seized his legs and clutched painfully at his chest. He'd caught glimpses of these kinds of scenes on the TV, had heard about them on his radio—disasters like school shootings—but that was the news, something that happened to other people, not something you just walked into.

Beyond the pine trees, elevated by a giant hill, the casino seemed to glow against the purple evening haze, lit up by long rows of neon pink lights that ran down its windows like columns. A crowd had gathered around the giant fountain at the casino entrance, now closed off by uniformed officers who had emerged from lit cop cars. A Humvee rolled in beside a parked fire truck, and cops in SWAT gear hopped off, carrying guns that were half their size, to take position in front of the casino doors. Cops with German shepherds patrolled the perimeter. People in yellow jackets were escorting or carrying the wounded to the grass; there were so many wounded.

Adeem hoped Reza and the others stayed in the basement. *Stay safe, Rez.*

He'd text him later, when he could. When he could *think.*

Adeem moved as fast as he could without breaking into a run toward his car. The gravel pathway to the parking lot crunched beneath his feet. He narrowly dodged another driver frantically trying to leave. Finally, he reached his own car and leaned against it to keep himself steady.

"Breathe," he repeated to himself. "Breathe." Miss Takemoto was right about the dangers of becoming a Mountain Dew–chugging zombie; Adeem was more out of shape than he'd thought. He imagined his heart gasping for air, its four chambers contracting and pumping in a desperate, clumsy dance to keep him functioning, if only barely.

He unlocked the car, pulled open the driver's seat door, and froze.

"I can explain."

A girl was huddled in the back seat of his Acura TSX with both hands up, as if she was worried he was going to try and shoot her. In the evening dark, he hadn't seen her from outside.

She had dark, liquid eyes set against her pale, freckled skin. Her forehead was a mess of sweaty bangs. And she was shaking.

"Jesus!" Adeem drew back, startled. "How'd you get inside?" he demanded.

"The door was unlocked." The girl gripped the seat in front of her.

Unlocked? *Oh no.* Panicking, he suddenly reached for a lever on the driver's seat—which made the girl flinch—and folded the seat down with a loud thud. But there it was, safe and sound: his Tecson radio and his external AM antenna, tucked in the back-seat pocket. The only remaining thread he had to his sister.

Adeem shoved the radio into the glove compartment and breathed a long sigh of relief. The girl, he realized, had inched as far away from him as she could, so he pushed the driver's seat up into place, gently, to put some space between them. The girl was obviously on edge, and he wasn't helping.

The faraway crack of something that sounded dangerously like gunfire, followed by the shattering of glass, gripped Adeem's attention toward the hill where the casino stood, only a quarter of a mile away.

Another bang. Adeem nearly jumped.

"What the hell's going on?" Adeem dove into the driver's seat and slammed the door behind him.

The girl wrapped the light cardigan she wore closer over her frame. "There's a gunman—we're not safe."

"No shit," he retorted. He'd been tense before, but now his entire body was rigid. A bead of sweat rolled down his face. It hit him then, what this girl must have seen. What she must have been through.

"Are you hurt?" he asked.

"No." She took a shallow, quivering breath. "I'm okay, I think."

She didn't look okay, but Adeem wasn't about to point that out.

Streams of people broke through the row of pine trees beside them, running into the church parking lot. Some were shrieking, sprinting with seemingly no intention of ever stopping. Others were moving toward the church for shelter. At one point, someone bumped into their car with a loud thud. It was a woman just a few years older than Adeem. Leyla's age.

Adeem's body wouldn't move. He wanted to disappear beneath the woman's desperate, frantic stare. Before he could even think to let her inside, a high-pitched whistle and a far-away popping resounded through the open sky. The woman's eyes widened in horror before she ran off.

The girl with the freckles whimpered behind him. She was watching the sky now through the window, an uneasy expression on her face. Adeem was almost afraid to look, but a flash of red forced him. A flare, maybe? Maybe the police were signaling to each other.

But suddenly, from up on the hill where the casino was nestled, screams broke through the hazy night air and throbbed between his ears. The crowd that had been waiting outside the entrance scattered. Silvery-gray fumes escaped from a series of shattered windows on the face of the casino and descended upon them, enveloping the entrance, sweeping over the row of police cars. Even from within the car, his nose picked up on a smell that burned his nostrils and stung his eyes.

An ocean of a crowd sprinted down the hill, toward the church. Toward *them*.

"Shit." That was all Adeem needed to convince him. He shoved his phone back in his pocket and jammed his finger against the Start Engine button. The radio blared to life, blasting some fast-paced electronica. Adeem raised his voice. "I'm gonna *Tokyo Drift* our way out of this. We'll figure out the rest later." Adeem turned to look at her. "You okay with that?"

More gunshots from the casino. Except they sounded louder this time, too loud for even the music to muffle. The shadowy evening horizon line was now raked by black plumes of smoke. The back of Adeem's neck tingled with painful awareness—the feeling he used to get, late at night, when he could feel some imaginary monster following him upstairs to his bedroom. Except this time, the danger was real. The monster was real. And somehow he'd fallen right in its path.

He opened his mouth to ask her again, but before he could, the girl put on her seat belt.

"Anywhere's better than here," she said.

He slammed the accelerator. "Roger that." He was thrown to the back of the seat by sheer force and barely wove through the incoming wave of people, speeding toward the main road and away from the church, the casino, and the haze of hungry flames. Hours of Mario Kart definitely had not prepared him for the real thing. Another bead of sweat rolled down his cheek.

"I'm Adeem, by the way," he half screamed.

The girl leaned forward. "Cate," she said, wiping her eyes. "My name's Cate."

FIVE DAYS

UNTIL THE END

OF DELIBERATIONS

[THE FIRST "MESSAGES" SENT OUT
IN BINARY BY JESSE'S MACHINE]

Testing, testing, one, two, three . . .

Commence message transmission:

Alma, if you can see this,
Please, for the sake of my unborn baby, you can't do this.

> Alma,
> Come at me, bro. If I can handle life, I can handle you.
> Kareem

> > Dear Vincent,
> > If we don't make it, know my love remains
> > in space forever.
> > Yours,
> > Sam

To the aliens,
Don't bother coming here. Humans taste awful.

> Seymour, my one and only,
> They say it'll all end soon. All I can do now is wish
> you were here with me. Aliens, Almaens, whoever—
> give my Seymour a sign that I love him.
> Love, Cora

Len,
They say this message should reach space, so maybe it'll reach you. If you're there, send down a little luck our way. We could use it.
Love,
Moira

Dear Pete,
I miss you.
Laura

Citizens of Alma,
I've already lost everything. I don't even have enough money to send a longer message. Just please reconsider.
Thank you,
Kai

I swear to all you alien colonizers out there,
If I die before Derek knows I've been crushing on him all year,
I'm taking you bitches down with me.
Up yours,
Mia

12

JESSE

Less than twenty-four hours after Jesse first posted about the Hewitt Electronic Communication Center on Reddit—HECC, for short—he woke up to a doorbell that wouldn't stop ringing and a small line of people running from the doorway to the mailbox.

There were twenty people milling in the front yard, give or take, old and young and everything in between. Most had backpacks and small cameras and wide eyes, like the tourists he used to see back at the Roswell Plaza Hotel. He even recognized some of the locals: Frank Gottlieb, the waiter at Cattle Ranch Steakhouse who swore up and down he'd been abducted by aliens in the '80s; Kit Newton, a freshman who charged kids at school fifteen bucks a jar filled with dirt from the old UFO crash site; and a few people he'd worked with at the hotel, including the assistant manager, Doug, who was probably happy the hotel closed down because it meant he'd have more time to spend with his exotic snake collection.

Realization dawned like a punch to his jaw. *The machine.*

A van rolled into the driveway, barely avoiding the line of people, and another group of tourists shuffled out. Jesse started counting heads—counting wallets—but kept losing track.

The photo he'd uploaded had captured the machine's towering, seven-foot-tall frame; it would be obvious to anyone the thing was massive, and with its glowing interface and back-lit keys, it looked straight out of a NASA laboratory. No one would know it was nothing more than a glorified printer—or, at least, a *lot* of people wouldn't know. And he didn't show up at school enough for people to know he was about as good at math and science as knitting blindfolded.

But he'd spent hours at the Roswell Public Library yesterday after he'd unearthed the machine and found several sun-faded astronomy journals from the '80s. Some forgotten would-be astronomer from Chile had written a thesis on gaseous planets in the TRAPPIST-2 system, long before Alma had been discovered, and bored Jesse to death with his theory that one of those gassy planets would complete its orbit around the system's sun-like star every 489 days. It sounded legit enough to Jesse, and the theory—and poor astronomer—were obscure enough that no one would discover Jesse's source. So Jesse banked on it, claiming on his Reddit post that Alma, through his machine, had given him all kinds of information about their solar system, including information about their orbits. Information that, as far as anyone could tell, only he and Alma could *ever* know—unless Jesse had a five-million-dollar telescope. Which he did not.

He couldn't believe it had worked.

The lie, that is.

Jesse shut the curtains, but already people had seen him. Now they were shouting his name. The local reporters must have been eager for a story, no matter how small—something different from the usual gloom-and-doom that every damn news station was showing nowadays.

He wished he had another working laptop, but he had to use the only one they had, an ancient, beat-up Gateway, for the inside of the machine. He wondered how many people had seen his Reddit post already. How many people in the world already knew his name?

Soon everyone will know the name Hewitt, J-Bird.

When he was alone in Dad's shed, the feel of wood grain beneath his fingertips had brought him a strange sense of familiarity, like the touch of an old friend; there was comfort in knowing he could easily transform a cheap block of wood, a spring, and some bolts into something sellable to make an easy few bucks, no sweat. With his own two hands, and a little effort, he could manipulate basic materials into something greater.

And with the machine, he could change things for himself—and for his mom, too.

He hadn't told her about his plans yet, and was glad she was as usual working a double at the diner. It wouldn't take long for rumors of the machine to reach her there, though. He hoped she wouldn't be too mad.

Mom never dreamed big. She'd never been able to afford big dreams.

And Ms. K. What would she think?

Impulsive.

Then again, she always told him the importance of finding hobbies. It's why she encouraged Tom Ralford and his stupid radio show. Why should this be any different?

He'd have to cancel his appointment with her today, though. He was technically supposed to go once a week ever since the incident, or else he'd lose insurance coverage or some state-mandated bullshit like that. But it was just one time, and some things were more important.

He washed his mouth out with Listerine and shoved on some old jeans and his cleanest T-shirt. He made sure his cuff was in place on his left wrist, doing his best to avoid looking at the thin, silvery scars, then tugged on his old leather jacket. The crow patch on his breast pocket seemed to be grinning at him.

Through the circular window on the door, people were peering into his house.

"All right, all right, coming," Jesse said. He tried to sound casual. Confident. Like he knew what he was doing.

He took a deep breath, reached out, and opened the door.

Mom never dreamed big. So Jesse would dream big enough for the both of them.

460, 480, 500 . . .

By afternoon, Jesse had already made $520. Not even close to paying off the bills they owed, but hell, it was enough to cover a few days of Mom's earnings. Enough for 120 poppy-seed loaves, even. And that was a start.

Jesse wiped the sweat that clung to his forehead. Keeping the line of customers in check—twenty-six visitors today and it was barely 1:00 p.m.—was harder than he thought. He almost couldn't believe how many people could just toss twenty bucks down the drain.

His hands had cramped hours ago, but he'd have to get used to it. At least the messages people wanted to send to Alma weren't overly long; the gist of most of them was along the lines of *Please don't kill us.* But others had messages that read more like wishes, as though Alma were a vast Santa Claus, or some kind of psychiatrist. Funny thing about people thinking it was the end of the world: people were suddenly more talkative, suddenly more open. Even the locals that recognized him seemed to forget that Jesse was the ghost of a kid at school who rarely showed up to class.

Instead, Jesse had become their messenger.

Aliens, Almaens, whoever, one of the first messages had read, *give my Seymour a sign that I love him.* Jesse had stared at the customer—an older woman with round Coke-bottle glasses—before shrugging and typing up her message into the machine. He wasn't sure what the logic was in asking Alma to help with her relationship troubles—and really, if Alma was real, what made her think they'd help at all?—but he kept his thoughts behind his charming smile.

And anyway, for all he knew, Seymour could be a cat. He wasn't about to ask.

"Now, there's no guarantee that Alma will respond to every message," Jesse said for what must have been the fortieth time that day as he finished typing the message. Tiny neon light bulbs that decked the face of the machine began to blink. "And I certainly can't guarantee Alma will do anything for your Seymour. But I'll broadcast your message for them loud and clear."

Jesse had done some basic research; he knew radio waves had long been proven the fastest—and potentially most reliable—way for scientists to send messages into space. But messages via radio waves could never reach Alma before the aliens made their decision. They just weren't fast enough. Nothing on earth was, anyway.

But Jesse didn't need to make people believe he'd found an impossibly fast way to transmit messages. People were already convinced that Alma had to have incredible transmitter power to send a message like the one they'd sent to NASA; it would have had to travel faster than the speed of light to reach Earth in a day. So an alien planet having that kind of technology meant it was at least possible they had some kind of powerful receiver, too. Who was to say Alma didn't already have some kind of super satellite receiver floating around Earth, ready and aimed to pick up our radio messages midflight?

All that mattered was the plausibility. The details didn't matter.

It was like Tom Ralford said. People just wanted to get their feelings out, to *feel* heard. And they'd pay money to do it.

"Bless you," said a large woman with skin the color of turned cheese. She fumbled through her oversized, stained leather purse until she found her wallet. Her skin was warm as she took Jesse's hand and gently enclosed in it over twenty-five dollars in cash. "A little extra for your trouble, dear. You keep doing the good work."

Jesse gave her the brightest smile he could muster. "Thanks, ma'am." He crammed a copy of her message into a folder on a shelf behind the machine. He'd decided to keep the messages. For posterity's sake.

Once the woman left, he slipped out of the shed, locking the door behind him and promising the guy next in line—some loser with a fanny pack—that he'd be right back.

He jogged across the short stretch of patchy desert lawn, trying to blink away a headache. He needed water. He needed a *break*. He'd talked to more people in one morning than he usually did in a month.

He wondered if that's why his dad had locked himself away in the shed, working on the husks of these weird, egg-shaped machines. Was this his plan all along? Not to make Roswell some kind of extraterrestrial communication hub, but to get rich off the dream that it might be?

Or had he actually believed in this shit?

Before Jesse could slip inside the kitchen, though, a hand came down on his arm, just above his leather cuff.

"Excuse me," a deep voice asked sheepishly. "Do you know if this HECC machine really works?"

Jesse nearly jumped out of his skin. It was the boy from the gas station—the cute guy who'd come in for coffee.

Jesse yanked his arm away as his brain frantically went through a mental checklist:

Had he put on deodorant that morning? Yes. Maybe. He couldn't double-check without looking like an idiot. Shaven? His five-o'clock shadow straddled the line between boyish and hipster lumberjack, so good enough. His clothes would have to do; his leather jacket hopefully gave him more of a vintage, hipster vibe than dirt poor. So at least he didn't look like total shit.

But *this* guy. If he was good-looking in the gas station, he was on an entirely different plane up close. His smooth, chiseled face and wide, round eyes screamed *earnest.* The boy's eyes were dark, so dark that Jesse couldn't see where his irises ended and his pupils began—obscuring, the kind that could hide secrets effortlessly. He wore a plain, dark blue T-shirt that hugged his taut body like a second skin. But despite his boy-band looks, he had a voice like sunset and smoke that left Jesse reeling.

Jesse tugged at his leather cuff, a nervous habit. For a second, he couldn't make his own voice function.

Then he cleared his throat. "Uh, yeah. I mean, I made the thing, so I guess I gotta say it works, right?" He gave a forceful bark of a laugh.

"Oh, wow. Sorry." The boy recoiled in surprise. "Man, I feel dumb. With the jacket and everything, I thought you were a bouncer or something. You're . . . a lot younger than I thought you'd be." His eyes swept Jesse up and down, and Jesse's whole body went tight beneath his gaze. "Gotta be honest, I've never been good with machines. Big ones like that kinda freak me out; I keep thinking it's gonna turn rogue or burst into 'Daisy Bell' or something."

Jesse nodded. "Yeah, I totally get that." But he didn't get it at all. Who the hell was Daisy Bell?

"Kinda ignorant to this stuff. How does it work?"

"Oh, it's easy. Nothing too complicated." Jesse cleared his throat. He'd explained it a hundred times before, but for some reason, he was having trouble keeping his head on straight now. "It . . . works kind of like a translator. Basically. I just type up people's messages, and the computer translates it into binary. I'd be lying if I said I knew Almaen, but binary is the next-best thing. The machine then beams up the message alongside an encoded key, so they can recognize it from static. The hope is that they receive it one day and decrypt it."

"Oh, cool, like the Arecibo message."

Fuck. Jesse made a mental note to look that up later, too. "Exactly."

"Huh." He smiled at Jesse, but it was wooden. Forced. "Interesting. How'd you learn how to do it?"

Jesse stiffened. He didn't like the way he'd said "interesting," the way he'd lingered on the word to give it that infuriating tang of skepticism. Maybe Jesse could buy a nice new button-down shirt, make himself look older, more official.

"People learn how to make bombs on the internet, how to become dictators on the internet. You can pretty much learn anything these days." He looked away. "You, uh, planning on using the machine today?"

"Nah, I'm just passing through. Was curious, is all." This time, his smile was genuine.

"My name's Corbin. Corbin Lee."

As Corbin ran his hand through his hair, Jesse caught a whiff of that familiar woodsy shampoo. Jesse swallowed, dazed. He suddenly felt tacky, like a cheap door-to-door salesman—or worse, like Kit Newton, with his alien dirt. All Jesse was missing was a briefcase full of Mason jars. At least if he were still working his respectful stint at the souvenir shop at the Roswell Plaza Hotel, he could sidle right down to his usual hit-and-run method: flirt a little, invite Corbin for a tour, take him behind Close Encounters—and call it a single night well spent.

Then again, Corbin didn't seem like the kind of guy who would be easy.

He cleared his throat. "Jesse. Um, Hewitt. Like the Hewitt Electronic Communication Center. My machine. Obviously." He cleared his throat again. Why was his throat so damn tight?

"Corbin! *¿Qué pasa?*" a man in a camo baseball cap called. "Shouldn't you be at the hospital?"

Corbin grinned and waved back. "Mr. Arroyo! *Estoy en camino ahora, prometo.*"

"*¡Apúrate!* Mariposa's waiting."

Hospital? Mariposa? For once, Jesse actually wished he'd paid attention in Spanish class.

Corbin gave him a tight-lipped smile. "I'll let you get back to it. Jesse, right?"

Jesse nodded. Corbin extended a hand to him, and for a second, Jesse could only stare.

Was he asking for a *handshake*? Such a simple gesture, and yet it felt so out of place when Jesse had spent the whole day reeling in the bleary-eyed, high-strung people who'd come from all over town just to take a stab at his machine. He'd had to break up a fight in line and threaten to call the cops, even though he knew damn well the cops were too busy trying to stop Roswell from going up in flames.

A handshake felt so old-school. So civil.

But he kinda liked it.

Jesse took Corbin's hand. Corbin had a great grip—confident, warm, just firm enough.

"Come back anytime," Jesse blurted out.

Corbin's gaze held Jesse in place. "I will," he said, "just as soon as I figure out what I want to say."

Jesse watched Corbin as he turned and stumped off to the street. Something about the way he walked—his broad shoulders ever so slightly slumped by an invisible weight—looked sad to him. Familiar, even. Then again, these days, almost everyone looked sad, no matter how much they tried to hide it.

"Excuse me." A scrawny girl no older than thirteen shouldered through the crowd. "I can take a Snap with the machine, yeah? I don't need to send a message or anything."

Her friend, another girl chewing bubblegum with more concentration than necessary, nodded.

Jesse sighed. "You got ten bucks?"

Maybe starting tomorrow, he would increase the price per message to fifty bucks. If he wanted to save his house before the bank knocked on their door, he had to: with the amount of hours it took to draft people's messages and Alma's responses, and the amount of hours it took for Jesse to comfort some of his customers, just to get them to cough up their money, he simply wasn't making enough. And the clock was ticking.

The girl forked over the ten bucks, and Jesse gestured her toward the machine.

"Then go for it."

Jesse slipped the money into his beat-up wallet, and the two girls sauntered to the shed, where Jesse had pulled the machine out for easy access and viewing. Quickly, he scanned the crowd for Corbin, but he'd already left.

Jesse touched the palm of his hand, where the warmth of Corbin's gentle grip still lingered.

Maybe his machine worked better than he'd thought.

13

ADEEM

"Shit," said Adeem. A small burst of anxiety flared in his chest. They'd only gone about a hundred and twenty miles, passing endless stretches of beige desert and lumpy mountain range, when the gas light came on. Adeem, distracted by the radio, hadn't even been paying attention to the tank.

Or maybe, subconsciously, he'd been trying not to think about it.

The next big city on the way to Roswell was Las Vegas, where Priti lived—still a good three hours away. So close and yet so freaking far. The apocalyptic levels of traffic leaving Reno had been the equivalent of wading through quicksand while wearing a weighted tortoiseshell, and even though Adeem had turned the engine off during the lulls, it must have still been a drain on the gas. Once they had finally squeezed out of the city, gas station after gas station was either closed or sold out of gas. But he'd hoped eventually they'd find one. Hoped and hoped and hoped.

Out *here*, though, on this back highway? There was no telling when they'd pass another one, and panic was beginning to curl inside his gut.

Worse still, he was dead tired; after driving through the night, the gas tank wasn't the only thing exhausted. But he couldn't afford to stop.

"What is it?" asked Cate. She had leaned forward so suddenly, Adeem recoiled, her voice surprising him.

She'd been pretty quiet on the road, and Adeem could tell she was scared—scared of what would happen, scared of what had happened, maybe even scared of him. She looked like she could barely sit still in her seat. Who knew what she might have seen, what kind of horrifying flashbacks she was trying to suppress in the back of her mind? Adeem hadn't been there, but even *he* was terrified. People might have died at the casino. Probably *had* died. How many times had he seen mass shootings on the news and dismissed it as something so unlikely, so remote, it could never happen to him? And yet it *had*, just across the parking lot of the church he'd been in. No wonder Alma was so disgusted with Earth, where shootings were as certain as death and taxes.

To fill the awkward silence between them, Adeem had put on the radio—the handheld Tecsun, since the car radio was too patchy. Though he half hoped he might catch another transmission from Leyla, he instead caught a report from a local pirate station about NASA officials scanning airwaves using satellite tech to find any sign of Almaen spacecraft, any sign of attack.

If the point of turning on the radio was to be distracted, he'd definitely succeeded. But it was the only thing to keep his mind off, to put it lightly, the *bizarro* situation he'd gotten himself into: Narrowly escaping a mass shooting. Running away with some white girl. Driving to *Roswell* with her.

Not exactly the original plan.

A few hours ago, when the cacophony of the casino and the gunfire was safely behind them, Adeem had asked her where he should drop her off, and was surprised when she'd said she didn't know.

"What do you mean, you don't *know*?" As much as Adeem wanted to help her, he had things to do. A sister to find. A sister to drag back home.

"I mean, normally I'd say the bus station, but . . ."

He understood. None of the buses would be running anymore. Even train service had been suspended. That left her completely stranded if she couldn't find a ride. He felt a pang of sympathy. They were probably about the same age, but there was something about her that wafted exhaustion, something sad and lost. Just how far was home for her?

Cate's mouth went lopsided as she began to chew the inside of her cheek, and though her long bangs covered most of her forehead, Adeem could see from the rearview mirror the emerging deep creases on it.

"Well, where do you need to go?" Adeem asked. "Because I'm heading to—"

"Roswell," she finished for him.

For a moment, Adeem was half-convinced Cate was an alien mind reader herself—what the hell had he gotten himself into? But he shook the thought out of his head. The radio reports were spooking him.

Sill, what were the chances? Roswell was a small town, and definitely not a popular tourist destination. No, it was *too* weird, *too* coincidental. Stranger things had happened, sure—there were fucking aliens in the sky watching all of humanity like some kind of ant farm, after all. But things like this didn't happen to *him*.

Adeem had begun to laugh like Cate had said the most hilarious thing in the world.

Was it really just coincidence? Or fate?

Leyla had been a big believer in fate. When he'd asked her about why she was so hooked on Urdu poetry, she'd said it was because Urdu poetry was about two things: *ishq* and *qismat*. Love and fate.

"Humanity's strongest driving forces," she asserted. "And when they work in tandem—when something's meant to be—the universe always has a way of sending you a message. Of telling you you're on the right track."

Maybe the sentiment had been comforting to Leyla, at least

at the time. But love, fate—Adeem wasn't sure if he believed in any of it. And yet, despite all odds, he'd heard her voice on the radio. If Leyla was right—that love and fate were the ultimate driving forces of humanity—then the universe really had pointed Adeem to Roswell. To her.

He just didn't know how Cate was supposed to fit in all this. Either way, it seemed *something* would have them traveling together.

But what should have been a relatively simple twenty-four-hour trip was getting more and more . . . problematic.

Now Adeem tightened his fingers on the steering wheel. "Bad news. My car's low on juice."

Cate pulled out her phone, typed, and searched her screen. "I'll see what's nearby—it's spotty as hell, but I actually have some service," she said, her voice barely carrying over a staticky piano cover of "What a Wonderful World" playing on someone's personal broadcast. "Looks like there's a town called Tonopah down the road. We can ask around, see what's open."

"Your best idea yet." His mouth was dry, anyway, and he was getting hungry.

A few minutes later, they reached Tonopah: a tiny town, devoid of any trees or green, but where it lacked in plant life—or life at all—it more than made up for in liquor stores and RVs and dirt. And hopefully gas stations, even though, at least on the surface, most houses and stores seemed empty if not outright boarded up. Some of the houses even had white crosses painted on their doors, which gave Adeem the chills.

Adeem pulled into the parking lot of a corner convenience store and, this time, locked the car doors. He wasn't in the mood for fate forcing him to bring along more stragglers. And with the way his parents kept texting him every hour—and the way he was ignoring them—he couldn't be away from home longer than a day without them imploding from panic.

By some miracle, the convenience store was still open, and was one of the few places in the area that still had light. It would have seemed almost normal on the outside, except that a cop in a gray patrol uniform was positioned just outside the entrance. Another effect of Alma, he supposed.

Adeem mumbled a polite "Hello" to the cop as they walked past him. Adeem made it a point to be polite to cops—especially since he was a brown guy who was always stopped by TSA or stared at by overly cautious store owners who assumed he might steal something. He simply grinned in return, a Cheshire-cat smile that kind of creeped Adeem out.

The doors slid open. Both Adeem and Cate froze.

Though the ceiling lights were on, they flickered dimly, casting the inside of the store in a cold, foreboding light. Some of the shelves had been overturned onto the ground, which was covered in spills and stains and broken things; a broom leaned against the broken glass door to the fridge where drinks should have been kept, as though someone had meant to start cleaning, but had given up. Most of the remaining shelves were empty, save for a few scattered sundries: packs of cheap mascara in the makeup aisle, some greeting cards and stationery no one had bothered to take, a couple tabloids and newspapers strewn across the front counter. Besides a ripped bag of Sour Patch Kids scattering the floor—a total travesty—the food aisle had also been entirely cleared, as well as the battery station next to it. He was sure if he ventured farther to the back, the medicine aisle would be empty, too. Either the place had been ransacked by panicked looters last night, determined to take everything they'd need in case of an alien attack, or they'd simply sold out of everything.

"Holy shit" was all Adeem could think to say.

"Looters," Cate said unnecessarily. She rubbed her bare arms. "I still can't believe this is happening."

Adeem could get a good look at her now, under the barely-there fluorescent light; she stood in front of an endcap covered in thick green dishwashing liquid from a broken bottle. Her short brown hair was a little greasy around her forehead, and though her fingernails had been painted a sparkly dark blue, the tips had been chewed and the nail polish was flaking. He'd probably find her bitten-off nails—lunules, he believed they were called—in the back seat of his car.

"I keep thinking none of it's real, like I'll wake up from a dream." She looked at him. "Do you think Alma's actually going to"—she scowled—"*terminate* us?"

"You know," he said thoughtfully, "every day, I find it increasingly difficult to justify human existence to an outside observer. But we domesticated *dogs*. I mean, that has to count for something, right?"

Cate blinked, as if trying to figure out if he was serious, before chuckling softly. "That sounds like something Ivy would say."

Adeem realized it was the first time he'd seen her smile. Hers was tentative and featherlight, revealing a single dimple on her left side.

"Who's Ivy?" he asked.

Cate's smile faltered. "My best friend. She was at the casino with me—but she got out before everything went down." She tapped a fallen, leaking shampoo bottle with her foot. "She was my ride."

He wondered what had happened between them. But he didn't prod. "So now you're stuck with me instead."

"Yep." She made her hands into fists, placed them on either side of her head. "Help me, Adeem. You're my only hope."

Adeem laughed. Maybe it wouldn't be so bad having her along for the ride. If they could crack each other up despite everything, then maybe everything would be all right.

The universe always has a way of sending you a message.

"Excuse me?" Adeem called out. But there was no one: no cashiers, no shoppers, either. He caught a glimpse of one of the newspapers fanned on the counter. *MOB ATTACKS KENNEDY SPACE CENTER.* He almost laughed at that. What did the mob think would happen? That they could commandeer a rocket and fly into Alma?

"Excuse me!" Cate tried again. Her voice echoed back to them, and she shrugged.

But finally a man with graying hair and a dark blue collared shirt emerged from the back. A pin on his left breast pocket read *MANAGER*. He was carrying a backpack. "We're closed," he said. His voice was gruff and rusted, as though he'd been yelling for days. "No stock."

"We're just looking for a gas station," Adeem said. "You know of one close to here?"

The man rubbed his eyes. He was tired, too. Hell, everyone was tired. "It's not about which one's closest," he said. "It's about which ones have fuel. You can try the Taylor Street Gas, but that'd be back the way you came, off the highway, twenty miles or so. Last I heard, the Chevron down the road was running low. And they'll charge you an arm and a leg for it, the bastards."

Adeem pushed his fingers against his forehead, where a ball of tension was expanding. It would be a risk to drive out of the way to get more gas, and worse, it'd be a waste of precious time. At this point, he was less worried about the War of the Worlds than being skinned alive by his parents.

"What about water?" Cate blurted out. "Do you know where we can find any water?"

The store manager eyed Cate hard, then slumped his shoulders. "Not officially . . ." He seemed to make a decision and opened his backpack to toss a water bottle over to her. "Take one of mine. I gotta rack up those karma points while I still can."

Adeem was surprised. It was a tiny gesture, but it was

something. A kindness he hadn't expected.

They thanked the store manager and headed for the door.

"Should we take our chances with the Chevron?" Cate asked. "I could put it on my credit card . . ."

"Yeah, but I'm *hungry*," said Adeem. "Think the Sour Patch Kids are still good?"

"The ones on the *ground*? What are you, *five*?"

The automatic doors shut behind them. Once outside, Adeem realized they were alone in the parking lot. The cop, strangely enough, had left.

As they approached his car, Adeem's blood suddenly ran cold, and his stomach clenched so painfully fast, he might have preferred a punch to his windpipe.

The hood of his car was open.

A wave of nausea struck him, and he had to hold the frame of the car to keep himself steady. Someone had stolen the battery. His phone charger was gone, too, as well as the bag of quarters he used for parking meters. Even Derek's baseball bat was gone.

No. Adeem ripped open the glove compartment and let go of the air filling his chest. The radio was still there, where he'd tucked it after he'd found Cate in his car. Whoever had robbed them must not have had a use for an old transistor. Freaking pleb obviously didn't know its worth.

The cop. The thought slapped him, hard, in the gut. That guy stationed outside the convenience store.

Not a cop.

Was the uniform a fake? Or maybe he was a real cop and just didn't care anymore about doing his duty, didn't care about ripping off some kids for whatever they had.

It felt like a hive of bees was trapped beneath Adeem's skin. It didn't help that his phone was vibrating in his pocket, a reminder of just how screwed he was if he didn't come home soon. And he was hardly any closer to finding Leyla.

Beside him, Cate was silent for a while. She swallowed. And then finally, she calmly asked him a simple question.

"So, what the hell do we do now?"

FOUR DAYS

UNTIL THE END

OF DELIBERATIONS

14

JESSE

Someone—or some*thing*—was watching Jesse.

It was just after six in the morning—and a few minutes after his mom, bleary-eyed from exhaustion, had once again departed for the diner—when he went to unlock the shed. The sun was just beginning its ascent, and long shadows made fingers across the stubbly yard. But just as he reached the door, he felt his back go rigid. As though eyes—a gaze hot with fury and malice—had pinned his feet to the grass. He knew the feeling well. He trusted it. It was the same way people looked at him in school as they whispered when they thought he couldn't hear. *Fruit. Fag. Freak*. Thankfully, no one had the balls to mess with him at school. His reputation was good for that, at least, even if it didn't stop them from staring.

He thought right away of the wolves from the Spring River Zoo, where his dad used to take him when he was a kid; someone had set the wolves loose, and Animal Control didn't give a shit anymore. The pack had been spotted last night, rummaging through the trash bins behind someone's house not too far from Jesse's neighborhood. But in typical Roswell fashion, some guy had gunned one of them down and injured another.

Late last night, after Jesse's mom trudged back home from her shift at the diner, and as she nibbled at a peanut butter sandwich he put in front of her, she mentioned she'd overheard the neighbors talking about it—the injured wolf had wound up bleeding out in the middle of Highway 101.

"Why didn't they do anything to help it?" he growled.

Behind his mom, a poster of a leaping cat with the caption *Nya-ver give up!* was beginning to peel off the wall. Another one of Ms. K's weird gifts, one that Mom had hung up despite Jesse telling her not to bother. Normally, the poster made her laugh every time she saw it. She didn't look amused now.

"Some tourists found the poor thing," she explained. Her tired eyes narrowed.

"Apparently, they were on their way to see that popular *machine* of yours."

Jesse stuffed his hands in his pockets, trying but failing to ignore the sudden prick of guilt. The news of his machine had reached Mom at work, and the fact that she wasn't asking for details meant she had taken their unspoken stay-out-of-my-business policy to heart. He didn't have to ask; her face had said it all.

It made Jesse sad: that wolf, separated from his pack, slowly inching toward a painful death. One of the only times he'd ever paid attention in biology class—and one of the few times he'd actually shown up—was during their animal behavior unit. Mr. Weaver had explained how most predator species were actually afraid of humans. Wolves were misunderstood, with complex social behaviors—nothing like the mindless, bloodthirsty monsters they were made out to be on TV.

Humans were the real monsters.

Though he was pretty sure Ms. K would scold him for saying so.

He turned around, scanning the stubbly yard, the stunted desert trees, the slump of weather-beaten houses extending toward the horizon. Nothing.

Still. Something was definitely watching him.

It was afternoon when Corbin came back.

Corbin tossed him a dazzling smile. "We meet again."

Jesse felt the urge to smile right back, except he was sure it would make him look overeager, and he hadn't checked his teeth since he'd scarfed down a sandwich for lunch. He opted for what he hoped didn't look too much like a demented, tight-lipped smirk. "Small towns, am I right? Just can't avoid each other."

A little girl, half-hidden, clung to Corbin's arm. She gawked at Jesse with dark brown eyes, as clear and huge as the old tea plates Mom used on the rare occasion she had a friend over. Her hair was gone, and she wore a baby-blue headband that threatened to slip off her head. Her blue checkered T-shirt, with a small white daisy adorning its center, cascaded over her tiny frame. And her skin was pale, Jesse thought with a fluttering of unease in his chest, like thin, wet paper. Too pale. He'd seen little kids that looked like her on brochures he'd get in the mail sometimes, asking for donations for the Ronald McDonald House or places like that. Places for kids with cancer.

"Who's your friend . . . ?" Jesse asked, his throat tight.

Corbin gently pulled the little girl in front of him but kept his hands on her shoulders. "Jesse, I'd like you to meet Mariposa. She prefers Mari, though. My sister."

"Oh." Jesse relaxed. A sister—of course. Not a love child or anything like that; he'd dealt with that kind of thing before, back when he'd hooked up with a guy named Mark who'd come with one too many strings attached for Jesse's comfort. But little sisters? He was pretty sure he could handle little sisters.

Jesse bent down until he was face-to-face with Mari and put on his best, most charming smile. "It's very nice to meet you, Mari. I'm really loving that headband of yours. Do you think I could wear one, too?"

She giggled and buried her head in Corbin's stomach.

Jesse had sometimes wondered what it would have been like if he had had a sibling growing up, too. Most times he'd dreamed about a brother—an older brother, someone to teach him the ropes and help keep the dirtbags in school off his back. Ms. K had sometimes joked that Jesse was like her kid brother—and she acted like a big sister, the way she nagged and annoyingly tried to insert herself into his life, the way she'd pat his head after their one-on-one sessions.

But looking at Mari, he wondered if he could have ever hacked being a big brother himself.

"So. Business is booming, huh?" Corbin's gaze trailed the long, unattended line of people behind Jesse, some locals and mostly tourists now, beginning at the entrance to the shed and reaching past the mailbox. Today, they'd lined up even before he'd finished slugging his coffee. Eager. Desperate. Squirming with impatience. In their minds, they only had four more days left.

Jesse couldn't believe what other people would believe. In a few days, the government would announce some big triumph over the fake threat, and in the meantime, no one would notice they'd launched a war with North Korea or whatever. Politics was all a scam. This one was just bigger than usual.

"You could say that. Got almost fifty people already." And Jesse had the money to show for it. Plus countless messages on his home phone from local papers and radio stations, promises of press coverage and *more* money. *Even with all the fires and killings, people are looking for hope*, one journalist had claimed. *Your machine can be part of that.*

It almost made Jesse laugh.

Even if his mom didn't approve now, she would change her mind when she saw how much he'd earned—when she saw, too, that no one had been hurt, not really. The whole Alma thing was a hoax. What was a tiny scam compared to an enormous one?

"Long odds are better than nothing, right?" Corbin's face was unreadable.

Jesse hesitated, his fingers itching toward the leather cuff on his wrist. "Sure. I mean, that's why I fired up the machine in the first place. To give people a voice, a fighting chance."

Lies. They came so smoothly for him but saying them to Corbin and his kid sister left a bitter taste in his mouth. The truth was, he didn't give a shit about any of these people waiting outside his house. It was ridiculous; some of them were coming from out of state, now, desperate to send out a translated message to Alma, as if their words would somehow convince these imaginary aliens that their lives had value—as if Alma was real, and would actually care about what humans would think.

Conning those people was easy because people *wanted* to believe.

"Our dad brought us to Roswell so we could all stay together, with our grandparents. They own a bakery here: Creciente," Corbin explained. "We're not too far—just off North Montana and London Court—" He paused. Mari was tugging on his pant leg. He bent down to her level, and Mari whispered something to him.

Corbin's ears reddened.

"What?" asked Jesse, curious. "Uh," began Corbin, rising. "Mari wanted me to tell you that I"—he put his hand on his chest—"know how to make the bread laugh."

Jesse looked at Mari, then Corbin. "Oh?" A grin slid across his face. "Do tell, Mari."

"Cori can tell you," giggled Mari.

Corbin sighed. His ears were still red. "It's nothing, it's just—our grandma makes these apple empanadas at Creciente, and they look kind of like mouths, so sometimes I put them on my face . . . it's not important."

"He makes funny noises," added Mari.

Corbin threw her a look that instantly melted away when she smiled back.

Jesse knew Creciente Bakery; the place was one of the few beloved local spots to have remained standing since the '80s. Mom and Dad had loved the bread there, back when they had the pocket money for it. Jesse definitely knew London Court, too. The nice houses. Jesse should have figured. Poor people didn't smell like Corbin. He felt suddenly ashamed of his house, then ashamed for feeling ashamed, then angry for feeling ashamed.

"Anyway," continued Corbin, determined to change the subject, "one of Mari's nurses told her about your Wish Machine." He put a hand on her head and tousled hair that wasn't there. At least, not anymore. "She's been stuck on it ever since. After she heard I met you yesterday, she said she wanted to see the Wish Machine, too."

Jesse felt his stomach seize. "Wish Machine?"

"That's what some people are calling it. No offense, but 'HECC machine' doesn't quite stick as well."

If people were talking about it at the hospital, had already nicknamed the damn thing, then Ms. K had definitely heard about the machine by now. He wasn't looking forward to the inevitable chew-out, and he was pretty sure she'd already left a message on the home phone to ask why he'd missed his last appointment.

Even with the supposed end of the world, she'd find a way to lecture him.

Jesse sighed and rubbed the back of his neck, where the sun was beating down on his skin like a big, angry eyeball. "So you really want to send a message to Alma, huh?" he asked Mari.

She nodded enthusiastically, and Jesse suddenly felt the urge to hide behind the shed like he used to when he was hiding from Dad, filled with both shame and longing. He had known his machine would attract naïve tourists and desperate locals with cash to spare, but hopeful children? With fucking cancer? Was this the kind of person he wanted to be?

"If that's what you want," he said. "Your wish is my command."

The change was subtle—the smile hadn't left Corbin's

face—but Jesse caught a flicker of something in Corbin's expression that made him feel like he'd said something wrong.

"Here ya go." Corbin handed Jesse a folded piece of paper, and his warm fingers grazed Jesse's. "This is the message Mari was hoping you'd translate for her. If, by any chance, Alma does actually respond, could you, maybe, print out a copy for us to pick up?" Corbin looked at him hard, and Jesse read the meaning behind it: he wanted Jesse to make up a response. He *knew* Jesse was full of shit. But he was going along with it. For Mari. And maybe for Jesse, too. "Mari would really love that. I'll bring payment when I come back, if that's okay."

It all made sense now. Corbin was only putting up with Jesse's bullshit for his little sister's sake. But the worst part of it was that Corbin was still so fucking nice about it. Nice to him, a liar and a thief. If Jesse were in his shoes, he would have punched the con artist out for taking advantage of people, circumstances be damned. And he'd deserve it, too.

After all, Jesse was a heartless piece of shit.

Just like Dad.

If Corbin would come back again, Jesse would print out fifty copies. And then print out fifty copies of the word *LIAR* and tape them all over himself. "Yeah, of course. If they respond, we should get it twenty-four hours after our transmission is sent. Actually, no, you know what? It's on the house."

"Really? Wow, thanks, man. Seriously." Corbin seemed to mean it.

"Better yet, pay me in empanadas."

Corbin snorted, which brought an unfamiliar swell of warmth to Jesse's chest.

"Hey, and let's hang out later, yeah? I don't really know anyone around here. Maybe tonight, if you're not too busy? I'll come back after Mari's settled."

"Yeah," Jesse replied as casually as he could. "Should be free tonight."

Corbin grinned. "Good. Looking forward to it, Hewitt."

Jesse couldn't help it. He smiled, too.

He said his goodbyes and waited until they were down the street before he opened the paper. A child's scrawl read:

Please help the world get better.
And please make Corbin feel okay if I don't get better.
I don't want him to be sad.
Love, Mari

He'd had at least a few hundred different messages to translate in the past couple days, but this one hit him right in the chest. Mari's wish wasn't even about her. And somehow that made him feel all the more shitty.

But at the bottom of the page, Jesse noticed in tiny, neat letters, a phone number, followed by the initials *CL*.

He stared at the numbers.

Despite everything, despite outright lying to this perfectly nice brother and sister, Jesse had still gotten *his* wish granted.

That was the kind of world they lived in. No justice.

. His mom had once told him that as soon as he'd learned to talk, he'd learned to lie. She'd laughed when she said it—at the time, she had caught eight-year-old Jesse watching cartoons way past his bedtime, and he told her he'd been doing homework. The lie had been so ridiculous, she hadn't even gotten mad at him. She'd just shaken her head, still laughing, and waved him back to his bedroom.

But she was right. Talking and lying—they were one and the same for him.

Jesse felt the impatient glare of his customers. He forced a smile. He needed to keep the customers happy. Needed to keep them talking and tossing more money for more messages.

Most important, he had to keep lying.

It was the only thing he knew how to be good at.

15

CATE

"The more I think about it," said Adeem, kicking a pebble across the blanched desert dirt, "the more this reminds me of an episode of *SpongeBob SquarePants*."

"What are you *talking* about?" Cate's tone came out snappier than she'd meant. She'd gotten an email from Dr. Michel assuring her that her mom was okay, but service was spotty out here, and she hadn't been able to reply. Were they feeding her enough? Was she safe? Did she sleep well? The more questions that cropped up in her mind, the more panicked she felt. She couldn't remember the last time she'd been away from her mom this long—even if it had only been three days.

Mom, who loved old sci-fi movies, who asked too many

questions about Cate's nonexistent social life, who made the best mint chocolate chip brownies. Mom, who heard voices in the walls, and starved herself, and begged Cate to forgive her in spite of everything.

God, she missed her, all of her.

It's okay, it's okay, it's okay, it's okay.

After they'd explained the situation to him, the manager at the convenience store in Tonopah had been kind enough to drop them off at a nearby service station, just outside town, to buy a new car battery. Being the middle of the night, it'd been closed. Too tired to do anything else but wait for it to open again, they used some folded-up cardboard boxes they'd found behind the store as beds and slept, shivering, until the sun rose. She woke to find Adeem had taken off his shirt and draped it over her in the night for warmth; he blushed but said nothing when she handed it back to him in the morning, and they sat in silence waiting for the station to open.

But the station never opened.

So they'd walked for an hour along a two-lane road paralleled by power lines, hoping to find some kind of civilization; only, they hadn't. There was nothing around them, it seemed, except sun-bleached plateaus and mountains, like oversized globs of dough, half melting under the newly risen sun. The pale blue sky, devoid of clouds to break up the monotony, was dizzying to look at, so Cate had to keep her tired eyes glued to the ground, which, after a while, also made her dizzy. Occasionally, she would catch a glimpse of a lizard, scurrying through dirt and dust and rock in search of shade. She was practically becoming one herself; her skin was cracked and flaking off by the minute.

At this rate, they were going to die out here. Aliens would find their bones, dig them up from the sand like they were fossils, and hang them up in an alien museum.

You've been out here a day, girl, she could hear Ivy chide in her head. *Stop freaking out all the time.* But Ivy didn't understand. It was Cate's fault her mom felt like she was safer in the hospital than with her own daughter. It was Cate's fault why the real Ivy wasn't here. By now, Ivy was probably home, or hidden away in some bunker in Arizona. She couldn't believe the last conversation they might ever have with each other was a stupid fight. She wished she had enough service to call Ivy, even just to hear her say, *I told you this mission was* literally *impossible.*

"Oh, come on, you *must* have seen it," Adeem huffed. His glasses were coated in dust. "That episode when SpongeBob and Squidward have to deliver a pizza, but then they lose their car and get stranded in the middle of the desert?" He chuckled. "For the record, you'd be Squidward."

Cate pushed her bangs off her sweaty forehead. "I'm really starting to regret jumping in your car."

Adeem looked at her over his shoulder and tossed her a grin. "Exactly."

Cate had yet to figure out how he always managed to seem so upbeat. They should have been in Roswell by now, and the thought yanked at her bones, tugging her body like a rubber band pulled taut. But ahead of her, Adeem was whistling, though his lips were either so dry, or he was so drained, that the song felt halfhearted, wrung of any real life. Even his radio, slung around his shoulder in a black carrying case, weakly crackled with static alongside him. The boy was easygoing, no doubt about that; maybe that was why he had agreed to take her all the way to Roswell, no questions asked. But she wondered how much of his cheerful disposition was a mask.

She still had no idea what to make of him.

"Is that it?" Adeem asked suddenly, and Cate looked up.

Another gas station in the distance, supposedly with an ATM, that Adeem had tracked on Google Maps before his battery began blinking red threateningly. A smaller station, but maybe the ATM . . .

Cate broke into a sprint.

"Wait!" Adeem called after her, but Cate could not. They should have been back on the road, like, yesterday. No, *actually* yesterday. She would move her sore, burning legs for Mom alone in the hospital, and for her dad, who didn't even know she existed.

She ignored the stabbing of pebbles in her dusted-up shoes and slowed when she saw the ATM, covered in Sharpied graffiti and band stickers, leaning against the side of the shuttered station building. But the screen, missing a few pixels, dashed her hope faster than she could catch her breath.

"It's busted." Cate pounded on the ATM with her fist.

Someone had drawn an arrow pointing to the card slot and written *INSERT HOPE HERE*. A cruel joke.

Adeem came up from behind, his breathing ragged, and peered over her shoulder to look at the screen. "The network must be down."

Cate lifted her head. She still wasn't used to how tall he was. "You think?"

They'd already tried calling four different towing companies in the morning, but none of them picked up—that is, until the fifth, which demanded three hundred dollars up front. With no other options, the plan had been for the both of them to take out cash and pay off the greedy tow truck driver needed for Adeem's car to drive them south. So much for that.

He patted his black bag. "We're not totally screwed yet. My radio's still on, searching for signals. There's a chance I can catch another HAM nearby . . ." Seeing her expression, he added, "It's amateur radio. If you're a HAM, you can use special frequency bands for long-distance communication. And if someone's listening in through a receiver, if their timing's right, they could catch my message. It means I can get someone to send help."

Cate didn't understand half of what Adeem said, but she knew that finding someone using a radio would take time they didn't have.

They had no time. No water. No car. No money.

No hope.

"No." Whether she was rejecting Adeem's plan or their dwindling prospects of safety or *everything*, she didn't even know. "No, no, *no*."

For so long, Cate had felt like she was drowning in the stress of her life, and it was all she could do to cling to a piece of driftwood floating by, a piece of stability—getting a job at Lickity Split Creamery, hanging out with Ivy. And then she'd hate herself—because what right did she have to feel overwhelmed when it was her mom who was the one struggling more than anyone?

"Don't hate on my baby." Adeem yanked his radio out of his bag. "Oh, shit."

"What now?"

"It's low on battery."

He looked at her hesitatingly, as though afraid to see how she'd react. But this time, Cate threw her head back and laughed. They were so screwed. It was all so ridiculous.

"Quick," she said, closing her eyes to stop the tears from flowing—from laughing or crying, she wasn't sure. "Gimme another reason."

"Another reason?" Adeem asked cautiously.

"Like before, when you said humans domesticated dogs. Give me another reason why Alma won't kill us. Why we won't die." *Here and now.*

"Mmm . . ." He scrunched his mouth in thought. He didn't even question her, didn't pry.

She swallowed, her throat painfully dry and her cheeks painfully wet as she waited for his answer.

Waited for him to throw her a line.

"Pizza," he said finally, stone-faced, before amending: "Pineapple pizza."

There it was again, that deadpan expression as he'd said something ludicrous. Of all the reasons in the universe to hold on, of all the pieces of driftwood he could have tossed her, he'd chosen food.

Cate laughed, a sound so loud she thought she'd burst her ribs.

"Oh no, Cate cracked!" she heard Adeem say, but she didn't care.

She clutched her aching stomach and laughed until it hurt. And the more she thought about it, the funnier it all was: she was in the middle of the desert with a strange boy, thousands of miles from home, trying to find her dad before aliens wiped them all out. She'd been scared for so long, but now, the absurdity of her situation made her feel freer than she'd ever felt in her life. Delivering a letter on foot, even with how bad things were, almost felt easy compared to her day-to-day life. She didn't have to stress over Mom refusing to take her medication. Didn't have to cook dinner for the two of them or hear Ivy talk about all the cool things she got to do during the weekend. No school, no classes, no teachers or school counselors asking her, *Are you sure you're okay?* as though she were a porcelain doll, as though she couldn't handle it.

She was tired and hungry and dehydrated, and her belly cramped like hell.

But for once, she was free to do what she wanted.

She turned away from the useless ATM and made her way back to the main road. She still had a bucket list to complete. A whole life yet she hadn't begun to live.

"What are you doing?" asked Adeem, trailing behind her.

"What does it look like?" Cate trained her eyes on the horizon. She stuck out her thumb. Hitchhiking wasn't on the bucket list Ivy had made for her, but now was as good a time as any to add it.

"I love random encounters as much as the next person," said Adeem, sliding his glasses up the bridge of his nose, "but, uh, normally I'm equipped with a Poké Ball. Or a sword. I don't know, but I'm pretty sure this is how we get on a true crime podcast, if aliens have that sort of thing."

"Not all strangers are serial killers. I trusted you, didn't I?"

"Not everyone you meet is going to be like me."

Cate snickered. "You can say that again."

They'd just have to hope a car would come along soon.

It took another half hour and a pool of sweat before Cate heard the road rumble. She squinted her eyes at the edge where the road met sky, praying for movement.

It wasn't a car that emerged, but a van, as blue as a fallen piece of the sky, rolling right toward them.

"Stop, please!" Cate yelled. She nearly jumped into the road to block it off.

Thankfully, the van slowed to a halt, its engine wheezing as a small smoke plume leaked from its backside. Cate noticed only after it stopped the swirl of psychedelic graffiti overlying the paint job, including a shoddy painting of a lime-green alien head, complete with bug-like black eyes. Underneath it, in pink spray-painted letters, were the words: *STAR VOYEURS*. Cate could practically hear her mom yelling at her in her head about not trusting strangers—but she'd already trusted Adeem.

Besides, she was pretty sure that normal rules didn't apply when the world was ending.

The van door slid open.

"Ayy, fellow pilgrims!" A girl popped her head out. She was probably in her early twenties. Her long bubblegum-pink hair reached past her suntanned shoulders, and she wore a tiny crop top that revealed a diamond piercing on her belly button. She could have been on her way to Coachella, not bunkering down for the end of times. "Where's your final destination?"

"Roswell."

The woman beamed. "Hop on in. We're going south to Truth or Consequences. Should take you almost within spitting distance."

Cate wasn't sure if that was the name of a town or some kind of weird festival, but if it brought her closer to Roswell, or any place with water, she was in.

"Cate . . ." Adeem spoke quietly. "Are you sure we can trust them?"

"Plans one through four failed. What choice do we have?"

"I just feel the need to point out that you're telling me to get into a stranger's van."

Cate shrugged.

"Right. Safety's for squares. Who needs it? Not us," Adeem mumbled as he finally clambered into the van, maybe partially persuaded by the sight of a cooler and the beckoning blast of air-conditioning. Inside, Cate let out a sigh of relief. Sweat had pooled at her lower back and neck, and whenever she swallowed, she tasted only salt. Being able to sit, even on upholstery that smelled faintly of wet dog, felt like heaven. And she didn't see any axes or weapons or dead bodies, so that was a plus.

"You can call me Alice," the woman with pink hair explained. "Our driver with the blue hair is Ty." She giggled. "My partner in crime."

"Yo," said Ty. He wore a green army vest covered in pins; his arms were half slumped over the steering wheel, revealing an incredible array of vivid tattoos on every spare inch of skin.

"Nice to meet you," Cate said. "I'm Cate, and this is my . . ." She paused and glanced over at Adeem, who still looked nervous. "This is my friend Adeem. Thanks again for picking us up."

"Don't mention it," said Alice. "Ty wanted to keep going, but I told him, Children of the Anthropocene have to look out for one another."

Cate glanced at Adeem. "Children of *what*?"

"The Anthropocene," Alice repeated. "You know, the current epoch we live in. The final epoch. Before humanity is expelled once more."

"Expelled . . . ?" Cate swallowed, her excitement dulling. "What, you mean like a Biblical expulsion? Like, the Fall?"

Alice clapped her hands. "Exactly."

Adeem's eyebrows furrowed. "But that would make Alma—"

"Our true Creators, yes." Alice smiled as the van engine revved. "But don't worry, humanity will probably be reborn again somewhere. Unlike Eden, our planet is one of many viable homes, a single grain of sand on an eternally growing cosmic beach. Who knows where humanity might end up next?"

"Unless Alma decides we truly are a failed experiment," Ty added. He wasn't smiling.

Cate's stomach gave a twist. There was something in their eager, welcoming acceptance that they might all die soon that made her . . . uneasy.

But they might actually have food now, and water, maybe even a chance to charge their phones, even if service out here was unpredictable, to say the least.

The conversation soon turned back to other things—like the bonfire parties and night carnivals strewn across the desert that Alice and Ty had discovered along their journey—the strange and absurd celebrations Alma's pronouncement had summoned. As Alice described one particular party hosted by some famous business magnate who claimed to be building "escape submarines," slowly Cate began to relax. Adeem, however, kept fiddling with his fingers.

They had just passed Corn Creek, a crumbling, desolate town twelve hours from Roswell, when Ty pulled over, saying they would camp out in the desert.

"Shouldn't we keep going?" Cate urged. "We haven't been driving long, and we really need to get to Roswell fast." Her gut had begun to throb with cramps, and she knew it wasn't just from hunger. She hadn't thought to bring any extra tampons. She wasn't supposed to be gone for this long.

"I can drive," Adeem offered.

Ty shook his head. "You've been sitting for almost three hours. It'll be good to stretch your legs." He pulled open the driver's-seat door and hopped out of the van. "The world's not going anywhere just yet."

Except that it was, Cate wanted to say. But she took a deep breath. Unless she and Adeem were prepared to trek through the now chilly desert all night, they were stuck here at the whims of these two boho buzzkills.

Alice set up a campfire while Ty built the tents, deftly and impossibly fast. Alice pulled out a few cans of food from the back of the van and cooked them in a cast-iron stew pot over the thriving flames of the campfire. Once they were ready, she offered one to Cate, who settled on a can of baked beans. Her mouth tingled with their unexpected sweetness. It was amazing how good things tasted when you were hungry.

Adeem took one, too, and cleared away the pebbles and sharp rocks with his shoe until the ground revealed soft, beige dirt. Ty took off his green army vest and spread it on the ground for him and Alice to share.

They were surrounded by an endless ripple of dark,

flat-topped hills, but it was the sky, an enormous canopy above them, that gripped Cate's attention.

"The stars are incredible," Cate whispered. And they were, truly. The view was nothing like anything she'd seen in San Francisco. She could imagine herself falling into the silk canopy of the night sky, swallowed whole, enveloped by starlight. She was so happy, she didn't even care if most of the stars were dead. Not all of them were. She knew that now. Now that they knew for sure alien life existed, she wondered how much of it was out there. How many hundreds of billions of planets. How many hundreds of billions of lives.

Mom had told her for so long to live life like everything was normal, but this just seemed . . . miraculous.

Alice chuckled. "And to think, so many people have never taken the time to see the sky for what it really is. A thing to be cherished. A thing to be one with. Worshipped."

A small, catlike smile spread across Alice's face. "But, of course, the real worship begins in Truth or Consequences."

"Until then," said Ty, "we're taking this chance that Alma has so graciously bestowed to see the country, before it all falls apart." He'd barely touched his can of food, as far as Cate could tell.

Cate swallowed. "What do you mean?"

Alice looked surprised. "Well, you've seen the way things are. Mass murders and jail breaks all across the East Coast. Power outages. Shooters bursting into the Capitol. Then there was a stampede in Jerusalem. At least a thousand people died, like, instantly. You really haven't heard?"

Cate couldn't speak. Only a few days had passed since Alma's message, and already so much had happened. How much had they missed? She hated being stranded in the desert, in the middle of nowhere, but maybe it was a blessing in disguise.

"No," she replied, her voice thick. "We've been pretty disconnected."

Silence fell upon them except for the crackling of the fire and Ty's spoon as he stirred his can of creamed corn.

"See," he began finally, "this is what happens when you disrupt humanity's status quo. We crack. We're egotistical little ants.

"Earth society has programmed us to keep our heads down and remain as these mindless drones. Everyone tells us we all have to follow the same blueprint: You gotta go to school. Graduate. Go to college, if you want the best job. Get married. Make babies. Work some more, get promoted. Then you retire. We want, and want, and want, and then we die. Then people say, *Oh, what a great life that person led*. But that's not living. It's just a way to exist."

Cate felt herself shrink beneath his words—wasn't *existing* all she'd ever done with her life?

"But Alma—the people on Alma never lost that spark, that streak of curiosity, that will to truly *live*, not just settle on mere existence. It's why they made us: the ultimate act of benevolence. They wanted to spread their glorious way of life."

"You think . . . we're Almaen?" Cate's heart rammed in her chest.

Ty grinned, and his white teeth gleamed. The crackling flames of the bonfire between them seemed to grow, scraping the edges of the night sky. "Not Almaen, per se. No, see, *we* are the aliens. An anomaly."

"What?" It was the first time Adeem had spoken in seemingly forever. His mouth dropped, like it was the stupidest thing he'd ever heard.

Ty continued, undeterred. "Almaens are the true mother race, don't you get it? The signs are all around us. They created us. Put us here to cultivate the planet, to live righteously. But we"—he tapped his chest—"we lost the spark. We're broken. God as you know it isn't going to save us. Just look at the state of the world! Look what we did to it!"

Alice rested her hand on his shoulder, her nails pointed at their ends and glazed with neon green and yellow. Ty leaned back into it, and took a deep inhale.

"So now," he said, calmer, "we all have to accept Alma's judgment. We deserve to be punished."

Cate was shaking, and not from the desert cold. She reached her hand into her pocket, clinging to her blackbird key chain. She needed something to hold on to. She needed to see her mom. To see Ivy. The scariest thing about Ty wasn't his horrible fanaticism, but that part of her *agreed* with what he was saying. She couldn't deny that she lived in a world where she had to spend her life hiding her mom's condition. The world had taught her to be ashamed of it. And she'd gotten caught in the idiotic stigma. Worse, she'd done nothing to fight it.

So didn't she—didn't humanity—deserve, on some level, to be punished?

But Adeem put down his can.

"Deserve?" repeated Adeem sharply. It was the first time she'd seen Adeem look angry. "How can you say that? For some people, living is enough of a punishment. Life's *hard*. And, sure, humans don't make it easy for each other, and we kind of suck as a species, but we also do a lot of *good*, too. No matter how shitty things get, the moment we stop seeing the good and start treating each other like ants or some kind of failed experiment—that's when the bad guys win."

There was a long, tense moment of silence. Cate shot Adeem a fearful look. Alice and Ty had helped them—*saved* them—and Adeem wasn't exactly making friends.

Ty smiled. But Cate could tell it was an effort. "I'm just sayin' no one here is completely innocent, little man," he said. "But punishment doesn't have to be such a bad thing. Human life means so little in the grand scheme of things, don't you think?"

Suddenly, it dawned on Cate. Ty didn't care if they all died. Ty *wanted* them all to die. What was it that Alice had said? The sky was *a thing to be worshipped, a thing to be one with.* What would they do once they reached their destination, then? She didn't want to think about it.

And she didn't have to. Adeem stood up abruptly, and though the light from the fire was warm and bright, the smile reappearing on his face was anything but cheerful. "That, *little man*, is one hell of a bad take." Without another word, he stormed toward the little red tent Alice had set aside for Cate and Adeem's use, his radio in tow.

The sound of a sleeping bag unzipping. Rustling. And then silence. Even the fire seemed to crackle and pop at a quieter volume.

Alice reached toward Cate with another can of baked beans. She was smiling. "Still hungry?" she asked.

16

JESSE

"Seriously? *Alien Zone?*"

Of all the places in Roswell Jesse and Corbin could have gone together that night—okay, of the few options they had—Jesse would have picked Alien Zone as the last. At best, Alien Zone had the charming quality of a UFO-themed haunted house built by a bunch of stoned high schoolers back in the '70s, and like most Roswell attractions, had never been updated since. The place was decrepit and dusty, filled with life-sized dioramas of gray-skinned aliens posed in human settings: barbecuing, lounging on ripped couches, shitting in an outhouse. It smelled of rubber and mothballs, coating your lungs the moment you walked inside, and Jesse felt sick when he breathed it in; thankfully, he hadn't been there since his mom forced him to go to Andrea Roos's birthday party in fourth grade, and barely anyone showed up, so Andrea cried. He had hoped to never come back. After the place closed down a few months ago due to lack of customers, he'd been certain he never would.

"What's wrong with Alien Zone?" Corbin asked.

Everything, Jesse almost answered. Hadn't Corbin had enough of fake aliens by now? But instead, he shrugged. "Just thought you'd want to explore Main Street, maybe check out Stellar Coffee. Like a normal person."

Corbin threw him a crescent moon smile. "Well, sorry, but I haven't *been* to Alien Zone yet."

"Okay, but why would you *want* to go?" If Jesse believed the world was ending in less than four days, he'd rather nap. Or rob a bank.

"Because unlike *you*, I haven't seen everything this town has to offer."

The thing Corbin clearly didn't understand was that there wasn't much to offer; Second and South Main Streets, where Jesse and Corbin stood now, was the closest thing to a *downtown* Roswell had—but really, it was nothing more than crumbling rows of tourist-centric alien-themed shops, book-ended by the International UFO Museum and the occasional *normal* store that seemed wildly out of place, like the Calico Cow Quilt Shop and Radio Amigo. Jesse had never seen more than two or three families of tourists at a time ambling down the sidewalks, donning the stupid green alien stickers all customers to the UFO Museum were forced to wear. And the tourists never stayed for more than a day, disappearing faster than dust clouds that ripped through the edge of the desert around them. Not that Jesse blamed them. For as long as he could remember, here, tumbleweeds had outnumbered people.

Then again, thanks to Alma, things were changing: like the woman who'd come all the way from Ohio in her RV to see Jesse's machine, currently camped down the street from Jesse's house, and the lines of customers—tourists—the machine was slowly pulling in. Even now, across the street, uniform-clad students from the New Mexico Military Institute were lined in formation, patrolling the town. More and more locals—beyond the Frank Gottlieb types who lurked in Stellar Coffee and ranted about abductions—were actually beginning to believe in aliens; that was the weirdest thing.

The wind was picking up, and the dust in the air was settling on Jesse's cheeks. The lamppost by the side entrance, furnished with black alien eyes on the glass bulb, flickered on to a dull glow. As Jesse and Corbin approached the beige Alien Zone building, a crow, like a black wisp perched on the roof, regarded Jesse with a glint of amusement in its beady stare.

That was when they noticed the thin slabs of plywood covering the front entrance and windows of the Zone.

KEEP CALM AND SHOOT ALIENS, someone had spray-painted in black over the plywood.

"That's . . . one way to welcome tourists," said Corbin.

"That's Roswell's rustic hospitality for you."

Corbin paced the length of the entrance. "I thought this place would be bigger," he observed. "And not, you know, *closed.*"

Jesse snorted. "Even in normal circumstances, Alien Zone's never been popular with locals."

Across the street, the Military Institute students marched toward Third. With their crisp white shirts and dark pants, they almost looked like soldiers. It made Jesse feel uneasy.

The wind carried the faint howl of dogs. No, wolves. Jesse hoped they were faring better than he was. Hearing them made the uneasiness wedge deep inside him, and he wasn't sure why. Like the world really *was* changing, slower than he'd realized—stretching and stretching, becoming so thin it was bound to break any day. It was just a matter of how.

"So, then, what does anyone do for fun here?" Corbin's voice gently coaxed him from his thoughts.

"Shoot stuff," Jesse offered with a lazy shrug. "Chase stray cats. Drive around in pickup trucks. Or . . ."

He looked behind to make sure the patrol of Military Institute students was out of view. The front windowpanes were far too big to shatter without making a racket; he would need a few pillows, a blanket, things to muffle the sound. And the lock was big, shiny, practically sparkling. Though the front door wasn't boarded, breaking into a new commercial lock would be a pain in the ass. But the back door . . .

Jesse led Corbin to the corner, past the new tiny garden on Third and Main, which was nothing more than a glorified bench and a couple of trees, and into the alleyway leading to the back of Alien Zone. Just as he suspected: the windowless door where they received deliveries, like the greasy pizzas from Peter Piper Pizza for Andrea Roos's birthday party, was free of plywood. And the lock? Built into an ancient, rusted old doorknob barely clinging to the wood.

He peeled off his leather jacket, wrapped it around the doorknob until it was secure, and pulled it taut, gripping it for balance. "What are you—" Corbin began to ask, but stopped when Jesse kicked the knob once, twice—then broke it free, the sound muffled by his jacket. The door, now adorned by a crooked hole, creaked open.

Jesse casually plucked the busted knob from the inside of his oversized jacket and tossed it into a nearby bush.

Corbin froze. "But the alarm . . . ?"

"Have you *seen* this dump?" replied Jesse, slinking his arms back into his jacket. "Think about it. It'll be a miracle if it still has power."

Corbin grinned, a mischievous twinkle in his eye. "Huh. Full of surprises, aren't you, Hewitt?"

He wasn't sure it was a compliment, but a warm bloom of satisfaction nestled in Jesse's chest.

The inside of Alien Zone was cloaked in inky darkness when Jesse closed the door behind them. Corbin pulled out his phone, and a small burst of harsh light illuminated black shelves that carried ancient merchandise: key chains and mugs and shot glasses and the like. On the left, against a black backdrop, some of the life-sized alien models wore kitschy T-shirts with neon designs that glowed in the dark, giving the room a dim lime-green and pink and blue gleam. Someone must have gone a little overboard with the glow-in-the-dark paint.

Jesse found the front desk and went to switch on the main lights, but as he guessed, the power was out.

Corbin pocketed his phone. "I kind of like it like this. Good mood lighting, don't you think?"

He was right: instead of the pale gray-blue walls, Alien Zone was space itself, splattered with drops of neon like stars against the pool of darkness. In the silent void, Jesse felt, if only for a moment, untouchable by the world outside. "I gotta thank you," Corbin said. As Jesse's eyes adjusted to the dark, he could make out Corbin, leaning against one wall, watching him so earnestly.

"For?"

"Coming out with me. Here. On such late notice. I can't imagine how stressful it must be, working that machine all day." Corbin's words were like a deep hum. "I mean, I could barely wrap my head around the science of it all. I got lost just trying to understand *octal intermediary* and the basics of binary." He shook his head. "It's just, you know, amazing what you're trying to do. For people. For everyone. I can barely last a shift helping Grandma with her bakery, and here you are, changing the *world*."

Jesse tugged on his leather cuff. "It's not all that special."

Corbin took a step toward Jesse. "You sure have me fooled."

His blood pounded. *Did* Jesse have him fooled? Was Corbin really that gullible? Or was Corbin the kind of person who would believe what he *wanted* to believe?

The warmth fizzled out inside Jesse just as quickly as it'd sparked, leaving him cold and hollow. Being with Corbin was walking right into a mistake. He could feel it. Everything Jesse did was supposed to be about getting them out of the eternal hole they lived in. About *money*, money that he and Mom needed. Or at the very least, passing the time between making money—nothing more, nothing less, and definitely nothing personal. So what the hell was he doing with someone like Corbin?

He shouldn't have come out tonight. Good people like Corbin were supposed to be off-limits. He had no reason to invest in whatever the hell this was supposed to be. Plus, once Corbin figured out who Jesse really was, he'd leave. Just like Ian. Like all of them.

So why couldn't Jesse pull away?

Jesse cleared his throat. "So, you work a lot? At your grandma's bakery?"

"Yeah," answered Corbin, "when I'm not at the hospital. I really like it. I've always had fun messing around in the kitchen, even when I was little." He scratched the back of his neck. "Believe it or not, I used to be a pretty bad kid, actually."

"No freaking way."

"I know, I know." Corbin chuckled. "Grandma said I needed a hobby to refocus my anger. I turned to baking."

"Is that the secret ingredient to your empanadas? Anger?"

"Nah, only love now."

There was a lilt of suggestion hanging on Corbin's words, one that Jesse couldn't quite grasp. Like a secret wink from an attractive stranger across a crowded room. It brought an unexplainable momentary flush to Jesse's cheeks.

"Come on." Abruptly, Corbin turned away from Jesse. "Now that we're here, we might as well enjoy it."

Jesse immediately felt the absence of Corbin's nearby warmth. He didn't know whether to be relieved or disappointed as Corbin took off into the vast gymnasium space, which had played host to generations of Roswell children. Jesse trailed after him, full of an uneasy mixture of longing and regret.

Corbin hesitated in front of the spiny architecture of a massive jungle gym complete with enclosed tunnels—built in part to resemble an alien ship, and exuding the faintly nauseating smell of plastic and sweaty feet.

"What. Is. *That*?" Corbin asked.

"That," Jesse said, "is a relic."

But Corbin was already disappearing toward it. Soon, the thump of footsteps against plastic cut through the silence of the main room of the Alien Zone. Apparently, Corbin had found the entrance into the winding tunnels.

"It's gonna break," warned Jesse. The jungle gym was

archaic—it had practically fallen apart even at Andrea Roos's birthday, a full eight years ago.

"O ye of little faith." Corbin's voice was slightly muffled; he must have been deep inside the jungle gym already, that beautiful idiot. Jesse squeezed his wrist again; his own veins felt hot against his fingertips.

"Come on!" Corbin shouted. "It's no fun if it's just me in here."

"Pass," Jesse shouted back. For a moment, he heard the faint sound of rustling.

Then silence.

And Corbin screamed.

"Corbin?" Nothing. "Corbin? Are you okay?" Still nothing.

Jesse waded through the dark and found the entrance into the jungle gym. His heart raced as he crawled inside and climbed through the tunnels, his palms sweaty. His weight sank against the plastic precariously as he moved higher and higher into the structure. A faint whiff of Corbin's familiar cedarwood-and-vanilla scent pulled him farther in.

Finally, he found Corbin, lying on his back.

"Are you okay?" Jesse was breathless. He dropped to his knees next to Corbin.

"I . . ." Corbin slowly rolled over to face Jesse. "I thought I saw an alien."

It took Jesse a second to register that he was kidding. "You fucking idiot!" Jesse punched Corbin's shoulder as Corbin began to laugh. "Dammit, you actually *scared* me."

"Sorry, I'm sorry—I had to get you in here *somehow.*"

Jesse looked away so that he wouldn't be tempted to smile. He refused to let Corbin off the hook that easily. "I guess it worked," he said.

"I'm really sorry. Seriously. But look." He pointed ahead. They'd reached the top of the jungle gym and together were crouched inside a yellow plastic bubble with clear windows across its surface, letting them overlook the vast dark of the Alien Zone, studded with speckles and threads of neon. "Kinda feels like we're zooming through hyperspace, doesn't it?"

Jesse eyed him from the side, taking in the stubble across Corbin's sharp jawline, his black curls. Jesse had to fight the urge to bury his face against Corbin's neck, to imagine what his lips would taste like.

He was grateful for the dark—he could feel the heat spreading across his cheeks, and he'd rather not let Corbin see him blush like a goddamn idiot.

"See?" said Corbin. "Totally worth it."

Where Jesse had felt empty, something steely and tightly wound in his chest was allowed, for just a moment, to unfurl.

He was getting too close. Too close . . .

Jesse swallowed and shuffled back toward the tunnel, putting a few feet of distance between them, but something had caught his arm: his leather cuff had gotten snagged on the cheap black rope netting that encompassed the outside of the jungle gym.

"Shit. I'm stuck."

Corbin took out his phone again, turned on the flashlight, and angled it toward Jesse's wrist. "Oh, here, let me help . . ."

"No!" Jesse yelled without meaning to. He covered his wrist with a hand. He was sure the light from Corbin's phone would illuminate the scars his cuff kept hidden. "No."

Corbin's round, dark eyes bore into Jesse's face, and he could feel the gentle, featherlight weight of them, the questions that lingered there. But Corbin said nothing.

Jesse's chest shuddered. *Shake it off, Jesse.* The voice in his head was Ms. K's—it always was these days—but somehow, it calmed him.

Corbin left his phone's flashlight on, directing it toward Jesse but politely averting his eyes, as if to give Jesse some space. As if there were a cold, colorless glass between them, delicate, on the verge of shattering.

Jesse tugged his cuff free of the nettings.

"Come on," Jesse mumbled. "It's too hot in here."

17

CATE

It was around 10:00 p.m., the most normal hour Cate had been to bed in the past few days, when the campfire dwindled to a few measly embers. She hadn't sat by a campfire since that summer at Camp Escondido.

Except Camp Escondido's counselors were a lot less creepy than Ty, and now Cate found herself missing Mom all over again.

She'd asked Alice to borrow a portable phone charger, and as soon as her phone came back to life, she inhaled, let out a shaky exhale, and wrote her mom a long text. It didn't matter if the signal was totally unreliable—a bar or two one second, none the next—and it didn't matter if her mom probably didn't have her phone on her in the hospital. Writing to her was therapeutic, and Cate wrote as though she were talking to her mom on the family room couch like any other night, over a single mint chocolate chip brownie sundae they'd share before clambering into their beds.

You wouldn't believe where I am right now, or the incredible views out here, she typed. *Maybe one day, we should try movie night outside at the pier instead of the couch. Maybe save up for an outdoor movie screen, borrow Ivy's projector.*

Ivy. Another voice she missed.

I don't know why we never did it before, she continued. *But I'll invite my friends. You're always saying you want to hang out with them more.*

I think you'd love it.

When the text bounced back, Cate shoved her phone in her pocket, and let her head fall back against her aching neck. She'd never understood what people meant by being worried sick, but now, as her anxiousness rolled in her stomach like a barbed metal ball, she was beginning to.

If they left here by dawn, they could make it to Roswell by 3:00 p.m. Which would leave her with a little over three days to get back home. All hope wasn't lost, not yet.

Alice and Ty agreed. "We'll make sure you get to where you should be," Ty promised.

After they told her they would stay up a little longer to keep a lookout, Cate found a fat Joshua tree to relieve herself behind—another new and weird experience for her—and crawled into the safety of her tent. As helpful as they'd been, after Ty's gloomy pronouncement that they all deserved to die, frankly, Cate was more than happy to get away from them.

Her eyes adjusted to the darkness inside the tent, where Adeem had pulled a sleeping bag up and over his head like a cocoon, his glasses tucked safely in a corner and the rectangle of his radio peering from beneath the covers. But the tent was small, and Alice and Ty had only prepared one for them to share. Trusting Adeem to get her to Roswell was one thing, but sleeping next to him wasn't exactly something she was comfortable with. They'd technically slept side by side before already, last night behind the gas station, but that was different: they'd had quite a few feet separating them, and sleeping beneath the vast openness of the night sky hadn't felt so . . . intimate.

She bit her lip, unsure of what to do.

"Adeem?" she whispered.

No response.

"Are you asleep?"

Still nothing. She'd just have to catch him up on the plan to leave first thing in the morning, and if his reaction to Ty was any indication, he'd be just as eager to get out of here as she was.

Cate clambered deeper inside the tent, unfolded the spare sleeping bag, and laid herself down. Screw self-consciousness; she was too tired, and, strangely enough, she did feel . . . *safe*. Maybe there was something about having a little more than three days till the end of the world that was making all her walls come down. Or maybe there was something about Adeem. She wanted to trust him—how could she not? He was the one who'd offered to take her to Roswell, after all. Ivy would have called it fate.

There were no pillows, so she settled on folding her hands behind her head after huddling deep inside her warm sleeping bag, safe from the desert chill. Her stomach hurt—from dehydration or cramps or sheer worry, or maybe all three, but she closed her eyes, grateful that, at the very least, Adeem didn't snore.

She was drifting into sleep when Adeem mumbled.

"It's your turn."

She rubbed her eyes and saw stars. "My turn for what?"

"To give a reason. I've given you two already."

A reason? Her mind was slow to stir awake, but she vaguely remembered: she'd asked him for one before. *Give me another reason why Alma won't kill us. Why we won't die.*

Cate propped her head up with her hand. "I thought we established pizza was the be all, end all."

"Pizza is up there, but alien court's still in session, so." Adeem rolled over to look at her, careful not to flatten the radio lying next to him. "Give me another argument, counselor." He knocked the ground with a fist as though it was a gavel.

Cate cracked a smile. Adeem's voice was raspy from sleep. Still, his voice carried the sound of a barely repressed smile.

She liked that about him.

"Okay . . ." she said slowly, thinking. "The library. The atrium in the San Francisco Public Library."

Adeem said nothing for a beat, but his eyebrows furrowed. "So you're from San Francisco. That explains the ridiculous Cali girl accent you've got."

"Oh my God, I do not!" Cate's fingers itched for a pillow to throw at his face. The thought made her miss Ivy even more. It was strange now to think that just a few days ago, she was sitting in Ivy's room, telling her about Mom's letter. San Francisco felt hopelessly far away.

Adeem sat up, grinning. "But seriously, the *library*?"

"You almost sound like Ivy." Cate rubbed her goose-pimpled arms and pulled up the sides of her sleeping bag; she hated that the desert could get so cold. "I have a lot of memories there, so maybe I'm biased. But the atrium at the library always felt so welcoming. Sunlight would beam through the ceiling windows, and everything was this beautiful pearly white. It felt like being inside a giant snail shell." Her bangs grazed the tops of her eyes. She pushed them out of the way. "My mom used to take me a lot when I was little."

But they hadn't been able to go for a long time. Cate wasn't sure what the hushed voices echoing through the atrium would do to her. Now whenever Mom offered to take her, she refused, opting instead for movie night on the couch and Chinese takeout. Safer options.

Still, she missed it. She missed a lot of things.

The letter suddenly felt so heavy in her pocket. A reminder that she'd only left her mom's side for a damn good reason.

"So you've mentioned your mom, but . . ." Adeem's voice trailed. "What about your dad?"

She shook her head slowly. "I've never met him."

Even in the dark, Cate could see Adeem's eyes widen. "Is that why you're going to Roswell? To find him?"

She looked away, opening her mouth and closing it again. She didn't even know where to begin.

"It doesn't have to be a secret," he said, with the smug smile of a kid who'd just been proven right. She imagined he made that face a lot. "Want to talk about it?"

She turned her head and looked at him in surprise. It was the first time Adeem had ever asked a personal question, a genuine one. Talking felt good. It felt *ordinary*, despite everything happening above them. Her heart swelled a little at the thought, dulling her stomachache, even if the question did make her throat tighten.

"It's a long one, but . . ." She pulled her sleeping bag up to her chin. "Basically, my dad left Mom before I was born. Or something like that. I don't think he even knew about me. When the news about Alma broke out, I think Mom started to regret that she never told him."

"So *you* have to be the one to drop the news? That's . . . awkward."

Cate hesitated, pushed her stubborn bangs aside again. She trusted Adeem on some level, but her mom's schizophrenia and her letter seemed too big a secret to spill. Too painful. She didn't want to begin to imagine what he'd think if he knew. "My mom couldn't come," she said finally. "She's been . . . sick. Sometimes, I think Mom is worried she failed me somehow, by raising me herself. But I know finding my dad—getting that closure—will make her feel better. But if we all die, well, at least I'll know I tried."

"You mean if Alma doesn't accept our ongoing legal arguments for our continued existence."

"Exactly."

Cate's throat felt swollen. It hurt, talking about Mom, telling Adeem the things that she'd wanted to tell Ivy that night in the casino, before she'd lost her temper. The night breeze rustled the tent. Crickets sang, only just concealing the sounds of Alice and Ty's muffled whispers from afar.

"I kind of wonder if Ty is right, in some ways," she continued. "Half the time, I have no idea what I'm doing. Life does feel small in the grand scheme of things, and sometimes it feels like I don't have control over anything. I get mad at everyone and everything because it feels like I have to do everything alone. Like, where the hell is God, you know?

"But I'm so freaking tired of living like that."

Adeem went quiet, and his eyes were trained on the ceiling of their tent. She wondered if bringing up Ty was a mistake.

"Ty," Adeem announced loudly, "is a grade-A douche bag."

"Adeem!" Cate shrieked, barely able to swallow her laughter.

"It's convenient to sit back and do nothing when everything

goes to hell," continued Adeem, only a little quieter. "People like him blame the problems we face on the natural order. Or God. Or a lack thereof. But the moment we sit back and do nothing while everything falls apart—that's why we have problems in the first place. That's why this is happening." He gestured vaguely to their tent, to outer space, to Alma. "But *you* are actually trying to do something. Even if it's just for your mom, you're still trying to bring your family back together. Even when everything feels hopeless. That can only be a good thing. And people see that, Cate. I see that."

Cate's eyes prickled. She hugged her knees to her chest, feeling a little shy beneath his genuine praise. "Is that why you agreed to take me to Roswell? Was that your way of trying to do some good in the world?"

"Now, *that*," he said, lying back down on his sleeping bag, "was a total coincidence."

"You never told me why you were heading to Roswell in the first place." Her question tiptoed: she'd been a little too nervous to outright ask him earlier—it was almost as though they'd had a silent pact to avoid personal questions. Until now.

"You really want to know?" He grinned mischievously.

Cate nodded.

"I'm on a quest," he began in hushed tones, "to find the seven Dragonballs—"

Of course. She should have known he'd turn it into a joke. "I'm going to throw my phone at you now."

"Okay, okay, the truth—listen now—the *truth* is that I'm on my way to Area Fifty-One so I can hack into Alma's main-frame—"

Cate pulled out her phone and raised it threateningly.

Adeem flinched. "Okay, fine, I'm serious, I'll tell you!" He sighed. "I'm looking for someone, too. My sister."

"You have a sister?"

"Yep, one runaway sister." He ran his hands down his cheeks. "One who apparently couldn't be bothered to say goodbye when she left."

Cate's arm fell. His words were cold, veiled by sarcasm, but she could feel the pain behind them.

"In other news, Earth is round and water is wet. Anyway, we should get some sleep," he said quickly. Dismissively.

He tugged his radio closer to him and rolled again, showing only his back. She had the urge to reach out and wrap her arms around him, to do anything to make this sudden coldness go away, but she had no idea how he would react, so instead, she rolled away.

Outside, the cool breeze grazed the sides of their tents, and Alice and Ty's whispering had been replaced by the hollow droning of the desert.

That's when it hit her:

All that big stuff he'd said about reuniting her family. About *doing* something despite how small she felt.

Had he only been telling her what *he* needed to hear?

18

JESSE

Fresh, crisp night air flooded Jesse's lungs. Main Street was empty; the Military Institute students were gone, and Jesse could hear nothing but the scrape of an empty Takis bag against asphalt and the rustle of dust in the breeze. Corbin was quiet, too. He'd been quiet since Jesse's little outburst in Alien Zone.

But when they rounded the corner toward Third, Jesse saw a figure sitting in the tiny park on the single bench. His breath nearly left him again. Even though the streetlight was out, Jesse recognized Ms. K instantly: tiny and tight-shouldered, wearing her usual crescent moon necklace and her harem pants she playfully called her "swagpants." Long, wavy hair thrown into an unruly bun, the way she did only when she'd been in a hurry. She was using a large cardboard box labeled *towels* as a footrest and her eyes were closed, like she'd been sitting there for a while.

And as though his recognition had summoned it, her eyes opened, and her attention landed on him in a sudden collision of awareness. For a moment, time seemed to stand still.

"Jesse?" She stood suddenly, her face mirroring the same expression of disbelief. "What on earth—ain't it past your bedtime, kiddo?" She was wearing glasses; she must not have been sleeping well lately.

He scowled. "Don't call me that."

No matter how hard he willed it to calm down, Jesse's heart thrummed wildly in his chest. Just what he needed. His counselor. Right in front of Corbin, of all people. Not that he was particularly ashamed that he went to counseling. But it was only natural that Corbin would start getting curious about *why* Jesse needed counseling in the first place—so much counseling that he and Ms. K were, sometimes irritatingly, close.

She was the one who'd given him the leather cuff, after all.

Ms. K clicked her tongue. "I'll stop calling you 'kiddo' when you stop calling me Ms. K. My last name's really not that hard to say."

To be fair, he *had* tried, once, but she teased him over how he couldn't nail the gutteral "kh" without sounding like a cat spitting a hairball. "I'll consider it," said Jesse, his lips curling at their edges, "when you stop stalking me."

"Ha! You sure it's not the other way around?" Her smile spread sluggishly across her face, barely meeting her dim, dark eyes. The past couple days must have taken a toll on her.

Are you okay? he wanted to ask. She'd looked a little tired the last time he'd seen her, a few days ago at the group counseling session. Now she looked *drained*. But she wouldn't tell him; she never did. For someone so nosy, she was awfully good at deflecting anything personal: questions about where she was from, what her family was like. He'd long given up on asking. Maybe some things were better left unknown.

"So?" he asked instead. "What are you really doing out here?"

She stretched her arms above her and barely suppressed a yawn. Even in the dark, her crescent moon necklace glinted. "I was just at the church dropping off some supplies. Got an influx of people coming through from the desert trying to find shelter, and the hospital had some extra blankets and whatnot to donate." She gently kicked at the box with her foot. "I got a bit of extra time on my hands since *some* people canceled their sessions on me."

She was subtle enough not to tip Corbin off to the nature of their relationship, but not subtle enough for Jesse to miss the jab. He looked away.

Satisfied, Ms. K's attention pivoted to Corbin. "Wait, you're Mari's brother, right?" she asked, casually changing the subject.

Corbin appeared lost in thought for a moment. Then his

expression cleared. "Oh! You were the counselor who talked with Mari at the hospital, yeah? First time I've seen her laugh like that since we moved here." He smiled warmly. "Yeah. I'm Corbin."

So they already knew each other. Jesse suppressed a groan. Somehow that made it worse. His chances of running away from this awkward-as-hell situation had dwindled to zero. And even if he did run, it was a matter of time before Corbin put two and two together.

"It was my pleasure, trust me," Ms. K replied. "If you're around the hospital again, let me know if you want to meet with me, too. I'm pretty much always there now for the volunteer program."

Corbin rubbed the back of his neck. "I might take you up on that. I think Alma's put everyone in therapy these days."

Ms. K's knowing gaze shifted back to Jesse, and a thick, dark eyebrow curled upward. "Well, look on the bright side. Impending global disasters inspire new . . . friendships." The word held the lilt of a question.

Jesse could feel himself shrinking, as if his body were considering a strategic retreat. "Aren't you supposed to act like you don't know me when we see each other in public?" he muttered. It was one of the first things she'd told him in their one-on-one sessions.

She laughed at that, a sound filled with color. "As far as I'm concerned, when the world's ending, rules go to shit."

Corbin nodded. "Amen."

"Speaking of shits . . ." Ms. K patted the bench. "*Jesse*, now that I have you here, can I talk to you for a second? Alone? If that's okay, Corbin."

Fuck. She was definitely going to irradiate him, maybe lecture him to death, if he was lucky. Jesse shrank even farther away. He glanced at Corbin pleadingly, but he didn't notice.

"Of course. I actually wanted to check out a mural that popped up over on Fourth. I'll wait there," Corbin offered, smiling.

Jesse cursed Corbin's politeness as he watched him walk away, leaving him alone with Ms. K.

She sat back down and patted the bench more forcefully.

He perched reluctantly on the edge of the bench, his back tensed.

"So, you canceled on me. Are you avoiding me or something?"

"No," he lied. "Just figured you needed more time with your other clients."

"Hmm." Ms. K leaned back and closed her eyes again. "That old shtick again."

"What, is this an impromptu therapy sesh?"

"And ruin your cute little evening?" Ms. K opened her eyes, but at least had the decency not to look at Jesse, whose face suddenly grew warm. "Nah. I just wanted to check in. I mean, things are hard right now. Stressful. Scary."

"Don't worry. I'm keeping busy."

"Right . . ." She looked at him now, her gaze soft. The night shadows made the line between her brows just a little deeper than usual. "I did hear about your machine." She chuckled. "Tom told me about it. He says people have stopped using his radio to try and find their loved ones because they think broadcasting messages to Alma is more effective. He sounded kind of bummed."

Jesse's breath stilled. He wondered if she'd figured out the machine was a hoax. He'd been wanting to talk to her about the machine. Besides his mom, she was the only one he *could* tell, even though part of him knew she'd be disappointed. It's why he'd been putting it off. She'd call the machine another kind of coping mechanism, an unhealthy one. But he also knew if she understood the extent of their money problems—and what he was willing to do to fix them—she'd be the first to try to help.

Somehow, that was worse than her disappointment.

Jesse was tired of needing help.

He shoved his hands in his warm pockets. Above them, an entire squadron of fighter jets from the nearby base thundered through the night sky. It was unusual for them to be out at this hour, and something about seeing them now made Jesse chilly.

"You're still wearing it," Ms. K whispered once the jets passed.

He didn't have to ask what; he knew she was talking about the cuff. ". . . Yeah. Haven't taken mine off once. Dunno about your other clients, though."

He didn't know why he added that last part. He knew he was the only one of Ms. K's clients to get a gift from her. Self-sabotage, he was pretty sure Ms. K had called it: his inability to accept something good. A small piece of his depression.

The thing about wanting to die was that people always assume it's the constant pain that gets to you, the pain that convinces you to do something, anything, to make it stop. Jesse's depression *was* painful at first, all sporadic tugs and pulls beneath his skull, like a stubborn specter that clung to his mind with sharp teeth. And with the pain came a parade of dark thoughts: like how his dad had left them behind like it was nothing, weighing them with his debts, how he and Mom had barely enough to survive, how Jesse would be stuck in this dumpster fire of a town for the rest of his miserable life, buried in the dirt, where he belonged. But eventually, Jesse became numb to the pain.

And soon Jesse became numb to everything.

That was what got to him: the inability to feel.

That was why he felt nothing at all when beads of red surfaced on his left wrist.

It was also why Ms. K, gently wrapping the leather cuff around his barely healed wrist, had told him how happy she was that he was still alive, and that she hoped one day he'd feel something, too.

"You remember what I said about the five-second rule?" she asked suddenly.

Jesse sighed and recited: "'Only five seconds of thought stand between you and a crap-ton of regret.'"

Ms. K nodded. "Exactly. The world's not exactly a warm and welcoming place these days. And I just want to remind you that you're not alone, even if it's hard to believe. *Especially* when it's hard to believe."

"Thought you said this wasn't going to turn into a therapy session," he said stiffly.

Ms. K stood and gently ruffled his hair. "I'm telling you this as a *friend*, not a counselor. I'm telling you this because loneliness tends to make people do shitty things. Things you can't take back. And I don't want you to ever find yourself in a position when you're in too deep, when you've said or done something you're going to regret. Now's not the time for that."

Jesse didn't know what to say. His throat had grown thick and the world spun beneath him. It was all he could do to grip the edge of the bench. He hated how easy it was for Ms. K to say exactly what he didn't want to hear. How easy it was for her to see right through him and make him spill all the fears he kept locked up inside.

How easy it was for her to make him feel when he didn't want to.

"Anyway, I don't want to take too much time from your hot end-of-the-world date," she teased.

"Ha."

Jesse lifted the box by her feet and handed it off to her.

She took it with a smile and stepped back toward Third. "Don't be a stranger, ya hear? And tell Corbin I said bye."

"I will."

As her footsteps grew farther and farther away, Jesse

exhaled, relieved without quite knowing why.

But suddenly, Ms. K called him back. "Hey, Jesse?" she said, spinning on her heel to face him again.

"Yeah?" he asked, his nervousness flooding back.

Ms. K bit her lip, then shook her head. "Just . . . stay out of trouble. Promise?"

His head throbbed with a thousand things he wanted to say to her. He couldn't shake off the prickling feeling that this was some sort of goodbye. But all he heard himself say was another lie:

"I promise, Ms. Khan."

One of his customers had spray-painted a giant red heart on the side of Jesse's shed, and it seemed to mock him. His fingers hovered over the shed door's fat metal padlock, grazing the cold steel. It felt like hours since he'd seen Corbin and Ms. K, since he'd stood in front of the shed, his eyes boring holes into the peeling wood.

Tonight had been long. Too long.

He couldn't get Ms. K's words out of his head, the stuff about loneliness and regret. Stuff that made it sound like she knew something he didn't, and it was pissing him off. What the hell did she know? She had no idea what it was like to grow up your whole life in a broken family, barely struggling to survive. Loneliness was for people who were stupid enough to want to rely on other people. You'd be better off asking for a monthly indefensible ass-kicking from behind.

And regrets? Jesse had no regrets. Everything he did, he did because he was the kind of person who'd do whatever it took to pay off his family's debts and finally get rid of his dad's ghost once and for all. He had no doubts about the machine—about his plan, either. For once in his life, he had the opportunity to do something good for his mom, an opportunity that he'd made for himself. He wouldn't feel so useless anymore. He wouldn't be like his old man. In just a few days, he and Mom would be free.

If that meant he had to keep up a lie and push someone like Corbin away, then he wouldn't hesitate. He couldn't.

He pulled his hand away from the shed's lock and held his wrist in his hand. The wrist Corbin had almost touched.

If he had any regret—and it was a big "if"—it was pulling his hand away so fast. He let himself imagine, for just a moment, what Corbin's touch would have felt like.

Something cracked behind him.

Jesse whipped around. The hair on his arms stood straight. "Who's there?"

Footsteps, rushed footsteps, and then a burst of pain exploded in his cheek. Before he could raise his fists, a foot came flying into his stomach.

"Not such a tough guy now, huh?" The guy attacking him had a clean-shaven head, pale under the dim moonlight.

Jesse doubled over, gagging. Another kick to his legs sent him on the ground. His body felt like lead. Another guy emerged from behind the bushes, but Jesse's eyes felt like they were spinning in his head. He couldn't see straight; he could only make out a black beard.

"What do you want?" Jesse spat, finally finding a breath of air. His face was pressed on the driveway, and pebbles embedded into his bloody cheek. Someone pinned his arms behind his back, and he could feel his shoulders pop in protest, imagined them ripping out of the sockets with just another hard tug.

"You know damn well what we want, you little shit," the guy growled.

One of the guys—the shaved guy, maybe—pushed his boot on Jesse's head. He could squish his head like a grapefruit if he wanted, Jesse thought fearfully. He could die right here, alone and in the dark. He thought of the wolf, then, the one that had crawled onto the highway to die.

"Emmit, go easy." Bearded Guy nudged Jesse with his foot. "We're here to collect for what you did to our friend."

"Come on, Samuel. It's nothing he doesn't deserve."

"Friend, what friend?" Jesse asked breathlessly, squirming under the shaved guy's weight. "I don't know who you're talking ab—" But another kick in the ribs silenced him, and he choked on his own tongue.

"Marco Castillo. My best friend. Like a brother to me. You might remember him as the guy behind the counter at the gas station you tried to steal from."

Marco. Of course.

He'd almost forgotten him. Forgotten what he did to them.

"I'm so sorry," said Jesse. He truly was. He felt sick and ashamed and hurt. God, everything hurt.

"Sorry isn't going to do shit. And poor Marco, you know, he's pretty injured. He'd love to see his grandmother. Maybe his sister. And they sure would love to see him in the hospital. Only problem is, they're stuck in Mexico."

Samuel bent down so his mouth was mere inches away from Jesse's throbbing ear.

"But you're going to fix that. You're gonna pay for some plane tickets."

"What are you talking about . . . ?" said Jesse weakly. "They shut down . . . airspace . . ."

Samuel chuckled. "They might not be running now, but once all this alien bullshit dies down, you and I both know things'll go back to normal. And you are going to give us all the money you made from that stupid machine of yours, you hear me? Every fucking dollar. Don't even think about trying to run out on me, or I swear to God"—his voice went lower, guttural—"I will find your dear little mom, and I will make her pay for your crime."

Jesse was fading in and out of consciousness. For how long, he couldn't tell. But he was alone now. He could swear he heard a wolf howl in the distance.

"We'll be back in three days," growled Samuel. He took Jesse's chin in his hand. Jesse saw a wheel of blurry skies behind his head. "It's the end of the world, kid."

THREE DAYS

UNTIL THE END

OF DELIBERATIONS

TRANSCRIPT
EXCERPT FROM TRIAL

SCION 12: Rest assured, terminating the local population of Project Epoch has never been a task taken lightly. But we have also invested countless reserves modifying the planet's climate and ecosystem to be compatible with our microbiomes. To spurn this resource when we need it most is unthinkable.

SCION 13: Do our investments in the planet outweigh the value of all human life?

SCION 12: I am merely suggesting another consideration.

SCION 6: We have considered enough. The reality is that Alma has long surpassed the peak of its vitality despite persistent efforts to maintain its biosignature. But in the right hands, Project Epoch can remain habitable. We may yet still restore its equilibrium temperature. The answer here is clear. We are wasting time.

ARBITER: May I remind the grand jury we must

---

deliberate for the full length of eight days. Propriety demands it.

SCION 6: What value is there in propriety when our time runs short?

SCION 3: Our scientists determined *Homo sapiens* to be the only species with intelligence adequate enough to create civilization remotely comparable to our own. The Arbiter is right. We owe them the respect of a full-length deliberation.

SCION 8: Have we not further considered revisiting the division of Project Epoch's reserves? With our technology, better allocation of reserves could provide an opportunity for both species to create an unprecedented planetary union.

SCION 4: Share the planet? With our own specimens? And how do you suppose they would welcome us when they discover our scientists have implanted a biological agent that could inoculate them at our will?

SCION 2: I agree. Their own history reveals that the specimens of Epoch are often unreceptive to change. If we disable the Anathogen diffuser and

allow their species to remain, they would likely
interfere with any attempt to cultivate the planet's habitability.

SCION 6: These specimens are worse than children—
utterly incapable of sustaining their own planet.

ARBITER: Scion 6, your tone is not constructive
here.

[Scion 13 stands.]

ARBITER: Scion 13, proceed.

SCION 13: I have been studying Earth's contri-
butions to issues of significance since our last
recess.

SCION 7: What have you found of note?

SCION 13: The recorded history of humankind is
only six thousand years old. It is short. The human
life span is even shorter—laughably so in compar-
ison to our own species'. Despite this, on a grand
scale, the speed of humanity's intellectual evolution is exponential. Their history reflects this.

ARBITER: Continue.

SCION 13: But our own species has had over two hundred fifty thousand years of evolution. Imagine what humanity could be capable of, if only given a little more time.

DEREK

Doko the fuck are you, my Deemodatchi??

Your parents keep asking me, as if you actually *tell me*

stuff

And it's stressing out boku no kokoro

ADEEM

Is that Japanese

Are you marathoning anime again

DEREK

OH THANK GOD HE'S ALIVE

Yes lulz, Goku has saved the universe like 42 times, he's the

only thing giving me hope right now

BUT THAT'S BESIDES THE POINT

Answer my question: Where tf ARE YOU??????

Did you find Leyla yet?

ADEEM

. . . lol

Lolololololololol

LOLOLOLOLLODOFDFJSHFDJHFDJ

Abandon all hope, ye who are Adeem.

DEREK

Damn son

That bad huh

Just hurry, okay?

The computer lab at school got trashed by looters

My parents want us to hide out at our church

I can't hold off your parents forever, they're worried as hell

And keep us updated, you freaking clam

Hello? Hi? You dead yet?

ADEEM

T_T Sorry, service sucks right now.

I'll text more when my phone's not running on 2%

and I actually have proper phone service

I think my texts keep getting lost

DEREK

Apology accepted

May the force be with you and your power always be over 9000

ADEEM

Omfg why are you like this.

DEREK

Lulz love u too bro~

19

ADEEM

"Cate, wake up." Adeem shook her hard, but she was a deep sleeper, even worse than Derek at their sleepovers back in middle school. "Wake *up*."

Finally, her eyes fluttered open. When she realized Adeem was hanging over her, she shot up, startled.

"What? What happened?" She was breathing heavily. Her bangs were sticking up at full mast, like they'd been shocked into awareness, too. In any other circumstances, Adeem might have found it a little funny.

If it were Derek, he would have answered with something snarky like *An Unexpected Error Occurred,* but it wasn't Derek because Adeem was in the middle of a desert with some girl he barely knew.

He squeezed his fists to his sides. Somewhere along the way, Adeem's knuckles had cracked and begun to bleed, but he could barely feel it because every part of him hurt. He was so sure sleeping in the desert wouldn't be so bad; the desert always looked so soft and pillowy in Dad's *National Geographic* mags, but that was the Sahara and this was the Boonies, USA. God-freaking-dammit.

"They're gone. Alice and Ty—they're gone. They took the van and left us behind."

They'd probably stolen a lot of their stuff off unsuspecting people like them—their food, their phone chargers, their van, who knows what else. The thought made Adeem's veins throb. If Derek were here, he would have pointed out that Adeem looked like that angry Arthur meme right about now, but again, Cate was not Derek. So instead, she stared back at him blankly. "I don't understand."

"They took my wallet." He was trembling, and he couldn't stop. The inside of his chest was on fire. "At least a hundred bucks, gone." Not to mention his debit card, his school ID, his Amateur Radio Quick Reference Card, and his driver's license.

"Please tell me you still have yours."

Cate threw off the top of her sleeping bag. With a loud jangle, her keys, a bottle of pepper spray, and her weird blackbird key chain flung to the other side of the tent. Her wallet—teal with a gold strap—was still there, too, tucked safely inside her sleeping bag. She fanned open the wallet: she only had a couple one-dollar bills, some crumpled pieces of paper, and a few different business cards of various doctors.

"I didn't have much to begin with," Cate said apologetically. "I didn't think we wouldn't find a single working ATM. Did they really take *everything*?"

"No, I had my radio on me, and I had my phone in my pocket." He flexed his fingers; for some reason, he couldn't feel them. "I went to go pee for, like, two seconds." His phone died trying to text back Derek and Reza, who'd been frantically trying to reach him, so he'd used the last of the radio's battery to see if he could get a signal. But of course, he couldn't, and he'd returned to their camp, trying his best to stay calm even though it'd been the longest he'd gone without being connected.

Then he'd heard the van pull away. Gone so fast, they'd left their tent behind.

"What about your phone? Any bars? Maybe we can call, I don't know, *someone*."

She clicked on her phone; the battery symbol glowed threateningly red, and her bars were nonexistent.

"I'm sorry—I spent half the night trying to send texts to my mom, and I guess it drained my battery." Cate shuddered, as if cold. "I thought I'd be able to use Alice's charger again in the morning."

Adeem could practically hear his heart fall into his empty stomach and shatter into a million pieces.

They only had three days left until Alma made its announcement about humanity's fate. *Three days*. He could barely wrap his head around the thought. This was supposed to have been a day trip. He was supposed to have brought Leyla home by now; they would have pulled into the driveway last night, talking as if nothing had changed. A big, tearful reunion over big, heaping bowls of steaming daal chawal with raw onions, Leyla's favorite. Then Adeem could have shown her the office, all the modifications he'd made to the radios, all the weird messages he'd plucked from the airwaves over the years. Spent all night playing Mario Kart while puzzling through codes from the broadcast recordings. Maybe it was stupid to think everything would have been the same—Leyla had been gone for almost three years now—but he could hope, and that wasn't stupid. Was it?

Cate suddenly started giggling.

"What's so funny?" Adeem asked, exasperated.

"It's so *stupid,*" she said, barely composing herself. "Technically, stealing something was on *my* bucket list, and so far, we've somehow managed to be stolen from *twice.*" She wiped one of her eyes and shrugged. "I don't know, it's . . . absurd. Like, how can things get any worse?"

"How is that even remotely funny?" Adeem ran his hand down his sweaty face. "And why the hell is *stealing* on your bucket list? Why not plant a tree, adopt a puppy? Like a decent human being?"

She snorted. "For your information, petting more puppies was *also* on my bucket list."

Adeem felt a rush of blood to his head so sudden it made him dizzy. He closed his eyes. It had crossed his mind to at least try and get his phone charged before bed—he'd seen Alice's portable charger—but then he'd let his pride get in the way. So now they had nothing. He'd been so careless. And somehow, Cate found it hilarious.

If they made it out of here alive and if, by some miracle, Alma decided to spare Earth or humanity or whatever in three days, he would definitely start praying five times a day and apply to the MIT robotics program and listen to every damn thing Ms. Takemoto and his parents told him.

"Screw this. I have to get home," Adeem blurted out. It was the only thing that made sense. It would take half a day just to reach Roswell from where they were in Corn Creek, assuming they found a car this second. But they had no money, no mode of transportation, and most important, no time. He wasn't even sure he'd be able to bring Cate back to San Francisco before the end.

His parents must have been worried sick. It was bad enough they'd lost one child. Did they think he'd left them, too?

He squeezed the radio in the palm of his sweaty hand, though the chance of him finding Leyla now was slipping through his fingers like sand.

Cate stared. "What about Roswell?" She wasn't laughing anymore.

Adeem's head hung. "It's over. It doesn't matter anymore."

"What do you mean?" she pressed.

"It doesn't *matter*," he snapped, his voice raised. "We're stranded in the middle of nowhere." And, really, it was nowhere: besides Alice and Ty—if they even counted—Adeem hadn't seen another soul for miles. Almost like Alma had already struck.

"It's game over. Bucket lists be damned. I just wanted to find my sister and survive, but at this rate, it'll be a miracle if we live long enough to hear Alma blow us all up or whatever the hell it is they plan to do to us all."

He felt sorry for practically yelling at her, but right now, his nerves were frayed, and he was pretty sure he had grit burrowed in every corner of his body. He wanted to dry heave all his frustrations out. And it was technically her fault for hitchhiking and relying on a bunch of batshit, alien-worshipping Extraterrestrialists. Why did Cate have to be so damn trusting of everyone?

Shit, she'd trusted *him* to get her to Roswell, even though she barely knew him.

"So we just turn around? Go home?" Cate's big brown eyes trembled. "After everything?"

"Unless you have another great idea," he said, not bothering to stave off the sarcasm from his voice. "Maybe we can hitchhike again. Maybe this time with some axe murderers."

"We can't go back. I—I left my mom and Ivy for this," Cate argued, clutching her stomach like his words physically hurt. "We've already come this far. We still have a chance. Please."

She had a point. But relying on mere chance wasn't good enough. Leaving his parents all alone during the end of the world was *not* the plan. He hadn't even said goodbye to Derek

FARAH NAZ RISHI

yet. Hell, none of this was the plan.

"What about all that stuff about actually trying to do something?" she continued. "You can't tell me how great it is that I'm trying to bring my family back together and then just ditch me out here!"

The hurt on her face reminded him so much of Ms. Takemoto, the look she gave him every time he lied through his teeth to avoid Coding Club.

"I'm sorry." And he meant it. But now he could barely stand to look at her. He backed quickly out of the tent, letting the flap drop behind him.

He'd known those weirdos who called themselves something as ridiculous as the Star Voyeurs weren't to be trusted. This was their fault. Hell, if humanity was destroyed, it would be because of people like them. Adeem had gotten nothing but bad vibes the moment they opened the van door: Alice kept speaking in that creepy baby voice, and Ty was a sanctimonious little shit. People like Ty were the very reason that Adeem stayed inside with his radios. If he overheard something annoying, he could just flip a switch and change the channel.

Now his radio was dead, and his phone was almost out of batteries, too—barely at two percent, after he'd managed to send a couple texts to Derek. But it might be enough to find a station, find someone nearby, find someone who could help.

Poor Cate. She'd sounded so determined. He shouldn't have said all that stuff to her last night about finding her dad.

248

But he'd wanted to believe she could. That it would be worth it just to bring her family together again, no matter what the cost.

Well, they tried, right? That still counted for something, right?

Or maybe he was even more naïve than Cate. This plan to get Leyla back? It wasn't like a broken code: he couldn't just throw a semicolon somewhere and a car would suddenly materialize and all their problems would be miraculously fixed. There was no debugger for real life.

```
if (meant To Be) {
findLeyla ( );
} else {
goHome ( );
}
```

Sometimes, it was better to reset the code altogether, Ms. Takemoto had once told him. It didn't mean your code was a failure.

It just meant it was time to cut your losses.

(((20)))

JESSE

Jesse's lip throbbed from the new stitches. He should have taken the doctor up on his offer of the good painkillers. Even his mom was urging him to, although that would have cost them more money.

But *everything* hurt: his ribs, his back, his head, where a bump the size of a peach had begun to form—almost as much as it had hurt to take out his wallet at urgent care and dish out over one thousand dollars to pay for the split lip and lacerations on his cheek. And the bruises to his skull, of course. Can't forget that.

All that money, gone. A good chunk of the profits he'd painstakingly collected, the money they needed to load up and get the hell out of Roswell. He couldn't see they had much choice, with Samuel pumping him for money he had no chance of getting. But if Samuel wanted the money so badly, then why beat Jesse to a pulp and make it that much harder to get?

It made no sense. Nothing made sense.

The urgent care facility was only a little over a mile from his house, but the wait just to be seen took ages. His mom even had to take a shift off from the diner just to wait with him. Roswell General Hospital wasn't even an option; the last time he'd been there was the night he'd gotten the scars on his wrist, after his mom found him bleeding out on the bathroom floor.

The same night he'd met Ms. K.

Now that tourists were flocking back to the town, more people were surging the health-care centers. It didn't help that most of these tourists, unlike the family-friendly ones of a few years ago, were high off the apocalypse and had begun a small but steadily growing tent city, rows of propped-up blankets and cardboard boxes around an abandoned grain warehouse in the old Railroad District. They'd brought little more than their pets in carriers, stolen red shopping carts filled with necessities to last the next two and a half days. The rest of their worldly possessions they'd given up in a desperate attempt to convince Alma they were worth sparing, and passed the time with songs and prayer circles that lasted long into every night. There were just too many of them, and police had outright given up on trying to control them. Jesse was almost certain his real neighbors had fled town before things got any wilder, their abandoned house now replaced by at least five shroom dealers offering "temporary escapes"—they were probably responsible for a quarter of the hospitalizations in town.

In a way, this was *supposed* to be what Jesse wanted. Roswell was now bustling, thriving in the discord; people were more than willing to throw away money they might not need in a couple days. Even Pluto's Diner, where Mom worked, with its shitty, tacky, alien-themed food, had become something of a hot spot.

But the frenetic high of seeing Corbin, of things finally going his way even just *slightly*, had been pounded out of him. Where he'd been a money-making genius yesterday, today he was just Jesse, a beat-up kid who had to wait in the urgent care waiting room with his mom for hours and hours just to be seen by an exhausted doc, along with a bunch of idiots who'd nearly drunk themselves to death and some meth-heads.

They needed out. Out of the house, and out of this circus of a town. Away from Roswell, away from the ghost of Jesse's father.

Maybe Marco's friend was right. Once all the Alma bullshit blew over, Jesse could buy plane tickets to California for him and his mom and never look back.

His mom now heaved open the door of the urgent care

center. "I still think you should have told the doc about a possible concussion."

Jesse lunged for his mom's arm and pulled her out of the way of a breathless nurse, running with a child in a wheelchair.

"And yet my reflexes have never worked better." His vision, though, had seen better days.

His mom gently tugged her arm out of Jesse's grasp. He looked at her, hurt.

But she looked away. "I saw Ms. K by the front desk," she said. "You should talk to her before we go."

"What?" Jesse suddenly felt light-headed. Since when did Ms. K work at the urgent care center, too? No wonder she'd looked so beat. Counselors all over must have been stretched thin. "Oh. Well, I don't really have anything to talk to her about." He tried to ignore the urge to scratch at his wrist.

His mom's jaw tensed, emphasizing her hollow cheeks. He could see the disappointment clear as day all over her face. "Fine," she said. "I'm gonna go bring the car around. Don't want you wading through these shady crowds. People keep . . . eyeing you, more than usual."

Her eyes flicked up at a trio of whispering townies; Jesse recognized one of them as his old algebra teacher, who he was pretty sure hated his guts to begin with. Now, most locals seemed to want to punch Jesse out. After all, it was his fault all these weirdos had come scurrying into Roswell, making trouble.

If he felt like he was being watched all the time, it was probably because he was.

They finally arrived home late in the afternoon. He and his mom had to beeline through the eager, trespassing crowd of would-be customers lining up behind the old velvet stanchion he'd nicked from a garbage dump a couple days ago. The crowd would have been gone by now, normally, but since he'd been out all day, he imagined all of these people had been waiting for him to finally show.

But instead of the usual excitement at the prospect of more money, he felt a flare of annoyance. All kinds of garbage had been strewn across his front lawn—chip bags, plastic wrap, a perfectly good half-eaten sandwich, which really set him off.

So it was easy to part through the crowd like a stone-faced Moses and ignore the calling and pleading to use the Hewitt Electronic Communication Center.

All those people carrying regret around, as if life were one big bramble patch and every regret they'd collected clung to their skin like a prickly bur. But instead of nursing vodkas at the bar, like most people Jesse knew who shouldered regrets, they were here. Waiting for him and his stupid machine.

If it was vindication they wanted, then these poor fools were better off at the bar.

No, he corrected himself. They weren't all fools.

As he entered the safety of his house, Jesse felt his bones relax a little. He took in familiar smells, like his mom's watered-down perfume, and dry tuna casserole, still pungent from when he microwaved a serving last night—a strong enough scent to cover the sour smell of mold lingering beneath the kitchen cabinets.

His mom suddenly flicked the kitchen light on. Jesse flinched hard, banging his elbow on the counter, his eyes struggling to adjust.

"So, now that we're home, you gonna finally tell me what the hell happened?"

His mom sat at the kitchen table, leaning her head on one hand, and looking as haggard as he felt.

Behind her, the microwave blinked with neon green light: 2:46 a.m., it read, but that couldn't have been right; it was almost 4:00 p.m. now. He wondered if the neighborhood had lost power in the middle of the night or if the clock had just given up like everything else lately. They all only had less than two days left now, supposedly.

Jesse's mind raced. All he could hear was the rush of blood in his ears. She was better off not knowing, wasn't she?

"I know it has something to do with your"—she waved her hands around—"bullshit alien communication machine or whatnot. Did someone jump you for it?"

"Sort of."

The sunlight pouring through the window hit his mom's hair, making it appear lighter—*whiter*. They hadn't even cele-brated her thirty-seventh birthday yet, but already, the hair at her temples was beginning to gray. Jesse felt his heart sink a little. When had she started to age? "I've been more than fair with you. I've stayed out of a lot of your business with this machine, giving you the space I thought you needed." She squeezed her eyes, probably subduing memories of blood on white tile, of Jesse ghostly pale and breathless. Memories that haunted them like barely hidden scars. "I still don't even know half of what you're doing out there, but now you've gotta be straight with me. Are people trying to hurt you? Are they mad because you're lying about talking to aliens or whatever the hell it is you've been telling people? Or are you the one picking fights?"

"I didn't pick a fight," he said, struggling to keep his voice level. But watching Mom angrily grip the tablecloth between her fingers made something in his chest feel raw and frayed. He tried not to think of that night in the QuikTrip, his fists flying at Marco's face as he begged Jesse to stop.

She sighed. "Please don't lie to me right now, J-Bird."

He grit his teeth. "I'm *not*. You're right. I got jumped."

The front door pounded. The customers waiting outside were getting impatient.

Mom frowned and released her grip on the tablecloth. "I knew that machine would bring nothing but trouble. Of course it would. It was your father's, after all. It's brought the whole town trouble; people keep talking about it at the diner, telling me all sorts of crap. But it's troubling me now, Jesse. They say you're the reason all these, these *vagabonds* in their damn tents keep stumbling into Roswell. You've been attracting the wrong kind of attention with that thing."

Jesse thought of the wolf the tourists let bleed to death, of what Ms. K had said about doing things you can't take back. But he shook it out of his head.

"And I told you we need this money. Mom, I *know* about the eviction notices. The late payments."

His mom recoiled. Her breath stilled.

Jesse went on. "What I'm doing? It's so we can get a new *life*. We can get a brand-new start. We could go to California, like Dad promised he'd take us. But we'll make it on our own. You won't have to work eighteen-hour shifts anymore. We can leave the shed and all the memories of Dad behind us. I'll start going to school more, working more part-time jobs to help support you. We've earned it. The money's for a good cause." He wouldn't tell her the part about Marco's friend coming to claim that money for himself.

His mom folded her arms across her chest. "Just like the peanut butter? The bread? Is that all for a good cause? I looked the other way for a long time, Jesse, but this—scamming people with your dad's machine—it's going too damn far."

Jesse gestured vaguely toward the window, toward the shed surrounded by paying customers. "Mom, these people are idiots. They want a place to pour out their problems, and I'm giving it to them. They just want to believe they can talk to Alma to make themselves feel better. If they think the machine actually works, then that's their own damn fault." He swallowed, but it wasn't enough to ease his dry, aching throat. "What I do isn't bad or wrong or a crime. People do this kind of stuff all the time. I'm no different from, I don't know, a fortune-teller or something."

"No, you're taking *advantage* of people's legitimate fears." Her face was unreadable now, and it unnerved Jesse. Why was she so angry? "I know you think you can get away with all this because of the way things are right now, and trust me, you're not the only one preying on desperation. But you've got to be better than that. You need to start caring about other people, especially now. Get these thoughts out of your head. I never wanted us to go to California. Those pipe dreams were your dad's. All I ever wanted was for us to be together. All I want is to spend time with my boy. Not a scam artist."

"Pipe dreams . . . ?" He couldn't hide the acid in his voice, and his chest frantically quaked, barely wresting back control.

He couldn't help but feel he was missing something. He didn't need to care about other people, just himself and his mom. What was so wrong with that? The machine was supposed to make him the opposite of his dad, but here Mom was, looking at him with an expression she had only ever used for Dad: disappointment. He hated it.

"I don't get it," he said coldly. He went to the sink and ran some water into a glass. It tasted dusty. "Why are you acting like you think the message from Alma is legit?"

"Because maybe I do," she said simply.

For a long time, neither of them said anything. Jesse's mind went numb; he felt like his feet had fused to the floor. The worst part was watching Mom's chest rise and fall, as though she was fighting to keep herself calm. But that just left the silence between them.

That's when it hit him: She hadn't just taken off her last shift at the diner to keep him company at the urgent care. She'd taken off work for good.

Finally, Jesse found his voice. "What happened? What happened to 'this is all one big government conspiracy'?"

His mom shook her head. "Jesse . . . we've gone through some horrible shit, you and me. Horrible things, they happen all the time. So who are we to say all this isn't real, too?"

But you know better, he wanted to say. *You know none of this can be real. Because if it's real . . .*

"I already almost lost you once. I didn't see it coming, and I should have, and now, more than anything, I just want you to be safe," she said, her words heavy and deliberate. "Your dad never knew when to stop. Never knew when to ask for help. And you know what? He died a lonely man."

"I'm not lonely," Jesse said. But it was Corbin's face, once again, that came to mind. Stupid. They barely knew each other.

"There is nothing wrong with being lonely. I don't—I don't ever want you to feel ashamed." His mom glanced at his wrist, her lightless eyes like nebulas, and stood. "But I don't want you to keep pretending you're okay. I don't want you to keep downplaying the hurt you feel like you're not even human. You keep it up—all these lies to yourself, to other people, and soon you're not going to know who you are."

"That's not true," he said softly. He knew *exactly* who he was; that's why after that bloody nightmare of a night, when he'd almost died, he'd promised himself to never let anyone close.

But now, Ian's face, illuminated by the neon lights of Close Encounters, flashed through his mind, followed by Joey, and Ryan, and Mark. Each face another kick to his gut.

Those weren't even friends. So who did he have, really?

Who had he ever had?

She grabbed her purse from the table and gave him one last hard look. "I'll be upstairs if you decide what's really important."

She went upstairs and slammed her bedroom door.

21

ADEEM

A giant signboard, painted a faded neon pink and yellow with peeling black letters, announced they'd reached Sun-free Grotto Park, where RVs littered the grounds and the afternoon sun really did beam freely—too freely. From afar, rows of white RVs looked like gapped, crooked teeth divided between dusted paths browned by sand. The narrow ribbons of pavement that snaked between them shimmered in the heat. Adeem's eyes ached. The desert and everything in it was so blindingly beige, like the hairy, exposed back of a man sunbathing on a white beach. What little greenery there was—occasional dry shrubs and cacti—had been bleached to the same dull color.

His phone was still very much dead, and according to

the dubious GPS on Cate's barely charged phone, it was an eight-hour walk from Corn Creek to Las Vegas, the closest actual city where they had any hope of finding help and rides home. Two hours into their stumbling through the desert like a couple of robots learning how to walk, the heat became unbearable, and his one-pound radio felt like a cement block at his side. They needed water, fast; the desert out here was lifeless and dead as a Fallout video game, and as much as he loved playing it, he didn't exactly want to live it.

He'd been right to give up on Roswell; even finding a way back home was feeling more impossible by the minute.

"I don't get the name on the sign," said Adeem, wiping off his forehead with his T-shirt. "Is it a 'grotto' or is it a 'park'? Those are two very different things. And why even call it a 'park' when it's just a bunch of RVs?" He was trying to get Cate to laugh. It was bad enough they could die out here, but he didn't want to do it with her like this. She'd been silent for hours—still angry at him, probably, for abandoning their plan to get to Roswell. Not that they had much of a choice. As soon as they found civilization, he'd told her, he would head back home.

At least he could die true to himself: half-assing things and not following through.

Now Cate shrugged. "I don't know. Maybe a gathering of RVs is a park, the same way a bunch of crows is a murder, or a group of antelope is a herd." At least she was talking to him again.

"And you know what that makes us?" he asked. "Hella lost."

Cate smiled for the first time all day. "Now, that right there is a good reason why Alma won't nuke us: our sense of humor is so bad, they'll just leave us alone."

Adeem smiled, too, despite the emptiness of his stomach, the chafe of burst blisters in his shoes, and the desert sun, still relentless even in September, turning his neck into jerky. It wasn't funny. None of it was funny. But the thing about the end of the world was this: either everything mattered, or nothing did.

Plus, he liked making her smile. It let him forget, for just a moment, that they would either have to turn back together or go their separate ways.

He knew he might never see her again. But in three days, he might be able to say the same for everyone he'd ever met.

For Leyla, even.

The RV park was at capacity. Some RVs seemed to have been here for years; those had little garden setups lining their weather-battered frames, and blue and green retractable awnings over their front doors, and power generators clinging to their sides. A couple of them even had chicken coops. But other RVs had just arrived: the dirt around them had been overturned by the fresh tracks of people and tires, and they still radiated the heat of engines. As Adeem passed them, their exteriors clicked like freshly poured bowls of Rice Krispies, the sound of metal barely cooling in the heat. The thought made him hungrier.

But he was relieved to see *life*. At least in this moment, where there were people, there was hope, if only a little.

Dogs barked frantically as they went by. Some of the residents were busy setting up tents—little pops of color: reds, blues, and yellows. No, not just people—entire families. A group of people of all ages was gathered around a table, playing a board game. Civilization, from the looks of it. And nearby, someone had set up a makeshift Popsicle stand.

Were they all extraterrestrialists, like Alice and Ty? Unlikely; he didn't see any lime-green alien or UFO flags, or people openly spreading the good word of their Almaen overlords. Had they all been displaced from their homes? Even before he'd left home, he'd caught radio reports of riots and stampedes, people fighting and even killing one another over supplies. According to Alice and Ty, the violence had only gotten worse since then, and the deserts—far away from other people—were probably safer for those who weren't survivalists. Either way, here, he didn't feel the same unease he'd felt with Alice and Ty. These people could still laugh. These people were still trying to hold on.

Some kids had started a game of tag; they zigzagged past Cate and Adeem, giggling as they disappeared behind the rows of RVs and ignoring the glares from weary adults. Desi parents would've slapped them for less, he thought—amused at first, then sick with guilt and worry.

He missed his parents.

Bad.

He missed Derek.

He missed his bedroom. His laptop. His radio.

There was so much he was going to miss.

Sand had leaked into his shoes, and now his blisters stung more than ever—Cate had been limping, too. They reached what appeared to be the main office: another trailer, adorned with large, crooked antennae on its roof, which beckoned them with a cheerful plastic pink flamingo standing beside an overly enthusiastic neon sign that read *Welcome to Sunfree!* Across a shimmering strip of asphalt was a mini-mart, miraculously open. Even better, it appeared from the rotation of people passing in and out that there were actually things for sale.

"You can wait here," Adeem suggested. She looked even more exhausted than she had the day before; he didn't blame her after trekking all morning in the desert. But he thought she might be hungry, too—she kept wincing, as if she was in pain, and pressing her hands to her stomach.

She straightened up when she realized Adeem was staring.

"I'll check out the mini-mart," she said. "Maybe they have a working ATM."

Adeem doubted it. The problem, most likely, wasn't just the servers. He'd seen enough end-of-the-world movies and video games to know that by the time people resorted to making tent cities, things like banks had already long fallen. If he could get his radio working, he wouldn't be surprised to hear ham reports of Wall Street itself and federal government buildings around the country all getting caught in the cross fire of apocalyptic chaos. But there it was, that spark of hope in her eyes. He was too tired to extinguish it.

Adeem knocked on the trailer door. "What?" a voice called from within, and Adeem opened the door.

The first thing Adeem noticed were the animals: there were at least four—no, five cats scattered throughout the office, some sleeping, others sunbathing. One was sleeping next to a watercooler nestled beside a large, leafy green tree in a pot, and it took all of Adeem's willpower not to stumble toward the cooler and drink his body weight in water. The place was a hidden oasis; from the ceiling hung several other plants with dangling vines. But then he saw the giant bulletin board, plastered with handwritten messages alongside *MISS-ING* posters, hundreds of strangers' faces all staring back at him.

Despite the heat, he shivered.

Finally, he noticed the tiny, old, brown-skinned woman sitting at a small counter, a fat pair of headphones wrapped around her neck. Her round, metal-rimmed glasses sat at the edge of her nose. There was a large black dog curled up by her feet where a small metal fan whirred. Adeem made a mental note to tell Cate about the dog—she could finally cross something off that ridiculous bucket list of hers.

"*No tenemos teléfonos que funcionen,*" the woman said.

"Sorry. I don't speak Spanish." Adeem got that a lot. People saw his skin color and assumed.

"And why the hell not? We live in a global society." She adjusted her glasses. "What are you, then?"

Adeem's skin prickled. He hated that question, and yet, it was one that somehow people always found reasonable to ask. "I'm from Nevada," he said firmly, "and my parents are from Pakistan." He looked for signs of judgment or mistrust on her face but found none.

"Hmm." She wasn't even looking at him; she had spun around in her chair to fiddle with something on the table. "Getting transmissions to Pakistan'll be difficult, if that's what you're here for, but: 'Verily, with every hardship comes ease.'"

That, he hadn't expected: a line from the Quran was not the usual response to his heritage.

Seeing his expression, she explained: "I'm hearing that one a lot on the waves. That and a lot of psalms. 'Though I walk through the valley of the shadow of death, I will fear no evil.'" She chuckled. "So? You got a message for me?"

Adeem stepped closer; only then did he notice the modest ham radio station rig hidden behind wires and the hanging plants, set with multiple shelves filled with two—no, three different radio transceivers, a wattmeter, a linear amp, and an HC-5 microphone. In the corner, a large black box covered in dials: a quantum phaser, a device to block any interference from a radio signal bigger than hers. Two of her computer monitors displayed rows of fluctuating frequencies. He couldn't even begin to compare his setup back home to hers.

She had to have at *least* one generator powering it all.

But his breath snagged when he saw the grand piece de resistance: a gorgeous vintage beast of a transceiver—a Yaesu FT-101B—with a shiny oak inlay. A custom job, probably, one that put the chipped Philco back home to shame.

The whole rig must have been hastily put together; wires were everywhere, snaking down the backside of the table like vines, and the monitors were at odds with the single silver keyboard, missing a few of its keys. Notebooks were scattered across every available surface; sheets of paper covered in different handwriting styles had fallen on the floor.

Just like that, just for a split second, he thought she was the most beautiful woman he'd ever seen—even though she must have been pushing seventy and was wearing a pit-stained Mr. Spock T-shirt. He even forgave her for asking where he was from, especially since she was only trying to figure out how far her waves would have to travel. She was probably asking everybody.

"No, I— Are you operating the whole station by yourself?" He moved closer to her without meaning to. The gentle hum of the generator and her radios soothed him like the purring of a giant cat. This was *exactly* what he needed.

The woman spun in her chair to face him. "Of course. What do you take me for?" She shoved her glasses up the bridge of her nose. "Name's Rosie. You're in the Command Ops Center of southern Nevada, as I like to call it. With most of the local cell towers losing their backup power, I'm taking messages and broadcasting them where they need to go. Cell towers got nothing on good ol'-fashioned tech," she boasted.

She had a point: even if he and Cate had gotten their phones charged, power outages were screwing with cell towers. But with two-way radios, they could contact their parents from all the way out here, put their minds at ease.

They could find a way *home*

"You'll send messages anywhere?" Adeem asked. A ginger cat began weaving between Adeem's legs, nuzzling against him. "For free?"

"'Whoever has a bountiful eye will be blessed, for he shares his bread with the poor,' as they say." Rosie winked. "I'll send messages anywhere but Alma. You'd have to go to Roswell for that."

His shoulders tensed. "Roswell?"

"Guess you wouldn't know about it if you're not plugged in, eh?" she chuckled. "Everyone's talking about it on the waves. Some kid in Roswell supposedly created some kind of superpowered transmitting device—been beaming messages toward Alma for days now. Pretty sure half the population of New Mexico has already sent messages, begging the aliens to spare us." She shook her head.

"You don't seem to approve very much," Adeem observed.

"Honey, I've lived long enough to know that begging your oppressors to spare you never works. You either fight back, or"—Rosie tapped one of her transceivers— "remind the ones you love there's something still worth fighting for."

Adeem wondered if Leyla had heard about the transmitter. Or if it even worked.

He pulled his dead radio from its carrying case. "I've kind of been off the waves lately. Do you think you could hook me up?"

Rosie beamed and plucked off her headphones from around her neck. "Another radio enthusiast, I see! I bet I can scrounge up an extra charging outlet for ya—just hang tight. Help yourself to some water, in the meantime, and for Pete's sake, wash your face or something; you look like you got into a fight with a sand dune and lost."

Adeem let out a long breath of relief. "Thanks. Thank you. So much," he said, before nearly tripping over the ginger cat in a rush to the watercooler.

Rosie stood up from her chair and tiptoed around him toward the trailer door, careful to avoid any snoozing cats. "Anything for a fellow Hammie," she said before closing the door behind her.

With a few huge gulps of the cold, crisp water, Adeem could practically feel his cells buzzing with life. Osmosis had never felt so good. He couldn't wait to tell Cate to come in here and fill up, too.

The thought surprised him—how much he wanted to see Cate's face light up with a smile. Not with the delirious, end-times laughter she'd already offered in response to his terrible jokes, but with real happiness. Maybe all that crap he'd said to her about hope last night hadn't all been BS.

He looked around and could hardly believe their luck. Now he understood why all those people were camping out here: to use Rosie's radio. The woman was a certifiable desert flower. Maybe they had no way of getting to Roswell now, but at least they'd be able to reach their families back home.

With this huge a rig, he could probably even send a message to Leyla . . .

The realization jolted him. *He could send a message to Leyla!*

He set down his cup and sidled into Rosie's chair, his breathing shallow. Slowly, he traced her keyboard with his fingers, savoring the feel. God, he'd missed this. If Rosie'd do anything for a fellow Hammie, surely she wouldn't mind him borrowing her equipment for a second.

He scoured through her equipment to find an anchor to something familiar. Rosie's rig was beyond unfamiliar: it was three times the size of his, and ten times more powerful. But like code, radio worked the same any- and everywhere. He let out a huge breath and switched to an empty high-frequency band. The monitor closest to him glowed with confirmation. If he could broadcast his own message, the transmitter station would relay it until another station received it and relayed it onward—until maybe, just maybe, his message would find Leyla. He could do this.

A bead of sweat rolled down his spine as he put on Rosie's headphones and set the transceiver to broadcast. He picked up the microphone. Adjusted his glasses.

But he hesitated. The words wouldn't come.

What could he even say? *Hey, it's me—your little bro, in case you forgot—just letting you know I tried to find you, but hey, that's life, I guess. Hope you have a safe, fun-filled apocalypse!*

He groaned. Even if he did figure out the perfect thing to say, on public broadcast, no less, what if she didn't hear? She could be in a radio quiet zone, for all he knew. Or worse.

Even if she did hear, what if she didn't care?

The words his dad had spoken still echoed between his ears: *You could have been out there finding her yourself, but I've never once seen you make an effort.*

He'd said it out of anger and frustration, but the thing was, his dad had been *right*. And it wasn't just about finding Leyla. Adeem never made an effort for *anything*, whether it be in Coding Club, or actually doing something with the games he made, or even being a good friend to Derek. It was why poor Ms. Takemoto constantly hounded him with flyers from MIT robotics, and why his parents constantly lectured him about wasting away his talents. For him, life was a series of RPG-style random encounters, and he chose *Flee* every time. Like a coward.

But this time, he *had* made an effort, hadn't he? He'd traveled across desert, gotten stranded, nearly died trying to find his sister. His wallet and car had both been stolen, for God's sake. And yet, what did he have to show for all his effort? Nothing but shredded feet and wounded pride.

He set down the microphone.

There was no point in trying anymore, he thought, queasy with misery. Maybe some things weren't meant to be.

Outside, a door slammed and someone shrieked. He jumped in his chair, and several cats bolted for the corners. Rosie's dog raised its head.

Cate? His heart pumping wildly, Adeem pushed his way outside. At the entrance of the mini-mart, a man in a dark green apron had Cate in a tight grip.

"You really thought I wouldn't notice, huh?" The man was practically spitting at her.

Cate squirmed, trying to wrench away. "Get off me."

"Hey!" Adeem stormed up to them. "What the hell is going on?"

"You her partner in crime?" The man glared at Adeem and pointed a red, sausage-like finger at him. "Goddamn criminals like you are the reason this whole world's gone to shit in the first place. You have any idea what I've had to do just to protect my store from people like you?"

"We're not criminals," Adeem said. At the same time, he caught sight of Cate's face and his stomach sank. What had she done?

"Please," said Cate, attempting to wrench her arm from the man. "Let me go."

"Listen. I think you're confused." Adeem's mouth was dry. "We're just passing through—"

But before Adeem could finish, the man cut him off. "Yeah? Then why the hell did I catch your little *friend*"—the man replied, shaking Cate's arm with every word—"stealing shit from my store?"

Adeem noticed for the first time that he had Cate's balled-up cardigan in his fist. He shook it: a granola bar, a small bottle of aspirin, and a couple of weird plastic tubes slipped from the pockets. Then he dug his fingers through the pockets until her blackbird key chain, mini-Taser, and wallet landed on the dirt—the latter of which only made her look guiltier.

Cate let out a small whimper.

"You picked the wrong store to mess with," the manager of the mini-mart said, puffing his chest. "My cousin's the local sheriff, and you bet he's gonna throw your little asses in jail."

Adeem's brain went numb. Her bucket list. Her stupid freaking bucket list.

"Why?" he said dumbly. But he knew she wouldn't be able to explain.

Either way, it was too late. The manager was speaking into a portable radio he'd pulled off his apron, and his red-rimmed eyes were pinned to Cate.

And Adeem didn't dare move, didn't dare argue.

After all, he'd already learned the hard way that making an effort only made things worse. And it didn't look like this situation came with an option to hit *Flee*.

(((22)))

JESSE

With a loud click that pierced through the quiet—a goddamn blessing, considering the other night a parade of people in alien masks had been blasting horns and banging drums down his street—Jesse locked up his shed for a break. He was starving and about to faint. It was around 7:00 p.m., and a vast portion of the crowds of people waiting for him to return from the hospital had all but given up for the day and left, many of them probably returning to their tents down the street. The smell of charring meats drifting through the air made his mouth water. From his home, he could see plumes of smoke from their bonfires raking across the murky depths of the night sky.

Jesse could have sworn there were more tents than yesterday.

He shivered and shrugged his black leather jacket back onto his shoulders, where it had been slipping. He didn't normally get cold easily, but now, no matter how hard he tried, he just couldn't stay warm.

The chirp of crickets punctuated the relative stillness, and the usual clamor of the growing tent city—the bongo drums and singing and dancing—had dimmed to a dull, faraway hum.

But when the grass rustled behind him, his hand shot toward the knife tucked in his pocket. Ever since last night—ever since Marco's goons had jumped him—he'd decided to carry a switchblade he'd found in one of his dad's old utility cabinets. His fingers gripped the cold metal of the handle so tightly they hurt.

The source of the sound came closer. Even obscured by the night shadows, Jesse would recognize that gait, that soft, calm stride anywhere. Corbin.

"Hey, you."

Jesse slowly pulled his hand out of his pocket. He should have been happy to see him again.

But his stomach only ached with a painful cocktail of guilt and anxiousness, feelings he wasn't used to. He didn't want Corbin to see him like this.

"Man, I haven't seen you all day. I thought people were gonna start rioting. Where have you . . ." Corbin recoiled at the sight of Jesse's bruised face. "Oh God, what happened?"

Jesse smiled as charmingly as he could without hurting his

lip any further. "Would you believe me if I said my machine turned sentient and attacked me? Kept calling herself HAL." Jesse had figured out the Daisy Bell reference Corbin had made earlier; he'd forced himself to watch *2001: A Space Odyssey*, even though he'd almost fallen asleep halfway through it. He barely had time to finish it, anyhow.

Corbin briefly smiled back. "Ha. And here I thought HAL was a gentle soul. You gonna be okay?" He looked at Jesse, his eyes focusing only on his—not the bruises, the nasty cuts, or the split lip. Corbin wasn't grossed out at all. He just seemed genuinely worried.

Jesse let out an inward breath of relief that Corbin didn't pry too much. "Yeah, should be. But what about you? What are you doing here?"

"Mari's not doing too hot at the hospital. More fatigue than usual. And they're starting to get concerned about their generators." Corbin put his hands behind his neck, stretching out his shoulders. "Been trying to keep myself distracted. Thought maybe I could take you to dinner."

As he got closer, Jesse noticed the exhaustion etched on his face: the dark creep of stubble on his chin, the bloodshot eyes cupped by sunken, shadowed skin.

"Jesus. Is she okay?" Jesse was surprised by how scared he sounded. "Are *you* okay?"

"I don't know, it's"—Corbin rubbed his eyes—"a freaking madhouse, Jesse. Some guys broke into the hospital and tried to steal medical supplies. Nurses had to rush into Mari's room and barricade the door. With all the craziness happening, more people are taking it upon themselves to go vigilante, I guess. But a bunch of people from the waiting room tackled the guys and tied 'em up until some cops finally showed." Corbin laughed tiredly. "Mari's . . . still safer there than anywhere else right now. Except she really wants to see you again. She's really excited about the machine."

Jesse's fingers buzzed with the urge to comfort Corbin, but he squeezed it away. Maybe painkillers could ease his guilt; the feeling was eating at his stomach, and it hurt ten times worse than the split lip. *You're lying to these people, people just trying to survive.*

"I haven't seen an, um, response back from her message yet, but I'll check when I reopen tonight."

Corbin looked at him, and it was impossible to read his expression. "Night shifts, too, now, huh? Maybe you should be resting after HAL went rogue on your face?"

"Oh yeah. That." Jesse tugged at the collar of his leather jacket, which he could have sworn had gotten tighter. "Had to show her who's boss. And then had to do some repairs."

He couldn't tell Corbin he'd been locking up the machine with new, steel chains and installing more locks all because he'd gotten the shit beat out of him. And he definitely didn't want to admit that his argument with Mom had left him a little unsettled; if he tried to sleep now, he'd be tossing and turning all night with a ghoulish parade of thoughts banging around in his head.

Corbin chuckled. "As long as she's good now. Gotta take care of that machine of yours. It's basically become a beacon of hope, you know? Not just for Mari, but for hundreds and hundreds of people."

Jesse squirmed uncomfortably. A beacon of hope. Wish machine. A pipe dream. People kept calling it that, but even the money it had brought him wasn't going to be his anymore. Which meant he had no way out anymore. Eventually, he'd have to give up everything, and with no way to escape, it'd be a matter of time before Corbin and Mari would find out he'd been scamming them all along.

Corbin and Mari would be left with nothing but a handful of dead hope, just like Dad's scratched-off lotto tickets clutched in her trembling fists.

Tell him the truth. The voice was screaming inside his head, but his throat was squeezing shut, and his head wasn't working right. Even if he did tell the truth now, he had no idea how Corbin would react. What if Corbin got furious, decided to tell the world that the machine was a lie?

Then again, what if Corbin already *did* know, and was holding his breath, testing Jesse, waiting to see if he'd pass? Waiting to see if he'd own up to it.

No. It wasn't over until it was over, and if Corbin was keeping quiet, so would Jesse.

So instead, Jesse asked, "So are your parents with Mari right now?"

Corbin kicked at a pebble on the ground. It bounced down Jesse's empty driveway until it hit a crushed soda can some asshole tourist had left behind. "It's kind of complicated. My mom and dad are divorced. Mom's in Chicago, and Dad's here. He's with Nan and my grandpa back home, catching up on sleep." He exhaled, his breath shaky. "Everyone's so exhausted. There's just so much going on and not enough time. It's kind of scary."

Jesse wanted to run. Like a selfish coward, he wanted to ghost Corbin and forget any of this had ever happened.

"I'm really sorry you guys are going through this," he said, his voice grating from his throat.

But Corbin shrugged. "Don't be. It's not your fault. She really loves your machine, you know. You're practically her hero. You've only been good to us." He rubbed the back of his neck sheepishly. "Maybe when Mari's feeling a little better, you could go see her?"

The suggestion made Jesse uncomfortable. It wasn't that he didn't want to see Mari again. She was actually really cute, for a little kid. Mom used to be good at sewing; she'd probably make her another one of those headbands, if he asked. If she wasn't still mad at him.

He stamped out those thoughts. He was getting carried away, letting himself get closer.

"I'll . . . I'll think about it," said Jesse.

His feet felt leaden on his front porch. Part of him wanted to run, but part of him wanted to stay, too. Words played across his lips. He wanted so badly to spit it all out, just tell Corbin everything. Maybe Corbin would be different. Corbin *was* different.

The problem wasn't Corbin, he realized. The problem was

him. Jesse was the same selfish piece of shit as everyone else.

"I should probably skip dinner and get a nap in now, like you said," he said, swiveling the cuff on his wrist. "Need my beauty sleep. It's gonna be a long night."

Corbin grinned. "Oh, you have no idea. You got less than three days left."

He was right. At midnight tonight, it would be two days left, technically.

Jesse smiled back weakly, shoved his hands in his jacket pockets, and walked past Corbin, fighting the urge to inhale the subtle cedarwood-and-vanilla scent wafting off his body.

"Hey, Jesse?" asked Corbin as he passed.

Jesse looked over his shoulder. "Hmm?"

"You gonna tell me what really happened to your lip?"

Jesse was so startled by this question, he froze. But, hidden safely behind his chest, his heart began to race all over again.

Corbin, he realized, wasn't smiling anymore. And the way he was staring at Jesse's face, at his mouth, at the swollen parts and the not-swollen parts, sent a thousand different feelings pushing up through him.

Jesse turned back and pulled his jacket closer over his body. "Maybe later."

And as Jesse began to head to his front porch, he tried to drown out the most terrifying thought of all: If Corbin could read him so easily, what else did he know?

23

CATE

As far as jail cells went, this one wasn't *so* bad—not that Cate had much experience, of course. But she'd always imagined jail cells as dark, cold, cement blocks; windowless walls and, above, dripping ceilings that could barely contain the shouts of frustrated prisoners.

Sure, the metal toilet fastened to the wall gave off a sour, murky smell, and the flickering light bulb gave off the worst lighting in all of existence—the kind of light that tugged at your eyes until they hurt—and she'd watched a long, ruddy bug too big to be anything but a cockroach scurry beneath a wall.

But getting thrown in jail definitely wasn't on the bucket list.

At least she was having new experiences, and at least they'd been brought to a sheriff's station just outside Las Vegas, which meant Roswell was only an eleven-hour drive away.

It also meant that, when they got out of here, she'd probably have to part with Adeem soon.

But at least he'd be happy—at least he could go home.

She thought to point it out to Adeem, but his face was scrunched in a scowl and she was too afraid to look into his eyes.

When the local sheriff showed up at the Sunfree mini-mart, Adeem had adamantly refused to let Cate be taken alone, and started making such a scene that the sheriff had finally shrugged and nudged both of them into his vehicle. She was touched by the gesture. But, of course, that meant they were now stuck here together, and Adeem made it clear he blamed her: he hadn't spoken a word to Cate since she'd gotten them both in trouble. Worse, he didn't seem to have his radio anymore; in his rush to help her, he must have forgotten it in the office. Yet another thing that was her fault.

God, he must have hated her right now.

Sheriff Beeson, the "*second* cousin to the obnoxious mini-mart owner, and definitely not his *personal on-call muscle*," as he'd bitterly corrected them in the patrol car, led Cate and Adeem into the only free cell in the Clark County Sheriff's Office; the others had been filled to capacity. Every phone on every sheriff's desk seemed to be ringing off the hook.

He unlocked the cell and gestured them on in; Cate reluctantly shuffled inside, and, to her relief, Adeem joined her. If they were obedient, for now, it'd be easier to talk herself out of the situation later. She just had to think of a plan.

The sheriff closed the cell door. But he didn't lock it. "Now before you start panicking, you can both breathe easy. I'm not going to charge ya. Legally speaking—and yes, the law still reigns in my book despite what those Alma worshippers might tell ya—you do not have to get in there if you don't want to."

Adeem jerked his head up, his expression confused.

"Then why'd you bring us here?" Cate asked.

Sheriff Beeson looked at her from beneath his thick ginger brows. With his whiskery sideburns, he looked a little like a walrus. "To keep you *safe*. I can't in good conscience let ya out there, and trust me, you're safer in here than ya are out there. I've got people stealing trucks of supplies. Just yesterday, I had to help bust a damn drug party at Kingston Peak—pardon my French. But we had twenty-two ODs and one bus to ship them thirty miles to the hospital. People are losing their goddamn minds, and I do not"—he wagged his finger at them—"need a couple of lovesick kids getting caught up in it."

Cate couldn't help it; she made a face. "We're not . . ." she started. "It's not like that." Of course, she liked Adeem, but not that way. She was relieved that Adeem seemed to feel the same way, relatively speaking. He looked like he was trying to swallow a brick. "We're friends," she assured the sheriff.

He folded his arms across his chest. "Either way, I'd strongly advise you both to stay here until your folks get here. If I had a nicer place to put ya, I would, but, seeing as the way things are . . ."

Behind him, two other sheriffs were leading a man with long, greasy hair, draped in nothing but a towel. "I didn't do anything wrong! Your authority means nothing!" the man shrieked. The all-too-familiar smell of smoke wafting off his body burned Cate's nose.

She was beginning to doubt Sheriff Beeson on the relative safety of the sheriff's office. Just how long would they have to sit here? She'd already wasted three days. Three days that should have been one.

Her stomach still hurt, even more now, and her heart hammered in her chest. Even if she could call Mom, there was no way she could pick them up. And what would it do to Mom's state of mind to hear her daughter was calling from a jail cell in the middle of nowhere? As if Mom needed more bad news on top of everything else.

She wasn't even close to finding her dad yet.

The sheriff scratched his chin, ignoring the toweled man's hollering. "Now, our phone lines are still in operation. I can call the station nearest home for you to track your family down, let your parents know we found ya."

"Actually, could you maybe give us a minute?" Cate asked, hoping he couldn't hear the panic in her voice.

Beeson pushed away from the bars. "Sure. Just think about who you need to contact. You have IDs? I want to see if anyone's filed a missing persons report."

"Both of ours got stolen," Cate quickly lied. "But I'm Catherine, ah, Holloway, and he's Adeem"—she swallowed—"uh, Minhaj."

Sheriff Beeson nodded, satisfied. "Great. I'll let you know what we can do on our end," he said, before disappearing into the throngs of people crowding the station.

Adeem raised an eyebrow. "Why would you lie to a cop who can actually reach our parents for us?" he hissed out of earshot. "And Minhaj? Really?"

"I know, I know." It wasn't exactly the first time she'd lied to a cop, but it was still terrifying. "I panicked. I can't have him looking me up in his system and finding out where I live. He's acting like he won't keep us here against our will, but if he finds out just how far away from home we are, I highly doubt he'll just let us go out on our own. He said he'd make us sit here and wait for our parents to show up." As if that would happen. As if it *could* happen.

The radio in the background switched to a report on riots breaking out in financial districts in cities all over the country, big corporate buildings targeted by arsonists. San Francisco was one of them. Cate's stomach lurched. Lickity Split Creamery was close to the Financial District. She'd just been there a few days ago, scooping ice cream into waffle cones.

She couldn't even check if Bethany had made it out okay. She couldn't do anything, as long as they were stuck in here.

Since she'd gotten them into this mess, she had to help find a way out.

"Look, before we do anything, I think I owe you an apology," she said. "I honestly didn't think that guy'd react so freaking violently over a couple toiletries." She could barely hear herself over the bustle in the station: sheriffs shouting orders, people protesting their arrests in the jail cells beside them, and a loud, crackly radio in the corner of the office broadcasting safety warnings about traffic conditions in Las Vegas.

Adeem let out a derisive snort. "Welcome to the life of every brown and black kid in America." His voice was like a bucket of cold water.

She clenched her teeth. Yep, he hated her. So much for talking him into continuing the trip to Roswell together.

"You should have *waited*. We could have asked someone for help. Stealing aspirin? Really?" His eyes narrowed. "Was it really worth it?"

"As a matter of fact, yes, it *was*," she said defensively. Because of course, on top of everything else, Cate just had to get her period with a side of cramps during the end of the world. Apparently, the end of days wasn't enough to fend off the wrath of Aunt Flo. "And . . . I kind of had to take a couple tampons. So. There you have it." She swallowed, awaiting his reaction.

"Oh." His eyes widened. He understood. "You got your . . . ?"

"Yep," said Cate, her face growing hot.

Adeem's head slowly fell. And then his shoulders began to tremble.

He was laughing.

Her jaw fell in horror. She didn't exactly find her period a laughing matter.

"*Man*," he choked. "Your body doesn't give a shit about timing, does it? That's why we're in jail? Seriously? Did it not get the memo about the impending alien attack?"

"Are you . . ." Cate blinked back her disbelief. *"Adeem, are you asking me if my uterus knows about Alma?"*

Somehow, this only made Adeem laugh harder.

Relief flooded Cate in an instant. She had hated the idea of Adeem being angry with her, even if she still barely knew him. More than that, though, whether he realized it or not, Adeem had reminded her of something substantially important that she'd forgotten: her body was still functioning, preparing for the future. She was still breathing. Which meant that despite everything she'd gone through, and all the bad luck that had followed them, she was still *alive*.

"So you forgive me?" she asked quietly.

He looked up at her, his eyes red-rimmed but watery. He smiled. "Jesus, I'm not going to be mad at you for *that*."

A squad of helicopters thundered above the sheriff's office. The chatter from the cells next door quieted down to an uncomfortable silence. Everyone knew what it all meant: the coming storm, the one no one wanted to talk about, but everyone could feel in the air.

"Well?" asked Adeem. "I need to figure out a way home, but what do you want to do?"

"I'm still trying to figure that one out." Cate pulled out her dead cell phone out of habit, and with it slipped out her black-bird key chain.

"Is it so bad to ask your mom for help? She can convince him to let us out. I know you said she's sick, but it's kind of an emergency."

"She can't help."

"She can't or she won't?"

"Both. It's . . . complicated." Cate shoved her phone back in her pocket but held on to the key chain. If her dad really was a shape-shifting magic pirate, then his stupid bird key chain should have magically changed into a real bird by now and offered to fly off, carrying her mom's letter for her in its chipped beak. Wishful thinking. Maybe this whole trip had been driven by wishful thinking.

It was unfair, really, to live in a world where aliens were real but magic was not.

Adeem gave an exaggerated shrug. "Guess we'll die."

"What?" She was surprised by the unusual lifelessness in his voice. "Why? Don't you have someone we can call?"

"Nope."

Cate stared at him. "There must be *someone*. Your parents?"

"Look," Adeem began tiredly, "if I know my parents—and trust me, I do—they are definitely freaking out, and probably have the rest of the Muslim community freaking out with them in our mosque basement in a never-ending cycle of panic. I haven't even had a chance to let them know I'm okay.

Imagine a couple of freaked-out brown Muslims trying to get cops to help their son come home. They'll be totally ignored, at best. But my parents have enough to deal with as it is without me telling them I screwed up so bad trying to find my sister that I ended up in a freaking jail cell in Las Vegas. I got myself into this; I need to find out how to get home like a big boy."

Cate bit her dry, chafing lips. So he really had given up on finding his sister. Which meant she'd been right: as soon as they got out of here, their journey to Roswell together would be over.

Not that she could blame him for calling it quits. They'd traveled almost five hundred miles together, and she knew as much about him now as she did the night she crawled into his car. She hadn't known he was Muslim, for one thing, not that it really mattered. But she especially hadn't thought of all the things he must have gone through before she'd even shown up in his car. All the things that must have led up to him planning this journey alone.

Cate didn't even know *why* he was out here trying to find his sister in the first place.

She'd been content with knowing they both were heading to Roswell. That had been enough. But it wasn't. Of course it wasn't. Even if *she* wanted to keep moving forward, Adeem had a family back home.

But she had a promise to keep to her mom. And maybe she was doing this for herself, after all. Meeting her dad, having him know she existed, would make her not feel so alone anymore. And that was the last thing she wanted to feel at the end of the world: alone.

Either way, she was *not* going back to San Francisco without delivering the letter.

And yet, why did the idea of going to Roswell without Adeem feel so wrong?

Cate squeezed the key chain hard, its sharp edges digging into the palm of her hand, grateful for the hot pinch of pain against her skin. Another reminder she was alive, that Alma hadn't killed her yet.

She took a deep breath. "I can't call my mom because she's in the hospital," she said slowly, tasting the sound of her secret for the first time.

Adeem's eyes widened in surprise. But he said nothing. She continued.

"She has schizophrenia. She's been dealing with it for years. *We've* been dealing with it for years. Barely. For better or worse, the last thing she asked me before she was taken to the hospital was to go find my dad." Cate looked down, surprised to find that she felt like crying. "I don't know why it's so important to her—why it's so important to *me*. Maybe . . . maybe after so many years of stories, I just wanted the truth."

For a long second, there was silence. Even the din of the sheriff's office sounded so far away. And then:

"I can't even begin to understand what you both have gone through. But wanting to find the truth . . ." He clasped his hands together and stared at the dark space between them, as if contemplating hiding inside.

"My sister," Adeem began slowly, "ran away from home after she came out to me and my parents. Left with no warning. And I'm her only sibling. Her little *brother*. I used to tell her everything. I practically worshipped her—and she just up and left without even talking to me about it. And, I get it, it's not easy to come out, and I can't even imagine how scary it must have been when none of us knew what to say, but . . ." His voice cracked, and he swallowed. "She didn't even give me a *chance*."

Seeing him suddenly spill all the pain he'd kept locked inside—all the pain he'd kept covered with his geeky sense of humor—wrenched at her chest, tight like a fist. Her eyes grew hot and cloudy, making Adeem appear to be drowning behind a watery film.

"I told my parents I'd be the one to bring her home, but I just don't even know why I'm bothering anymore." He shut his eyes tightly for a moment before opening them again. "I wanted answers so freaking badly, but I should just have left her alone. It's obvious what she wanted. She could have found me a long time ago. She could have come back anytime. But the world's ending, and she *still* hasn't reached out. I only happened to catch some obscure *radio* message that she might have sent from Roswell, but I don't even know for sure." He held his head in his hands, squeezed tightly. "I had a chance to send her a message, you know. Back at the office at Sunfree. But I didn't. Because I realized right then and there that I'd already gotten the truth I needed. She obviously doesn't give a shit about me, so why should I expect anything to change?"

Cate's breath stilled. Was that why Adeem had clung so desperately to his radio all this time? She'd caught him trying to use it so many times, randomly checking into frequencies, scouring the invisible threads of sound and light, before she'd made him leave it behind.

Cate didn't have a sibling, but she imagined losing one would feel like losing an irreplaceable piece of your history, your home. Yourself.

"What do *you* want?" she asked. Her voice was shaking, too.

Adeem rubbed his nose. "I want her back," he said quietly. "I always have."

She felt heat rise through her fingertips. Like she'd suddenly received some sort of missing piece of the puzzle, understood something crucial—a sudden, immeasurable desire to help Adeem. And in some way, help herself.

"Then screw the details," she said. "This is literally your only chance to find her." *At least I don't need to explain what "literally" means to him,* she thought, almost laughing in her delirium. God, had it only been a week since she'd been living her normal life—a week since she'd kissed Jake? It felt like lifetimes had passed since then.

He smiled sadly. "If only it were that easy."

293

Cate felt herself deflate. *It* can *be that easy*, she wanted to scream. But he'd already made up his mind.

Suddenly, Adeem stood.

"I still can't call my parents," Adeem said finally. "But I think I know someone who could help."

24

ADEEM

Back at the old house in Albuquerque, when Adeem was nine and Leyla was fifteen, black thunderclouds rolled in so fiercely, the power went out for two long, miserable days. He'd lost count, but by around the twentieth time Adeem had complained about being bored out of his mind, his mom finally slammed her book onto the kitchen table, the force of which blew out a nearby candle. "Only boring people are bored," she snapped. But before Adeem could retort with something stupid, Leyla—who was taller then—grabbed him by the back of his hoodie with her free hand, snatched a still-lit candle off the counter with the other, and dragged him to the library.

She closed the door behind them as Adeem stumbled in after her, and set the candle down on the desk. Lightning shattered the tranquil darkness, dousing the library in a momentary silver glow. Outside, a dogwood tree sagged precariously beneath the torrent of rain and shrieking winds. There was no sign of the storm letting up.

Adeem spun to face her. "What?" he whined. "What'd I do?"

"Oh, Adi-jaan, my dear baby brother," Leyla began cheerfully, "did you know that *books* are a thing?"

Adeem blinked in confusion.

Leyla bounded, fairy-like, to a bookcase. The flickering-heartbeat light of the candle danced across shelves filled with fractured-spined books and Dad's collection of old radios—including the Philco, recently chipped.

She yanked a small green hardcover book from the shelf, waved it toward him. Dad had given her that book a couple months ago; the cover was already showing signs of wear and tear. "See, there's something you can do called *reading*. Whole worlds appear in your mind! Like VR, but better."

"Shut up," Adeem grumbled. "I *know* what reading is, but *I* prefer my Switch."

"Yeah, but, see, your Switch is dead, and you don't have to charge books." She patted the plush red Oriental rug on the floor with her foot. "Come, Adi, sit. I can read to you."

Adeem stared back incredulously. "Who even reads poetry anymore?"

"For your information, *I* read poetry." Her eyes trailed to the window. "And so does Priti."

Priti was new at Leyla's school, and the two of them had

become fast friends. It wasn't long before she was coming over almost every day, and now Leyla wore a crescent moon necklace around her neck—a friendship necklace from Priti—and Adeem had yet to see her ever take it off.

Leyla becoming obsessed with poetry was one of many things that were beginning to change.

"What about Reza?" Adeem challenged. "What does *he* think?"

"He . . ." Leyla hesitated. "Well, he doesn't love it as much as Priti and I do."

Adeem followed Leyla's gaze toward the window, too, wondering what kept her attention. But he saw nothing beyond the unrelenting rain.

He sighed and took a seat on the rug, spreading his spindly legs out in front of him. "At least *someone* has enough sense."

"You never know if you don't give it a try," she lectured. "You of all people should like poetry. Let me put it in a way you'll actually understand."

As Adeem glared, Leyla sank onto a plush armchair in the corner of the room, book in hand. "Poetry is like code. Each word is its own variable, each carrying a different associated value, depending on the author's intent. And every string of words comes together, like a data structure, to create a *message*. So reading poetry is running a program in your brain; if you understand the meaning of the words, then the poet's code—their message—succeeded."

Adeem had only just started learning the basics of coding.

He didn't exactly understand the metaphor. He definitely wasn't much of a reader, either. But Leyla had known exactly what to say to pique his interest.

At least, a little bit.

He'd listen, if only to prove her wrong. "Whatever you say, but," he said, sighing, "fine. If I die of boredom, though, it's your fault."

Leyla grinned, victorious. She peeled open the book, a collection of Sufi poetry, and read a few poems from Rumi, another by Rabia Basri. It was when she'd chosen a *ghazal* by Hafez that Adeem started to really listen.

"'With looks disheveled, flushed in a sweat of drunkenness, / His shirt torn open, a song on his lips and wine cup in his hand / With eyes looking for trouble, lips softly complaining, / So at midnight last night he came and sat at my pillow . . .'"

Leyla paused, catching Adeem's wide-eyed expression. "Maybe I'll just skip this one."

"Wait, is Hafez talking about another *dude*? On his *pillow*?"

She smiled tentatively. "It kind of sounds like it, doesn't it?"

"That's . . ." Adeem made a face, like he'd eaten something sour. "Weird. So, like, he's gay?" He had nothing against it, but homosexuality was one of those topics swept under the rug in Sunday school. The one time he'd asked one of his Sunday school teachers, Auntie Aminah, about it, she simply sighed and said, *It's complicated*, and left it at that. Being gay was a thing, an identity, that existed, and that was all he really knew.

Leyla's smile faltered. "Who really knows?" she said, chuckling. "All right, Adi. I think that's enough torture for one night."

She held the book close to her chest and stood. "Hey, I just remembered—I might have a portable charger in the storage room. Wanna help me find it?"

He was so excited by the prospect of playing Pokémon, he barely noticed the flicker of pain across her face, lingering like the shadow of candlelight. But now, his memories of Leyla were like a blurry photograph, slowly coming into focus. It was funny almost; he'd always been so good at fixing things, at solving puzzles, but he couldn't even decode his sister's signals.

The only sign he'd ever understood was when the night Leyla disappeared, her favorite green book of poetry was gone, too. A sign she wasn't coming back.

You okay? Cate now mouthed, pulling him from his memories.

"Yeah," said Adeem. "Just . . . defragmenting."

She tilted her head and stared at him quizzically, but Adeem had too much on his mind to elaborate.

He'd already asked Sheriff Beeson if he could make a couple phone calls using the office landline. "Please do whatever it takes to get yourselves back home," the sheriff said after he'd lead them out of their cell and to the back of the office where a row of volunteers were fielding incoming phone calls. The sheriff handed him a greasy black landline phone.

Adeem first called Reza. After apologizing that he hadn't

been able to call sooner and assuring him again and again that he truly was okay, he explained the situation, leaving out the part about Cate's attempted—albeit hilarious—tampon theft. Then, when Reza promised to let his parents know he was safe, Adeem asked for Priti's phone number.

The line went quiet. Adeem understood Reza's shock; putting himself in close proximity to Priti, especially now, was asking for a fight. But he'd remembered Reza saying she lived in Las Vegas, and his options weren't exactly . . . broad.

"Unless you have someone else you can send over," said Adeem eagerly, "because I would gladly take literally anyone else in your magical Muslim network to bail us out."

"I'm sorry, bud," Reza apologized. "Priti's the only one I know; Las Vegas isn't exactly a huge HQ for Muslims. I can call her for you, if you want."

Adeem bit down hard. His gut reaction was to scream *YES*, but:

"I should probably do this. I think."

If he had to face her, he may as well talk to her sooner than later.

"Just don't be too hard on her, okay?" Reza warned. Adeem made no promises.

Now he squeezed the phone tightly in his sweaty hand as he waited for someone to pick up.

"Hello?" a voice on the other line said, deep and warm and familiar, like a fresh pot of *doodh pati* on a cold evening. It made Adeem bristle.

She picked up. She actually picked up, Adeem thought, panicking.

"Hello?" Priti asked again. "Anyone there?"

Her voice sounded exactly the same. In his head, he'd half imagined her transforming into some kind of manipulative, homewrecking witch the moment Leyla agreed to run away with her, complete with a throaty Disney villain laugh. But she was still just Priti, the same girl who'd come over almost every day after school and helped Mom do the dishes, who'd done so much of her homework on the kitchen table with him and Leyla and Reza.

The same girl who'd left with Leyla, and without a word.

"Hey." Adeem cleared his throat. "This is Adeem."

"Holy shit," Priti breathed. *"Adi?"*

He'd suddenly felt a horrible concoction of embarrassment and shame brewing in his stomach. This was a stupid idea. Why would Priti travel out of her way to save him, the kid who'd, as far as she knew, done jack shit to support Leyla when she'd needed him most? That's probably why she hadn't stopped Leyla from leaving her family behind. For all Adeem knew, Priti might have encouraged it.

The conversation was short, awkward, stilted; Adeem could barely hear Priti over the constant ringing of telephones and the shouting of police officers and volunteers issuing instructions for those who'd gotten themselves stranded in the desert outside Las Vegas, finding safe haven from nearby riots. And he could barely think with Cate staring at him like a curious bird. Maybe she could see the discomfort on Adeem's face.

"I need you to pick me and a friend up. Unfortunately, we're stranded, and you're the closest person to us. I don't really have a choice."

He knew she probably had a million questions, starting with how he'd finally gotten hold of her new number and whether he was looking for Leyla. But she didn't ask any of those things.

As he glanced at the clock hanging on the wall above one of the sheriff's desks, he wondered if Priti had expected this phone call to come someday.

"I can do that," she said. "Where are you? Do you need help getting back home?"

He glanced at Cate. "Clark County Sheriff's Office."

He heard her take a deep breath. "Wow. You, uh, wandered a little far from home."

"Like I said, unfortunately, you're the closest person to us."

Adeem had no idea what the state of the roads would be anymore; most people would have run out of gas by now, unless they'd stocked up ahead of time. For Priti, the drive to the Clark County Sheriff's Office probably wouldn't take long under normal circumstances. Now, though, it could take hours.

And going back home would take days, would take until the end of the world.

Priti would send the Great Eagles vis-à-vis her car: he'd head back to Hobbiton, back to the safety of his office library, and Cate, the raging little dingus, would find some way to fly right into the all-seeing alien eyeball of Alma-uron. Alone.

He gave Priti the address, his throat strangely tight.

"Got it," said Priti. "It's gonna take me a while, so hang tight. I'll leave right now. I'll be there as fast as I can."

Adeem bit his lip and hung up. He looked over at Cate, who was still fiddling with her blackbird key chain while she waited for him to finish.

The radio broadcast in the background had long moved on from local traffic conditions to some breaking news about a mass poisoning of water supplies across the Northeast. He could have sworn the broadcast sounded even weaker than before.

"So who did you call?" asked Cate. She had traded away her key chain for her nails, picking at them mercilessly, though they were barely anything more than keratin stubs.

"My sister's ex." It sounded weird saying it out loud.

"And she's actually agreed to pick us up?" Cate let out an exasperated puff of air. "Is she a saint or something?"

Adeem clenched his teeth and looked ahead.

It was a little past 9:00 p.m. when Sheriff Beeson approached their cell again.

"Your ride's here," he said. Following him was a young brown woman with bruise-colored bags under her giant, round eyes. Her once-long black hair was now cut short, barely reaching her pierced ears, but she still wore dark colors like she had back when she and Leyla were in high school: a dark gray athletic jacket, black leggings, black sneakers.

Adeem remembered his mom asking her over dinner why she always wore those kinds of clothes—*You'd look so pretty in a dress!* she'd lamented—but Priti replied that her own family had bounced around so many times as a kid, she was used to being on the move.

And here she was again: a walking memory.

Priti. That acidic feeling of anxiety chewed harder at Adeem's gut.

"Adi?" Priti asked, hesitant.

"Long time no see," Adeem replied stiffly. He had so many things he wanted to say to her, so many words scrabbling at his throat. But he had to focus. He had to be numb. He just needed to use Priti to get into the city and find another way to get home. This could be easy. Painless, even.

"What the hell happened?" Panic crept into her voice. "You didn't tell me you were in *jail*."

"I'm not." Beside him, Cate became very interested in destroying her nails again. "Not technically, at least. Unless you count charm and intelligence as crimes."

Priti didn't smile; instead, she looked at Sheriff Beeson with narrowed eyes. "You really didn't have to lock them up in a cell, did you? They're kids. That seems unnecessary."

Sheriff Beeson sighed and took his ring of keys off his belt. "As I told them earlier, it was for their own protection."

Priti turned toward Cate with an uncertain smile. "And you must be Adeem's . . . friend?"

"Cate," she introduced herself. The smile hadn't left her

face since she'd come back from a trip to the ladies' room and gleefully informed Adeem that the sheriff's bathroom had free tampons.

"Thank you so much for coming all this way to save us."

Priti rubbed the back of her bare neck. "I'd say it was no trouble, but, not gonna lie, I thought traffic was going to murder me."

She stepped back while Beeson unlocked the cell. As Cate and Adeem filed out, Adeem could have sworn he saw Priti move toward him, as if going in for a hug, but suddenly decide against it. Adeem was glad. He didn't want Priti getting the wrong idea about a reconciliation, even if the world was ending in little more than two days.

Sheriff Beeson led the three of them past a row of desks and blue filing cabinets to a waiting area by the main entrance. "I'll give the three of you a moment to catch up while I get some paperwork ready."

Priti's eyebrows twitched. "Paperwork? Really?"

"Like I told these kids before, if I start getting lax with the law, we get chaos," he replied. "More than we already got. It's just for our records, and I reckon you could use a moment to talk." With that, he stepped away, leaving no room for argument. Adeem was pretty sure the sheriff hadn't been off his feet in hours. Around them, the bustle of other officers and frantic people begging for help finding loved ones they'd lost contact with made Adeem feel like they were in the eye of a storm.

"Ridiculous," Priti muttered. She looked Adeem over. "So? Are you okay? Are you going to tell me what you're *doing* out here so far from home? Do your parents know where you are?"

"Oh, cool, are we gonna do that thing where we pretend to care about each other?" Adeem asked.

Priti flinched. Which, Adeem realized, didn't make him feel any better.

"You're right," she said weakly, her voice almost drowning in the flurry of the sheriff's office. "But I drove through hell to get here, so I think you owe me that at least."

"Owe you?" His head flared with quiet, cold rage. "*Owe you?* You really want to talk about who owes who right now?"

Pull back! Pull back! he could hear his inner voice of reason command.

"I get that you're mad, trust me. You have no idea how guilty I . . ." Priti ran a hand down her tired face. "Just trust me, okay? You don't know the whole situation."

"We can all catch up in the car," Cate suggested, tugging on Adeem's sleeve.

"No," Adeem said, shaking her off. "Please do educate me on this whole situation you speak of, because you, at the very least"—he glowered at Priti—"owe me a freaking explanation."

"Now's not the time, Adi."

"Don't call me that. Don't you *dare* call me that."

"Is everything all right?" a gruff voice belonging to another sheriff called out from behind his desk, observing them with an irritated expression.

"Yeah," Cate answered calmly, "just figuring out transportation plans so we can get out of your hair!" She glared at Adeem. "We've got two days left; we don't have time for this."

"She's right," said Priti. "I know you want answers, but we need to get you *home*. I have friends that are running a shuttle out of Las Vegas tomorrow morning—"

"Just tell me something, okay," Adeem interrupted, "because I'm having difficulty understanding." He was wrong to think he could stay calm. It was Priti, *Priti* who'd helped wedge his family apart. She was a half of a whole problem. And now the words gushed up his throat faster than he could will them down, an inner Wall of Jericho all but crumbling into nothingness. He couldn't stop them if he tried.

"And don't get me wrong, I'm thankful you're helping me now. But you can't just help me now and think that's going to somehow make up for everything. I've waited two long-ass freaking years for you both, and I am not letting you put me on some shuttle back to Carson City without telling me why you didn't have the decency to tell me and my parents what happened to my sister. You of all people knew how close we were.

"But even now, with Alma, with everything happening, you still didn't call. I had to be the one to chase Leyla, all by myself. So why? Why didn't you say anything? Why didn't you *tell me*?"

"Because Leyla broke up with *me*. Because Leyla left home with little more than the clothes on her back, and all she had was me, and we weren't ready for that kind of pressure on our relationship. Leyla didn't want me to . . ." Priti swallowed. "Fuck, just . . . forget it. I should have been better. Is that what you want me to say?"

"No. No, no, wait. What do you mean, Leyla didn't want . . . ?"

Priti stared at the floor and bit her lip. She had the look of someone who'd been caught with a secret that had slipped out of her grasp and writhed on the ground for all to see.

"Leyla didn't want you to know. She thought it'd be better that way."

Adeem slowly blinked away the blur edging his eyesight. It all made sense. Maybe it'd always made sense, but he just didn't want to see it: Priti hadn't said anything only because *Leyla* had told her not to.

Leyla had left with no intention of ever seeing him again. It's what she had *wanted*.

"So it's true, then." Adeem's voice shook. "It was Leyla's idea. All of it. Leaving us, changing her number, making it impossible to find her. She didn't even tell us you broke up, didn't even tell . . ."

He blinked hard. "Leyla really wanted to cut us out for good, didn't she? Was it really better that way?"

"I didn't say that. It's not *like* that."

Pain quivered down Adeem's veins like a viscous, inky-black thing that made his skin itch. "Even me, huh? Even now?"

"Sorry to interrupt." Sheriff Beeson returned, carrying a manila folder than looked unusually small in his ruddy hand. He waved it toward Priti.

"I . . ." Priti sighed. "I'm going to get this crap over with, but . . ." She stared at Adeem with an expression that bore into him so deeply, he wanted to pull Cate in front of him as a shield. But to his surprise, Priti suddenly tossed him her car keys; he fumbled but caught them before eyeing her with suspicion.

As she passed him, following Sheriff Beeson, she gently squeezed Adeem's shoulder.

"Wait." He spun to face her, jangling the keys out in front of him. "What's this for?"

She paused. Her shoulders slumped. "So you can get answers," she said. "I told her I'd give her the space she needed, but that doesn't mean I can't help you now."

Priti shut her eyes for a beat and nodded, as if reassuring herself before continuing. "And, for what it's worth, I'm sorry we hurt you. Leyla had her reasons, and I respected them. I hope you can, too."

Adeem swallowed. Priti seemed smaller somehow. Younger. Adeem had always felt Leyla and Priti were so much older and wiser than he was; a six-year gap was not nothing, and somehow, those years made them less prone to making mistakes. Less vulnerable. And maybe that was too unfair an expectation. Honestly, he wasn't sure what he would have done in Priti's situation. She was older, sure, but she was human. She didn't mean to hurt him. She'd only wanted to do right by the person she had loved. At the end of the day—at the end of the world, even—that was all anyone could ever do.

"There's still no excuse for leaving without saying goodbye.

Unless Leyla's actually an Almaen spy," he grumbled.

"Be kind, Adi. Life's too exhausting as it is to hold on to anger so tightly."

He didn't correct the nickname. "Whatever. I'll stay mad at my sister for as long as I very well please."

"That you will," said Priti, chuckling weakly. "Do me a little favor when you do finally see her, please? Tell her—just, tell her I said hi."

"Tell her yourself."

Priti took a step back and smiled.

"Maybe one day," she said softly, before following a patient Sheriff Beeson down the hall, disappearing behind a line of cabinets.

She was gone. Adeem squeezed the car keys in his fist, savoring the pinch of metal against his palm, and breath came roiling out of him all at once. But he couldn't shake off all the residual anger he'd suppressed for so long. He thought he heard Cate say something like *Earth to Adeem?* beside him, but he couldn't be sure; blood thudded far too loudly between his ears, and her voice was too muffled, too distant, as if she were underwater.

Leyla. *Dammit, Leyla.* Why hadn't she waited? If she'd waited just a few more hours that night, they'd all have calmed down. Their parents could be old-fashioned sometimes, he knew that, but he also knew they'd have accepted her. The worst part about her coming out wasn't that she was gay, but that she'd left. They missed her. That's all that mattered, all that ever mattered. Especially now.

And yet, even with the world ending, she still wanted to leave Adeem alone in the dark. Did it make any sense?

So what about the radio message? Did she actually want to see Adeem one last time? He'd been sure it was her way of reaching out, of telling him she wanted to see him again. But hope was a funny thing. It made him hear exactly what he wanted, and not what the message actually had been: her final goodbye. Her idea of the goodbye that she owed him.

Well, fuck that.

Priti could respect Leyla's wishes, but he was tired of letting his big sister get what she wanted.

He was going to find her.

And punch her in her selfish face.

TWO DAYS

UNTIL THE END

OF DELIBERATIONS

TRANSCRIPT
EXCERPT FROM TRIAL

ARBITER: We must bring our deliberations to an end by Earth's next sunrise. But I must remind you that although we approach the deadline for the Anathogen release, the gravity of this discussion remains.

SCION 12: The sooner we can bring this discussion to a conclusion, the sooner we can begin preparations. Our planet's core is cooling at unprecedented levels; our magnetic field is failing. Time is of the essence.

SCION 6: Then by all means, let us expedite the process by getting to the true question, the one no one dares mention.

ARBITER: Get to it, then.

SCION 6: The true question here is regarding potential. Humanity is a biologically and socially dysfunctional species. They have failed to genetically adapt to the pressures of a globalized society. It is encoded in their DNA to be hereditarily myopic.

SCION 13: That is wholly speculation.

SCION 9: I agree with Scion 6. Even with the knowledge of another sentient species with whom they share the galaxy, the subjects of Project Epoch have continuously proven to be a selfish species intent on their own annihilation. The reality is that the earliest iterations of their species would likely not have survived but for our own interference.

SCION 2: Irrelevant, Scion 9. You bring up a negative claim. My concern is, following this unprecedented rate, how do we know humans will not continue to degrade the composition of their planet's atmosphere if left to their own devices, or worse? This deliberation is about not only the potential loss of an entire species, Almaen and human alike, but the potential loss of not one but two of the rarest planetary systems in the galaxy as a result of our final decision.

SCION 6: Almaens can restore equilibrium on planet Earth. Humans will invariably destroy it. It is as pragmatic an argument as any.

ARBITER: Is everyone in agreement? Or can evidence be provided for an alternative conclusion?

25

CATE

"I still don't think this is a good idea."

Adeem stared ahead and gripped the steering wheel, his knuckles white. "A little too late to complain now."

Cate's heart kept drumming impatiently. She couldn't lean back, instead settling for the edge of the passenger car seat, sitting on her hands to keep them still. They'd been on the road for most of the night, and the tug on Cate's conscience was becoming unbearable. Even if she was grateful Adeem had finally decided to see their journey through.

Earlier, when she'd watched Adeem sidle into the driver's seat of Priti's Honda Civic in the Clark County Sheriff's Office parking lot, she'd been conflicted. Eleven hours stood between her and Roswell—just eleven hours between her and her dad, if she could find him—but a small part of her wanted to grab Adeem by the hem of his hoodie, drag him out, and tell him it was wrong to leave Priti all by herself, even if time was slipping between her fingers like sand.

Whatever grudges Adeem might have against Priti, it didn't feel right.

"Come on," Adeem had said impatiently, avoiding her eyes. "Do you want to get to Roswell or not?" With a click, he fastened his seat belt, locked in his decision.

Cate had stood rooted in front of the hood, tugging nervously at an oily lock of her still unfamiliarly short hair. She wondered what the chances were of Adeem driving away without her. She wondered how long she could cling to the hood of the car if he *did* try to drive away.

"Come *on*," he'd pressed. "If we're doing this, it has to be now."

"But what about her? We're really just ditching her like this?"

"She said it was fine. And besides, what better place for Priti to stay safe than a police station?"

Cate had rolled her eyes. Adeem was being ridiculous, not to mention he didn't even have his driver's license anymore after Alice and Ty had stolen his wallet. It was kind, *too* kind, for Priti to give them this chance—it felt wrong actually taking it.

And yet . . . her legs had moved on their own.

The worst part was the car itself: Priti's car had been meticulously vacuumed, was completely scratch-free and stainless inside and out; it was an older model, but one that was so clearly loved. Cate could have taken it for a rental car if it weren't for the sandwich bags thrown haphazardly on top of the dashboard, filled with snacks like dry Corn Pops, chocolate pudding, and clementines, the easy-to-peel kind. There was even a first aid kit and a couple hurriedly folded T-shirts on the back seat that filled the car with the smell of flowery detergent. Unopened water bottles claimed every available cup holder, and a folded phone charger sat next to the gearshift. Priti had even managed to get her hands on a spare gas can, the bright red container peeking from beneath the back seat.

Guilt flared inside Cate to add another layer of pain in her stomach. Everything in this car, Priti had intended for them. Maybe giving them her car, giving them this chance, had been her plan from the start. Cate silently thanked her.

That had been almost nine hours ago.

Though the moon had swelled to almost full as the night had passed, its light had done little to fade the desert stars, which had seemed to be watching them like millions of cold, pale eyes. Though daylight would soon hide them, the reality was that they *were* being watched, that there *was* life above them, planning. Studying. Judging. The thought made Cate's skin prickle.

Now they were due to pass through Albuquerque by sunrise, and as they soared down Route 66, the twilight sky—a bruised haze of intermingling blacks and blues and purpled edges—was beginning to brighten by the minute. It was painfully quiet. The quiet held an unnatural stillness that frightened her, like the world was holding its breath, suspended in air before its inevitable fall. Maybe Adeem felt it, too, because he reached over to turn on the radio. But most of the channels were dead. Adeem frantically tapped his finger against the channel-changer button until Cate slapped his hand away, telling him to focus on the road. Then, sound: a barely functioning AM news channel. The reporter's voice was half-drowned in the scrape of static.

"The question on everyone's minds has begun to pivot from 'how' to 'when.' I'm talking, of course, about the Message and forthcoming deadline," the reporter began. Adeem let out a sharp breath of air.

"The intercepted September thirteenth missive from the newly discovered planet scientists have dubbed Alma warned that they would give Earth seven days, but as the deadline approaches, scientists are in disagreement over precisely when that judgment is due to be delivered. The consensus has landed on the September twenty-first sunrise, GMT. However, others argue that, similar to the Y2K scare of 2000, we will receive our answer at midnight, the twentieth, and still others believe Alma has its own clock and thus we cannot possibly calculate the exact moment of the message's arrival. Joining us in the studio right now is Jim Horace from the United States Naval Observatory . . ."

Cate dug her fingernails into her car seat. They were down

to less than forty-eight hours. Was Mom listening to the news? Was she waiting to hear from Cate, to hear that she'd found Dad and delivered the letter? She clutched her blackbird key chain, running her fingers against the carved grooves of its wings.

"Your phone's done," Adeem said suddenly. The two of them had agreed to take turns charging their phones with Priti's extra charger, because charged phones with no service were probably still better than dead ones. Adeem yanked her phone off the plug. His own phone, now fully charged, sat on top of the dashboard.

Cate snatched her phone from Adeem's clammy fingers. Still no service. It was stupid to expect anything else. Before her phone had died, she'd had, at best, a bar or two. Cell towers must have been blinking out, one by one, every hour. Still, she checked her texts; it was bad enough she couldn't reach Mom, but getting no word from Ivy, too? Certifiable torture. Her fight with Ivy felt so stupid now. Ivy had only ever been worried for her, and yet Cate had gotten so defensive.

All she could do now was pray Mom and Ivy were safe.

Sweat pooled in the palms of Cate's hands as she squeezed her phone and typed out another message to her mom: **Love you. I'll see you soon.**

Seconds, then minutes passed. She imagined her message floating in the air among hundreds of thousands of other frantic messages, all going nowhere. Her chest ached with every moment of silence. When a tiny red exclamation point appeared on her screen, confirming the message couldn't be sent, Cate put down her phone. The whole world was turning into a dead zone.

With less than two days to hunt her dad down, and still no cell phone service, how was she even supposed to find him? Her head hurt the more she thought about it.

She wanted to roll down the window, but she'd only get a mouthful of dirt. She'd do anything to feel the San Francisco sunlight on her skin, just one more time.

As she leaned her forehead against the cool glass of the car window, she pulled out her bucket list from a pocket inside her wallet. Even seeing Ivy's handwriting right now was a balm.

Adeem noticed her movements. "What are you doing?"

"Need a pen," she said, unfolding the paper. "Should probably add 'grand theft auto' to my bucket list."

"Ah yes, the infamous bucket list. Didn't expect you to actually have a physical list." He smirked. "Also, for the record, we didn't steal Priti's car. She offered it willingly."

"Yeah, well, it sure didn't feel like she had much of a choice, the way you were glaring daggers at her." She opened the glove compartment with a click and shuffled through some papers: Priti's car insurance, a car manual, receipts from auto repair shops. She began emptying the compartment, searching. She had to pass the time somehow to keep herself from imploding, and working on her bucket list, on all the things she still had left to do, was strangely comforting. Before, the idea of a bucket list had made her feel empty and unfilled, but now, it lit a fire inside her.

"So? What else's on your list there?" asked Adeem.

"Finding Dad," she read. "Petting puppies, as you remember. Also sneaking out to a party, seeing the world—nothing too exciting. Yet."

"Wait, what's the one you skipped?" He peered over her shoulder for a moment. "Did that one say *kiss someone for real*? You loser. As opposed to, what, kissing someone *falsely*?"

"Shut up and drive," she muttered, blushing as Adeem laughed. She briefly wondered if Adeem had ever kissed someone. He was probably more likely to kiss his radio.

She finally found a pen, hidden inside a small green hardcover book in the back of the glove compartment. "Bingo. Now I can add 'Kick Adeem in the balls' to my list, too."

Adeem's laughter abruptly died.

"What? I wasn't serious. At least, not entirely—"

"That book."

The way he said it made Cate suddenly feel nervous. She examined the book as though it were made of glass. The words *Classical Urdu Poetry* in small, gold calligraphy adorned the deep green cover. She opened to a random page and skimmed. "'If nothing else, we have at least dared to dream of dawn, / That which we'd never glimpsed, to that place our gaze has gone.'

"It's beautiful," Cate uttered.

"That book is my sister's," Adeem said incredulously. "But

why does Priti have it?"

"Maybe Priti bought a copy of her own?"

"No, there's no way. My dad got it from Pakistan for her as a gift. It's not easy to get. See that tea stain on the front?" He gestured toward a faded brown blotch at the curled bottom pages of the book. "That's Leyla's, all right."

Cate gently laid the book on her lap. "Maybe Leyla lent it to Priti?"

"But Priti and Leyla broke up," said Adeem, shaking his head, "and if Leyla *actually* let Priti borrow it, the first thing Leyla would want is her book back. That thing is precious to her; it's the only thing she took from home when she left."

"Unless they *didn't* break up? Or," she added softly, "they still love each other." After watching Priti talk about Adeem's sister, Cate was convinced Priti still had feelings. And if that book was so precious to Leyla, then what if she'd left it behind as an excuse?

"I don't know." Adeem's voice was thick. "It doesn't make sense."

Cate opened her mouth to ask what he meant when a blur of color on the road, barely noticeable in the nighttime darkness, distracted her. "Watch out!" she screamed.

With a string of curses, Adeem slammed the brakes and swerved the car; they nearly careened into a crowd of people standing by a roadside gas station. They tore through patches of shrubs and bumps in the sand before coming to a halt.

"What the hell was that?" Adeem asked, breathing hard.

Cate tasted hot metallic liquid in her mouth; she had bitten her tongue. Her blood was pumping too fast. She threw open the door and hopped out of the car. As she took a couple calming breaths, she looked to her surroundings, or at least, to what she *could* see in the dark. A couple signposts along the way had warned them they were about to pass through some big national forest; a dark line of trees in the near distance cast a jagged shadow against the ink-stained sky. At the edge of the forest, where they were now, sat a run-down truck stop, and twenty or thirty people were filed in some semblance of a line to use it. But the truck stop didn't appear open; it only had a machine to fill tires, which had been smashed in, and two gas pumps with bright yellow *Out of Order* signs plastered on the side. As for the attached mini-mart—too small to be called anything but a hut, really—it was a mess of broken windows illuminated by a single flickering streetlamp.

Then she saw it: a pay phone. One that, judging by the line of people beside it, actually worked.

Adeem appeared beside her. She grabbed his arm excitedly.

"I can try Mom again!" She'd tried calling the hospital from the police up in Clark County, but no one had answered, and eventually the sheriff had come around and ripped the phone away, saying they had to keep the still-working lines open as much as they could. But now she'd have another chance. She could make sure her mother knew she was all right, and get her dad's full name so she could actually stand a chance at finding him in time. She dug through her wallet. "I have seventy-five cents—wait, no, make that eighty-two cents. I think that should be enough."

"Look at this line! We'll be here waiting all night," protested Adeem.

"The sooner I find my dad, the better chance we have of getting back home before it's too late, right?"

Adeem hesitated.

Before he could answer, Cate was already moving. "Excuse me," Cate called out as she walked the length of the line. "Is there any way we can maybe cut in? I need to call my mom. It's an emergency."

"Everything's an emergency these days," a young man in a camo hat retorted. He was probably fourth or fifth in line. "You'll have to wait in line like everyone else."

"I don't think Ranger Rick is going to let us butt in," Adeem whispered behind her.

"So, what, we just give up?" Cate said angrily. "Jesus, you have, like, the least drive of anyone I know."

A woman standing behind the man with the camo hat gently placed a hand on his shoulder. "Come on, they're kids. If you won't be kind now, when will you ever be?" She waved Cate over. "You can take my spot."

Cate beamed. "Thank you, ma'am!"

"You just have to promise me you'll pass on good karma," the woman said with a wink.

Cate made a mental note to add that to her bucket list, too.

Ivy would be proud if she knew. If only Cate ever got a chance to talk to her again.

The wait to use the phone wasn't as long as she feared; maybe a lot of them weren't getting through, or, like Cate, they'd already blown off most of their money, left with nothing more than a couple quarters—only enough for a short phone call.

Or maybe it was just hard for people to find the right words to say with only two days left.

Cate glanced behind them; it'd only been thirty minutes, but the line to use the phone had grown, with several dusty vans and RVs now parked beside Priti's car. So many people with bags—the kind to carry things in and the kind beneath their eyes. And even more had brought young kids, as young as toddlers. Where were they all going? Were they all headed to some makeshift sanctuary like Sunfree? Or were they all on a journey to find something, or someone, lost?

Cate shivered. The desert became unbearably cold during the nights; San Francisco hadn't built her for anything below fifty degrees. Another reminder that she was far away from home. That if they didn't hurry, she'd never see it again.

"Your turn, Cate," Adeem said softly beside her. His face, cast in shadows, looked even more gaunt than usual, like the exhaustion had whittled at his cheeks.

She nodded slowly, dazed.

A week ago, the idea of calling her mom in front of all these people would have terrified her. Once, during a math test,

Mom had called her, trying to stay calm but unable to hide the panic in her voice because she'd misplaced her medication—and maybe did Cate know where it was? But when Cate snuck into the girls' bathroom to comfort her mom, cradling her phone close to her chest, half the softball team walked in. She hung up on Mom without a second thought. She'd been so mortified at the thought of one of the girls overhearing her conversation and spreading rumors about her and her mom, she spent the rest of the school week tense and on edge, as though a million eyes were watching her.

She'd been so, so stupid.

Cate stepped toward the pay phone. "Are you sure you don't want to call your parents first?" she asked Adeem.

"Nope," he said, sheepish. "Not really in the mood to hear my parents crying at me. Or asking if I've been accepted to MIT yet. Low drive, remember?"

"Right." Even exhausted half to death, Adeem was stubborn as always.

"Anyway, we don't have enough quarters for that."

That part was true, at least. Next time they came across a phone, though, she'd *make* him call his parents. Even if they had to beg for more quarters.

Nervous butterflies rammed against the inside of Cate's stomach as she dropped in a few quarters into the pay phone, hovered her finger over the keypad, and dialed the number she'd copied onto her cell phone. After a few rings, a woman's voice answered: "Saint Francis Memorial Hospital, psychiatric unit." Her voice strained against the background noise in the hospital.

Cate nearly dropped the phone; a tiny sob of relief escaped her throat. God, phones were magical. She couldn't believe she was talking to someone back home, someone who might have been only a few feet from Mom. Even though she was in the middle of the freaking desert, hundreds and hundreds of miles away.

She gripped the phone tighter. "I'm trying to reach my mom," Cate explained, her voice shaky and thin. "She—she was admitted a few days ago in the unit. Molly Collins? She's a patient of Dr. Michel's."

Someone screamed in the background, a doctor or nurse maybe, issuing frantic commands, before a sharp beeping overpowered them.

"Let me transfer you. One moment, please."

With a click, an elevator jingle, cheerful and light, began to play on the other line, which felt all levels of absurd considering Cate was standing in the middle of nowhere, Arizona, in the middle of the night, filthy and dehydrated, with a bunch of strangers and Adeem.

Cate closed her eyes. *Mom.* Her one and only mom. It felt like forever since she'd heard her voice. She'd been trying so hard not to think about how much she missed her. But now she could let everything around her, like Priti's car, and the stupid desert, and Alma, just fade away, and in this moment, she could just be Cate Collins again: a normal high school girl who just wanted her mom despite it all, despite everything.

The jingle stopped. Had they been disconnected? She panicked. And then—

"Catey?"

"I'm here, Mom." Relief and longing poured through her together. Cate squeezed her eyes tighter, but they ached, heavy with warm tears that threatened to spill. "It's me."

"Oh God, I was so worried, I thought I'd"—static interrupted, making her mom sound robotic—"again. Where are you? Ivy tried to fill me in, but—but I don't understand."

Ivy? Had Ivy visited Mom at the hospital? Her heart clenched at the thought.

Cate quickly wiped her nose. "You broke up a little there. I'm okay, I'm safe. Are you safe? What about Ivy? Are they treating you right?"

There was silence on the other end of the line. Then the undeniable sound of muffled crying.

Cate's eyes opened. "Mom?"

"Where—you?" begged her mom, her voice barely carrying over another surge of static. "Catey, I need you *here*."

Cate took a breath. "Mom, I'm heading to Roswell. I'm trying to find Dad, remember? The letter? I just need his full name, I'm so close—"

A loud, robotic screech emanated from the phone, so sudden that Cate ripped the phone away from her ear and cringed. "Hello?" she asked when the sound finally faded.

"I'm so sorry." Cate heard something like a sob on the other end. "I—I can't remember. I'm trying to remember what happened—I can't. I need you."

"What do you mean?" Cate clung to the phone now, as if it were the only anchor left in the world to her mom. The wind whipped at her hair and stung her eyes, forcing the tears to leak down her cheeks.

The phone beeped.

"Hello? Mom? Mom!"

The dial tone blared against her ear.

Cate let the phone dangle from its cord. Her vacant-eyed reflection stared back at her in the metal side of the phone booth. She felt sick. Mom had sounded awful. And what did she mean, she couldn't remember? Did she not remember calling the police, going to the hospital, anything about that night?

Or did she not remember giving Cate the letter for her dad?

Cate bent forward, suddenly feeling dizzy, and hugged her stomach. Her mind swirled with dark emotions she couldn't understand. She couldn't believe how horribly she'd misread the situation. If she'd just taken the time to *think*, she would have stayed home or with Ivy, where she'd be safe, where she'd be near her mother. But instead, she'd ditched her mom when her symptoms had been flaring, when she'd been enduring one of her hallucinations—when Mom needed her most.

Cate should have known better. This really was all just a wild-goose chase.

Unless . . .

Unless some part of her had been looking for an excuse to run away.

She swallowed down the metallic feeling tingling in the back of her throat. That woman at Ataputs said she'd *known* Dad. He *had* to be in Roswell. Maybe Mom was alone and scared right now, but finding Dad would ultimately help her. Help them both. She had to believe. She'd been clinging to it. There was nothing else *to* cling to.

She had to believe that this would all be worth it.

Or else she might just break.

"What happened?" Adeem asked, reaching out an arm to her.

"The call died," Cate answered weakly, leaning into him, suddenly having a hard time standing upright.

Adeem helped her move out of the line. Someone else had already grabbed the phone and begun dialing their own call. "Maybe we'll find a place with cell service again," he said soothingly, rationally. "Or even a satellite phone—that could totally work, too. God, I wish I still had my radio. But don't worry, we'll find a way to reach her, okay? Come on, Squidward. We're so close. We got this."

His voice was soft. Cate looked at him now, really looked at him, and realized that somewhere along the road, she'd begun to trust him, fully and utterly. Or maybe she always had, since the moment he'd found her huddled in his car in the church parking lot and asked if she was okay. And for whatever reason, he seemed to trust her, too, even though she'd done nothing but make mistakes. He was no Ivy, that was certain; where Ivy was ambitious and self-assured, Adeem was nebulous and lost. Maybe as lost as Cate was.

But maybe right now, he was exactly what she needed.

26

JESSE

Jesse's head was broken.

Maybe his mom was right: he had a concussion. He should've eased up on the painkillers. He should have had that nap he'd told Corbin he was going to take.

As if he could sleep.

He couldn't rest—and he couldn't *think*, either; his thoughts meandered aimlessly between the crevices of his brain, spelunking so deep into the darkest depths they were never heard from again. And worse, when he did finally grasp a thought, it was all numbers.

Numbers! Him! The kid who fell asleep in Algebra II while sitting in the first row! If he hadn't known any better, it really was the end of the world.

First, the time: 10:03 a.m. The last time he'd properly slept: forty-eight hours ago. Customers he'd served and messages he'd transcribed in the past twelve hours straight (in part because sleeping was a lost cause): fifty-eight, with no end in sight. Price per message: fifty dollars, raised to make up for the thousand dollars he lost at the urgent care center. The decibel levels of sound due to the nearby growing tent city: five billion, give or take—he didn't know how decibel levels worked, but whatever. Times he'd heard fireworks/vehicle crashes/random explosions: seventeen.

Number of nonpaying customers Jesse had to chase off: six, including none other than Tom Ralford, distributing cards for his UFOs & U radio channel.

Channel your regrets and transitory wishes into lasting change! Tom had declared. *From now until the end, only UFOs & U is offering the chance to send your messages to the people you care about, free of charge!*

Jesse just shook his head. *Too late to use your dumb radio channel now, Tom.* The way he figured, if it took the world ending for people to reach out to their loved ones, then they'd never loved them anyway.

He pushed his mind back to the numbers, such as the number of steps he'd taken toward Tom before the guy pulled his embroidered safari hat farther down his face and skulked off: two.

Times Jesse could have sworn he'd seen Marco's fisty friend

in the crowd: three. A reminder that at least *some* numbers would soon no longer need keeping track of, like the amount of dollars he'd have if Marco's friend got his way: zero.

For now, though, the numbers went on and on and on, dancing like a bunch of Alma-loving revelers around his burning skull. Lack of sleep was affecting him more than he'd thought.

But he didn't mind taking messages. Some of his customers were suckers—hopeful nutjobs, maybe, but not *all* of them were bad; some, Jesse *enjoyed* talking to. A lady from Illinois brought boxes full of graham crackers she'd pilfered from a Walmart; she was making s'mores over a tiki torch and handing them out to people in line for free. Jesse hadn't had one since he was a kid, when his mom had taken him "camping" in their backyard. An older man from Portland even donated a secondhand, but exceptionally powerful, generator to make sure the machine stayed running. "This machine's too important to let die," he'd insisted. Jesse was almost touched.

Most important, taking messages gave him an excuse to get out of the house. For at least a little while, he could pretend he was a normal kid with a relatively normal summer job (even if it meant pulling all-nighters)—a summer job that just happened to include seeing the worst and weirdest of humanity. He could forget that he was out here because his mom wouldn't leave her bedroom and he couldn't figure out how to comfort her. He could forget that he was out here because

Marco's friend was going to take everything he had because he was a giant fuckup.

He could forget the itch in his ribs. The need to see Corbin.

Maybe that's why he couldn't stop thinking about numbers. They were a defense mechanism against his thoughts of Corbin.

Either way, the numbers kept up their stubborn dance behind Jesse's eyes, and now he kept making typos. His customers were starting to notice.

He'd just finished typing one such message.

"Does this look good to you?" Jesse asked, turning the screen toward the customer, a young guy/skinny chihuahua hybrid with bulging eyes and a shaking frame, probably not much older than Jesse.

The guy brought his face close to the screen, and his nearly nonexistent lips narrowed as he read. "There's a typo here." He pulled away, tutting indignantly. "Her name is spelled *C-e-c-i-l-i-a*, not *C-e-c-i-l-i*. You haven't sent it to Alma yet, right? I want them to protect my Cecilia—I don't even *know* a Cecili."

"I'll correct it right away," said Jesse, rubbing his heavy eyelids.

"Cecilia deserves to be safe, do you understand? Cecilia Eaton. She's—she's everything to me. And I can't have you typing it wrong and Alma protecting the wrong person."

As if Almaens, if they existed, could. As if they *would*.

"Of course, I totally understand," assured Jesse. "I know you want to protect her. I get that. We'll get the message out there."

The guy folded his arms across his chest. "So, how much does this cost again? Because my little brother, Louis, came three days ago. Said it was twenty bucks."

"Fifty dollars for one message."

"Is that right? Because I could have *sworn* Louis said it was twenty—"

"Prices go up with inflation. And thanks to Alma, things are inflated."

"Even for a fellow classmate? I went to Roswell High—you went there, right?"

The vein on Jesse's left temple throbbed. He was done feigning politeness. "Honestly? Even if we did go to school together, I have no clue who you are. But lucky for you, now Alma does." With a loud hum and whirl from the machine's drive, two white ultra-perforated sheets of paper printed from a narrow slot. Jesse picked up the papers: two copies of the guy's message for his beloved Cecilia with the same message translated in binary beneath it, and instructions for him for when to pick up Alma's response, if they "deemed his message worthy" of one.

"The machine's encoding." He put away his copy to keep and reached out a hand toward him. "Fifty dollars, please."

"Fine," the guy said coldly, snatching his copy. "You weren't exactly a ball of sunshine in stats class, either. Just seems a little wrong to charge so much for something people *need* right now."

His voice was dripping in sarcasm, and Jesse almost laughed. If only he knew. Hope was pricey.

Fighter jets rumbled overhead like storm clouds; airspace was still closed to commercial jets, but the sky had never looked more crowded with glittering red lights. Jesse's customers looked up, too; hundreds of faces of people lined up from the shed to his mailbox and down his neighborhood street. Some sitting in lawn chairs, still drinking last night's cheap beer though it was morning now, their faces in a tight, nervous grimace as they awaited their turn with the machine. Others stood in their worn, dusty sneakers and lumpy hiking backpacks they refused to set down, probably for fear of their belongings getting snatched away.

And all of them with desperation etched into their faces like raw scars.

As the guy fished out the cash from his wallet, Jesse's eyes trailed to his house, to Mom's window. Sure, to the people in line, Jesse was some benevolent kid hacker who'd snatched NASA's Almaen language code for public use, charging only a small fee—okay, a relatively small fee—to help them send their messages. To them, he was trying to make people happy, provide comfort in these potentially final days.

But then, what about Mom? Her window curtains were drawn. Maybe because she was sleeping in today. Or because she didn't want to look out the window and see him.

This machine was supposed to be for her, for their fresh start in California. For *them*. What was the point of all this effort if she was too disappointed in him to even accept his help?

No, that wasn't even right anymore. The machine was supposed to save them from their debts—debts that were all his dad's fault. But now the machine would barely pay off Jesse's own debts to Marco.

He was an idiot to think he could ever be of any help to Mom.

Like father, like son.

Something caught Jesse's attention—a shuffling in the crowd, someone shoving their way through like a rogue tide—and for a moment, his heart soared up his throat to choke him: Was it Marco's friend, coming to collect early? As Jesse's panic bubbled over, it was clear *someone* was desperately clambering through the lines to reach him; heads bobbed as they were knocked over by some invisible force. Could he get away with hiding a portion of his earnings from him, quickly, before he showed?

He heard the panting first, saw the hands reach out from between two tightly knit bodies of the next customers in line, then:

Ms. K emerged, stumbling, her hair sticking up in more directions than Jesse thought possible.

"Um, hi?" said Jesse, surprised. Lack of sleep was screwing with him worse than he thought.

"Cell towers down . . . pissing me off . . ." She heaved.

"Oookay . . . ?" When he decided she wasn't a sleep-deprivation-induced hallucination, he asked, dreading her response, "Do you need something? Water, maybe?"

He hadn't expected her to show up at his house. He hadn't even had a chance to explain everything to her. She'd made it clear she knew about the machine, but she still didn't know the circumstances, and what if she called him out on his bull-shit just to make a point, right here, in front of everyone?

He sighed inwardly. He was being stupid. Even he knew Ms. K was too nice to pull something like that.

"I saw Corbin . . ." She swallowed. "At the hospital. Mari's in surgery."

"What?" The world suddenly swayed around him.

She just nodded. "It's not good, Jesse. I tried to calm him down, but . . ." Ms. K chewed her lip. "I really think you could help him."

"I . . ." A sudden chill bit at Jesse's skin. He gripped his scarred wrist tightly through the cuff and squeezed; it cracked from typing all day. What the hell had happened to Mari since he'd last seen her? The thought of her going through something like cancer . . . the thought of what that must be like for her whole family . . . it just didn't seem fair. People like Corbin and Mari, people like his mom: bad shit happened to them all the time, when they hadn't done a thing wrong—like goodness was a lightning rod, meant only to attract bad luck. There was no justice in it. How could anyone explain it?

He wondered if that's why his old man had been so horrible. In Jesse's experience, bad things rarely happened to bad people. Maybe Dad had had the right idea.

But he had to stay calm. He couldn't let his emotions get the better of him. He couldn't *afford* to: he only had two days to make enough money to be acceptable to Marco's friend, who was still watching him closely. Any less than at *least* a couple thousand, and he'd know Jesse was holding out on him.

Jesse stopped fighting the chill that crept up his chest and let it swallow him whole. "I can't," he said evenly.

Ms. K recoiled like he'd suddenly spoken in tongues. "You can't? Can't or won't? Jesse, I don't want to force you to do anything you don't want to do, but please, think about it. The machine can wait. I don't want you to regret not being there for him, and I know you're scared, but this could actually be a chance for you to open up, let someone in." She took a step closer. "And he could use a friend right about now. You're the closest thing he's got here."

Jesse smirked. "That's the stupidest thing I've ever heard."

Instead of looking angry, as he would have expected her to, Ms. K only looked hurt.

"People are in surgery all the time," he continued, keeping his demeanor cold as steel. "If Corbin can't even handle that on his own, how the hell does he expect to handle the rest of Mari's treatments? Or Alma?" He beckoned the next customer over with a flick of his wrist. "I have more important things to do here."

Ms. K opened her mouth to say something, then closed it just as quickly. Her fingers fumbled at her neck to grab her crescent moon necklace. She closed her eyes and took a deep breath, the same thing she told him to do before he said anything he might regret.

"Jesse," she said finally, her voice pleading, "I need you to know I care about you when I ask, What on earth do you think you're *doing*?"

Jesse swallowed and turned his back to her.

He wished he knew how to answer.

It was strangely warm for September. All that panic in the air, maybe. Jesse took off his leather jacket and tossed it over a scraggly bush by the shed. He had just finished counting his earnings—he'd made $3,900 just since last night, the most money he'd held in his hand.

He should have felt happier. Accomplished. But he didn't feel anything at all.

This sun was almost at its peak, and he was sweating through his clothes. The neighborhood had lost power about an hour ago, so Jesse decided to use the donated generator that had been powering the machine as a phone, radio, and battery charging station for anyone who needed it—for a nominal fee of twenty dollars every five minutes, of course. While someone volunteered to try and procure another backup generator for the machine, Jesse took the opportunity to finally give himself a break—after all, mankind had yet to invent a *human* power generator, and the lack of sleep was finally getting to him. He'd resume, he promised his remaining customers, just as soon as a new power source was found. For now, he was locking up, and he was finally going to take that nap he so desperately needed.

Many of his customers complained they had no time to wait anymore, but for now, most of the line had miraculously disappeared to do whatever the hell it was people did before they thought the world would end. Break shit. Or sing campfire songs under the water tower next to Hangar 84.

Jesse reached for the first padlock on the shed to lock up; rows of locks and chains hung down the side of the shed like metal vines, glinting in the newly emerging sunlight. He paused. The paint on the shed had once been close to nonexistent, having peeled off throughout the years and storms that relentlessly chipped at it. But the customers who'd begun spray-painting the shed had managed to finish an entire mural, mostly when he wasn't looking. He'd meant to stop them earlier, certain they'd just drawn a bunch of crudely rendered dicks. He was wrong. Upon closer inspection, he now saw the intricacies, the love and care that went into their art. He was entranced. A giant silver-and-gold UFO ornamented the entire side of the shed, gilded with glitter that caught the light, while on the other side, smiling faces stared back at him: realistic portraits of famous people, like Malala and Mr. Rogers, Anne Frank and Albert Einstein, and several others he didn't recognize.

These people had accomplished something with their lives. Made the world a better place. And now he had to look them in the eyes, all while pretending to be something he wasn't: someone who believed in humanity. Someone who cared. Someone that Corbin and Ms. K wanted Jesse to be.

The worst part was the spray paint above the shed door. White wings outstretched, a dove stared up toward the sky. A symbol of peace between the alien UFO and the best of humanity.

Jesse laughed bitterly. It would have been far more appropriate to put a crow.

Once, when Mom had forced them out of the house for some father-son bonding time at the Spring River Zoo, Dad had finally explained why he'd sewn the strange crow patch on his leather motorcycle jacket. They'd been standing outside the wolf exhibit when Jesse admitted they were his favorite animals, and Dad had tutted disapprovingly.

"Everyone knows crows are the best," said his dad, his pale yellow grin wide against his thick black beard. "Crows are tricky bastards, so smart that they can get other animals to do their bidding. Even your gullible little wolves get fooled by them all the time."

"How . . . ?" asked Jesse, though he was almost afraid of the answer.

His dad bent down low to meet Jesse at eye level and whispered conspiratorially: "They lead wolves to the prey they can't kill themselves. And the wolves, well, they're stupid enough to listen. The crows wait for the wolves to take the bait, and once the wolves make the kill, the crows chase the wolves off to keep the fresh meat for themselves."

Jesse imagined sharp beaks and talons digging into the wolves' skin, wolves that were no doubt already tired and weak from the hunt. "That doesn't seem fair."

Dad only laughed, then tapped at his crow patch on his jacket. "It's a crow-eat-dog world, J-Bird. You'll learn soon enough."

When Dad died, Jesse had no choice but to learn. Sure, crows manipulated. Crows deceived. But crows also *survived*—it was their trickery that *kept* them alive. It was what Jesse had been doing: leading people here, to Roswell, while they were none the wiser, only to steal from under their noses.

Except now, he didn't hear the sense in it. All he heard was that his thoughts were starting to sound more and more like Dad.

Fucking *Dad*.

This was all because of him. This entire mess. Being stuck in this shithole town. His whole *life*. It was all a failure. The only real shock was that Dad hadn't run off on them sooner.

Mom liked to insist to Jesse that "you always have a choice, in anything you do," but sometimes, people didn't have choices.

Suddenly, Jesse wasn't tired anymore. He was burning. He was on fire with anger.

Suddenly, there was a craving in his fists.

Come on, J-Bird.

The hammer was in his hands before he had time to think much about what he was doing. Thoughts—plans, schemes—were what had gotten him here. Maybe it was time now to let himself go, let himself be free. Destroy the lies.

Break something.

Maybe break everything.

He wondered, wildly, if this was how the folks up in Alma—if they even existed—felt about Earth. That it was all just a dressed-up joke, a failed experiment, a big fat lie, full of promises never meant to come true.

He wanted to break something the way that Ms. K's eyes looked broken when she looked at him earlier—from disappointment or worry or fear, he didn't know and it didn't matter.

Break something the way his relationship with Mom was, who'd left so much unspoken, dead words long abandoned on the kitchen linoleum floor.

Break something the way Jesse had broken his chances with Corbin, all because he couldn't allow himself to taint someone so fucking good. The kid was smart—how did he not see what a loser and a liar Jesse was? Why did he keep coming back? Couldn't he take the hint?

Well, maybe now he'd get the message.

Pressure built in Jesse lungs and joints, choking him like water. The doors to the shed protested with a sharp creak as he yanked them open. The muscles in his forearms rippled in anticipation, and he moved as if controlled by some invisible force.

The first hit was so hard, the force of contact reverberated through his aching bones. The crash was deafening in the stale quietude of the shed. The beautiful white metal façade of his machine, his own personal Frankenstein, now had a giant crater, and Jesse hit it again and again until it started to look like the moon. Soon, the shed floor was littered with nuts and nails and glass and metal pieces. It felt crazy. It felt almost good. Sweat trickled down the side of his face. Maybe it was tears. He couldn't tell the difference.

He smashed the computer screen in.

He hit it until his biceps ached and his shoulders cramped.

He hit it until he had nothing left to give, until he fell to his knees, heaving. He wasn't crying—not really—he was panting, but the breath tore through his throat like angry fire. He felt dizzy. When had he last eaten? Maybe he was going to die here, right next to his dead joke of a machine. Maybe that was the greatest and cruelest joke yet—maybe the world wasn't going to end, only *his* world.

He remembered this feeling. This tingling numbness that was beginning to descend over him like a welcome blanket—eerie, silent, yet deafening. It was the feeling of giving up. Of being *done*.

Only as he swayed forward, he noticed something sparkling . . . something caught between the shed floorboards. He blinked.

He wiped sweat from his eyes.

He reached out, yanking the thing—a piece of paper?—from the cracks, and smoothed out its edges.

No, not just paper.

A Lucky Star Lotto ticket.

Unscratched.

Like a sign.

Jesse gingerly wiped the sweat that had collected on his upper lip.

He brought an unsteady finger to the silver glitter at the bottom of the ticket and scratched.

WINNER—$5

His laughter cut through the shed. His chest hurt, but he laughed so hard, he almost lost his balance, and had to hold out a hand on the shattered machine to keep himself steady.

Was this the sign? Was this all that was left of hope? Five bucks.

But then:

A creak at the doorway killed his laughter.

They'd come. They'd come for their pay. When he turned around, he prepared for the worst. Another beating—maybe this time one that would send him to his grave.

Instead, there was just a figure standing at the entrance to the shed with his hands stuffed into his pockets, staring at Jesse.

Corbin.

"Jesse," he croaked, his eyes filled with fear. "What are you doing? What have you . . . ?"

Jesse was still on his knees on the floor, the scratch card in his hand, the hammer—and remains of his machine—scattered around him.

"Why are you here?" he demanded. His voice scraped through him, raw. Hurt. "You're supposed to be at the hospital."

"I was"—Corbin's eyes trailed down, resting on the hammer, then back to Jesse—"but Mari's in the operating room. They're putting in a stent now, so there's nothing else I can do but wait." He was speaking fast. Nervously. "Ms. Khan said she told you, but, I guess you were . . . busy. Which sucked, because, you know, where else was I supposed to go? Except the strange thing is, I found myself really wanting to see you. At first, I thought I was being silly; I mean, I barely know you; we only went on *one* date together, and with the apocalypse and all, does it even count? But then I thought, Maybe that's exactly why it counts, and before I knew it, my legs just . . . brought me here."

Corbin swallowed and took a step closer.

Jesse went stiff. "Leave. Please."

An uncomfortably heavy silence smothered the air around them. Nothing but the rhythmic thud inside Jesse's chest.

Corbin didn't leave, though. Instead, he inched forward again, hesitantly, letting the hot sunlight leak into the depths of the shed, sending dust swirling and dancing through the air.

"Jesse," he whispered.

"Leave," Jesse tried to say, but his voice shook.

"No." Corbin stood his ground. "Jesse, listen. Listen to me. People rely on this machine. They need it—they need *you*. And I do, too. So tell me what's going on. Please."

Jesse stared at the scratch card, at the hammer, at the pieces of metal now glinting in the streak of sunlight.

"When we first met," he said, "you asked me if my machine worked, and, well, in a way, it does. Or did. It worked in the sense that it ripped people off and took money from those stupid enough to believe aliens would find them worth listening to. *That's* how it worked."

Corbin's eyes slowly searched Jesse's face, but the usual smile in his eyes, like a gentle, flickering flame, had dwindled to cold, ashen embers.

Jesse had always been good at reading faces. He knew how to put on a mask, how to manipulate his own face to get other people to read him wrong, so he knew what to look for in other faces, too. But Corbin was different. So beautifully, frustratingly, painfully different.

"Jesse," Corbin said, "I knew the machine didn't work. I mean, how would you know there are actually Almaen satellite receivers in orbit? How would you pick up their messages through all that cosmic background radiation? It just didn't make sense. And I'm probably not the only one who's figured it out. But that's not the point."

"What?" Jesse felt sick with shame and embarrassment. He hated how easy it was for Mom and Ms. K to see right through him—to see the flaws and fears he tried so hard to hide—but now, to hear *Corbin* confirm he'd seen through him, too, made Jesse feel like an outright fool.

He'd almost have preferred Corbin telling him from the start that he'd known the machine was a fraud. At least it would feel better than Corbin going along with it all, like a game of make-believe. Like Jesse was a child.

Corbin's eyes softened. "You wanna know why people believe in you? It's because hope gives people something to hold on to. It makes them feel better. It gives them a reason to keep fighting. People need hope right now, Jesse. Desperately. And there's nothing wrong with that."

Jesse chuckled darkly. "There are some things hope can't fix, Corbin. Maybe it's time you learned that." *He'd* learned it the hard way. He'd been stupid enough to believe the machine would be enough to save him and Mom, save their house. But false hope never saved anyone.

"I know." Corbin's voice cracked. "But isn't that the point of hope? And faith, even? That you have it and you hold on to it and you protect it, even when it's impossible? Isn't that when you need hope the most? You can't blame people for wanting to feel better."

"But I *can* blame you for lying to a little kid to make her believe talking to aliens is somehow going to cure her," Jesse snapped. "Holding on to false hope is going to hurt you both." He'd stood up and was brushing off his jeans. "I did you both a favor."

The punch came so fast, Jesse felt more shock than pain. He

stumbled, catching the edge of what was left of the machine to hold himself upright. His cheek burned.

Jesse pressed a hand against his face and stared back at Corbin, slack-jawed and silent.

Corbin was breathing hard. "I don't know *what* your reasons were for putting on this whole scam of yours," he growled, "and I don't know what the hell changed. Let's be real, you wouldn't tell me if I asked. But just because things aren't going your way does not mean you get to pull the rug out from under everyone. Just because *you've* lost all hope doesn't mean you get to throw out hope for all of us."

Jesse's eyes burned. "You have *no* idea what I've gone through." The scars on his wrist seemed to tingle with remembrance.

Corbin grabbed him by the collar of his shirt, and Jesse suddenly didn't know if Corbin was going to kiss him or knee him in the gut. Their faces were so close. Corbin's voice was husky, his smoky vanilla scent pouring over Jesse as he said, "My sister is barely hanging on to her life, and I refuse to let you disappoint her just to clear your own conscience. Got it?"

Corbin's usually perfect hair was disheveled and greasy around the bangs, and his eyelids were swollen. Jesse clearly hadn't been the only one to pull an all-nighter. Except Corbin had been by Mari's bedside all night. And Jesse was standing here whining to him like a selfish asshole.

"Let go of me," Jesse said slowly.

Corbin did, and Jesse was almost sorry when he took a step back. Despite everything—despite the fact that he had just punched Jesse in the face—it had felt good to be so close to him. So close to somebody.

No, so close to *him*.

Jesse fussed with the small buckle on his leather cuff.

"You know, the worst part of it all," said Corbin, "isn't that you were profiting off people's hope. It's that you look down on people for having any hope at all."

Jesse clenched his fist. It hurt. God, his words hurt like hell.

He had wanted to tell Corbin about just why he'd needed to make the HECC machine. He wanted to tell Corbin everything: about his dad, about their money troubles. About his scars. There were probably a thousand things he could say to fill the space between him and Corbin, words with warmth and weight. But he didn't know *how* to tell him. Or maybe he did, but he was too afraid of what would happen. Didn't Corbin get it? Good things leave you. You can't get attached.

"If you feel that way, then why the hell are you wasting your time?" Jesse asked—he was angry, and he was also curious. "Why are you still here?"

Corbin shook his head slowly. "Because I know you're better than this."

"No, Corbin, I'm really, really not."

Corbin had moved farther away. Now he gripped the door frame of the shed, edging farther into the light, becoming hazy at the edges. "You *are*, Jesse," his voice said. "I have to believe it." Corbin threw him one last unreadable gaze. "I have to."

Then he was gone.

27

CATE

"This is it," announced Adeem.

Roswell emerged in the distance, unceremonious and unwelcoming.

After they'd left the abandoned gas station and its endless line for the phone, Cate and Adeem had barreled through the morning daylight in Priti's car, untouchable on the empty road—though Cate had half expected at every turn that some new disaster would hit them. An accident. Another cop. The gas tank running out, even after using the spare gas can. Or even that Alice and Ty would somehow reappear to accost them again, take what they'd forgotten last time.

But now, as they reached their destination, Cate felt a shift in the air, like they'd entered some sort of invisible bubble that muted the low rumble of the car engine beneath them and the brush of sand against their tires. The feeling made her skin bristle. She should have been relieved, but if anything, she was nervous.

They were . . . *here*.

Cate had never been to Roswell before—she'd never even been outside California—but she certainly knew of Roswell's quirky reputation. She was prepared to find metallic UFO statues suspended in air, signs proudly indicating various crash sites, graffiti murals on shop walls depicting alien abductions—the usual silly props all over the place. Aliens had always been the status quo.

Instead, a blockade of police vehicles greeted them at the town's border, and Adeem had to swerve out of the way of an overturned electric-blue car lying on its side in the middle of the road like a beached whale. An officer directed them to leave Priti's car behind at the blockade alongside several other abandoned cars, parked beside an electronic road sign that had been hacked to say *BELIEVERS WELCOME*.

She didn't like it one bit. Leaving behind Priti's car was the equivalent of leaving their one and only lifeboat. Dread brought an aching in her chest.

"The tent city's blocked up all the main roads inside," one of the officers had told them. "No one's going to drive off with your car anyway, not with the roads being the way they are and us being right here."

At the very least, he *sounded* right: although Roswell seemed dead at its edges, if Cate strained her ears, she could hear the faraway hue and cry of a crowd huddled at its epicenter, like the beating heart of the town itself. And after they passed the cement police barricades, the deeper into the town they went, the louder the sound grew, and the more the streets filled with clamoring bodies and tents. But the music was nothing like the shitty dance music at the party with Jake. It was *live* music, the ebb and flow of an orchestra, and they found an entire street blocked by orchestra players clad in black tuxedos, sitting in rows of chairs with their eyes closed in deep concentration as they played in the street like it was the most ordinary thing in the world. She found herself enraptured by the sight, until Adeem gently tugged her shirt and mouthed something to her that looked a lot like *Time*.

The officer at the blockade had pointed them to a pay phone a couple blocks away, just outside an abandoned auto shop called Keller's. The place was a mess of graffiti and broken windows and cracked cement, but the pay phone still worked. Cate pulled out a couple extra quarters she'd found in the glove compartment of Priti's car and slipped the coins inside the slot. She tried not to cringe as she dialed; the buttons were sticky, and she didn't want to begin guessing with what.

Adeem waited patiently a few feet away, his back turned to her, allowing a million worries to race through her mind, echoing in the quiet spaces between the ringing.

A bead of sweat rolled down her spine. At first, she'd thought to call Mom again at the hospital. But after the last conversation, and how much it had upset her mom, she decided to take a different route. A harder one.

The phone kept ringing. She slipped her hand into her pocket, gripped the letter against her palm. All of Cate's worst fears raced through her mind: What if she wasn't home anymore? What if something had happened to her and her family?

What if Cate never got a chance to say she was sorry?

Cate closed her eyes and tried desperately not to cry.

"Hello?" a voice called out to her.

Cate squeezed the phone tightly. "Ivy," she breathed.

"Jesus. Cate?" Ivy's voice went up ten octaves. "Please tell me that's you. Please tell me you're not calling from an alien spaceship."

Cate bit her lip and nodded. "Yes. It's me. I'm alive."

"Cate. Oh God, Cate, I'm so, so freaking sorry. I was such a dick to you. I love you so much, and I want you to know that I never ever meant to hurt you. Our fight at the casino—it was so stupid and I miss you and everything is on *fire*." Ivy was spilling words faster than Cate could keep up.

"Slow down, you dummy. I should be apologizing to you," said Cate, wiping her eyelids. How had she ever been mad at her best friend? "I know you were only trying to protect me."

"A lot of good *that* did," said Ivy, irritably. "Did you at least make it to Roswell?"

"Yeah." Cate glanced at Adeem, who a few feet away was talking with some people carrying hiking backpacks. "With some help. Lots of help. But I don't have much time—I'm on a pay phone. Have you seen my mom?"

"I've been going to see her every day," said Ivy. "My family was supposed to hide out in freaking Alcatraz. There's some underground tunnels or something there. Supposedly safe. Relatively. But I convinced Mom and Dad to let us stay at home, somewhere familiar, ya know—so we're in our basement. I guess it was the right move because it's forced Mom and Dad to talk to each other. If we survive this, I think they might actually try counseling. I don't want to jinx it, but . . . baby steps."

"Holy crap, Ivy." That was the first bit of good news Cate had heard in what felt like forever.

"I know. They even came with me to check on your mom. But the hospital stopped taking visitors last night, after the power got spotty. I guess they're in lockdown mode now. They're not taking any chances."

Cate's jaw clenched. If the hospital was on lockdown, that at least meant her mom would be safe. Hopefully.

"Don't worry," Ivy went on, as if reading Cate's mind. "She'll be fine. My mom's already thrown a bunch of medical malpractice jargon at them to make sure of it."

"And you? You're all safe?"

"Us Huangs are tough." Cate could imagine Ivy winking. "Probably also helps that the hospital's walking distance from our house, and my mom's got a couple of cop friends who escorted us last time we checked on your mom."

Cate closed her eyes, blinking back moisture. Ivy was the best. She'd never fight with her again.

But first, priorities: Cate had less than two days left, and she still didn't even know her dad's last name. Even if she broke into the county clerk's office and had an infinite amount of time to search through all those files, there were probably a hundred Garretts in town.

She could feel it in the air. She was so close. She just needed some kind of hint.

"I need you to tell me if she said anything about my dad. *Any* information that can help me find him."

Nearby, she heard the shattering of glass, like someone breaking through a window. A dog barked frantically.

"I'm sorry." Ivy sighed. "She didn't really say a word about your dad. And, frankly, I didn't ask. She didn't exactly seem in the mood to talk, Cate. I think she's really worried about you. So many people have already had to evacuate the city; my parents and Ethan just finished packing to head to Lakeport. I think your mom just wants you home safe."

Cate's chest tightened. The thought of Mom, alone in the hospital, calling out for her only daughter made guilt flood her all at once. But Cate knew what was best for her mom. The time apart was only a temporary hitch. Finding her dad would be good for both of them in the long run.

If there *was* a long run.

"I know," said Cate in a strangled voice. "But I'm already

here, and I need to make sure this trip wasn't a waste. I mean, she never even had a chance to tell him about me. I can give her that chance."

"Are you really sure this is about what *she* wants, Cate, or about what *you* want? What *do* you want out of all this?" Ivy's voice was quiet but pointed.

Cate tugged at a tendril of her hair, her confidence melting. She'd never really thought about what *she* wanted. Adeem had once praised her for helping her mom find Dad: *Even if it's just for your mom, you're still trying to bring your family back together. Even when everything feels hopeless.* Sometimes, Mom herself had to push Cate out the door, begging her daughter to live her life like a normal sixteen-year-old. Most of the time, Cate would sneak back inside through the window, unless Ivy was there to drag her away.

But what *did* Cate want? To be reunited with a long-lost father who didn't even know she existed? An apology for all those years Cate and her mom were left to fend for themselves? Or maybe she just needed someone to pat her head and acknowledge how hard she'd tried.

She wasn't so sure anymore. Maybe she'd never been.

Cate swallowed. "My time's running out."

Silence on the other line. Then, "Okay, just . . . come home soon, okay?"

"I promise."

"I saw Jake Owens, by the way," said Ivy, suddenly remembering. "He and his family rented an RV to get out of town, two days ago."

"Oh," said Cate. A week, a lifetime—it still wasn't enough to make memories of Jake any less gross. "Ew."

Ivy chuckled. "But it hit me then. He never deserved to be on your bucket list. You were way too good for him." Her voice softened. "I hope you know you're too good for anyone."

"Except you."

"Yeah. Except me."

A warm tear rolled down Cate's cheek. "I love you, Ivy."

"I love you, too."

Her hand trembling, Cate hung up with a click. A siren warbled in the distance.

She wiped away dust and tears from her face with the hem of her sleeve and took a deep breath. She had to be strong for Mom. She had to be strong for her because, for better or worse, that's who Cate was: stupidly, stubbornly dutiful, until the end. And that was okay. Living for her mom wasn't such a bad thing. She loved her.

Maybe sometimes you had to live for someone else until you learned to live for yourself. Sometimes, they could be one and the same.

"Did you get a name?" Adeem looked at her worriedly, his warm brown eyes gentle.

"Not yet," said Cate. "But I will."

28

JESSE

In Jesse's experience, a quick nap cured anything.

But this time, he woke up to find his pillow damp, his lip still throbbing, and his chest empty, aching for breath. It'd been the worst nap of his life. Also, his last. His last *here*, at least.

That didn't mean much, though. It wouldn't have been the first time he'd woken up with a headache like he'd been beaten senseless. If he was lucky, it meant that his little "rage against the machine" was some kind of paranoid stress dream, that he'd imagined it all.

And yet, the stacks of paper he'd printed containing every single one of his customers' messages to Alma took up all the meager space on his desk. *Those* were real.

Which meant everything he'd said to Corbin was real, too.
Jesse was never lucky.

He'd heard something like the crack of gunfire outside. It must have been what had woken him. After the week he'd had, he was surprised he wasn't used to it.

He sat up slowly and held his head in his hands, trying to steady his breath. His brain wheeled in his skull.

When the frantic beating in his chest subsided, and the rush of blood in his ears quieted, he craned his neck to listen. Not gunfire. Someone was banging on the front door. Again.

Jesse trudged downstairs, and the steps creaked beneath his bare feet, though he could hardly hear it over the chanting of his name and the impatient banging of fists against doors and windows, all fueled by a desperate need for his now-broken machine. It was midafternoon, and the din of people from the tent city, hovering around the padlocked shed, was overwhelming. The noise outside was almost enough to tear the house down. Maybe that was the point.

And in the midst of it all sat his mom, sitting at the kitchen table like it was the most ordinary thing in the world. Except she had a faraway look on her face and a lit cigarette between her fingers. He hadn't seen her smoke since the funeral they could barely afford. Thin gray fumes wafted like dead trees to the yellow-stained ceiling. She was wearing her old, faded bathrobe covered in tiny blue flowers. He'd bought it for her back when he had a job at the hotel gift shop. He didn't remember it fitting her so loosely back then, though. Even her face was all sharp angles and lines, weathered from years of disappointment.

She drew on her cigarette, surrounded herself in her own little cloud.

"We're out of bread," she said.

"Should I steal some for you?"

"No." She almost looked amused.

"You should get somewhere safe." Jesse double-checked the locks, closed the blinds. Another crash outside. The snapping of wood.

"Now, you know I can't leave you all by yourself," she said, killing the stub that remained of her cigarette. "We're family. In case you forgot."

That stung. But Jesse deserved it.

"I destroyed the machine," he said.

His mom looked up at him and said nothing.

"It's just a matter of time before people find out." He swallowed hard, like he had stones wedged in his throat. "And I don't want you around when they do."

His mom's eyes flickered with something Jesse couldn't recognize.

Outside, the banging of wood was rhythmic and unrelenting. Some people—locals or outsiders, he couldn't tell—left his neighbor's house in ruins the other day for fun before driving off in a stolen golf cart spray-painted black and green. He almost wondered what they'd do to his. Set it on fire, most likely. Or maybe Marco's friends would feel so bad for him when they came to collect, they'd back off and everyone would leave him and Mom alone.

Wishful thinking.

Suddenly, his mom pushed her chair back with a screech and stood.

"Well, guess I better hurry and pack my things."

"Wait, just like that?"

She approached him, her worn-out slippers brushing against the linoleum floor. She put her hand on his cheek. Her hand was warm. Jesse felt a little shy beneath her stare. Like he was a little kid again.

"They've opened up Goddard as a safe house," his mom said. "I'll be safe."

Goddard was a planetarium a half-hour walk from their home. He'd been there a couple times for elementary school field trips, but he'd never really paid attention to the presentation; in the safety of the dark, starry beads of light floating overhead, he'd been too busy staring at Vance Wagner, his first crush. He'd gotten beaten up for it, too. The thought made him sick with shame now. He'd fallen in love so many times not even knowing what the hell love was.

"What about you?" she asked, her shaking voice betraying her outward veneer of calm. "Or am I not supposed to ask?"

Jesse smiled sadly. "I have some stuff to make up for. But as soon as I'm done, I'll come find you."

She tapped his cheek before pulling her hand away. "Better late than never. Just make it quick, 'kay? I want to spend some time with my boy."

"Okay."

He watched his mom begin to climb the stairs back up to her bedroom. She looked so thin from behind. It made his chest ache.

"Hey, Mom?" Jesse scratched his wrist nervously.

She paused. "Hmm?"

"I'm sorry." *And I love you.*

Her warm eyes crinkled. "I know."

The UFOs & U HQ was a crudely built extension behind Tom Ralford's house, painted an uneven black and made with reclaimed materials, mostly pilfered from a school construction site. Jesse only knew this because he was there when Tom first launched UFOs & U a year ago—before his big breakdown and subsequent resurrection of the channel—right in the middle of a group counseling session. He had pulled out one of his portable radios, tuned in to some random channel, and filled the room with the sound of the *X-Files* theme song. He beamed brighter than a young mother showing her newborn to the world. The rest of the session involved Ms. K trying to get back on track, her voice barely carrying over Tom's overly detailed explanation of how and why he launched a radio channel dedicated to "the rich alien lore" of Roswell. Jesse had laughed his ass off.

Being at Tom's house now made his stomach curdle with guilt.

Jesse's heart drummed unsteadily as he pulled down his hood; he'd worn it beneath his leather jacket to blend into the crowd as he escaped his house and ran to Tom's, carrying a wheelbarrow he'd found in the back of the shed before the crowd had arrived and filled with about twenty pounds of paper, as well as all the money he'd made from the machine, tucked inside a leather knapsack. The last thing he saw behind him was a man with a green bandanna covering his face, approaching the shed with something that looked like a lit glass beer bottle. An image that would haunt him for the rest of his life.

He was still trying to catch his breath.

Mom had already packed her things and snuck out from the back of the house. She was probably already halfway to Goddard Planetarium by now.

Which left only the messages to deal with. And Marco's friends.

He knocked on Tom's front door. If he knew Tom—and he did—he'd still be home. He wouldn't leave Roswell, even if he could. Even now. Tom wasn't a coward.

"Tom?" Jesse called out. "Tom Ralford? It's me. Jesse. From counseling."

Silence. The shuffling of feet. Then a gruff voice from behind the door said, "You mean Jesse from the machine."

"Hey, that'd be a good band name," said Jesse amicably.

"But yes. I'm Jesse, formerly of the machine. I was hoping you'd give me a chance to talk to you."

The door pried open an inch, and Jesse caught Tom's beady eye staring back at him.

"Talk about what?"

"Your radio. Believe it or not."

Tom's eye narrowed to a sliver, as if considering.

"I've got a lady friend over. You can try again tomorrow." The door slammed shut.

Jesse groaned. He leaned his forearm against the door. "Tom! Please?"

Again, silence.

"Tom!"

Jesus, how many people had Jesse pissed off?

"Tom, I think he gets the point," a familiar woman's voice sounded from behind the door.

The door opened once more, this time to reveal Ms. K.

"Sorry about that, Jesse. What are you doing here?"

"What the hell are *you* doing here?"

"I just stopped here on my way back from the hospital." She looked at him meaningfully. "Mari is out of surgery."

"Oh, that's . . . good."

Ms. K smiled knowingly. "She's stable, in case you were wondering. Corbin is very relieved. So then I came here to see if I could get a message back home. Tom's one of the only ones left in town with a working radio channel—well, maybe 'working' is a bit of a stretch. But we're trying to fix it in case the others need to use it. And he's got a generator."

"Funny you should say that," Jesse said, "because I also need to use the radio."

"Tell him I have a rifle!" Tom shouted from somewhere inside the house.

"You do not have a rifle!" Ms. K retorted. She turned to Jesse. "Shouldn't you be with the machine? What's going on? Where's your mom?"

"Mom's fine. And the machine . . . it's gone." If she knew how he'd hammered it to death, and barely escaped with the jacket on his back and a wheelbarrow full of wishes before his former customers and/or Marco's friends probably set the shed and his house on fire, she'd sit him down on a couch and ask him how he felt about it. "My machine wasn't exactly built for the people I need to reach, anyway."

"Who do you need to reach?" asked Ms. K, looking confused.

Jesse slipped past her and went inside, dragging his wheelbarrow behind him. The UFOs & U radio station had walls painted black to match the outside, but Tom had left the carpet a hideous green plush covered in what Jesse hoped were coffee stains. The back wall was taken up entirely by a thick wooden table with layers of weird blinking devices and boxes and radios. Tom had two matching computer monitors, both showing a screen saver that was some kind of cat slideshow.

A red-and-black *ON THE AIR* sign hung from the ceiling, but it was off. For now.

This was it. This was Jesse's chance to make it up to all those people he'd conned. He'd promised he would send out their wishes like messages in a bottle. It was time for him to keep that promise.

Just because you've *lost all hope doesn't mean you get to throw out hope for all of us.* Corbin's words still echoed in his head, raw and undeniable. Jesse was so tired of taking out his hopelessness on others.

Tom was sitting on a chair, his arms folded across his chest. A circular black microphone held by a skinny metal support attached to the table floated above his head like a halo. Tom was pouting.

"So, Tom, you got any open slots on your radio?" Jesse lifted the first stack of paper from his wheelbarrow. "Because I've got a ton of messages to send out, and I'm going to need some help."

29

ADEEM

Adeem swayed. The sun burned overhead, hazy and terrible and blinding. He sat down on a curb.

"Don't you dare sit down!" There Cate was in a second, pulling on his arm. "We are down to the wire, and my dad is still out there somewhere. Not to mention your sister. We don't have time to rest."

Cate was adamant about continuing their search—she was downright buzzing with renewed energy.

Adeem, on the other hand, had reached the point of exhaustion where his blood throbbed with a fever heat, even worse than that time he'd stayed up for a forty-eight-hour game jam. He wasn't sure if he was fully conscious anymore, or maybe now he was a ghost, or a tiny corneal floater beneath Alma's watchful eye, destined to be scooped up with an alien Kleenex and tossed into the trash void. But it wasn't even the exhaustion that was killing him. It was the nervousness. His sister was near. Breathing the same air—theoretically. Anger had powered him through before, the sheer desire to punch Leyla for ditching him, but now he was *here*. He couldn't believe they'd actually made it this far. He'd barf if he had anything in his stomach.

To think he'd gotten this close, only for his body to betray him in the last twenty-five hours. How did that poem go again? *So dawn goes down to day. Nothing gold can stay.* He'd actually paid attention that time in English. Poetry reminded him of Leyla, after all.

Adeem rubbed his eyes. Cate's determination was practically making her glow.

"I don't want to *die*," Adeem said. "I get that we have a time limit and all, but in case you didn't notice, for better or worse, we are still *human* with human bodies and human *needs*."

"Why do you have to say it so gross like that?" said Cate, scowling. "What do you think we should do, just snooze our way through the freaking apocalypse?"

It was probably the delirium setting in, but Adeem almost laughed. She sounded like a little kid throwing a temper tantrum. He wished he could meet her mom and shake the woman's hand; they could swap stories and share a good chuckle.

The thing was, Cate had been able to nod off a bit on the long drive, but Adeem hadn't had a full eight hours' rest since three *days* ago. Cate, being from San Francisco, had never driven a car before and decided their luck had been too bad to take unnecessary risks, so it couldn't be helped. But Adeem had never been more tired in his life.

Besides, his legs and feet ached; Cate's had to as well. And his skin felt like it was sizzling.

He and Cate had spent *hours* in the sun today, asking strangers if there was a government building still open, or a place to go to find missing loved ones. But most people laughed at them and said they had enough problems to deal with. Not to mention a group of kids stole an army tank from the military academy, wreathed it in Christmas lights, and crashed it into the country clerk's office.

He wanted to find Leyla and Cate's dad, but it was starting to feel like they were better off finding two guppies in a giant ocean blanketed with an oil slick and set on fire.

A siren blared in the distance; volunteers with megaphones were shouting instructions along with directions to nearby fallout shelters all around them. Somewhere, he was pretty sure the orchestra they'd seen earlier was performing Beethoven's Fifth.

Midnight tonight would mark the start of the final day.

"Just"—Cate rubbed her temples, exasperated—"stay here for a second, okay?"

"Happily." Adeem rested his chin in his hands. His head

pounded. His eyes struggled to adjust to all the movement and color around him. His ears hurt trying to pick up threads of sound from the cacophony. There was just too much of it. He wasn't used to any of it. He wanted to be home, in the quiet dark of the library, surrounded by the gentle hum of his computer.

A few feet away, a group of people was huddled around a small portable radio, their ears glued to a staticky news broadcast from the State Department.

Adeem felt a surge of envy. He missed his radio, too; he'd never been this disconnected from the wider world for this long. At least he'd left it behind with Rosie. It was probably safer there than with him.

Down the street, a small white van had somehow managed to maneuver through the crowd; the back of the van was wide-open, and people were distributing hazmat suits throughout the tent city. They barely had enough for twenty, maybe thirty people, from the looks of it. Others had to settle for improvised gas masks made of plastic water bottles. Adeem wasn't even sure if any of it would protect them from whatever Alma had planned. That was the worst part of Alma's warning: no one knew what to expect.

Adeem suddenly felt cold. And vulnerable.

It was real. All of this was real, and really happening. Little more than twenty-four hours dividing humanity from destruction. Sixty miles dividing humanity from outer space. He wanted to kick himself for not taking the chance he'd had earlier to call his parents. Like a stupid coward. Now they were probably still huddled in the unfinished basement of the mosque, surrounded by other families less broken than his—and that was the best-case scenario. He wasn't even sure where they were.

God. He'd been so focused on the journey itself, he hadn't even taken the time to accept that the world might really end.

Behind him, the radio news broadcast went on: "The White House today has issued guidelines for protective measures, and suggests staying indoors and in basements. Fallout shelters have been designated in all major cities . . ."

"Hungry?"

He looked up, flooded with sudden joy and relief. Cate was back. It felt like she'd been gone for several rotations of Earth. But she was back. And not only that, but she was holding two water bottles and a couple granola bars wrapped in paper towels.

"They're homemade," she said, handing him one of the granola bars, "but the lady who gave them to me assured me they weren't laced with anything."

"Oh my God," he said, snatching a granola bar and tearing into it. "May Allah bless you, you sweet angel." He swallowed and felt the weight of the food nestled comfortably in the emptiness of his stomach.

After a moment, he realized she was still standing.

"What's up?"

She sighed. "I just feel like we're no closer than we were

at the start of the day. It doesn't help that most people here aren't even from Roswell—no one has any idea who Garrett is. I keep trying to describe him—Mom said he had dark hair and eyes—but, you know."

"So do thousands of other people."

"Exactly." She sat down beside him, finally, and they finished eating in silence.

He didn't know what to say to give her hope.

He was too tired for hope.

He hated how he'd taken his own parents for granted for so long. Parents who were healthy enough to support him, even with all his idiosyncrasies and indecisions.

"I showed someone my mom's letter," Cate said at last. "And they told me to beam it to Alma." She snorted. "I guess my odds are just as good at this point that he's actually an alien."

Adeem scratched his chin. *Odds.* Odds were something Leyla loved to talk about.

Odds. Hope. Leyla.

Odds. Hope. Leyla.

Finally, it occurred to him. "Maybe we *do* need to find my sister here."

Cate stared at him. Then, slowly, a smile bloomed across her face, and she reached out to hug him. He was surprised that he didn't mind.

"So you're ready to see her, then? Even after what Priti said?"

"Honestly, I'm not sure. But, I'm thinking, if anyone could

help us find your dad, it's her." His mouth was so dry, he could feel his tongue expand the moment the water bottle touched it. "We need her."

"But how are we going to find *her*?"

"A friend back home told me she got a job at a counseling center. Maybe we could find a clue there."

It wasn't much of a lead, but it was the only one they had.

According to one of the only locals they'd found roaming through the tent city, the closest counseling center—and the only one in Roswell—was called La Familia Crisis Center, about a forty-minute walk from where they were now on North Main Street.

Or it should have been forty minutes. But navigating through the crowds and taking detours to avoid the more dangerous-looking roads, where people were shooting off fireworks and setting fires and bashing in windows, set them back over an hour.

Alma hadn't even done anything yet, and already people were falling apart at the seams. Almost like they were proving Alma's point. It was getting harder and harder for Adeem to convince himself they were better than this.

When they finally reached La Familia Crisis Center, the sky had gone gray and whispery with dusk. What little hope Adeem had had before promptly burned down to ashes. The small, tan, boxy building had been splattered with graffiti, and the door was nothing but a jumble of glass on cement.

Broken beer bottles scattered the sidewalk leading to the entrance, and one of the trees had been ripped clean out of its roots; they had to step over it to reach the remains of the door. Adeem thought he heard music, too, coming from inside, but he couldn't tell for sure—there was so much noise everywhere, it was impossible to filter.

"You still have the pepper spray?" Adeem asked. He didn't want to go inside. His heart slammed hard against his ribs, making his breathing shallow. What if Leyla had been caught up in all the destruction? What if she was hurt? He didn't want to imagine. But it was all the more reason for him to keep going.

Cate nodded, looking as nervous as he felt, and pulled the pepper spray out from her bag.

Together they went inside.

A thin layer of smoke tinged the air. Dirty shoes had trekked dirt and sand all over the gray carpeted hallway. His parents would have had a fit. A couple of overturned plants contributed to the mess on the floor—these, Cate quickly turned back to their rightful place.

The music inside grew louder: a woman's voice, melodic and calming, undulating like gentle ocean waves on a hot summer day. But there were no screams, no moans—nothing that would indicate they were in any sort of danger. Nothing but the music.

Adeem stopped walking. "Cate?"

"What?"

They'd reached another door labeled *MULTIPURPOSE CHAMBER* at the end of the hall.

"I think we're safe here. Relatively."

Cate lowered the pepper spray. "Why do you say that?"

He slowly opened the door. "Because they're playing Enya."

A group of at least fifteen people were arranged in a circle around a small bonfire, contained by chunks of cement and debris arranged in a ring. They sat on yoga mats, their legs crossed, and their hands together at their hearts in prayer. The room was dim, lit only by the flickering fire, and smelled entirely of lavender and sage.

It was . . . strange, to say the least. Like Adeem and Cate had entered some kind of magical vortex existing outside the confines of time and space. It was probably the most ordinary thing they'd seen since arriving in Roswell.

One of the people by the bonfire, a young man with a bun at the top of his head and a long, rumpled beard that almost covered his concave bare chest, opened his eyes. There was a tiny brass gong to the left of his feet.

"Greetings, friends," he welcomed them. "Please, stay with us a little while. This is a sanctuary for the lost and afraid."

Adeem and Cate stood awkwardly at the doorway, unsure of what to do.

"Thank you, but we're kind of in a hurry, actually," explained Adeem, clearing his throat. "We're looking for Leyla Khan. Do you know her, or have you maybe heard of her?"

The young man unfolded his hands and placed them on his knees. "Leyla . . . Leyla . . . that name sounds familiar."

"You should pray," one of the others chimed in, an older woman with long black hair that reached the floor. "Send your message out into the universe."

"Or perhaps they could use the Hewitt Electronic Communication Center?" added another.

The bearded man shook his head. "Unfortunately, it's been destroyed."

Adeem wondered if that was the alien communication machine Rosie had mentioned.

"But the name Leyla Khan *does* sound familiar . . . If she comes around here, we will tell her another soul searches for her."

"Sure," sighed Adeem.

After checking a few other rooms, they had come up with nothing. They found an office, but the entire thing had been turned upside down, and if there were any files or documents, they were gone, or ripped to shreds. No sign of Leyla anywhere. Besides the eclectic group of meditators, and a couple dead goldfish left behind in a broken fish tank near the lobby, the crisis center was completely empty. It was almost ironic, considering the entire world was in a crisis. The place should have been swamped.

Adeem dragged his feet toward the exit. He felt numb. Blank. Like nothing but static was left in his head. Why couldn't anything go their way, just once? Was this the kind of divine punishment Ty thought he deserved?

Where are you, Leyla?

Suddenly, footsteps bounded behind them.

"I just remembered." It was the young man with the beard again. His baggy orange pants barely fit around his waist. "Leyla Khan, you said, right?"

"Yeah . . ." said Adeem, hesitatingly.

The man pointed behind them. "There. That poster."

He was pointing to a large purple poster board that hung crookedly on the wall. Metallic, bubbly letters spread across the top of the board spelled out, *Working to Care for You!* And beneath that were several photos of counselors, smiling back at them.

Adeem searched frantically. Jessica Shaw: Marriage Counseling. Linden Lucas: Rehabilitation Counseling. Taylor Griffin: Substance Abuse Counseling.

Leyla Khan: Mental Health Counseling.

His breath hitched.

There she was. The picture had been taken midlaugh; her mouth was wide-open, showing rows of straight white teeth Mom had had no problem reminding her had cost a fortune at the orthodontist. She looked darker, and her hair was longer than he remembered, but in the picture, it was tied up in a horribly messy nest. She still wore that crescent moon necklace Priti had given her. There was a handwritten quote beneath the picture, too.

"Never lose hope, my dear heart,
miracles dwell in the invisible."
—Rumi

It was her handwriting.

His sister. She was here. She was right *here*. Adeem felt his knees buckle with relief, but Cate gently held his hand and squeezed.

"We'll find her," Cate whispered.

Adeem closed his eyes and squeezed back.

When they got back to the tent city, Adeem was shocked to find the orchestra still playing, though it looked like some of the musicians had traded off with others who'd brought their own, less traditional instruments for a classical orchestra, like banjos, and homemade drum kits made out of plastic bins and bottles. He also noticed a new, albeit small tent structure that definitely hadn't been there before, suspended between two lampposts; someone had spray-painted the words *TENT CITY LIBRARY* in neat, flowy cursive across its canvas side. A woman sat outside the makeshift library's entrance, a Carl Sagan book in her lap, eating from a tan MRE food ration packet. Among the inevitable fire and brimstone that came with knowing humanity only had a little more than a day left of its existence, Adeem hadn't exactly expected to find spots of beauty. Or relative calm. With raw music casting a warm filter over the prophetic bleakness of night's descent, it almost felt . . . hopeful. Though it probably helped that there were soldiers from the nearby military academy with rifles slung over their shoulders, hawk-eyed and silently watching from their posts around the tent city. Adeem shuddered to imagine the state of cities like New York and San Francisco.

"Now what?" asked Cate.

Adeem ran his hand through his soot-covered, oily hair. It was a good question, but he had no idea *how* to answer.

The radio broadcast was still going. The owner of the radio, a thin, balding man with round glasses, turned at the knob and scrolled through different channels. Adeem rested his gaze on the radio and let his eyes blur at their edges. For a moment, he thought he'd fall asleep, right there, standing.

Until he heard a voice.

"Testing, testing . . . This is the UFOs & U channel, your local source for all things alien and, now, all things human. We're out here with Jesse Hew—I'm sorry, folks, I'm being told he would like to stay anonymous. But I'm here with a special guest, and today, we'll be on the air with your messages, locally, and soon, internationally. As soon as we find out how. But as soon as we do, prepare your earbuds, because love, my friends, is on the air. Stay tuned."

Adeem turned around suddenly.

His brain buzzed with a thousand thoughts at once. Of *course*. Radios still worked. Hell, they were the only things that still worked. Maybe he didn't have his radio on him anymore, but his portable radio wouldn't have been enough to reach Cate's dad and Leyla, anyway. He needed a bigger rig, something like Rosie's. A rig like a radio station. He knew how to make an internet radio station, and though he'd never used a radio station before, he'd figure it out.

Leyla had reached him through the radio. Radio could help him again.

"Hey, Cate . . ." said Adeem, slowly. "Any chance your dad would be the type to listen to the radio?"

"I wouldn't know, but I imagine everyone would be listening to the radio right now. Why?"

He grinned, his chest flooding with a much-needed swell of energy.

"Because I think I have a plan."

ONE DAY

UNTIL THE END

OF DELIBERATIONS

TRANSCRIPT
EXCERPT FROM TRIAL

SCION 12: If we disable the Anathogen virus, Earth itself will be rid of humanity in due time, and rid itself of any chance we have to restore the composition of its atmosphere back to a hospitable state. We are at risk of losing our best chance at a new habitat, all in the name of continuing a project that has long proven to be a failure. Our choice here is clear.

SCION 4: We have conflated their value for far too long. Humanity arose as an accident of evolution. Who is to suggest such an accident will not happen again?

SCION 11: Even so, such a mutation is exceedingly unheard-of.

ARBITER: We are far beyond discussing the value of humanity. We must come to a decision.

SCION 7: Indeed. The problem we face is not simply finding a solution that helps us sleep at night. The problem we face is deducing a solution to finding a home where we may survive. Project Epoch is but a single factor; our best chance, perhaps, but not our only chance to find a new Alma.

SCION 3: Alma may be old and weary, but I am proud of our home. It has sustained our people and allowed us to reach levels some on Earth would call godlike. Almaens may boast of no disease, no war, and no corner of the universe left unexplored. We have accomplished far beyond what humans can possibly comprehend. But we must face the fact that now, our people are our home. What gives us the right to storm the home of anyone else?

SCION 13: And for all their faults, humans are imaginative and creative and capricious and full of possibility. I am curious to see what they do. I believe they deserve the chance to show us.

SCION 6: At what cost?

SCION 13: The same cost we all must face one day.

ARBITER: Are we closing in on a decision? We have but hours left to disable the Anathogen.

~~Dear~~ Alma:

Ms. Khan says sometimes putting thoughts to paper can help sort out your feelings. Laying down tangled strings, she calls it. I call it bullshit. But I figure I'm full of bullshit anyway, so what have I got to lose? Gotta sit here anyway, since Tom won't let me help with the radio.

Anyway, I don't think you exist. I don't think there are aliens out in the universe, and if there were, I don't think they'd give a damn about what us humans do out here. I don't even know if God exists.

And if you did exist, you probably wouldn't care about me, anyway.

But in case you do, or in case you're watching, or in case you're mad at me because I made a dumb machine that supposedly talked to you, I just wanted to say thanks.

Sometimes, it feels like no one's watching me at all. I guess it was nice to feel like I mattered, if only for a little while.

So I'm going to make things right. Maybe that'll matter in its own way.

J.

30

CATE

Adeem worked fast—relatively speaking, considering the end of the world was coming even faster. Maybe it was the prospect of being able to use a radio again, or maybe it was because they were in the eleventh hour, but before Cate could come up with a better idea, Adeem was already fighting his way toward a group of people around a portable radio, inspecting the radio, and jotting down some numbers.

It was all Cate could do to follow and keep up.

A little past midnight, they were standing in front of a seemingly ordinary house: olive-green panels, a flat green roof, peeling white-painted windows. Small—not much bigger than a trailer home. But modest. Cozy, even. Except that the roof was covered in antennae.

"That radio station broadcasts from here," Adeem explained.

"Why does that not surprise me?"

Jets soared overhead. Apparently, Roswell had an air force base, and Cate was beginning to realize why so many people congregated here, of all places. With a military and air force base, and a history of alien encounters, maybe Roswell was actually a relatively safe place to hunker down.

"So, what, we go in, and you borrow their radio?"

"That's the plan."

Adeem took a deep breath and knocked on the front door. No one answered.

A crash followed by a scream resounded in the distance; Cate couldn't tell whether it was a scream of terror or one of bliss.

Probably terror.

"They were just broadcasting, so I know they've got to be home." Adeem chewed the inside of his mouth and began walking to the side of the house.

"Please don't tell me you're going to peek through the window."

"I wasn't, but that's actually a really good idea."

"Adeem!"

Adeem grinned and sidled through some tall grass to get to the backyard.

Cate followed.

The back of the house had an extension that jutted out awkwardly, and the windows were covered in blackout curtains.

There was a single door here, too, painted bright red. Adeem raised a fist to knock, but instead, he swiveled around so fast, Cate thought to duck so as not to get punched in the face.

"What are you—?"

"Sorry, sorry," Adeem said. "I just thought of something."

"*Another* plan? We're not even done pursuing this one, and—"

He nudged his glasses onto the bridge of his nose. "Cate. I was thinking of your . . . your . . ." She noticed, even in the darkness, he seemed to be blushing. "Your bucket list. I know you said you wanted to kiss someone, and there's only one day left, and in case the world really is ending, I was just wondering . . . since, uh, last time I checked, I have a mouth and all . . . Would you maybe want me to? Because I could, if you want."

Now it was Cate's turn to blush. "I mean, that's really sweet, Adeem, but here's the thing. I *have* been kissed before. But this time, I don't want it to be just a *Hey, the world is ending, so let's do this* kind of kiss. I would rather hold out. You know, for the real thing."

Adeem actually looked relieved, and Cate was glad. She didn't want to hurt his feelings. In just a short time, she'd come to care for him, maybe even love him in a weird way. But in a *friend* way.

"Okay, good call. Just thought, you know, that I should offer. A kind gesture, really."

Cate burst out laughing, all of a sudden. She couldn't help

it. "Save those kind gestures for the next chick."

Then he was laughing, too. "I'll add it to my extensive repertoire."

After they'd calmed down, he looked at her and reached for her hand in the darkness. "Let's do this, yeah?"

"Yup," she said. "And get on with it—my feet kill."

Adeem turned back around, and banged on the red door. "Hello?" he called. "Anyone in there?"

A few minutes passed, and she was beginning to think it was a dead end, when the door opened, only just, revealing a gray, beady, sleep-deprived eyeball.

"You're not her. Who are you?" said a gruff voice.

Adeem fell back, startled, and nearly tripped over Cate.

"I'm Cate, and this is Adeem." She took a step forward, around him. "Is this where you broadcast the UFOs & U radio show?"

Another voice called out from inside the radio station. "Is she back? She should've been back by now."

"Nope, just some kids," the voice belonging to the eyeball replied. It stared down at Cate now. "So? Who are ya? Are you fans?"

"Um. Yes," Cate lied. "Yes. I'm a huge fan. Such a big fan, in fact, I was actually hoping to see how you run it all. It's on my bucket list."

The source of the eyeball grunted. The door swung open.

Cate went inside, followed closely by Adeem.

The eyeball belonged to a tall, thin man, with graying hair

half-covered by a safari hat. He wore a black button-down shirt decorated with small red-and-orange flames on the hem.

"This is where the magic happens," the man said, gesturing behind him.

The first thing she noticed was the electricity. No wonder they'd put up the blackout curtains. To avoid looters.

It was a radio station, all right. The air in here felt different, both stagnant and buzzing with life, like staying here too long would make her hair staticky. And the back wall was covered floor to ceiling in radio equipment and computers; what little room was left had been claimed by red and white and black wires. A three-foot-tall generator sat purring in the corner of the room like a fat white cat.

There was no one else here, save for a boy, sitting in front of the equipment with his back facing them, a large leather jacket hanging off his chair. He didn't turn to greet them. Instead, the table space in front of him was covered with sheets of perforated paper, and he was speaking into a microphone.

"'Seymour, my one and only. They say it'll all end soon. All I can do now is wish you were here with me. Aliens, Almaens, whoever—give my Seymour a sign that I love him. Love, Cora from Roswell, New Mexico.' Seymour, wherever you are, we hope you catch this. Call in anytime, and we'll do what we can on our end to connect you to Cora."

The boy clicked something off—the microphone, maybe— and stretched his arms above his head. His shoulder popped.

Then he picked up another slip of paper.

But before he read its contents, he said, "Tom, I really hope you're not letting some random strangers in here. We've got way too much work on our plates to be entertaining." His voice was soft and deep, the kind that vibrated against your skull.

Tom grumbled. "I'm helping you out of the goodness of my heart after what you pulled."

The boy stopped moving but didn't respond. Cate thought she saw his head fall a little.

Tom cleared his throat.

"So you're taking classifieds and reading them on the radio?" Adeem asked.

"It's a new feature of UFOs & U. Figured we would do our part to help any way we could."

"So let me get this straight," Cate interjected. "You can use the radios to reach anyone, anywhere?" With hours left until Alma killed them all, the frantic need to hear her mom again was so overwhelming, she was sure it would sprout arms and drag her back to San Fran, Alma's plans be damned. Knowing Ivy and her parents were looking after her mom was the only thing keeping her need in check. There was no one else Cate would ever trust more with her mom than the Huangs.

Tom grinned, revealing yellowing teeth. "Basically, you just need to broadcast on a particular frequency and someone tunes into that same frequency. That's how they can hear you.

"The problem is getting a broadcast across the country. You

need power for that. Tons of it. Antennae, too, of course. But you also need other special antennae around the country for your waves to bounce off. That's how you get the reach. And that's where we're struggling right now." Tom took off his hat.

"So you said you two are fans . . . ?"

Cate flinched. "Oh, yes. Right. But, to be honest, we were also hoping we could send a message on your station. And we figured this would be the best place to go."

"We're trying to find some people," Adeem added. "We think they're right here in Roswell, but we're having trouble finding them."

The boy at the table spun his chair to face them.

He had a dark, hard stare, and thick black hair in desperate need of a good brushing. A cut on his lip hadn't quite healed yet, and a green bruise graced his pale upper cheek. Cate wondered what had happened.

"We're not offering that kind of service," the boy said, adjusting the leather cuff on his wrist. "The messages we've been sending out are priority. People paid for those."

"Then we'll pay you," said Cate.

"No, no, that's not . . ." The boy ran a hand down his face. "That's not what I mean. We don't take payments anymore. All I'm saying is, we have *hundreds* of messages we need to send out. From people who came before you. I can't have you cut in line. It wouldn't be fair. And what happens when you leave and run your mouth? This place'll get torched, and then everyone loses. I can't have that."

"You said you're having trouble with getting your broadcast to have a wider reach, right?" asked Adeem, adjusting his glasses. "What if I help give your radio signal a little more reach, and you give me a little, I don't know, quid pro quo?"

The boy hesitated. "We do need help. There are a lot of messages here from people out of Roswell. *For* people *out* of Roswell. And I'd really like to get them out there."

Adeem beamed. But Cate sensed something pained behind the boy's emotionless eyes.

"So it's a deal?" Adeem confirmed. He reached out a hand.

The boy took it. "Fine." They shook on it.

"Name's Jesse, by the way." He stood. "Not that it matters, seeing as how we're all going to die tomorrow."

Tom made a face. "I thought you said you didn't believe in Alma."

"Starting to believe in a lot of crazy things these days.

"You two stay here," the boy, Jesse, commanded. "Tom, I'm heading out." He stood and swung the leather jacket over his shoulder. "I might not be back for a bit, so you just keep it up with the messages, all right?"

"Don't boss me around like it's your radio." Tom was standing over Adeem, who had already made himself comfortable in Jesse's spot at the radio rig, starry-eyed. "I've got a thousand things I need to do, too, for your inform—"

"Thanks, Tom."

"Wait," said Cate. "Where are you going?" She didn't want to let this kid out of her sight. He was the closest thing they had to a lead.

"Out," he said flatly.

"Before you go." Cate bit her lip. "It's kind of a shot in the dark, but do you maybe happen to know anyone named Garrett?"

For a moment, the boy's eyes glinted. She thought she'd imagined it, it was such a subtle change.

"Yeah, I know a Garrett," said Jesse. "What's it to you?"

Cate took a step toward him. He took a step back.

"He might be my dad. I'm looking for him."

Jesse smirked. "The Garrett I know is not your dad."

"You don't know that. And my dad didn't even know I existed."

"Trust me. He's not."

"I *don't* trust you. I don't even know you."

"That's probably a good thing."

Cate felt herself flush with indignation. This boy was—what was the word?—*moody*. And impossible.

But her eyes followed him out the door, into the veil of night, and she couldn't help but notice the slump in his shoulders beneath his oversized leather jacket, and the way he shoved his hands in his pockets, like a boy trying to hide every piece of himself from the world.

31

JESSE

The roar of army tanks moving into position thundered in the distance, met by cheers and chants of *Alma, Alma, we won't go—Earth is better than you know.*

Jesse chuckled tiredly to himself. The crowd outside was getting more creative by the hour, and it was barely two a.m.

The last day.

The day of reckoning.

Finally, it had come.

He'd already seen a giant UFO crafted from at least a hundred silver balloons released into the air, and a horde of therapy dogs march down Tom's street. It was utter chaos. He was lucky Tom's radio station was soundproof.

He double-checked to make sure he wasn't being followed, and continued down the familiar path to his house. For a moment, he held on to hope. His fingers trailed the chain-link fence that lined his neighborhood sidewalk, taking in its familiarity. He'd only been away from his house a day, but it felt like years.

He looked up. His stomach went into free fall so fast, he couldn't breathe.

There was nothing of his house left. Nothing but charred remnants and beams, and the stone foundation.

At least now they wouldn't have to worry about the eviction notice.

He almost wished he'd kept a copy for posterity's sake. He could have left it on the pile of ashes and stubs of wood for the landlord.

All he'd brought with him was a fat leather knapsack filled with over fifteen thousand dollars in cash.

He sat on the stone foundation as though it were the stoop leading to the porch. In a way, it was the stoop now.

And then he saw them: Marco's friend Samuel and the guy he'd called Emmit, standing beside the black husk that remained of the shed. Watching him. And when they realized Jesse could see them, their faces split into wide smiles, Emmit's revealing a silver front tooth.

Every hair on Jesse's body stood, and he shivered in the cool night air.

It was time for him to pay.

Jesse's heart pounded violently in his rib cage. They had found him. He had no reason to believe they wouldn't show up to collect, even with Roswell flooding with tents and bodies. But he'd hoped. He'd actually hoped. He wondered what Corbin would think.

But his thoughts came to a halt as Samuel and Emmit prowled toward him.

Panic welled. He had more than enough money to pay for the plane tickets. But there was something hungry in their eyes. Something wrong.

If they wanted a fight, then fine. He deserved it. But as they came closer, he felt his confidence shrivel. He was completely alone. What if he died here? As he watched them come closer, his own throat tightening, he felt like a wolf pup caught in a leg trap.

Except you made this leg trap, he corrected himself.

He clenched his fists.

But at least Mom was safe. It didn't matter what happened to him now. He'd pay up the money he owed, and if the sun came up tomorrow, she could start a new life with the money left over. She'd never have to worry about him or the debts for the house ever again.

"Amazing how three days can feel like a lifetime." Samuel was only a few feet away, and Jesse could smell the sour scent of beer wafting off him. "But I see your little source of income's been destroyed. How tragic."

"Source of income?" Jesse mockingly put his hand on his

chest, if only to hide the thrumming of his heart, the frantic rise and fall. "Now, I think we both know I was the real machine behind the operation."

Samuel rolled his neck. If it cracked, Jesse couldn't hear over the noise wafting from the tent city. "And now it's time to pay up."

He reached out a sweaty palm. "Hand it over."

Jesse swallowed but quickly folded his arms across his chest, feigning confidence. His mouth slid into a smirk. "Hand what over?"

Samuel threw his head back and laughed. "Ah, Jesse, Jesse, Jesse. You play dumb so convincingly."

But then his face hardened. "No more games. Hand it over. All of it."

Jesse recoiled, confused, and for a moment, his mask slipped. "All? I thought you only needed enough for plane tickets. A couple thousand should have covered it."

Samuel grinned. "Interest's a bitch."

Jesse's shoulders shook. He wasn't scared anymore. He was furious. Sure, he owed Marco, and he was sorry. So fucking sorry. But this didn't feel right. He'd thought Samuel was doing this *for Marco*—and some part of Jesse had been almost jealous that someone would go to such lengths for another, to see justice was served—no one would ever pull that for him.

But it was clear this piece of shit didn't care about Marco at all.

"Is Marco even in the hospital . . . ?" asked Jesse carefully.

Samuel glanced at Emmit, whose face broke into a feral grin. Jesse felt a flare of fear.

"Where is Marco?" he asked again.

Samuel ran a tongue across his cracked lips. "A shame. I thought we could do this peacefully."

And then he punched Jesse.

Jesse stumbled, winded, and clutched his chest. He couldn't see ahead of him—he was doubled over in pain—but he wondered if anyone else had seen, if anyone would step in.

Samuel shoved him, hard, and he flew backward before landing on the ground with a thud. His head throbbed from the impact. His knees buckled, and he collapsed to the ground, gasping for air.

No one would step in. No one was at the shed anymore, now that the machine was gone. Jesse was nothing without the machine.

Then again, no one had *ever* helped Jesse. It had always been him, out to fend for himself. Nothing would ever change.

Fine. Hurt me.

He felt his body lift up into the air; Samuel had him by his jacket.

Hurt me, Jesse screamed inside himself. Searing pain exploded at his nose as Samuel punched him in the face again, narrowly missing his stitches. A wet gagging sound escaped from Jesse's lips.

But before he was tossed to the ground again, he saw something sparkle in Emmit's hand. A hammer. His dad's hammer, from inside the shed. How had they gotten it?

No, Jesse tried to shout, but no words came, only blood. Samuel was closing in again. Jesse thought he heard shouting, but he couldn't tell; his ears were throbbing.

Emmit cocked the hammer toward him. Toward his legs.

Jesse scrambled on the dirt to get away, but a foot was on his back, pinning him as if he were nothing but a bug. "Wait!" he finally managed to choke out, even as his spine threatened to crack.

Suddenly, the weight on his back was gone. He looked up slowly, his vision hazy; his left eye was swollen. But he could see him now: Emmit crumpling to the ground and a kid—no, a girl—jumping backward to avoid the fall of his body. In her trembling hand was a pink pepper spray bottle. More movement, and a sudden crash drew Jesse's attention to his periphery. Samuel was off him and on his knees, clutching the space between his legs.

Behind Samuel's buckled form stood a boy in glasses, sweat dappling his brown face, eyes wide in surprise like he couldn't believe what had just happened. What he'd just done.

Samuel growled and got to his feet. Jesse heard the angry thump of his footsteps as he approached the boy and girl. But then there was a familiar blur and the sound of an impact: a fist against skull. Another thump. Samuel was back on the ground. This time, he didn't get up.

Ms. K. She was breathing hard. Then shouting instructions. The girl brushed her bangs out of her round dark eyes.

Even in the dark, and with the dizziness blurring his vision, Jesse recognized her as the pushy girl from UFOs & U. She was breathing hard, too, but still, she smiled, hesitatingly, and reached out her hand toward him.

Jesse caught a flash of something glinting off her purse. A key chain. Shaped like a crow.

32

ADEEM

It was only a few hours before dawn by the time they made it back to UFOs & U; Adeem and Cate had to hoist Jesse up on their shoulders, sharing the weight, to carry him back.

Adeem almost felt bad for Jesse's attackers. Cate had been intent on pepper-spraying them both in the face—twice for good measure.

And then Leyla—

She'd shown up out of nowhere. *Protected* them. And then tied up the attackers with freaking extension cords.

There'd been a moment when their eyes locked in place, and the world around them froze. This was their moment, their big reunion. Adeem couldn't move.

But then Leyla started giving orders, telling them to get

Jesse to safety so she could go get help, and Adeem, balloon-headed and dazed as all heck, listened.

They hadn't meant to follow Jesse, exactly. But Cate kept going on about some hunch she had that the boy knew something about her father and she didn't want him to get away. Plus, it hadn't taken Adeem very long to fix their little radio problem.

The answer was Rosie. He used the shortwave radio to reach her. She was listening to her radio all the time, and relaying the messages she heard from those who couldn't reach their loved ones in time. Adeem knew which frequency she picked up, so all he had to do was broadcast to her so she could, in turn, hear *him*. He'd been so relieved to hear her voice again.

"You left your beautiful little radio here!" she scolded as soon as she'd realized it was him.

He smiled from ear to ear.

With some coordinating, the UFOs & U radio channel would tap into her network and get a wider reach. With her resources, they could reach the entire country. It'd been done before, with people all throughout Europe sending messages to one another via radio to keep tabs on one another's locations during World War II; Adeem had read about it in some book on the history of the radio.

It was Tom who'd given them the tip that Jesse would probably be at his house, and he'd freely given him the address. Adeem got the impression Tom had mixed feelings about Jesse.

Nonetheless, he cleaned up Jesse's face, and Jesse was now resting in the corner of the room. Meanwhile, Adeem had taken the helm at the radio, rather gratefully, in fact—he needed something to distract himself from the fact that he'd just seen his sister for the first time in nearly two freaking years.

He'd just finished broadcasting a message for, to his utter amazement, Mia Jimenez in Texas, and was about to start another—this time for a Cecilia Eaton in New Jersey—when the door to the station opened.

It was Leyla. Still holding the extension cords.

He stood and cautiously approached.

Leyla looked away. "Hi, Adi."

He was filled with such an overwhelming sense of nostalgia that it physically hurt. Everything he'd been through for the past week—the blisters and the hunger and the race against time—it had all been for her, for this moment.

He held her tightly, somewhere between a hug and a choke hold.

"How could you leave me?" His voice cracked.

He was nearly half a foot taller than she was now. She felt so small in his arms.

"I'm sorry," she said.

"Why couldn't you *tell* me?"

"I'm sorry. I wasn't ready yet. *Couldn't* be." She trembled and pulled away. Her eyes were red. "I was so scared of disappointing you, Adi. I thought you'd never look at me the same way. I couldn't bear it. Even the thought of it killed me." She wiped at an eye with the back of her hand. "I kept thinking about Qasim Uncle and his son Tahir, when he came out and it became such a huge thing at the mosque. You know I heard Mom and Dad talking about it? Dad said, 'I can't even imagine what we'd do in Qasim's shoes.' As if there was something to imagine besides accepting your kid is gay."

She let out a half chuckle, half sob that stoked a warm ache behind Adeem's ribs.

"So when I—when I finally told you guys, when I came out, and I saw your reaction, I thought you hated me. You were so crushed, and I panicked. Like you'd had this vision of the future and you'd just watched it all come crumbling down, and I'd done that to you. Me, your big sister. I couldn't deal with that weight, with the thought that I'd disappointed you somehow. God, it hurt. It hurt so badly that I realized I'd rather be alone and free to live the way I needed to than risk living under our parents' roof and watching them pretend they're perfectly fine with it.

"And then you found me." She ran a hand through his hair affectionately. "I'm so sorry I didn't talk to you sooner. I should have had more faith in you, and I know I screwed up. But by the time I realized how much I missed you, I thought it might have been too late to reach out, to find out if you still, I don't know, hated me."

"I never hated you. Even if you did make me track you down through a freaking radio message." He groaned and squeezed at his throbbing temples. "So is that why you told Reza and Priti not to tell us anything? Out of *guilt*?"

Leyla nodded slowly. "I thought that if I could erase myself from your lives, you'd have an easier time. You know how people can be. One bad apple can ruin the barrel, and all that."

"Being gay is not a fruit-borne disease, you idiot."

"I know. I know it's stupid. But if there's anything I've learned, it's that fear"—she gestured around them—"makes people kind of lose their heads."

Adeem rolled his eyes. "Is that why you're a counselor now?"

"What better way to deal with my own problems, huh? Ignore them and deal with other people's."

"I think your stupid poetry was at least a healthier method." Then Adeem remembered: "Wait, what about the poetry book? And Priti—why does she have it? I saw it in her car, and are you guys even together anymore? I mean, it's clear she's still all about you. And then the radio message I heard—"

"Whoa, whoa," Leyla interrupted. "Easy there, tiger. One question at a time."

"I just need to know what's going on. Everything." He took a step closer. He was almost afraid she'd run away again. "Please."

Leyla looked up at the sky and slowly exhaled. She looked at Adeem and gave him a small, embarrassed smile. "After I ran away with Priti," she began slowly, "we went to Las Vegas. Priti had an internship lined up, and some family there, and they're a lot more . . . open about things. She let me live with her under the condition I talked to you guys again when I was ready. Otherwise, Priti wouldn't have supported me running away.

"But"—she bit her lip—"it took me a while, and I guess Priti realized I might never be ready, even though the guilt of leaving was eating me up. I started to depend on her too much, because in my head, she was all I had. It wasn't healthy. Priti kept begging me to reach out to you guys, said I was only hurting myself. Had a big fight over it. Typical Reza got himself involved and tried to play mediator."

"In the end, I left Priti, too. Like an idiot. I think I was angry at everything. Everyone. So I went to Roswell and finally got the counseling job. Fell in love with it. But I knew Priti was right. It's probably why I gave her my book of poems. I think I wanted to leave a piece of me behind, the way I'd totally failed to do with you. And then when I heard about Alma's message, I realized I'd formed this big bubble around myself. I'd pushed everyone away. I had to tell Priti I was sorry, and this guy I counsel in Roswell just happened to be offering free radio broadcasts to loved ones, so . . ."

"A public apology. You always did have a flair for the dramatic."

"What can I say?" said Leyla, shrugging. "But I guess the message worked. Except it didn't reach Priti. It reached someone far more important." She rested her hand on Adeem's shoulder and gave him a gentle squeeze. "I know my explanation's shit, and honestly, I still don't know what the hell I'm doing. But I guess the universe has a weird way of pointing us in the right direction."

"Idiot."

"I know."

It was strange. All the anger he'd held toward her for leaving him behind, for being so selfish, dissipated in an instant. Maybe that was the magic of siblings. They shared more than just blood, they shared roots. Home. Fighting with one was the equivalent of fighting with a more accurate mirror.

"If we survive whatever happens," said Adeem, "we should go see Priti. If you want. I'm sure you both have a lot to talk about, and after the last time I saw her, I kind of owe her an apology. She's, uh, probably not too far from us now." At least, she couldn't have gotten too far from the police station. If Cate were around, she'd probably be giving Adeem a death stare. Leyla's eyes glistened in the dark. They were wet. "I'd like that."

Adeem swallowed, let out a long breath.

Maybe he didn't know what the future held, or, soon, what home would look like—what home even was anymore. But at least they were alive.

At least now, they were together.

33

JESSE

Jesse must have passed out for a bit, because when he awoke, he was back at Tom's radio station, propped up by pillows on the carpet. It was still dark out. Someone had taken off his jacket and laid it over him like a blanket.

The girl, Cate, immediately noticed him awaken. She was at his side in half a second.

"Are we dead?" he asked. His voice was raspy.

She chuckled. "No. Alma hasn't killed us—yet. We still have a couple more hours until dawn, and then . . . who knows."

"Good." Jesse closed his eyes. "My mom's at the planetarium. I want to go see her."

And then, after a moment, he opened them again.

"Where'd you get that key chain?" he asked.

"Oh, this?" She tugged the key chain off her bag. He hadn't hallucinated: it was a crow made of wood—walnut, maybe—and exquisitely carved. But its beak had been chipped off. "My mom gave it to me. And my dad gave it to her. He's the guy I was talking about. Garrett. The one I'm trying to find."

He looked at her. Searched her face.

She had Dad's eyes. His eyes: big and round and dark. It was surreal. Was it even possible? The more Jesse searched his memories, the more he realized it *was*: all those "business" trips to California Dad had taken, all those promises he'd made to Mom to take her, but conveniently never fulfilling them. Who was to say he hadn't fathered another child on one of those trips?

But then, that would mean this girl . . .

Jesse swallowed painfully. "What's your name?"

Cate's eyebrows furrowed. "Um, Cate Collins."

"Cate Collins," Jesse repeated, testing the name in his mouth. "I'll remember that. What about your mom? Where is she?"

Cate looked away. "She's home. In San Francisco."

"You're a long way from home, Cate." Carefully, Jesse sat up.

"Yeah," she said, laughing a little. There was a tinge of sadness mixed up in there. "I guess I am."

Jesse still had the fifteen thousand dollars. More than enough for one plane ticket to San Francisco.

He made a mental note: If they were all still standing

tomorrow, he'd make sure she got back to her mom. Spend some more time with his own mom, too.

He gingerly threaded his arms into his jacket sleeves.

Cate's eyes widened in recognition. "That blackbird. It looks like mine." She ran her finger against the patch on his pocket.

Jesse smiled. "It's a crow, actually." He slipped his hands in his pockets. "The family crest of one Garrett Hewitt. My dad."

Cate looked confused. Jesse didn't explain. Instead, he stood tall on his trembling, nervous legs. "Hey, do you think you could help me get to the hospital downtown? There's someone I need to see."

He wanted to see his mom. He wanted to talk to Cate more. But there was something else he had to do first.

Cate got to her feet and let him lean on her. Slowly, her face broke into a smile. "Then I guess we'd better hurry, huh?"

Jesse found Corbin in the upstairs atrium in the hospital. He was sitting on the carpet with Mari in a wheelchair beside him.

Jesse greeted her first with a small, folded-up piece of paper.

"I never had a chance to get this to you," said Jesse. "I'm sorry it took me so long."

Mari gasped. Her tiny fingers carefully unfolded the paper, as though it were a bird that could come to life in her hands.

Jesse had written out a letter from Alma, with some suggestions from Ms. K. He was pretty proud of the final product.

He glanced over at Corbin shyly.

"You're here," said Corbin, matter-of-factly.

"Yeah. I'm here."

He took a seat next to Corbin, not even caring that his face was probably a mess, or that Corbin was still disappointed in him—for good reason. And Jesse tried not to think about how good it felt to see Corbin's warm smile again. But then he took a deep breath and counted to five and let himself settle into the feeling. Let himself feel.

Corbin shifted on the floor. "Tonight's the night."

"Mm-hmm."

"Not gonna lie," said Corbin, chuckling sadly. "I'm actually really scared."

Mari said nothing; her eyes were trained on the window, staring intently at the predawn darkness.

"You think we're not going to make it?" The thought of Corbin being worried made Jesse even more worried.

Corbin rubbed the back of his neck. "I don't even know if I'm afraid of dying anymore. I just keep thinking about all the things I have left to do. All the things I have left to say."

It didn't seem fair that the world could end like this. Jesse felt like he'd only just begun. He actually wanted to live.

Suddenly, Corbin started to laugh. "You know our neighbors—the Jarvises? In their backyard, their son keeps this stupidly huge, twelve-foot-tall playpen he made for his cat. But Mrs. Jarvis is really big on doing catch-and-release programs for feral cats, and I guess she does animal rehabilitation once in a while, so sometimes, they use the big pen for injured wild animals. Grandpa told me they had a fox in there last year, a family of orphaned racoons a couple months before that.

"Anyway, Mr. and Mrs. Jarvis went out last night thinking, Well, if the whole catch-and-release thing works on feral cats, what if it works on other animals? *Bigger* animals? They met up with some guy, a vet from Indiana, staying in the tent city down by Roswell City Hall, and long story short, they and a couple volunteers caught the wolves from Spring River Zoo.

"And it's amazing, right? What people can do. The *good* people can do. Maybe it doesn't sound like much, and maybe it makes no difference in the end, but when I heard about it, I felt so . . . relieved, you know? I felt so bad about the poor things out there, like—like because I'm human, it's partially *my* fault they were out there suffering. But now we have wolves for neighbors, and they're chilling in the playpen, safe and growing fat on cat food until the zoo can take them back."

Jesse let out a shaky laugh. He almost couldn't believe the wolves were together, were *safe*. He'd been so sure they'd be hunted down, one by one. It was practically a miracle.

Corbin continued, "If we all survive this thing, if Alma decides to spare us, I want to do stuff like that. I have to keep reminding myself that I don't have to sit here and feel helpless, for Mari's sake. I can *do* something—like the Jarvises."

He turned to look at Jesse. "Like what you did for so many people. Whether you realize it or not."

"It's not over," said Jesse.

His fingers found Corbin's.

"Look!" Mari cried suddenly. She was pointing out the window.

Jesse couldn't see it at first. An impenetrable silence nestled comfortably between them as he and Corbin looked to the horizon line, hand in hand.

And then, light.

Mari—

Intergalactic beings have watched Earth envelop itself in darkness for millennia. But in every shroud of darkness, there are small beings such as yourself who, when dealt a cruel hand by fate, still carry the strength to smile.

Your smile breaks through the dark. Your pain is where the light enters you. And your kindness is a guiding light for others.

And that holds a power that even we fear.

Small being, no matter what happens, never let that power go.

ACKNOWLEDGMENTS

This book would not have been possible without the countless number of people who dragged my tired soul across these pages.

I owe so much to Rosemary Brosnan and Alexandra Cooper at HarperTeen, who supported me when I needed it most. I also owe a world of gratitude to the rest of the wonderful team at Harper who've brought this book to life: Alyssa Miele, Allison Weintraub, Jon Howard, Janet Rosenberg, Monique Vescia, Allison Brown, Ebony LaDelle, Michael D'Angelo, and Jacquelynn Burke. You are all so magical to me.

Genius designers Erin Fitzsimmons and Catherine San Juan have truly humbled me with this cover, and having the illustration of living, breathing art god Adams Carvalho grace my debut is nothing short of amazing.

Endless thanks to my sensitivity readers, whose insight and advice helped make my book—make all books—just a little bit kinder. The work sensitivity readers do is invaluable.

I'm so lucky to have been able to work with the awe-inspiring fairy godqueens at Glasstown Entertainment, past and present: Lauren Oliver, Lexa Hillyer, Deeba Zargarpur, Emily Berge-Thielmann, Kat Cho, Lynley Bird, Rebecca Kuss, Diana Sousa, Kamilla Benko, Alexa Wejko, and Jessica Sit. Words cannot describe how thankful I am, which is a problem, because words are supposed to be my job now. Alas, you are all just that wonderful. Stephen Barbara and Lyndsey Blessing have also been behind the scenes, kindly guiding this little story on its own publishing road trip. Thank you for believing in me.

When I was still in law school and unsure of whether I should chase my writing dream, I found Marri and Kate, who gave me the support I needed to find my way. Thank you for being there, quietly and lovingly cheering me on through our shared writing adventures.

If my books are any good, it is because I learned from Jeanne Cavelos, wise sage of the Odyssey Writing Workshop and patron saint to all aspiring writers. Even as I write now, it's your voice I hear in my mind, helping me grow. A special thank you to Mary Robinette Kowal, whose fierce reassurance during the workshop is the reason why I kept writing.

Speaking of Odyssey, I owe all the hugs to my dear friends I made during those six fever-dream weeks: Gigi, Wendy, Rebecca, Mike, Michael, Matthew, Matt, and Hal. And the Tomatoes: thank you, Pablo and Linden, my favorite beautiful goth duo; Richard, a constant source of good cheer and good suggestions; Josh, my forever-favorite "frenemy," for reminding me the true meaning of strength; Jeremy, my most patient Turtle Sensei; and RK, my soul sister, my Jade Blossom, my behna. I love you all so much.

I would not be here without the work of the Muslim trailblazers before me who have convinced audiences that their stories—our stories—deserve to be told and fought for. Thank you to Khaalidah Muhammad-Ali, whose constant encouragement kept the fire in me alive, and Karuna Riazi, who held my hand and coaxed me down a path I never thought would be mine. Inshallah, I will pay it forward.

So many friends and family have buoyed me through this journey. For always being the first on my doorstep with a fire extinguisher whenever hell broke loose, I am forever grateful to Farheen, who has, for many years, made me a better person. I'm also grateful to Cara (my personal Ms. Takemoto) and Ethan. Thank you for your friendship, and for giving me video-game nights to look forward to in the midst of impending deadlines. Shaan and Alina, my Sea Salt Squad: even if we weren't related, I'd wish we were.

So much love to Stephen, my best friend, my partner: Thank you for feeding me and watering me and giving me sunlight. Your love keeps me alive. Literally.

I became an orphan while writing this book, but I'd like to think my parents are watching over me. So thank you, Dad, for showing me my capabilities, and Mom, for showing me my limits. Please look after me, okay?

Thank you, dear reader, who holds my heart in your hand. You've given me a chance and I will not squander it.

And last but by no means least: thank you, Shaz. If I could, I would drive across the world to find you just to hug you tightly and call you an idiot, one last time. I miss you, little brother. So very much.